William Richard Wood Stephens

Saint Chrysostom

His Life and Times

William Richard Wood Stephens

Saint Chrysostom
His Life and Times

ISBN/EAN: 9783337173098

Printed in Europe, USA, Canada, Australia, Japan

Cover: Foto ©Raphael Reischuk / pixelio.de

More available books at **www.hansebooks.com**

ὁ ἅγιος χρυσόστομος

'COPIED FROM A FRONTISPIECE TO THE EDITION BY FRONTO DUCÆUS,
A. D. 1636, OF ST. CHRYSOSTOM'S WORKS (IN THE CATHEDRAL LIBRARY,
CHICHESTER). THE ORIGINAL IS STATED TO HAVE BEEN ENGRAVED FROM
AN EIKON OF GREAT ANTIQUITY, AT CONSTANTINOPLE, AND AGREES WITH
THE NOTICES OF CHRYSOSTOM'S APPEARANCE BY GREEK WRITERS, WHO
DESCRIBE HIM AS SHORT, WITH A LARGE HEAD, AMPLE, WRINKLED FORE-
HEAD, EYES DEEP-SET BUT PLEASING, HOLLOW CHEEKS, AND A SCANTY
GREY BEARD.'

SAINT CHRYSOSTOM

HIS LIFE AND TIMES

A SKETCH OF THE CHURCH AND THE EMPIRE IN THE FOURTH CENTURY

By Rev. W R. W STEPHENS, M.A.

BALLIOL COLL. OXON.; VICAR OF MID-LAVANT, SUSSEX

𝔚𝔦𝔱𝔥 𝔞 𝔓𝔬𝔯𝔱𝔯𝔞𝔦𝔱

LONDON

JOHN MURRAY, ALBEMARLE STREET

1872

LONDON: PRINTED BY
SPOTTISWOODE AND CO., NEW-STREET SQUARE
AND PARLIAMENT STREET

PREFACE.

THE CONSIDERATIONS which moved me to undertake the preparation of this monograph are mentioned in the introductory chapter. How far the design there indicated has been satisfactorily fulfilled, it is for others to decide. I am of course conscious of defects, for every workman's ideal aim should be higher than what he can actually accomplish. The work has incurred a certain risk from having been once or twice suspended for a considerable period; but I have always returned to it with increased interest and pleasure, nor can I charge myself with having wittingly bestowed less pains on one part than another. I have endeavoured to make it a trustworthy narrative by drawing from the most original sources to which I could gain access; and where, as in those portions which touch on secular history, the lead of general historians, such as Gibbon or De Broglie, has been followed, I have, as far as possible, consulted the authorities to which they refer. To modern authors from whom I have derived valuable assistance for special parts of the work, such as M. Amédée Thierry and Dr. Foerster, my obligations are acknowledged in their proper place.

Neander's life of St. Chrysostom has, of course, throughout been frequently consulted. It is marked by the customary merits and defects of that historian. It is full of research, information, thought, and refined religious sentiment; but he fails to bring out strongly the personality of his subject. We have abundance of Chrysostom's sayings and opinions, but somehow too little of Chrysostom himself. The fact is that Neander seems always to be thinking more of those views and theories about the growth of Christian doctrine and the church, which he wishes to impress upon men's minds, than of the person about whom he is writing. Thus, the subject of his biography becomes too much a mere vehicle for conveying Neander's own opinions, and the personality of the character fades away in proportion. Some passages in the life of his subject are related at inordinate length; others, because less illustrative of Neander's views, are imperfectly sketched, if not omitted.

In extracts from the works of Chrysostom, the somewhat difficult question of the comparative advantages of translation and paraphase has been decided, on the whole, in favour of the latter. The condensation of matter gained by a paraphrase is an important, indeed necessary, object, if many specimens are to be given from such a very voluminous author as Chrysostom. A careful endeavour, at the same time, has been made to render faithfully the general sense of the original; and wherever the peculiar beauty of the language or the importance of the subject seemed to demand it, a translation has been given.

From an early date in the sixteenth century down to the present time the works of Chrysostom have occupied the attention of learned editors. The first attempts, after the invention of printing, were mainly confined to Latin translations of different portions.

(1) The first edition which was issued in Greek of the 'Commentaries on the New Testament' came from the press of Commelin, a printer at Heidelberg, in A.D. 1602.

(2) In 1612 appeared a magnificent edition of the whole works, in eight thick folio volumes, printed at Eton, and prepared by Sir Henry Savile. Savile, born in 1549, was equally distinguished for his knowledge of mathematics and Greek, in which he acted for a time as tutor to Queen Elizabeth. He became Warden of Merton in

1585, and Provost of Eton in 1596. Promotion in Church
and State was offered to him by James I., but declined,
though he accepted a knighthood in 1604. His only son
died about that time, and he devoted his fortune henceforth
entirely to the promotion of learning. The Savilian pro-
fessorships of Geometry and Astronomy in Oxford were
founded by him, and a library furnished with mathematical
books for the use of his professors. He spared no labour
or expense to make his edition of St. Chrysostom handsome and complete. He personally examined most of the
great libraries in Europe for MSS., and, through the
kindness of English ambassadors and eminent men of
learning abroad, his copyists were admitted to the libraries
of Paris, Basle, Augsburg, Munich, Vienna, and other
cities. He used the Commelinian edition as his printer's
copy, carefully compared with five MSS., the various
readings of which are marked (by a not very distinct plan)
in the margin. The chief value of the work consists in
the prefaces and notes, contributed some of them by
Casaubon and other learned men, though by far the best
are Savile's own. The whole cost of bringing out this
grand edition is said to have been 8,000*l.* Savile's wife
was so jealous of her husband's attachment to the work
that she threatened to burn it.

(3) Meanwhile, Fronton le Duc, a French Jesuit, had
been labouring independently, but in most amicable intercourse with Savile, not only to edit the works of Chrysostom complete, but accompanied by a Latin translation,
which he supplied himself for those pieces of which he
failed to find any good one already existing. His death
arrested the work, which was taken up, after a time, by
the two brothers, Frederick and Claude Morel, and completed by the latter in 1633. It was published in Paris
in 1636, in twelve large folio volumes. The Commelinian
was again used as the printer's copy, with fewer alterations
than in the edition of Savile.

(4) We now come to the great Benedictine edition, prepared under the care of Bernard de Montfaucon, who deserted the profession of arms at the age of twenty to become, as a member of the brotherhood of St. Maur, one of the most marvellously industrious workers in literature that the world has ever seen. In 1698, when the Benedictines had completed their editions of SS. Augustine and Athanasius, they began to prepare for an edition of Chrysostom, which they had intended to do for more than thirty years. Montfaucon was sent to Italy, where he spent three years in examining libraries; and, on his return, obtained leave from the presidents of the congregation to employ four or five of the brethren in collating MSS. in the Royal Library at Paris, and in those of Colbert and Coislin. Their labours extended over thirteen years; more than 300 MSS., containing different portions of Chrysostom's works, having been discovered in those libraries. Montfaucon, meanwhile, corresponded with learned men in all parts of Europe, in order to procure materials and further collations. His correspondents in England were Potter, Bishop of Oxford, Bentley, and Needham; and in Ireland, Godwin, Bishop of Kilmore. The result was that, after more than twenty years of incessant toil, Montfaucon produced an edition, in which several pieces saw the light for the first time, and others, imperfect in previous editions, were presented entire. The text after all is the least satisfactory part of the work. Mr. Field has discovered that the eight principal MSS. employed were not very carefully collated, and that, though Savile's text is extremely praised, that of Morel, by a curious inconsistency, is most closely followed, which is little more than a reproduction of the original Commelinian. The main value of the edition consists in the prefaces, written by Montfaucon to every set of homilies and every treatise, in which the chronology, contents, and character of the composition are most fully and ably discussed. The

chronological arrangement also of the pieces is a great improvement on the editions of Savile and Fronton le Duc, who had made no attempt of that kind. The last volume, the thirteenth, contains a life of St. Chrysostom, a most copious index, and dissertations on the doctrine, discipline, and heresies prevalent in his age, illustrated by notices collected from his works. On the whole, the edition must be pronounced a marvellous monument of ability and industry; especially when it is considered that at the date of its completion, 1738, Montfaucon was eighty-three years of age, and had been engaged for upwards of fifty years in literary work of a most laborious description. He died in 1741.

(5) The last edition, which leaves little or nothing to be desired, is that which I have used in preparing this volume—the Abbé Migne's, in 13 vols., Paris, 1863. It is substantially a reproduction of the Benedictine, in a rather less cumbrous size, and embodies some of the best corrections, notes, and prefaces of modern commentators, especially those of Mr. Field to the Homilies of St. Matthew, and some by the learned editor himself.

Such is a brief sketch of the several forms in which Chrysostom's works have appeared. It seemed an appropriate introduction to the history of the man himself. If the perusal of that history shall afford to readers half as much interest, pleasure, and instruction as I have myself derived from the composition of it, I shall feel amply rewarded for my labour; and I gladly take this opportunity of expressing my gratitude to my father-in-law for originally suggesting a work of this kind, and to many friends, and especially my wife, for constant encouragement, without which a mixture of indolence and diffidence might have prevented the completion of my design.

DENSWORTH COTTAGE, CHICHESTER:
All Saints Day, 1871.

CONTENTS.

CHAPTER VIII.

CHAPTER IX.

CHAPTER X.

CHAPTER XI.

CHAPTER XII.

CHAPTER XIII.

CHAPTER XIV.

CHAPTER XV.

Errata.

Page 7, line 1 from top, instead of ‘ Ambrose, only two—Augustine and Chry
sostom — survived into the fifth century,’ read ‘Ambrose, Jerome,
Augustine, and Chrysostom, the last three alone survived into the fifth
century.’

„ 8, line 9 from top, the words ‘ of Mariolatry’ should be omitted.

LIFE AND TIMES

OF

ST. CHRYSOSTOM.

CHAPTER I.

INTRODUCTORY.

I. THERE are many great names in history which have been familiar to us from almost our earliest years, but of the personal character, the actual life of those who bore them, we are comparatively ignorant. We know that they were men of genius; industrious energetic workers, who, as statesmen, reformers, warriors, writers, speakers, exercised a vital influence for good or ill upon their fellow-men. They have achieved a reputation which will never die; but from various causes their personality does not stand out before us in clear and bold relief. We know something about some of the most important passages in their life, a few of their sayings, a little of their writings; but the men themselves we do not know.

Frequently the reason of this is, that though they occupy a place, perhaps an important place, in the great drama of history, yet they have not played one of the *foremost* parts; and general history cannot spare much time or space beyond what is necessary to describe the main progress of events, and the actions and characters of those

who were most prominently concerned in them. Other
men may have been greater in themselves; they may have
been first-rate in their own sphere, but that sphere was
too much secluded or circumscribed to admit of the extensive and conspicuous public influence of which alone history takes much cognisance. They are to history what
those side or background figures in the pictures of great
mediæval painters are to the grand central subject of the
piece: they do but help to fill up the canvas, yet the
picture would not be complete without them. They are
notable personages, well worthy of being separately depicted, though in the large historical representation they
play a subordinate part.

To take out one of these side figures of history and to
make it the centre of a separate picture, grouping round
it all the great events and characters among which it
moved, is the work of a biographer. And by many it will
be felt that nothing invests the general history of any
period with such a living interest as viewing it through
the light of some one human life. How was this individual soul affected by the movement of the great forces
with which it was surrounded or brought into contact?
How did it affect them, in its turn, wherever in its progress it impinged upon them? This one consideration
will confer on many details of history an importance and
freshness of which they seemed too trivial or too dull to
be susceptible.

II. Among these side characters in history, characters
of men in themselves belonging to the first rank, men
whose names will be renowned and honoured to the end of
time, but precluded, by disposition or circumstances, from
taking the foremost place in the larger canvas of general
history, must be reckoned many of the great ecclesiastics
of the first four or five centuries of Christianity. Everyone recognises as great such names as Origen, Tertullian,

Cyprian, Basil, the two Gregories, and many more. Everyone would admit that the Church owes them a debt, but it may be safely affirmed that here the acquaintance of many with these eminent men begins and ends. A few scraps from their writings quoted in commentaries, one or two remarkable acts or sayings which have been thought worthy to be handed down, a few passages in which their lives flit across the stage of general history, complete the knowledge of many more. Such men, indeed, as Athanasius and Ambrose are to some extent exceptions. The magnitude of the principles for which they contended, the energy and ability which they displayed in the contest, were too conspicuous to be passed over by the general historian, civil or ecclesiastical. The proverbial expression 'Athanasius contra mundum' attests of itself the pre-eminent greatness of the man. But with other luminaries of the Church, whose powers were perhaps equally great but not exercised on so public a field or on behalf of such apparently vital questions, history has not dealt, perhaps cannot consistently with its scope deal, in any degree commensurate with their merits. Nor does this remark apply entirely to civil history. Ecclesiastical history, also, is so much occupied with the consideration of subjects on a large scale and covering a large space of time,—the course of controversies, the growth of doctrines, the relations between Church and State, changes in discipline, in liturgies, in ritual,—that the history of those who lived among these events, and who by their ability made or moulded them, is comparatively lost sight of. The outward operations are seen, but the springs which set them going are concealed. How can general history, for instance, adequately set forth the character and the work of such men as Savonarola or Erasmus, both in their widely-different ways men of such incomparable genius and incessant activity? It does not; it only supplies a glimpse, a sketch which make us long for a fuller vision, a more finished picture.[1]

III. It is designed to attempt, in the following pages, such a supplementary chapter in ecclesiastical history. An endeavour will be made not merely to chronicle the life and estimate the character of the great preacher of Antioch and Constantinople, but to place him in the centre of all the great movements, civil as well as religious, of his time, and see what light he and they throw upon one another.

The age in which he lived was a troublous one. The spectacle of a tempestuous sea may in itself excite our interest and inspire us with awe, but place in the midst of it a vessel containing human life, and how deeply is our interest intensified!

What was the general character and position of the clergy in the fourth century? What was the attitude of the Church towards the sensuality, selfishness, luxury, of an effete and debased civilisation on one hand, and the rude ferocity of young and strong barbarian races on the other? To what extent had Christianity leavened, or had it appreciably leavened at all, popular forms of thought and popular habits of life? What was the existing phase of monasticism? what the ordinary form of worship in the Catholic Church? what the established belief respecting the sacraments and the great verities of the Christian faith? In answer to such enquiries and to many more, much useful information may be extracted from the works of so prolific a writer and preacher as Chrysostom. Being concerned also as a preacher with moral practice more than with abstract theology, his homilies reflect, like the writings of satirists, the manners of the age. The habits of private life, the fashionable amusements, the absurdities of dress, all the petty foibles, as well as the more serious vices of the society by which he was surrounded, are

---

[1] In the case of the former this picture has on the whole been worthily executed in the pages of Villari; the life of Erasmus remains to be written.

dragged out without remorse, and made the subjects of
solemn admonition, or fierce invective, or withering sarcasm, or ironical jest.

IV. Nor does secular history, from which not a single
chapter in ecclesiastical history can without injury be
dissociated, want for copious illustration. Not only from
the memorable story of the sedition at Antioch, and from
the public events at Constantinople, in which Chrysostom
played a conspicuous part, but from many an allusion or
incidental expression scattered up and down his works, we
may collect rays of light on the social and political condition of the empire. We get glimpses in his pages of a
large mass of the population hovering mid-way between
paganism and Christianity; we are conscious of an oppressive system of taxation, a widely-spread venality in
the administration of public business, a general insecurity
of life arising from the almost total absence of what we
understand by police regulations, a depressed agriculture,
a great slave population, a vast turbulent army as dangerous to the peace of society as the enemies from whom
it was supposed to defend it, the presence of barbarians
in the country as servants, soldiers, or colonists, the con-
stantly-impending danger from other hordes ever hovering
on the frontier, and, like famished wolves, gazing with
hungry eyes on the plentiful prey which lay beyond it.
But in the midst of the national corruption we see great
characters stand out; and it is remarkable that they
belong, without exception, to the two elements which alone
were strong and progressive in the midst of the general
debility and decadence. All the men of commanding
genius in this era were either Christian or barbarian.
A young and growing faith, a vigorous and manly race;
these were the two forces destined to work hand in hand
for the destruction of an old and the establishment of a
new order of things. The chief doctors of Christianity in
the fourth century—Augustine, Chrysostom, Ambrose—are

incomparably greater than their contemporary advocates of the old religion and philosophy, Symmachus or Libanius; even as the Gothic Alaric and Fravitta, and the Vandal Stilicho, were the only generals who did not disgrace the Roman arms.

V. Some remarks on the theology of Chrysostom will be found in the concluding chapter. The appellation of preacher,[1] by which he is most generally known, is a true indicator of the sphere in which his powers were greatest. It was in upholding a pure and lofty standard of Christian morality, and in denouncing unchristian wickedness, that his life was mainly spent, rather than, like Augustine's, in constructing and teaching a logical system of doctrine. The rage of his enemies, to which he eventually fell a victim, was not bred of the bitterness of theological controversy, but of the natural antagonism between the evil and the good. And it is partly on this account that neither the remoteness of time, nor difference of circumstances which separate us from him, can dim the interest with which we read his story. He fought not so much for any abstract question of theology or point of ecclesiastical discipline, which may have lost its meaning and importance for us, but for those grand principles of truth and justice, Christian charity, and Christian holiness, which ought to be dear to men equally in all ages.

VI. But there is also in the struggle of Chrysostom with the secular power an ecclesiastical and historical interest, as well as a moral one. We see prefigured in his deposition the fate of the Eastern Church in the Eastern capital of the Empire. As the papacy grew securely by the retreat from the old Rome of any secular rival, so the patriarchate of the new Rome was constantly, increasingly depressed by the presence of such a rival. Of all the great churchmen who flourished in the fourth century, Athanasius, Basil,

---

[1] 'That godly clerk and great preacher,' is the description of him in the English Homilies. Hom. i.

the Gregories, Ambrose, only two—Augustine and Chrysostom—survived into the fifth century.   But the glory of
the Western Church was then only.in its infancy; the
glory of the Eastern culminated in Chrysostom. From his
time the patriarchs of Constantinople fell more and more
into the servile position of court functionaries. The working out of that grand idea, a visible organised Catholic
Church, uniform in doctrine and discipline, an idea which
grew more and more as the political disintegration of the
Empire increased, was to be accomplished by the more
commanding, law-giving spirit of the West.   Intrepid in
spirit, inflexible of purpose, though Chrysostom was, he
could not subdue, he could only provoke to more violent
opposition, the powers with which he was brought into
collision. Ineffectual was his contest with ecclesiastical corruption and secular tyranny, as compared with a similar
contest waged by his Western contemporary, Ambrose; ineffectual also were the efforts, after his time, of the Church
which he represented to assert the full dignity of its position.

VII. Chrysostom, and the contemporary fathers of the
Eastern Church, naturally seem very remote from us;
but, in fact, they are nearer to us in their modes of thought
than many who in point of time are less distant.   They
were brought up in the study of that Greek literature with
which we are familiar.   Philosophy had not stiffened into
scholasticism.   The ethics of Chrysostom are substantially
the same with the ethics of Butler.   So, again, Eastern
fathers of the fourth century are far more nearly allied to
us in theology than writers of a few centuries later.   If
we are to look to ' the rock' whence our Anglican liturgy
' was hewn,' and ' to the hole of the pit ' whence Anglican
reformed theology ' was digged,' we must turn our eyes,
above all other directions, to the Eastern Church and the
Eastern fathers.   It was observed by Mr. Alexander Knox,[1]
that the earlier days of the Greek Church seem resplen-

---

[1] 'Remains,' vol. iii. Letters to Dr. Woodward and Mrs. Hannah More.

dent with a glow of simple, fervent, piety, such as in a
Church, as a whole, has never since been seen ; and that
this condition is strikingly in harmony with our own
liturgy, so overflowing with sublime aspirations, so Catholic, so free, not bearing the impress of any one system of
theology, but containing what is best in all—holding
dogma firmly, but not inculcating it in a hard, dogmatic
spirit. We may detect in Chrysostom the germ of mediæval corruptions, of Mariolatry, of invocation of saints,
of a sensuous conception of the change effected in the holy
elements in the Eucharist; but these are the raw material
of error, not yet wrought into definite shape. The Bishop
of Rome is recognised, as will be seen from Chrysostom's
correspondence with Innocent, as a great potentate, whose
intercessions are to be solicited in time of trouble and
difficulty, and to whose judgment much deference is to be
paid, but by no means as a supreme ruler in Christendom.

Thus, the tone of Chrysostom's language is far more
congenial to that of our own Church than of the mediæval
or present Church of Rome. In his habit of referring to
Holy Scripture as the ultimate source and basis of all true
doctrine, ' so that whatsoever is not read therein, nor may
be proved thereby, is not to be required of any man as an
article of faith ;' in his careful endeavour to ascertain
the real meaning of Scripture, not seeking for fanciful
or mystical interpretations, or supporting preconceived
theories, but patiently labouring, with a mixture of can-
dour, reverence, and common sense, to ascertain the exact
literal sense of each passage ;—in these points, no less
than in his theology, he bears an affinity to the best minds
of our own reformed Church, and fairly represents that faith
of the Catholic Church before the disruption of East and
West in which Bishop Ken desired to die ; while his fervent
piety, and his apostolic zeal as a preacher of righteousness
must command the admiration of all earnest Christians, to
whatever country, age, or Church, they may belong.

CHAPTER II.

It has been well remarked by Sir Henry Savile, in the preface to his noble edition of Chrysostom's works, published in 1612, that, as with great rivers, so often with great men, the middle and the close of their career are dignified and distinguished, but the primary source and early progress of the stream are difficult to ascertain and trace. No one, he says, has been able to fix the exact date, the year, and the consulship of Chrysostom's birth. This is true; but at the same time his birth, parentage, and education are not involved in such obscurity as surrounds the earliest years of some other great luminaries of the Eastern Church; his own friend, for instance, Theodore, Bishop of Mopsuestia, and yet more notably, the great Athanasius.

There is little doubt that his birth occurred not later than the year A.D. 347, and some probability that it should be placed two years earlier;[1] and there is no doubt that

---

[1] The date may be approximated by the following landmarks. He was about twenty when he attended the lectures of Libanius (*Epist. ad Vid. Jun.* vol. i. p. 601). We may allow two years for his study there, and beginning to practise as a lawyer. He was then three years a catechumen under the Bishop Meletius (*Pallad. Dial.* c. v.): after this, six years were spent in monastic retirement, returning from which he was ordained deacon by Meletius. Now Meletius was in banishment from 370 to 378, and died during the Council of Constantinople in 381. If, then, he ordained Chrysostom reader just before his banishment in 370, and deacon just before his departure for Constantinople, we get 345 for the year of Chrysostom's birth. He was five years a deacon (*Pallad.* c. v.), which brings us to 386, and twelve years a priest, which brings us to 398, the year in which he was elected to the see of Constantinople. If we accept

Antioch in Syria was the place of his birth, that his
mother's name was Anthusa, his father's Secundus, and
that both were well born. His mother was, if not actually baptised, very favourably inclined to Christianity,[1]
and, indeed, a woman of no ordinary piety. The father
had attained the rank of 'magister militum' in the Imperial army of Syria, and therefore enjoyed the title of
'illustris.' He died when his son John was an infant,
leaving a young widow, about twenty years of age, in
comfortable circumstances, but harassed by the difficulties
and anxieties of her unprotected condition as mistress of
a household in days when servants were slaves, and life in
large cities altogether unguarded by such securities as are
familiar to us. Greatly did she dread the responsibility of
bringing up a son in one of the most turbulent and dissolute
capitals of the empire. Nothing, she afterwards[2] declared
to him, could have enabled her to pass through such a
furnace of trial but a consoling sense of divine support,
and the delight of contemplating the image of her husband as reproduced in his son. How long a sister older
than himself may have lived we do not know; but the
conversation between him and his mother when he was
meditating a retreat into a monastery, seems to imply
that he was the only surviving child. All her love—all
her care—all her means and energies, were concentrated
on the boy destined to become so great a man, and exhibiting even in childhood no common ability and aptitude
for learning. But her chief anxiety was to train him in
pious habits, and to preserve him uncontaminated from
the pollutions of the vicious city in which they resided.

347 for the year of his birth, no interval is allowed between his going to
the school of Libanius and becoming
a catechumen (vide *Tillemont*, vol. xi.
p. 347).

[1] Wall, on *Infant Baptism*, endeavours to prove that she was a Pagan,
in order to account for the delay in
Chrysostom's baptism, but his reasons
are far from convincing.

[2] De Sacerd. l. i. c. 5.

She was to him as Monica to Augustine, as Nonna to Gregory Nazianzum.

The great influence, indeed, of women upon the Christianity of domestic life in that age is not a little remarkable. The Christians were not such a pure and single-minded community as they had been. The refining fires of persecution which burnt up the chaff of hypocrisy or indifference were now extinguished; Christianity had a recognised position; her bishops were in kings' courts. The natural consequences inevitably followed this attainment of security; there were more Christians, but not more who were zealous; there were many who hung very loosely to the Church—many who fluctuated between the Church and Paganism. In the great Eastern cities of the Empire, especially Alexandria, Antioch, Constantinople, the mass of the so-called Christian population was largely infected by the dominant vices—inordinate luxury, sensuality, selfish avarice, and display. Christianity was in part Paganised long before it had made any appreciable progress towards the destruction of Paganism. But the sincere and ardent piety of many amongst the women kept alive in many a home the flame of Christian faith which would otherwise have been smothered. The Emperor Julian imagined that his efforts to resuscitate Paganism would have been successful in Antioch but for the strenuous opposition of the Christian women. He complains 'that they were permitted by their husbands to take anything out of the house to bestow it upon the Galilæans, or to give away to the poor, while they would not expend the smallest trifle upon the worship of the gods.'[1] The efforts also of the Governor Alexander, who was left in Antioch by the Emperor to carry forward his designs of Pagan reformation, were principally baffled through this female influence. He found that the men

---

[1] Julian Misopogon, p. 363.

would often consent to attend the temples and sacrifices, but afterwards generally repented and retracted their adherence. This relapse Libanius the sophist, in a letter [1] to the Governor, ascribes to the home influence of the women—' When the men are out of doors,' he says, ' they obey you who give them the best advice, and they approach the altars ; but when they get home, their minds undergo a change ; they are wrought upon by the tears and entreaties of their wives, and they again withdraw from the altars of the gods.'

Anthusa did not marry again ; very possibly she was deterred from contracting a second marriage by religious scruples which Chrysostom himself would certainly have approved.[2] The Pagans themselves admired those women who dedicated themselves to a single life, or abstained from marrying again. Chrysostom himself informs us that when he began to attend the lectures of Libanius, his master inquired who and what his parents were ; and on being told that he was the son of a widow who at the age of forty had lost her husband twenty years, he exclaimed in a tone of mingled jealousy and admiration : ' Heavens ! what women these Christians have ! ' [3]

What instruction he received in early boyhood, beside his mother's careful moral and religious training ; whether he was sent, a common custom among Christian parents in that age,[4] to be taught by the monks in one of the neighbouring monasteries, where he may have imbibed an early taste for monastic retirement, we know not.   He was designed, however, not for the clerical but for the legal profession, and at the age of twenty he began to attend the lectures of one of the first sophists of the day, capable of giving him that secular training and learning which would best enable him to cope with men of the world.

[1] Epist. 1057.
[2] Epist. ad Viduam Jun. vol. i.
[3] Ibid. p. 601.
[4] Advers. Oppug. Vitæ Monastic. lib. iii. c. 11.

Libanius had achieved a reputation as a teacher of general literature, rhetoric, and philosophy, and as an able and eloquent defender of Paganism, not only in his native city Antioch, but in the Empire at large. He was the friend and correspondent of Julian, and on amicable terms with the Emperors Valens and Theodosius. He had now returned to Antioch after lengthened residence in Athens (where the chair of rhetoric had been offered to him but declined), in Nicomedia, and in Constantinople.[1] In attending daily lectures at his school, the young Chrysostom became conversant with the best classical Greek authors, both poets and philosophers. Of their sentiments he in later life retained little admiration,[2] and to the perusal of their writings he probably seldom or never recurred for profit or recreation, but his retentive memory enabled him to the last to point and adorn his arguments with quotations from Homer, Plato, and the Tragœdians. In the school of Libanius also he began to practise those nascent powers of eloquence which were destined to win for him so mighty a fame, as well as the appellation of Chrysostomos, or the Golden Mouth, by which, rather than by his proper name of John, he will be known to the end of time.[3] Libanius, in a letter to Chrysostom, praises highly a speech composed by him in honour of the emperors, and says they were happy in having so excellent a panegyrist.[4] The Pagan sophist helped to forge the weapons which were afterwards to be skilfully employed against the cause to which he was devoted. When he was on his death-bed, he was asked by his friends who was in his opinion capable of succeeding him? 'It would have been John,' he replied, 'had not the Christians stolen him from us.'[5] But it did not immediately appear that the learned advo-

[1] Liban. de fortuna sua, p. 13–137.
[2] See concluding chapter.
[3] Ibid.

[4] Quoted by Isidore of Pelusium, l. 2, Ep. 42.
[5] Sozomen viii. c. 2.

cate of Paganism was nourishing a traitor ; for Chrysostom
had not yet been baptized, and began to seek an opening
for his powers in secular fields of activity.[1] He commenced
practice as a lawyer ; some of his speeches gained great
admiration, and were highly commended by his old master
Libanius. A brilliant career of worldly ambition was open
to him.   The profession of the law was at that time the
great avenue to civil distinction. The amount of litigation
was enormous.   One hundred and fifty advocates were required for the court of the Prætorian Prefect of the East
alone.   The display of talent in the law courts frequently
obtained for a man the government of a province, whence
the road was open to those higher dignities of vice-prefect,
prefect, patrician, consul, which were honoured by the
title of ' illustrious.' [2]

But the pure and upright disposition of the youthful
advocate recoiled from the licentiousness which corrupted
society ; from the avarice, fraud, and artifice which marked
the transactions of men of business ; from the chicanery
and rapacity that sullied the profession which he had entered.[3] He was accustomed to say later in life that ' the
Bible was the fountain for watering the soul.' If he had
drunk of the classical fountains in the school of Libanius,
he had imbibed draughts yet deeper of the spiritual well-
spring in quiet study of Holy Scripture at home. And like
many another in that degraded age, his whole soul re-
volted from the glaring contrast presented by the ordinary
life of the world around him to that standard of holiness
which was held up in the Gospels.

He had formed also an intimate friendship with a young
man his equal in station and age, by whose influence he

[1] Isidore Pel. l. 2 Ep. 42 ; De
Sacerdot. i. c. 4.
[2] Gibbon iii. 52, note. Milman's
edition.

[3] Ibid iii. 53 ; for an account of the
character of lawyers at this period,
see Amm. Marcellinus, lxxx. c. 4.

was diverted more and more from secular life, and eventually induced altogether to abandon it. This was Basil, who will come before us in the celebrated work on the priesthood. He must not be confounded with the great Basil,[1] Bishop of Cæsarea, in Cappadocia, who was some fifteen years older than Chrysostom, having been born in A.D. 329, nor with Basil, Bishop of Seleucia, who was present at the Council of Chalcedon in A.D. 451, and must therefore have been considerably younger. Perhaps he may be identified with a Basil, Bishop of Raphanea in Syria, not far from Antioch, who attended the Council of Constantinople in A.D. 381.

Chrysostom has described his friendship with Basil in affecting language:[2] 'I had many genuine and true friends, men who understood and strictly observed the laws of friendship; but one there was out of the many who exceeded them all in attachment to me, and strove to leave them all behind in the race, even as much as they themselves surpassed ordinary acquaintances. He was one of those who accompanied me at all times; we engaged in the same studies, and were instructed by the same teachers; in our zeal and interest for the subjects on which we worked we were one. As we went to our lectures or returned from them, we were accustomed to take counsel together on the line of life it would be best to adopt; and here, too, we appeared to be unanimous.'

Basil early determined this question for himself in favour of monasticism; he decided, as Chrysostom expresses it, to follow the 'true philosophy.' This occasioned the first interruption to their intercourse. Chrysostom, soon after the age of twenty, had embarked on a secular career, and could not immediately make up his mind to tread in the footsteps of his friend. 'The balance,' he says, 'was no longer even'; the scale of

---

[1] As Socrates, b. vi. c. 3, has done.   [2] De Sacerdot. l. i. c. i.

Basil mounted, while that of Chrysostom was depressed, by the weight of earthly interests and desires.[1] But the decisive act of Basil made a deep impression on his mind; separation from his friend only increased his attachment to him, and his aversion from life in the world. He began to withdraw more from ordinary occupations and pleasures, and to spend more of his time in the study of Holy Scripture. He formed acquaintance with Meletius, the deeply respected Catholic Bishop of Antioch, and after three years, the usual period of probation for cate-chumens, was baptized by him.

A natural question arises, why was he not baptized before, since his mother was a Christian, and there is abundant evidence that infant baptism was and had been the ordinary practice of the Church?[2] In attempting a solution of the difficulty, it will be proper to mention first certain reasons for delaying baptism which were prevalent in that age, and which may partially have influenced the mind of Chrysostom's mother or himself. It may sound paradoxical to say that an exaggerated estimation of the import and effect of baptism contributed in two ways to its delay. But such appears to have been the case. It was regarded by many as the most complete and final purgation of past sin, and the most solemn pledge of a new and purified life for the future. To sin, therefore, before baptism was comparatively harmless, if in the waters of baptism the guilty stains could be washed away; but sin after the reception of that holy sacrament was almost, if not altogether, unpardonable—at least fraught with the most tremendous peril. Hence some would delay baptism as many now delay repentance, from a secret or conscious reluctance to take a decisive step, and renounce the pleasures of sin; and under the comfort-

---

[1] De Sacerdot. c. iii.   [2] See references in Bingham, b. xi. vol. iii. Wall, vol. ii.

able persuasion that some day, by submitting to baptism, they would free themselves from the responsibilities of their past life. Others, again, were deterred from binding themselves under so solemn a covenant by a distrust of their ability to fulfil their vows, and a timorous dread of the eternal consequences if they failed. Against these misconceptions of the true nature and proper use of the sacrament, the great Basil, the two Gregories, and Chrysostom himself contend[1] with a vehemence and indignation which proves them to have been common. Many parents thought they would allow the fitful and unstable season of youth to pass before they irrevocably bound their children under the most solemn engagements of their Christian calling. The children, when they grew up, inherited their scruples, and so the sacrament was indefinitely deferred.

It is not impossible that such feelings may have influenced Chrysostom's mother and himself; but considering the natural and healthy character of his piety, which seems to have grown by a gentle and unintermitting progress from his childhood, they do not seem very probable in his case. A more cogent cause for the delay may perhaps be found in the distracted state of the Church in Antioch, which lasted, with increasing complications, from A.D. 330, or fifteen years prior to Chrysostom's birth, up to the time of his baptism by Meletius, when a brighter day was beginning to dawn.

The vicissitudes of the Church in Antioch during that period form a curious, though far from pleasing, picture of the inextricable difficulties, the deplorable schisms, into which the Church at large was plunged by the Arian controversy. Two years after the Council of Nice, A.D. 327,

---

[1] Basil exhort. ad Baptismum; Apost. vol. ix. hom. i. in fine, and in Greg. Nazianz. Orat. 40 de Bapt.; Illumin. Catechesis, vol. ii. p. 223. Nyssen de Bapt.; Chrysost. in Acta

the Arians, through the assistance of Constantia, the
Emperor's sister, won the favour of Constantine. He lost
no time during this season of prosperity in procuring the
deposition of Catholic bishops. Eminent among these
was Eustathius, Bishop of Antioch. He was ejected by a
synod held in his own city on false charges of Sabellianism
and adultery.[1] An Arian bishop, Euphronius, was appointed, but the Catholic congregation indignantly withdrew to hold their services in another quarter of the town.
on the opposite side of the Orontes.[2] The see remained
for some time entirely in the hands of the Arians. When
the Council of Sardica met in A.D. 342, and the Arian
faction seceded from it to hold a Council of their own in
Philipopolis, Stephen, Bishop of Antioch, was their
president. He was deposed in A.D. 349 by the Emperor
Constantius, having been detected as an accomplice in
an infamous plot against some envoys from the Western
Church.[3] But 'uno avulso non deficit alter;' he was succeed by another Arian, the eunuch Leontius.[4] He tried
to conciliate the Catholics by an artful and equivocating
policy, of which his manner of chanting the doxology was
an instance. The Arian form of it was 'Glory be to the
Father BY the Son IN the Holy Ghost'; this the bishop
was accustomed to slur in such an indistinct voice that
the prepositions could not be clearly if at all heard, while
he joined loudly in the second part of the hymn where all
were agreed.[5] He died towards the close of A.D. 357,
when the see was fraudulently seized by Eudoxius, Bishop
of Germanicia. He favoured the extreme Arians so
openly that the Semi-Arians appealed to the Emperor

[1] Philostorgius ii. 7; Socrates i. 23; Theod. i. 21.

[2] Socr. i. 24 : Theod. i. 22.

[3] Athanas. Hist. Arian. 20, 21 : Theod. ii. 9, 10.

[4] Socr. ii. 26 : he had been deposed from the rank of presbyter because he was a eunuch, in accordance with the provision of the Council of Nice. c. i. Labbe i. p. 28.

[5] Sozom. iii. 20 ; Theod. ii. 24.

Constantius to summon a General Council. Their request was granted; but the Arians, fearing that the Catholics and Semi-Arians would coalesce to overwhelm them, artfully suggested that Rimini, the place proposed for the Council, was too distant for the Eastern prelates, and that the Assembly should be divided, part meeting at Rimini, and part at Nice.[1] Their suggestion was accepted, and the result is well known. Partly by arguments, partly by artifices and delays which wore out the strength and patience of the members, the Arians completely carried the day; the creed of Rimini was ordered by the Emperor to be everywhere signed, and in the words of Jerome, 'the world groaned and found itself Arian.'[2] An Arian synod sat at Constantinople. Macedonius the archbishop, being considered too moderate, was deposed, and Eudoxius, the usurper of Antioch, was elevated to the see in his stead;[3] and Meletius, Bishop of Sebaste, in Armenia, was translated to the vacant see of Antioch, A.D. 361. But in him the Arians had mistaken their man. He was one of those who attended more to the practical moral teaching than to the abstract theology of Christianity; and, being not perhaps very precise in his language on doctrinal points, he had been reckoned an Arian.[4] After his elevation to the see of Antioch, he confined himself in his discourses to those practical topics on which all could agree. But this was not allowed to last long. The Emperor Constantius paid a visit to Antioch soon after the appointment of Meletius, and he was instigated by the Arians to put the bishop to a crucial test. He was commanded to preach on Proverbs viii. 22. 'The Lord *possessed* me'

---

[1] Sozom. iv. 12–16 : Theod. ii. 26. In consequence of an earthquake at Nice, it was removed to Seleucia in Isauria.

[2] Rufin. i. 21; Socr. ii. 36, 37; Sozom. iv. 19; Jerome c. Lucif. 18, 19.

[3] Socr. ii. 42, 43.

[4] Sozom. iv. 28.

(Septuagint ἔκτισε, that was the fatal word) 'in the beginning,' &c.   The interpretation put on the word 'formed'
(ἔκτισε) would reveal the man.   Two other bishops dis-
coursed first upon the same text; George of Laodicea,
Acacius of Cæsarea.   The first construed the passage in
a purely Arian sense : the Word was a κτίσμα, 'a created
being,' though the first in time and rank; the second
preacher took a more moderate line.   Then came the
turn of Meletius; short-hand writers took down every
word as it fell.   Meletius was a mild and temperate man,
but he had his convictions, and he was no coward.   To
the horror of the Arians (the secret joy, perhaps, of those
who disliked him) he entirely dissented from the Arian
interpretation.   The people loudly applauded his sermon,
and called aloud for some brief and compendious statement of his doctrine.   Meletius replied by a symbolical
action ; he held up three fingers, and then closing two of
them he said, 'Our minds conceive of three, but we
speak as to one.'[1]   This was conclusive ; the objection-
able prelate was banished to Melitene, his native place
in Armenia, thirty days after he had entered Antioch.
Euzoius, who had been an intimate friend and constant
associate of Arius himself, was put nto the see.   The
Church of Antioch now split into three parties; the old
and rigid orthodox set, who, ever since the deposition of
Eustathius in A.D. 327, had adhered to his doctrine, and
were called after his name ; the moderate Catholics, who
regarded Meletius as their bishop; and the Arians under
Euzoius.   The synod which had deposed him published a
thoroughly Arian creed, which declared the Son to have
been created out of nothing, and to be unlike the Father
both in substance and will.[2]

This first banishment of Meletius, which occurred in
A.D. 361, did not last long.   Julian, who became Emperor

---

[1] Theod. ii. 31 ; Sozom. iv. 28.   [2] Socr. ii. 15.

the same year, recalled all the prelates who had been
exiled in the two preceding reigns; partly, perhaps, from
a really liberal feeling, partly from a willingness to foment
the internal dissensions of the Church by placing the
rival bishops in close antagonism. Athanasius returned to
Alexandria amidst great ovations.[1]   One of the questions
which occupied the attention of a synod convened by him
was the schism of Antioch. Eusebius, Bishop of Vercelli,
a staunch Italian friend of Athanasius, was despatched to
Antioch in order to heal the division; but he had been unhappily anticipated by another Western prelate, Lucifer
of Cagliari, in Sardinia, a brave defender of orthodoxy,
for which with Eusebius he had suffered exile, but a most
unskilful peacemaker. He only complicated the existing
confusion by consecrating as bishop a priest of the old
Eustathian party, named Paulinus, instead of strengthening the hands of Meletius.[2] The unhappy Church at
Antioch, where the whole Christian community amounted
to not more than 100,000 souls,[3] was thus torn to tatters.
There were now three bishops—the Arian Euzoius; Meletius, generally acknowledged by the Eastern Church, and
Paulinus by the Western. And, as if these rival heads
were not sufficient, the Apollinarians soon afterwards
added a fourth. But the mild, prudent, and charitable
disposition of Meletius procured for him the affection and
esteem of the largest and most respectable part of the
population, as well as of the common people. Even when
he was banished for the first time after he been only a
month in Antioch, the populace endeavoured to stone the
prefect as he was conducting the bishop out of the city.
He was saved by Meletius himself, who threw a part of his
own mantle round him, to protect him from their fury.

[1] The Arian Bishop George having
been murdered by the Pagan population, Socr. iii. 5.

[2] Rufin. i. 27; Socr. iii. 6; Soz. v. 12.
[3] Chrysost. Hom. in Matt. 85, vol.
vii. p. 762.

And after he returned from exile the popularity of Meletius increased.   In paintings on the walls of houses and engravings on signet rings, his face was often represented, and parents gave his name to their children both to perpetuate his memory and to remind them of an example which was worthy of their imitation.[1]   Once more in A.D. 367, and yet again in A.D. 370 or A.D. 371, when the Arians recovered the favour of the Court under the Emperor Valens, he was sent into exile, but he returned after the death of Valens in A.D. 378; and it was as Bishop of Antioch that he presided over the Council of Constantinople in A.D. 381, and died during its session.[2]   His funeral oration, pronounced by Gregory Nyssen, is extant. The final reparation of that schism which he nobly and constantly endeavoured to heal, was not effected for nearly twenty years, when Chrysostom, the Archbishop of Constantinople, accomplished that good service for his native city.

It is interesting to dwell at some length upon the history of the Church in Antioch at this period, because it represents the painful feuds in which the Church at large became entangled through the baneful influence of the Arian controversy, that first great blow to the unity of Christendom; when bishop was set up against bishop, and rival councils manufactured rival creeds, when violence, and intrigue, and diplomatic arts were employed too often by both sides to gain their ends.   But the distracted state of the Church at Antioch also supplies a possible answer to the question why the baptism of Chrysostom was delayed so long.   One of the reasons frequently alleged for deferring the reception of that sacrament was the desire of the candidate to receive it at the hands of some particular bishop.[3]   Now who were the bishops of

[1] Chrysost. Hom. in Melet.
[2] Tillemont viii. 374.
[3] Greg. Nazian. Orat. de Bapt. 40 ;
Chrysost. Ep. 132 ad Gemellum.

Antioch during the infancy and boyhood of Chrysostom ? The Arians were in possession of the see at the time of his birth, and retained it till A.D. 361, when Meletius was appointed, but banished almost immediately. The pious sensible mother and the well-disposed youth would not unnaturally hold aloof from a Church over which presided such prelates as Stephen, Leontius, Eudoxius, Euzoius. Their minds may well have been so sorely perplexed and suspended between the claims of opposing factions as to delay the reception of baptism from the hands of any.

But the prudent, conciliatory policy, the mild and amiable disposition of Meletius, would attract the sympathy and respect of an affectionate, pious, and sensible character, such as was the youthful Chrysostom. He was about twenty when Meletius was banished in 367 by the Emperor Valens ; but the bishop returned in a short time, when Chrysostom's friend Basil had withdrawn into religious seclusion, and he himself was feeling an increasing repugnance to the world. He presented himself as a candidate for baptism to the bishop, and after the usual three years of preparation as a catechumen, was admitted to that solemn initiation into the Christian covenant.

There can be no doubt that baptism, from whatever cause delayed, must on that very account have come home to the recipient with a peculiar solemnity of meaning. It was an important epoch, often a decisive turning-point in the life, a deliberate renunciation of the world, and dedication of the whole man to God. So Chrysostom evidently felt it ; from this point we enter on a new phase in his life. He becomes for a time an enthusiastic ascetic, and then settles down into that more tranquil, and steady, but intense glow of piety and love to God which burned with undiminished force till the close of his career.

The wise Bishop Meletius, however, desired to employ his powers in some sphere of active labour in the Church. As a preliminary step to this end, he ordained him soon after his baptism to the office of reader. This order appears not to have been instituted in the Church before the third century ; at least, there is no allusion to it in writers of the first two centuries, and frequent references in writers of the third and fourth.[1] The duty of readers was to read those portions of Scripture which were introduced into the first service or 'Missa Catechumenorum,' which preceded the Communion, or 'Missa Fidelium,' so called because only the baptized were admitted to it. They read from the Pulpitum or Tribunal Ecclesiæ, or Ambo, the reading-desk of the Church, which must not be confounded with the Bema, or Tribunal of the Sanctuary. This last was identical with the altar, or rather the steps of the altar, and no rank lower than that of deacon was permitted to read from this position. By the Novells of Justinian,[2] eighteen was fixed as the youngest age at which anyone could be ordained to this office. But previous to this limitation, it was not uncommon to appoint mere children. Cæsarius of Arles is said to have been made a reader at the tender age of seven, and Victor Uticensis, describing the cruelties of the Vandalic persecution in Africa, affirms that among 500 clergy or more who perished by sword or famine, were many 'infant readers.'[3]

The ceremony of ordination appears to have been very simple. The Fourth Council of Carthage ordains that the bishop should testify before the congregation to the purity, the faith, and conversation of the candidate. Then in their presence he is to place a Bible in his hands with

[1] Tertullian is the first who mentions it ; de Præscript. c. 41.

[2] Just. Nov. cxxiii. c. 13.
[3] Quoted in Bingham, vol. i. p. 378.

these words: ' Take thou this book and be thou a reader of the word of God, which office if thou discharge faithfully and profitably thou shalt have part with those who have ministered the word of God.'[1]

[1] Conne. Carth. iv. c. 8. Labbe, vol. ii.

CHAPTER III.

COMMENCEMENT OF ASCETIC LIFE — STUDY UNDER DIODORUS — FOR-
MATION OF AN ASCETIC BROTHERHOOD — THE LETTERS TO THEO-
DORE. A.D. 370.

THE enthusiasm of minds newly awakened to a full perception of Christian holiness, and a deep sense of Christian
obligations, was in early times seldom contented with anything short of complete separation from the world. The
oriental temperament especially has been at all times
inclined to passionate extremes. It oscillates between
the most abandoned licentiousness and intense asceticism.
The second is the corrective of the first ; where the disease
is desperate the remedies must be violent. Chrysostom,
as will be perceived throughout his life, was never carried
to fanatical extremes ; a certain sobermindedness, and
calm, practical good sense eminently distinguished him,
though mingled with burning zeal. But in his youth
especially he was not exempt from the spirit of the age
and country in which he lived. He irresistibly gravitated
towards that kind of life which his friend Basil had
already adopted—a life of retirement, contemplation, and
pious study—'the philosophy' of Christianity, as it was
called at that time.[1]

It does not appear that Basil had actually joined any
monastic community, but merely that he was leading a
life of seclusion, and practising some of the usual monastic austerities. Chrysostom, indeed, distinctly asserts
that, previous to his own baptism, their intercourse had

---

[1] Vide quotations in Suicer Thesaur. sub verbo φιλοσοφί'.

not been entirely broken off; only that it was impossible for him, who had his business in the law courts and found his recreation in the theatre, to be so acceptable to one who never entered public places, and who was wholly devoted to meditation, study, and prayer.[1] Their intercourse was necessarily more rare, though their friendship was substantially unshaken. 'When, however, I had myself also lifted my head a little above this worldly flood, he received me with open arms' (probably referring here to his baptism or preparation for it); 'but even then I was not able to maintain my former equality, for he had the advantage of me in point of time, and having manifested the greatest diligence, he had attained a very lofty standard, and was ever soaring beyond me.'[2]

This disparity, however, could not diminish their natural affection for one another; and Basil at length obtained Chrysostom's consent to a plan which he had frequently urged—that they should abandon their present homes and live together in some quiet abode, there to strengthen each other in undisturbed study, meditation, and prayer. But this project of the young enthusiasts was for a time frustrated by the irresistible entreaties of Chrysostom's mother, that he would not deprive her of his protection, companionship, and help. The scene is described by Chrysostom himself,[3] with a dramatic power worthy of Greek tragedy. It reminds the reader of some of those long and stately, yet elegant and affecting, narratives of the messenger who, at the close of the play, *describes* the final scene which is not represented. Certainly it bespeaks the scholar of a man who had made his pupils familiar with the best classical writers in Greek. 'When she knew that we were meditating this course, my mother took me by the right hand and led me into her own chamber, and there, seating herself near the bed on which she

---

[1] De Sacerd. i. c. 4.   [2] Ibid. c. 3.   [3] Ibid. c. 5.

had given birth to me, wept fountains of tears; to which she added words of lamentation more pitiable even than the tears themselves. "I was not long permitted to enjoy the virtue of thy father, my child;—so it seemed good to God. My travail pangs at your birth were quickly succeeded by his death; bringing orphanhood upon thee, and upon me an untimely widowhood, with all those miseries of widowhood which those only who have experienced them can fairly understand. For no description can approach the reality of that storm and tempest which is undergone by her who having but lately issued from her father's home, and being unskilled in the ways of the world, is suddenly plunged into grief insupportable, and compelled to endure anxieties too great for her sex and age. For she has to correct the negligence, to watch against the ill-doings of her slaves, to baffle the insidious schemes of kinsfolk, to meet with a brave front the impudent threats and harshness of tax collectors." ' [1]

She then describes minutely the expense, and labour, and constant anxiety which attended the education of a son; how she had refrained from all thoughts of second marriage, that she might bestow her undivided energies, time, and means upon him; how amply it had all been rewarded by the delight of his presence, recalling the image of her husband. And now that he had grown up, would he leave her absolutely forlorn? 'In return for all these my services to you,' she cried, 'I implore you this one favour only—not to make me a second time a widow, or to revive the grief which time has lulled. Wait for my death—perhaps I shall soon be gone; when you have committed my body to the ground, and mingled my bones with your father's bones, then you will be free to embark on any sea you please.' Such an appeal to his

---

[1] For the oppressive manner in which taxes were collected see Gibbon, iii. 78. et seq., Milman's edit.

sense of filial gratitude and duty could not be disregarded. Chrysostom yielded to his mother's entreaties; although Basil did not desist from urging his favourite scheme.[1]

At the same time he assimilated his life at home as much as possible to the condition of a monk. He entirely withdrew from all worldly occupations and amusements. He seldom went out of the house; he strengthened his mind by study, his spirit by prayer, and subdued his body by vigils and fasting, and sleeping upon the bare ground. He maintained an almost constant silence, that his thoughts might be kept abstracted from mundane things, and that no irritable or slanderous speech might escape his lips. Some of his companions naturally lamented what they regarded as a morose and melancholy change.[2]

But the intercourse between him and Basil was more frequent than before; and two other young men, who had been their fellow students at the school of Libanius, were persuaded to adopt the same kind of secluded life. These two were Maximus, afterwards Bishop of Seleucia, in Isauria; and Theodore, who became Bishop of Mopsuestia, in Cilicia.[3] This little fraternity formed, with some others not named, a voluntary association of youthful ascetics. They did not dwell in a separate building, nor were they in any way established as a monastic community, but (like Wesley and his young friends at Oxford) they lived by rule, and practised monastic austerities. The superintendence of their studies and general conduct they submitted to Diodorus and Carterius, who were presidents of monasteries in the vicinity of Antioch.[4] In addition to his own intrinsic merits and eminence, Diodorus claims our attention, because there can be no doubt that he exercised a great influence upon the minds of his two most distinguished scholars, Chrysostom and Theo-

---

[1] De Sacerd. i. c. 6.

[2] Ibid. vi. c. 12.

[3] Socr. vi. c. 3.

[4] Ibid. vi. 3.

dore. Indeed, judging from the fragments of his works, and the notices of him by historians, it is not too much to say that he was the founder of a method of Biblical interpretation of which Chrysostom and Theodore became the most able representatives.

He was of noble family, and the friend of Meletius, who confided to him and the priest Evagrius the chief care of his diocese during his second exile under Valens about A.D. 370. And one of the first acts of Meletius, on his return in A.D. 378, was to make Diodorus Bishop of Tarsus. His writings in defence of Christianity were sufficiently powerful and notorious to provoke the notice of Julian, who, in a letter to Photinus, attacks him with no small asperity.[1] The Emperor finds occasion for ridicule in the pale and wrinkled face and the attenuated frame of Diodorus, wasted by his severe labours and ascetic practices; and represents these disfigurements as punishments from the offended gods against whom he had directed his pen. Being well known as a warm friend of Meletius, Diodorus was exposed to some risk from the Arian party during the exile of the bishop from A.D. 370 378. But he was not deterred from frequenting the old town on the south side of the Orontes, where the congregation of Meletius held their assemblies, and diligently ministering to their spiritual needs. He accepted no fixed stipend, but his necessities were supplied by the hospitality of those among whom he laboured.[2] Of his voluminous writings, a commentary on the Old and New Testament is that most frequently quoted by ecclesiastical writers. They expressly and repeatedly affirm that he adhered very closely to the literal and historical meaning of the text, and that he was opposed to those mystical

[1] In Facund. Hermian. pro def. trium. capit. lib. iv. c. 2 in Gall. and bibl. patr. xi. p. 706.

[2] Chrysost. Hom. in Diodor. vol. iii. p. 761.

[3] Socr. vi. 3.

and allegorical interpretations of Origen and the Alexdrian school, which often disguised rather than elucidated the true significance of the passage.[1] One evil of the allegorical method was, that it destroyed a clear and critical perception of the differences between the older Revelation and the New. The Old Testament was regarded as a kind of vast enigma, containing *implicitly* the facts and doctrines of the New. To detect subtle allusions to the coming of our Saviour, to the events of his life, to his death and resurrection, in the acts, speeches, and gestures of persons mentioned in the Old Testament, was regarded as a kind of interpretation no less satisfactory than it was ingenious. To believe indeed that the grand intention running through Scripture from the beginning to the end, is to bring men to Jesus Christ; that the history of the fall of man is given to enable us to appreciate the need of a Restorer, and to estimate his work at its proper value; that the history of a dispensation based on law enables us to accept with more thankfulness a dispensation of spirit; to recognise through the history of the Jewish system of sacrifices the immeasurable superiority of the one great Sacrifice as the substance of previous shadows, the fulfilment of previous types; to see, in fact, in the general course of Old Testament narrative, and in the voices of the prophets, intimations and hints, and significant parallels of the subsequent history to which they lead on and lead up;—this may be reasonable, profitable, and true: but it can be neither profitable nor true to see allusions, prophecies, and parallels in every minute and trivial detail of that earlier history.

From this vital error Diodorus appears to have emancipated himself and his disciples. He perceived, as we shall see Chrysostom perceived, a gradual development in Revelation: that the knowledge, and morality, and faith of men under the Old Dispensation were less advanced than

those of men who lived under the New. One instance
must suffice. He remarks that the Mosaic precept, directing the brother of a man who had died childless to
raise up posterity to his brother by marrying his wife,
was given for the consolation of men who had as yet received no clear promise respecting a resurrection from the
dead.[1] There is an approach to what some might deem
rationalistic criticism, when he affirms that the speech of
God to men in the Old Testament was not an external
voice, but an inward spiritual intimation. When, for
instance, it is said that God gave a command to Adam, it
is evident, he says, that it was not made by a sound
audible to the bodily ear, but that God impressed the
knowledge of the command upon him according to His
own proper energy, and that when Adam had received it
his *condition* was the same *as* if it had come to him
through the actual hearing of the ear. And this, he
observes, is what God effected also in the case of the
prophets.[2] A similar rationalistic tendency is observable
in his explanation of the relation between the Divine and
human elements in the person of our blessed Lord. His
language, in fact, on this subject is Nestorian: a distinction was to be made between Him who, according to his
essence, *was* Son of God—the Logos—and Him who
through Divine decree and adoption *became* Son of God.
He who was born as Man from Mary was Son according
to grace, but God the Logos was Son according to
nature. The Son of Mary became Son of God because He
was selected to be the receptacle or temple of God the
Word. It was only in an improper sense that God the
Word was called Son of David ; the appellation was given
to Him merely because the human temple in which He
dwelt belonged to the lineage of David.[3] It is clear that

[1] Niceph. *supd.* vol. i. p. 524 and
436.
[2] Ibid. vol. i. p. 80.
[3] Leont. Byzant. contra Nestor. et
Eutych. lib. iii. in Basnage thesaur.
monum. i. 592.

Diodorus would have objected equally with Nestorius to apply the title of 'God-bearer' (Θεοτόκος) to the blessed Virgin. Sixty years later, in A.D. 429, the streets of Constantinople and Alexandria resounded with tumults excited by controversy about the subject of which this was the watchword. But Diodorus happily lived too early for these dreadful conflicts, and his scholar Theodore was not personally disturbed; though long after his death, in A.D. 553, his writings were condemned by the Fifth Œcumenical Council, because the Nestorians appealed to them in confirmation of their tenets, and revered his memory. The practical element in Diodorus, his method of literal and common-sense interpretation of Holy Scripture, was inherited chiefly by Chrysostom; the intellectual vein, his conceptions of the relation between the Godhead and Manhood in Christ, his opinions respecting the final restoration of mankind, which were almost equivalent to a denial of eternal punishment, were reproduced mainly by Theodore.

It was inevitable that sometimes those who, in an access of religious fervour, had renounced the world and subjected themselves to the sternest asceticism, found that they had miscalculated their powers. The passionate enthusiasm which for a time carried them along the thorny path would begin to subside; a hankering after a more natural, if not more worldly life ensued; and occasionally the reaction was so violent, the passions kept down in unnatural constraint reasserted themselves with such force, that the ascetic flew back to the pleasures and sometimes to the sins of the world, with an appetite which was in painful contrast to his previous abstinence. The youthful Theodore was for a time an instance, though far from an extreme instance, of such reaction: the strain was too great for him; he relapsed for a season into his former habits of life; he retired from the little ascetic brotherhood to which Chry-

D

sostom and Basil belonged.   There is no evidence that he
fell into any kind of sin ; he simply returned to the occupations and amusements of ordinary life.   He was in love
with and desirous of marrying a young lady named Hermione.   But Chrysostom was at this period such an ardent
ascetic ; he was so deeply impressed with the evil of the
world, and regarded an austere and absolute separation
from it as so indisputably the highest form of Christian
life, that to him any divergence from that path, when once
adopted, seemed a positive sin.   The relapse of Theodore
called forth two letters of lamentation, remonstrance, and
exhortation from his friend.   They are the earliest of his
extant works, and exhibit a command of language which
does credit to the training of Libanius as well as to
his own ability, and an intimate acquaintance with Holy
Scripture, which proves how much time he had already
spent in diligent and patient study.   Since these epistles
have been justly considered among the finest of his productions, and represent his opinions at an early stage of
his life respecting repentance, a future life, the advantages of asceticism and celibacy, some paraphrases from
them will be presented to the reader.

He begins his first letter by quoting the words of
Jeremiah, ' Oh that my head were waters, and mine eyes
a fountain of tears.'

' If the prophet uttered that lamentation over a ruined
city, surely I may express a like passionate sorrow over
the fallen soul of a brother.   That soul which was once
the temple of the Holy Spirit now lies open and defence-
less to become the prey of any hostile invader.   The spirit
of avarice, of arrogance, of lust, may now find a free passage into a heart which was once as pure and inaccessible
to evil as heaven itself.   Wherefore I mourn and weep,
nor will I cease from my mourning until I see thee again
in thy former brilliancy.   For though this may seem im-

possible to men, yet with God it is possible, for He it is who lifteth the beggar from the earth and taketh the poor out of the dunghill, that He may set him with the princes, even with the princes of his people.' An eminent characteristic of Chrysostom is that he is always hopeful of human nature; he never doubts the capacity of man to rise, or the willingness of God to raise him. Theodore himself appears to have been stricken with remorse, and to have drooped into despondency, to rouse him from which and lead him to repose more trustfully on the goodness of God, was one main purpose of Chrysostom's letters. 'Despair was the devil's work;' 'it is he who tries to cut off that hope whereby men are saved, which is the support and anchor of the soul, which, like a long chain let down from heaven, little by little draws those who hold tightly to it up to heavenly heights, and lifts them above the storm and tempest of these worldly ills. The devil tries to extinguish that trust which is the source and strength of prayer, which enables men to cry, "as the eyes of a maiden look unto the hand of her mistress, even so our eyes wait upon the Lord our God until He have mercy upon us." Yet if man will only believe it, there is never a time at which any one, even the most abandoned sinner, may not turn and repent and be accepted by God. For God being impassible, his wrath is not a passion or an emotion; He punishes not in anger, since He is unsusceptible by nature of injury from any insult or wrong done by us, but in mercy, that He may bring men back to Himself. [1] The many instances of God's mercy; his relenting towards the Jews, and even to Ahab, when he humbled himself; the repentance of Manasseh—of the Ninevites— of the penitent thief—all accepted, although preceded by a long course of sin, prove that the words "to-day if ye will hear his voice" are applicable to any time:—it is

[1] C. 2–5.

D 2

always "to-day" as long as a man lives; repentance is
estimated not by length of time, but by the disposition of
the heart.' He acutely observes that 'despondency often
conceals moral weakness; a secret though perhaps unconscious sympathy with the sin which the man professes to
deplore and hate.' 'To fall is natural, but to remain
fallen argues a kind of acquiescence in evil, a feebleness of
moral purpose which is more displeasing to God than the
fall itself.' [1]

But although he speaks in the most hopeful, encouraging
language of the efficacy of repentance, however late, if
sincere, in *this life*, no one can assert more strongly the
impossibility of restoration when the limits of this present
existence have once been passed. In this respect he
differs alike from Origen, Diodorus, and his fellow-student
Theodore, and from believers in the later developed doctrine of purgatory. 'As long as we are here, it is possible,
even if we sin ten thousand times, to wash all away by
repentance; but when once we have been taken to that
other world, even if we manifest the greatest penitence, it
will avail us nought, but however much we may gnash
with our teeth, and beat our breasts, and pour forth
entreaties, no one will be able even with the tip of his
finger to cool us in the flame; we shall only hear the
same words as the rich man: "between us and you there
is a great gulf fixed."' [2] Nothing is more remarkably
characteristic of Chrysostom's productions, especially the
earlier, than a frequent recurrence to this truth: the existence of a great impassable chasm between the two abodes of
misery and bliss. Heaven and hell were no distant dream-
lands to him, but realities so nearly and vividly present to
his mind that they acted as powerful motives, encouraging
to holiness, deterring from vice. He paints the two
pictures in glowing colours, and submits them to the

¹ I. c. 8, 9.   ² C. 9.

contemplation of his friend. 'When you hear of fire think not that the fire in that other world is like it; for this earthly fire burns up and consumes whatever it lays hold of, but that burns continually those who are seized by it and never ceases, wherefore it is called unquenchable. For sinners must be clothed with immortality, not for honour, but merely to supply a constant material for this punishment to feed upon; and how terrible this is, a description would indeed never be able to present, but from our experience of small sufferings it is possible to form some little conception of those greater miseries. If you should ever be in a bath which has been overheated, then I pray you consider the fire of hell; or if ever you have been parched by a severe fever, transfer your thoughts to that flame, and you will be able clearly to distinguish the difference. For if a bath or a fever so distress and agitate us, what will be our condition when we fall into that river of fire which flows past the terrible Judge's throne.'[1] 'Heaven is, indeed, a subject which transcends the powers of human language, yet we can form a dim image of what it is like. It is the place " whence sorrow and sighing shall flee away" (Is. xxxv. 10); where poverty and sickness are not to be dreaded; where no one injures or is injured, no one provokes or is provoked; no one is harassed by anxiety about the necessary wants, or frets over the loftier ambitions of life; it is the place where the tempest of human passions is lulled; where there is neither night nor cold nor heat, nor changes of season, nor old age; but everything belonging to decay is taken away, and incorruptible glory reigns alone. But far above all these things, it is the place where men will continually enjoy the society of Jesus Christ, together with angels and archangels and all the powers above.'[2] 'Open your eyes,' he cries in a transport of feeling, 'and

---

[1] C. 10.   [2] Theod. i. c. 11 in initio.

contemplate in imagination that heavenly theatre crowded
not with men such as we see, but with those who are
nobler than gold or precious stones or sunbeams, or any
brilliant thing that can be seen; and not with men only,
but angels, thrones, dominions, powers ranged about the
King whom we dare not describe for his transcendant
beauty, majesty, and splendour. If we had to suffer ten
thousand deaths every day; nay, if we had to undergo
hell itself, for the sake of beholding Christ coming in his
glory, and being numbered among the band of saints,
would it not be well to submit to all these things?
" Master, it is a good thing for us to be here ": if such an
exclamation burst from St. Peter on witnessing a partial
and veiled manifestation of Christ's glory, what are we
to say when the reality shall be displayed, when the royal
palace shall be thrown open and we shall see the King
Himself; no longer by means of a mirror, or as it were
in a riddle, but face to face; no longer through faith, but
actual sight.'[1]   He passes on to some remarks upon the
soul, which are Platonic in character: ' Man cannot alter
the shape of his body, but God has conceded to him a
power, with the assistance of Divine grace, of increasing
the beauty of the soul.   Even that soul which has become
deformed by the ugliness of sin, may be restored to its
pristine beauty.   No lover was ever so much captivated
by the beauty of the body as God loves and longs for the
beauty of the human soul.[2]   You who are now transported
with admiration of Hermione's beauty' (the girl whom
Theodore wished to marry) 'may, if you will, cultivate a
beauty in your own soul as far exceeding hers as heaven
surpasses earth.   Beauty of the soul is the only true and
permanent kind, and if you could see it with the eye,
you would admire it far more than the loveliness of the
rainbow and of roses, and other flowers which are eva-

[1] C. 11.   [2] C. 13.

nescent, and feeble representations of the soul's beauty.'[1]
He tells some curious stories of men who had relapsed
from monastic life and subsequently been reclaimed to it.
One, a young man of noble family and heir to great
wealth, had thrown up all the splendour which he might
have commanded, and exchanged his riches and his gay
clothing for the poverty and mean garb of a recluse upon
the mountains, and had attained an astonishing degree of
holiness.   But some of his relations seduced him from his
retreat, and once more he might be seen riding on horseback through the forum followed by a crowd of attendants.
But the holy brethren whom he had deserted ceased not
to endeavour to recover him; at first he treated them
with haughty indifference, when they met and saluted him
as he proudly rode through the streets.   But at last, as
they desisted not day by day, he would leap from his
horse when they appeared, and listen with downcast eyes
to their warnings; till, as time went on, he was rescued
from his worldly entanglements, and restored to his desert
and the study of the true philosophy, and now, when
Chrysostom wrote, he bestowed his wealth upon the poor,
and had attained the very pinnacle of virtue.[2]   Earnestly,
therefore, does he implore Theodore to recover his trust
in God, to repent and return to the brotherhood which
was buried in grief at his defection.   'Now the unbelieving and the worldly rejoice, but return to us and
our sorrow and shame will be transferred to the adversary's
side.'   'It was the beginning of penitence which was
arduous; the devil met the penitent at the door of the
city of refuge, but if defeated there, the fury of his assaults
would diminish.'   He warned him against an idle confession of sinfulness not accompanied by any honest effort
to amend.   'Such was no true confession, because not
joined with the tears of contrition or followed by altera-

[1] C. 14.   [2] C. 17.

tion of life.'[1]   But of Theodore he hoped better things;
as there were different degrees of glory reserved for men,
implied in our Lord's mention of 'many mansions,' and
his declaring that everyone should be rewarded according
to his works, he trusted that Theodore might still obtain
a high place; that he might be a vessel of silver if not of
gold or precious stone in the heavenly house.[2]

In the second epistle Chrysostom expresses more distinctly his view respecting the solemn obligations of those
who joined a religious fraternity. 'If tears and groanings
could be transmitted through a letter, this of mine would
be filled with them; I weep that you have blotted yourself out of the catalogue of the brethren, and trampled on
your covenant with Christ.' 'The devil assaulted him
with peculiar fury, because he was anxious to conquer so
worthy an antagonist; one who had despised delicate fare
and costly dress, who had spent whole days in the study
of Holy Scripture, and whole nights in prayer, who had
regarded the society of the brethren as a greater honour
than any worldly dignity. What, I pray you, is there that
appears blessed and enviable in the world? The prince is
exposed to the wrath of the people and the irrational outbursts of popular feeling—to the fear of princes greater
than himself—to anxieties about his subjects; and the
ruler of to-day is to-morrow a private man : for this present life no way differs from a stage; as on that, one man
plays the part of a king, another of a general, a third of a
common soldier; but when evening has come, the king is
no king, the ruler no ruler, the general no general; so
will it be in *that* day; each will receive his due reward,
not according to the character which he has enacted, but
according to the works which he has done.'[3]   Theodore
had clearly expressed his intention of honourably marrying Hermione; but though Chrysostom allows that mar-

riage is an honourable estate, yet he boldly declares that
for one who like Theodore had made such a solemn renunciation of the world, it was equally criminal with fornication. He had wholly dedicated himself to the service of
God, and he had no right to bind himself by any other
tie : to marry would be as culpable as desertion in a
soldier. He points out the miseries, the anxieties, the
toils, often fruitless, which accompanied secular life, especially in the married state. From all such ills the life of
the brotherhood was exempt : he alone was truly free who
lived for Christ; he was like one who, securely planted on
an eminence, beholds other men below him buffetting with
the waves of a tumultuous sea. For such a high vantage
ground Chrysostom implores Theodore to make. He begs
him to pardon the length of his letter; 'nothing but his
ardent love for his friend could have constrained him to
write this second epistle. Many indeed had discouraged
what they regarded as a vain task and sowing upon a
rock; but he was not so to be diverted from his efforts:
he trusted that by the grace of God his letters would
accomplish something ; and if not, he should at least have
delivered himself from the reproach of silence.'[1]

These letters are the productions of a youthful enthu-
siast, and as such, allowances must be made for them.
They abound not only in eloquent passages, but in very
fine and true observations upon human nature—on penitence—on God's mercy and pardon. It is only the application of them to the case of Theodore which seems
overstrained. At a later period Chrysostom's views on
ascetic and monastic life were modified; but in early life,
though never fanatical, they were what we should call extreme. His earnest efforts for the restoration of his friend
were crowned with success. Theodore abandoned the
world once more and his matrimonial intentions, and re-

[1] C. 5.

tired into the seclusion of the brotherhood.   Some twenty
years later, in A.D. 394, he was made Bishop of Mopsuestia,
which is pretty nearly all we know about him, but the
extant fragments of his voluminous writings prove him to
have been a man of no ordinary ability, and a powerful
commentator of the same sensible and rational school as
Chrysostom himself.   We may be disposed to say what of
Hermione ?   Had she no claims to be considered ?   But
the ascetic line of life was regarded by the earnest-minded
as so indisputably the noblest which a Christian could
adopt, that her disappointment would not have been allowed to weigh in the balance for a moment against what
was considered the higher call.[1]

[1] Tillemont maintains that the Theodore to whom the first letter is addressed must have been a different
person from the fellow-student of
Chrysostom and eventual Bishop of
Mopsuestia, but he stands alone in
this opinion, and his reasons for it
seem inadequate.—Till. xi. note vi.
p. 550.

CHAPTER IV.

WE now come to a curious passage in Chrysostom's life ;
one in which his conduct, from our moral stand-point,
seems hardly justifiable. Yet for one reason it is not to
be regretted, since it eventually drew forth from him his
treatise ' De Sacerdotio ; ' one of the ablest, most instructive, and most eloquent works which he ever produced.

Bishop Meletius had been banished in A.D. 370 or 371.
The Arian Emperor Valens, who had expelled him, was
about to take up his residence in Antioch. It was desirable therefore, without loss of time, to fill up some vacant
sees in Syria. The attention of the bishops, clergy, and
people was turned to Chrysostom and Basil, as men well
qualified for the episcopal office.

According to a custom prevalent at that time, they
might any day be seized and compelled, however reluctant, to accept the dignity. So St. Augustine was dragged,
weeping, by the people before the bishop, and his immediate ordination demanded by them, regardless of his
tears.[1] So St. Martin, Bishop of Tours, was torn from his
cell, and conveyed under a guard to his ordination.[2] The
two friends were filled with apprehension and alarm. Basil
implored Chrysostom that they might act in concert at the

---

[1] Possid. Vit. August. c. iv.

[2] Sulp. Sever. Vit. St. Martin. l. i.
p. 224. The affectation of reluctance
to be consecrated became a fashion in
the Coptic Church. The patriarch
designate of Alexandria is at this day
brought to Cairo, loaded with chains,
as if to prevent his escape.—Stanley,
Eastern Church, lect. vii. p. 226.

present crisis, and together accept or together evade or
resist the expected but unwelcome honour.

Chrysostom affected to consent to this proposal, but in
reality determined to act otherwise. He regarded himself
as totally unworthy and incompetent to fill so sacred and
responsible an office; but considering Basil to be far more
advanced in learning and piety, he resolved that the Church
should not, through his own weakness, lose the services
of his friend. Accordingly, when popular report proved
correct, and some emissaries from the electing body were
sent to carry off the young men (much, it would seem from
Chrysostom's account, as policemen might arrest a prisoner), Chrysostom contrived to hide himself. Basil, less
wary, was captured, and imagined that Chrysostom had
already submitted; for the emissaries acted with subtlety
when he tried to resist them. They affected surprise that
he should make so violent a resistance, when his companion, who had the reputation of a hotter temper, had
yielded so mildly to the decision of the Fathers.[1] Thus
Basil was led to suppose that Chrysostom had already submitted; and when he discovered too late the artifice of
his friend and his captors, he bitterly remonstrated with
Chrysostom upon his treacherous conduct. 'The character of them both,' he complained, was compromised
'by this division in their counsels.' 'You should have told
us where your friend was hidden,' said some, 'and then
we should have contrived some means of capturing him,'
to which poor Basil was ashamed to reply that he had
been ignorant of his friend's concealment, lest such a confession should cast a suspicion of unreality over the whole
of their supposed intimacy. 'Chrysostom, on his side, was
accused of haughtiness and vanity for declining so great a

---

[1] C. 5. This word may refer to the
bishops or the people. Ambrose calls
the people his 'parentes,' because they
had elected him bishop.—Comment.
in Luc. l. viii. c. 17.

dignity; though others said that the electors deserved a
still greater dishonour and defeat for appointing over the
heads of wiser, holier, and older men, mere lads,[1] who had
been but yesterday immersed in secular pursuits; that
they might now for a little while knit their brows, and go
arrayed in sombre robes and affect a grave countenance.'[2]
Basil begged Chrysostom for an explanation of his motives
in this proceeding. 'After all their mutual protestations of
indivisible friendship, he had been suddenly cast off and
turned adrift, like a vessel without ballast, to encounter
alone the angry tempests of the world. To whom should
he now turn for sympathy and aid in the trials to which
he would surely be exposed from slander, ribaldry, and
insolence? The one who might have helped him stood
coldly aloof, and would be unable even to hear his cries
for assistance.'[3]

We may be strongly disposed to sympathise with the
disconsolate Basil. But the conscience of Chrysostom
appears to have been quite at ease from first to last in
this transaction. He regarded it as a 'pious fraud.'
'When he beheld the mingled distress and displeasure of
his friend he could not refrain from laughing for joy, and
thanking God for the successful issue of his plan.'[4] In the
ensuing discussion he boldly asserted the principle that
deceit claims our admiration when practised in a good
cause and from a good motive. The greatest successes in
war, he argues, have been achieved through stratagem, as
well as by fair fighting in the open field; and, of the two,
the first are most to be admired, because they are gained
without bloodshed, and are triumphs of mental rather
than bodily force.[5] But, retorts poor Basil, I was not an
enemy, and ought not to have been dealt with as such.
'True, my excellent friend,' replies Chrysostom, 'but this

---

[1] μειράκια; vide note at end of chapter.   [2] I. c. 5.   [3] C. 7.
[4] C. 6.   [5] C. 8.

kind of fraud may sometimes be exercised towards our
dearest acquaintance.' 'Physicians were often obliged to
employ some artifice to make refractory patients submit
to their remedies. Once a man in a raging fever resisted
all the febrifugal draughts administered to him, and
loudly called for wine. The physician darkened the
room, steeped a warm oyster shell in wine, then filled it
with water, and put it to the patient's lips, who eagerly
swallowed the draught, believing it, from the smell, to be
wine.'[1] In the same category of justifiable stratagem
he places, not very discriminatingly, the circumcision of
Timothy by St. Paul, in order to conciliate the Jews, and
St. Paul's observance of the ceremonial law at Jerusalem
(Acts xxi. 26), for the same purpose. Such contrivances
he calls instances, not of treachery, but of 'good management' (οἰκονομία). There is something highly Oriental,
and remote from our Western moral sense, in the sophistical tone of this whole discussion. If Basil really submitted to such arguments, he was easily vanquished. He
says, however, no more about the injustice of his treatment, but apparently accepting Chrysostom's position
that for a useful purpose deceit is justifiable, he begs to
be informed 'what advantage Chrysostom thought he had
procured for himself or his friend by this piece of management, or good policy, or whatever he pleased to call it.'

The remaining books on the Priesthood are occupied
with the answer to this enquiry. The line which Chrysostom takes is to point out the pre-eminent dignity,
difficulty, and danger of the priestly office, and then to
enlarge upon the peculiar fitness of his friend to discharge
its duties.[2] 'What advantage could be greater than to

---

[1] C. 9.

[2] The words priest and bishop are
employed in the following translations
and paraphrases, to correspond with
ἱερεύς and ἐπίσκοπος, which are used in

the original without much apparent
distinction. Chrysostom is speaking
of the priesthood generally, and it is
not easy to say which Order he has in
his mind at any given moment.

be engaged in that work which Christ had declared with
his own lips to be the special sign of love to Himself.
For when He put the question three times to the chieftain
of the apostles (κορυφαῖος), "Lovest thou me?" and had
been answered by a fervent asseveration of attachment,
he added each time, "Feed my sheep," or "Feed my
lambs." "Lovest thou me *more* than these?" had been
the question, and the charge which followed it had been
always, "Feed my sheep"; not, If thou lovest Me, practise
fasting, or incessant vigils, and sleep on the bare ground,
or protect the injured and be to the orphans as a father,
and to their mother as a husband; no, he passes by all
these things, and says, "Feed my sheep." Could his
friend, therefore, complain that he had done ill in com-
passing, even by fraud, his dedication to so glorious an
office?[1] As for himself, it was obvious that he could not
have refused so great an honour out of haughty contempt
or disrespect to the electors. On the contrary, it was
when he considered the exceeding sanctity and magnitude
of the position, and its awful responsibilities—the heavenly
purity, the burning love towards God and man, the sound
wisdom and judgment, and moderation of temper required
in those who were dedicated to it—that his heart failed
him. He felt himself utterly incompetent and unworthy
for so arduous a task. If some unskilled person was suddenly to be called upon to take charge of a ship laden
with a costly freight, he would immediately refuse; and
in like manner he himself dared not risk, by his present
inexperience, the safety of that vessel which was laden
with the precious merchandise of souls.[2] Vain-glory, indeed, and pride would have induced him not to reject, but
to covet so transcendent a dignity. The office of priest
was discharged indeed on earth, yet it held a place among
heavenly ranks. And rightly; for neither man, nor angel,

[1] II. c. 2.　　　　[2] III. c. 1, 2, 5.

nor archangel, nor created power of any kind, but the Paraclete Himself, ordained this ministry. Therefore, it became one who entered the priesthood to be as pure as if he had already taken his stand in heaven itself among the powers above. "When thou seest the Lord lying slain, and the priest standing and praying over the sacrifice, when thou seest all sprinkled with that precious blood, dost thou deem thyself still among men, still standing upon this earth; art thou not rather transported immediately to heaven, and, every carnal imagination being cast out, dost thou not, with soul unveiled and pure mind, behold the things which are in heaven? O miracle! O the goodness of God! He who is sitting with the Father is yet at that hour held in the hands of all, and gives Himself to be embraced and grasped by those who desire it. And this all do through the eye of faith. Do these things seem to you to merit contempt? does it seem possible to you that anyone should be so elated as to slight them?"[1]

'Human nature possessed in the priesthood a power which had not been committed by God to angels or archangels; for to none of *them* had it been said, "Whatsoever ye shall bind on earth or loose on earth shall be bound or loosed in heaven." Was it possible to conceive that anyone should think lightly of such a gift? Away with such madness!—for stark madness it would be to despise so great an authority, without which it was not possible for man to obtain salvation, or the good things promised to him. For if it were impossible for anyone to enter into the kingdom of heaven, except he were born again of water and the Spirit; and if he who did not eat the flesh of the Lord and drink his blood was ejected from life eternal, and if these things were administered by none but the consecrated hands of the priest, how would any-

[1] III. c. 4.

one, apart from them, be able to escape the fire of hell, or obtain the crown laid up for him ? ' [1]

There are, perhaps, no passages elsewhere in Chrysostom expressed in such a lofty sacerdotal tone ; but it must be remembered that on any supposition as to the date of this treatise, he was young when it was composed, holding therefore, as on the subject of monasticism, more enthusiastic, highly-wrought opinions than he afterwards entertained ; and moreover, that the whole treatise is written in a somewhat vehement and excited style, as by one who was maintaining a position against an antagonist.

Having proved that his evasion of the episcopal office could have arisen from no spirit of pride, but from a consciousness of his infirmity and incapacity, he proceeds to point out the manifold and peculiar dangers which encompassed it. ' Vain-glory was a rock more fatal than the Syrens. Many a priest was shipwrecked there, and torn to pieces by the fierce monsters which dwelt upon it—wrath, despondency, envy, strife, slander, falsehood, hypocrisy, love of praise, and a multitude more. Often he became the slave and flatterer of great people, even of women who had most improperly mixed themselves up with ecclesiastical affairs, and especially exercised great influence in the elections.' [2]

The scenes, indeed, which often took place about this period at the elections to bishoprics, occasioned much scandal to the Church. In earlier times, when the Christians were less numerous, more simple in their habits, more unanimous ; when liability to persecution deterred the indifferent, or pretenders, from their ranks, the episcopal office could be no object of worldly ambition. The clergy and the people elected their bishop ; and the fairness and simplicity with which the election was usually conducted, won the admiration of the Emperor Alexander

[1] III. 5.   [2] III. 9, 10.

Severus.[1] But when Christianity was recognised by the State, a bishopric in towns of importance became a position of high dignity; and warm debates, often fierce tumults, attended the election of candidates. Up to the time of Justinian at least, the whole Christian population of the city or region over which the bishop was to preside possessed a right to elect. Their choice was subject to the approval of the bishops, and the confirmation of the metropolitan of the province; but, on the other hand, neither the bishops nor the metropolitan could legally obtrude a candidate of their own upon the people. A charge brought against Hilary of Arles was, that he ordained several bishops against the will and consent of the people. A just and legitimate ordination, according to Cyprian, was one which had been examined by the suffrage and judgment of all, both clergy and people. Such, he observes, was the election of Cornelius to the see of Rome in A.D. 251.[2] If the people were unanimous, there were loud cries of ἄξιος, dignus; ἀνάξιος, indignus, as the case might be; but if they were divided, it was usual for the metropolitan to give the preference to the choice of the majority; or, if they appeared equally divided, the metropolitan and his synod selected a man indifferent, if possible, to both parties. Occasionally, also, as in the case of Nectarius, the predecessor of Chrysostom in the see of Constantinople, the Emperor interposed, and appointed one chosen by himself. Sanguinary often were the tumults which attended contested elections. The greater the city, the greater the strife. In the celebrated contest for the see of Rome in A.D. 366, between Damasus and Ursicinus, there was much hard fighting and copious bloodshed. Damasus, with a furious and motley mob, broke into the Julian Basilica, where Ursicinus was being consecrated by Paul, Bishop of Tibur, and violently stopped

---

[1] Lamprid. Vita Alex. Sev. ch. 45. Paris edit.   [2] Cyprian Epis. 52.

the proceedings. Frays of this kind lasted for some time. On one occasion, one hundred and thirty dead bodies strewed the pavement of the Basilica of Licinnius, till Damasus was eventually triumphant. It is especially mentioned that the ladies of Rome favoured his side.[1] It seems scarcely possible to doubt that as these events must have been fresh in Chrysostom's recollection, he must be specially referring to them when, insisting on freedom from ambition as one grand qualification for the priest-hood, he says, 'that he will pass by, lest they should seem incredible, the tales of murders perpetrated in churches, and havoc wrought in cities by contentions for bishop-rics;' and when also he alludes indignantly to the inter-ference of women in the elections. 'The elections,' he says, 'were generally made on public festivals, and were disgraceful scenes of party feeling and intrigue. The clergy and the people were never unanimous. The really important qualifications for the office were seldom consi-dered. Ambitious men spared no arts of bribery or flat-tery by which to obtain places for themselves in the Church, and to keep them when obtained. One candidate for a bishopric was recommended to the electors because he belonged to a distinguished family; another because he was wealthy, and would not burden the funds of the Church.'[2] The provocations to ambition and worldly glory were so great, both in the acquisition and in the possession of the episcopal office, that Chrysostom says, he had 'determined partly for these reasons to avoid the snare.[3] He shrunk also from many other trials incident

---

[1] Ammian. Marcell. l. xxvii. c. 3. Socrat. l. iv. c. 29. See a multitude of evidence carefully collected on this subject in Bingham, vol. i. b. iv. ch. 2.

[2] III. 15.

[3] Comp. in Ac. Apost. Hom. iii. 5. 'Men now aim at a bishopric like any secular office. To win glory and honour among men we peril our sal-vation. . . . Consuls and prefects do not enjoy such honour as he who pre-sides over the Church. Go to court, or to the houses of lords and ladies, and whom do you find foremost there? no one is put before the bishop.'

to the office.   There were always persons ready to detect
and magnify the slightest mistake or transgression in a
priest.   One little error could not be retrieved by a multitude of successes, but darkened the man's whole life.
For a kind of immaculate purity was exacted by popular
opinion of a priest, as if he was not a being of flesh and
blood, or subject to human passions.   Often his brethren,
the clergy, were the most active in spreading mischievous
reports about him, hoping to rise themselves upon his
ruin; like avaricious sons waiting for their father's death.
Too often St. Paul's description of the sympathy between
the several parts of the Christian body was inverted.   "If
one member suffered, all the others rejoiced; if one
member rejoiced, the others suffered pain."   A bishop had
need be as impervious to slander and envy as the three
children in the burning fiery furnace.[1]   What a rare and
difficult combination of qualities was required for the
efficient discharge of his duties in the face of such difficulties!   "He must be dignified, yet not haughty; formidable, yet affable; commanding, yet sociable; strictly
impartial, yet courteous; lowly, but not subservient;
strong, yet gentle; promoting the worthy in spite of all
opposition, and with equal authority rejecting the unworthy, though pushed forward by the favour of all;
looking always to one thing only—the welfare of the
Church; doing nothing out of animosity or partiality."[2]
The behaviour also of a priest in ordinary society was
jealously criticised.   The community was not satisfied
unless he was constantly paying calls.   Not the sick only,
but the sound desired to be "looked after" ($\epsilon\pi\iota\sigma\kappa\sigma\pi\epsilon\tilde{\iota}\sigma\theta\alpha\iota$),
—not so much from any religious feeling, as because the
reception of such visits gratified their sense of their own
importance.   Yet if a bishop often visited the house of a
wealthy or distinguished man to interest him in some

---

[1] III. c. 14.   [2] III. 16.

design for the advantage of the Church, he would soon
be stigmatised as a parasitical flatterer. Even the manner
of his greetings to acquaintance in the streets was criticised: "He smiled cordially on Mr. Such-an-one, and
talked much with him; but to me he only threw a commonplace remark." ' [1]

It is amusing and instructive to read these observations. They prove what important personages bishops
had become. The interests of the people were violently
excited over their elections. They were subjected to the
mingled reverence, deference and court, criticism, scandal,
and gossip, which are the inevitable lot of all persons
who occupy an exalted position in the world.

In the fourth book Chrysostom speaks of some of
the more mental qualifications indispensable for a priest.
Foremost among these was a power of speaking: 'That
was the one grand instrument which enabled him to heal
the diseases of the body entrusted to his care. And in
addition to this, he must be armed with a prompt and
versatile wit, to encounter the various assaults of heretics.
Jews, Greeks, Manichæans, Sabellians, Arians, all were
narrowly watching for the smallest loophole by which to
force a breach in the walls of the Church. And, unless
the defender was very vigilant and skilful, while he was
keeping out the one he would let in the other. While he
opposed the blind deference of the Jews to their Mosaic
Law, he must take care not to encourage the Manichæans,
who would eliminate the Law from the Scriptures. While
he asserted the Unity of the Godhead against the Arians,
there was danger of slipping into the Sabellian error of
confounding the Persons; and, while he divided the
Persons against the Sabellians, he must be careful to avoid
the Arian error of dividing the substance also. The line
of orthodoxy was a narrow path hemmed in by steep rocks

' III. 17.

on either side. Therefore it was of the deepest importance that the priest should be a learned and effective speaker; that he might not fall into error himself or lead others astray. For, if he was seen to be worsted in a controversy with heretics, many became alienated from the truth, mistaking the weakness of the defender for a weakness in the cause itself.' [1]

'But there was yet another task fraught with peril,—the delivery of sermons. The performances of a preacher were discussed by a curious and critical public like those of actors. Congregations attached themselves to their favourite preachers. Woe to the man who was detected in plagiarisms. He was instantly reprobated like a common thief.

'To become an effective preacher two things were necessary,—first, indifference to praise; secondly, power of speech; two qualities, the one moral, the other intellectual, which were rarely found coexisting. If a man possessed the first only, he became distasteful and despicable to his congregation. For if he stood up and at first boldly uttered powerful words which stung the consciences of his hearers, but as he proceeded began to blush and hesitate and stumble, all the advantage of his previous remarks would be wasted. The persons who had secretly felt annoyed by his telling reproofs would revenge themselves by laughing at his embarrassment in speaking. If, on the other hand, he was a weighty speaker, but not indifferent to applause, he would probably trim his sails to catch the popular breeze, and study to be pleasant rather than profitable, to the great detriment of himself and of his flock.' [2]

He makes some remarks eminently wise and true on the necessity of study for the preparation of sermons. 'It might seem strange, but in truth study was even more

---

[1] IV. c. 3–5 and c. 9.   [2] V. c. 1–4.

indispensable for an eloquent than for an ordinary preacher.
Speaking was an acquired art, and when a man had attained a high standard of excellence he was sure to decline
unless he kept himself up by constant study. The man
of reputation was always expected to say something new,
and even in excess of the fame which he had already
acquired. Men sat in judgment on him without mercy,
as if he was not a human being subject to occasional despondency, or anxiety, or irritation of temper; but as if
he was an angel or some infallible being, who ought
always to remain at the same high level of excellence.
The mediocre man, on the other hand, from whom much
was not expected, would obtain a disproportionate amount
of praise if he said a good thing now and then.[1] The
number of persons, however, in any congregation, who
were capable of appreciating a really learned and powerful preacher, was very small; therefore a man ought not
to be much disheartened or annoyed by unfavourable criti-
cisms. He should be his own critic, aiming in all his
work to win the favour of God. Then, if the admiration
of men followed, he would quietly accept it; or, if withheld, he would not be distressed, but seek his consolation
in honest work and in a conscience void of offence.[2] But
if a priest was not superior to the love of admiration, all
his labour and eloquence would be wasted: either he
would sacrifice truth to popularity, or, failing to obtain so
much applause as he desired, he would relax his efforts.
This last was a common defect in men whose powers of
preaching were only second-rate. Perceiving that even
the highly-gifted could not sustain their reputation without incessant study and practice, while they themselves,
by the most strenuous efforts, could gain but a very slender
meed of praise, if any, they abandoned themselves to indolence. The trial was especially great when a man was

[1] V. c. 5.   [2] C. 6, 7

surpassed in preaching by one who occupied an inferior rank in the hierarchy, and who perhaps took every opportunity of parading his superior powers. A kind of passion for listening to preaching possessed, he says, both Pagans and Christians at this time; hence it was very mortifying for a man to see a congregation looking forward to the termination of his discourse, while to his rival they listened with the utmost patience and attention, and were vexed only when his sermon had come to an end.'[1]

In the sixth book, Chrysostom enlarges on the dangers and trials which surrounded the priest as compared with the tranquillity and security of the monk,—that life to which he still felt himself powerfully attracted. 'Who watch for your souls as they that must give an account.' 'The dread of the responsibility implied in that saying, constantly agitated his mind. For if it were better to be drowned in the sea than to offend one of the little ones of Christ's flock, what punishment must they undergo who destroyed not one or two but a whole multitude?[2] Much worldly wisdom was required in the priest; he must be conversant with secular affairs, and adapt himself with versatility to all kinds of circumstances and men; and yet he ought to keep his spirit as free, as unfettered by worldly interests and ambitions as the hermit dwelling on the mountains.'[3]

The trials, indeed, which beset the priest, so far exceeded those of the monk, that Chrysostom considered the monastery, on the whole, a bad school for active clerical life. 'The monk lived in a calm; there was little to oppose or thwart him. The skill of the pilot could not be known till he had taken the helm in the open sea amidst rough weather. Too many of those who had passed from the seclusion of the cloister to the active sphere of the priest or bishop, proved utterly inadequate

---

[1] V. c. 8.   [2] VI. c. 1.   [3] VI. c. 4.

to cope with the difficulties of their new situation. They lost their head (ἰλιγγιῶσιν) and, often, instead of adding to their virtue, were deprived of the good qualities which they already possessed. Monasticism often served as a screen to failings which the circumstances of active life drew out, just as the qualities of metal were tested by the action of fire.'[1]

Chrysostom concludes by saying that he was conscious of his own infirmities; the irritability of his temper, his liability to violent emotions, his susceptibility to praise and blame. All such evil passions could, with the help of God's grace, be tamed by the severe treatment of the monastic life; like savage beasts who must be kept on low fare. But in the public life of a priest they would rage with incontrollable fury, because all would be pampered to the full—vain-glory by honour and praise, pride by authority, envy by the reputation of other men, bad temper by perpetual provocations, covetousness by the liberality of donors to the Church, intemperance by luxurious living.[2] He bids Basil picture the most implacable and deadly contest between earthly forces which his imagination could draw, and declares that this would but faintly express the conflict between the soul and evil in the spiritual warfare of the world. 'Many accidents might put an end to earthly combat, at least for a time—the approach of night, the fatigue of the combatants, the necessity of taking food and sleep. But in the spiritual conflict there were no breathing spaces. A man must always have his harness on his back, or he would be surprised by the enemy.'[3]

It is not surprising that Basil, after the fearful responsibilities and perils of his new dignity had been thus powerfully set before him, should lament that his trouble

---

[1] VI. c. 6–8.   [2] C. 12.   [3] C. 13.

now was not so much how to answer the accusers of
Chrysostom as to defend himself before God. He besought his friend to promise that he would continue to
support and advise him in all emergencies. Chrysostom
replied that as far as it was possible he would do so; but
that he doubted not Christ, who had called Basil to this
good work, would enable him to discharge it with boldness. They wept, embraced, and parted. And so Basil
went forth to the unwelcome honours and trials of his
bishopric, while Chrysostom continued to lead that
monastic kind of life which was only a preparatory step
to the monastery itself. His friendship with Basil is
curious and romantic. Their intercourse was brought to
a singular conclusion by the stratagem of Chrysostom.
Basil may have, according to his own earnest request,
continued to consult his friend in any difficulty or distress.
But he is never mentioned again. Although so intimately
bound up with this passage in Chrysostom's life, there is
something indistinct and shadowy about his whole existence. He flits across the scene for a few moments, and
then disappears totally and for ever.

The books on the Priesthood may be regarded as containing partly a real account of an actual conversation
between the two friends. But, as in the dialogues of
Plato, far more was probably added by the writer, so that
in parts the dialogue is only a form into which the
opinions of the author at the time of composition were
cast. It is impossible to decide with certainty the exact
time at which the treatise may have been written. It is
not likely to have been later than his diaconate in 381,[1]
but more probably[2] the work may be assigned to the six
years of leisure spent in the seclusion of the monastery

---

[1] Which is the date assigned by
Socrates vi. 3.

[2] As stated by Palladius, at least in
the Latin translation by Ambrose
Camaldulensis.

and mountains—that is, to the period between Basil's election to the bishopric, and his own ordination as deacon. The treatise reads like the production of one who had acquired considerable experience of monastic life, who had deliberately calculated its advantages on the one hand; and on the other had keenly observed and seriously considered the temptations and difficulties which attended the more secular career of priest or bishop. It is a more mature work than the Epistles to Theodore, and is free from such rapturous and excessive praise of the ascetic life as they contain.

NOTE TO FOREGOING CHAPTER.

It may excite surprise that men so young as Chrysostom and Basil, the former at least being not more than 25 or 26, and not as yet ordained deacon, should have been designated to the highest office in the Church. The Council of Neocæsarea (about A.D. 320—vide Hefele, vol. i. Clark's transl. p. 222) fixed 30 as the age at which men became eligible for the priesthood. The same age, then, at least must have been required for a bishop.

The Constitutions called Apostolical fix the age at 50, but add a clause which really lets in all the exceptions, ' unless he be a man of singular merit and worth, which may compensate for the want of years.' And, in fact, there are numerous instances of men, both before and after the time of Chrysostom, who were consecrated as bishops under the age of 30. The Council of Nice was held not more than twenty years after the persecution of Maximian, which Athanasius ('Epist. ad Solitar.,' p. 382, Paris edition) says he had only heard of from his father, yet in five months after that council he was ordained Archbishop of Alexandria. Rhemigius of Rheims was only 22 when he was made bishop in A.D. 471. In like manner, though it was enacted by the Council of Sardica 343–344, that none should rise to the

Episcopal throne *per saltum*, yet there are not a few examples that this rule was transgressed.

Augustine, when he created a bishopric at Fassula, presented Antonius, a reader (the very position Chrysostom now filled) to the Primate, who ordained him without scruple on Augustine's recommendation. Aug. Ep. 261 (ad Cælest.) Cyprian, Ambrose, and Nestorius are celebrated instances of the consecration of laymen to bishoprics.

CHAPTER V.

ABOUT this time, 372–373, while Chrysostom was still
residing in Antioch, he narrowly escaped suffering the
penalties of an imperial decree issued by Valentinian and
Valens against the practisers of magical arts, or possessors
even of magical books.   A severe search was instituted
after suspected persons ; soldiers were everywhere on the
watch to detect offenders.   The persecution was carried
on with peculiar cruelty at Antioch, where it had been
provoked by the detection of a treasonable act of divination.   The twenty-four letters of the alphabet were
arranged at intervals round the rim of a kind of charger,
which was placed on a tripod, consecrated by magic songs
and frequent ceremonies.   The diviner, habited as a
heathen priest, in linen robes, sandals, and with a fillet
wreathed about his head, chanted a hymn to Apollo, the
god of prophecy, while a ring in the centre of the charger
was slipped rapidly round a slender thread.   The letters
in front of which the ring successively stopped indicated
the character of the oracle.   The ring on this occasion
was supposed to have pointed to the first four letters in
the name of the future Emperor, Θ Ε Ο Δ.   Theodorus,
and probably many others who had the misfortune to own
the fatal syllables were executed.   There were, of course,
multitudes of eager informers, and zealous judges, who
strove to allay the suspicious fears of the Emperors, and
to procure favour for themselves by vigorous and whole-

sale prosecutions. Neither age, nor sex, nor rank were spared; women and children, senators and philosophers, were dragged to the tribunals and committed to the prisons of Rome and Antioch from the most distant parts of Italy and Asia. Many destroyed their libraries in alarm—so many innocent books were liable to be represented as mischievous or criminal; and thus much valuable literature perished.[1] It was during this dreadful time, when suspicion was instantly followed by arrest, and arrest by imprisonment, torture, and probably death, that Chrysostom chanced to be walking with a friend to the Church of the Martyr Babylas outside the city. As they passed through the gardens by the banks of the Orontes, they observed fragments of a book floating down the stream. Curiosity led them to fish it out; but, to their dismay, on examining it, they found that it was inscribed with magical formulæ, and, to increase their alarm, a soldier was approaching at no great distance. At first they knew not how to act; they feared the book had been cast into the river by the artifice of an informer to entrap some unwary victim. They determined, however, to throw their dangerous discovery back into the river, and happily the attention or suspicions of the soldier were not roused. Chrysostom always gratefully looked back to this escape as a signal instance of God's mercy and protection.[2]

It must have been soon after this incident and previous to the edict of persecution against the monks issued by Valens in 373, that Chrysostom exchanged what might be called the amateur kind of monastic life passed in his own home for the monastery itself. Whether his mother was now dead or had become reconciled to the separation, or whether her son's passionate enthusiasm for monastic retirement became irresistible, it is impossible to deter-

[1] Zosimus, l. iv. 13-15. Ammian.   [2] In A. Apost. Hom. 38, in fine.
Marcell. xxix. c. i.

mine. His mother is not mentioned by him in his
writings after this point, except in allusion to the past,
which is a strong presumption that she was no longer
living. Bishop Meletius would probably have endeavoured
to detain him for some active work in the Church, but
he was now in exile; and to Flavian, the successor of
Meletius, Chrysostom was possibly not so intimately known.

During the first four centuries of the Christian era, the
enthusiasm for monastic life prevailed with ever-increasing
force. We are, perhaps, naturally inclined to associate
monasticism chiefly with the Western Christianity of the
Middle Ages. But the original and by far the most prolific parent of monasticism was the East. There were
always ascetics in the Christian Church; yet asceticism
is the product not so much of Christianity as of the East;
of the oriental temperament, which admires and cul-
tivates it; of the oriental climate, which makes it tolerable even when pushed to the most rigorous extremes.
Asceticism is the natural practical expression of that
deeply-grounded conviction of an essential antagonism
between the flesh and spirit which pervades all oriental
creeds. Even the monastic form of it was known in the
East before Christianity. The Essenes in Judæa, the
Therapeutæ in Egypt, were prototypes of the active and
contemplative communities of monks.

The primitive ascetics of the Christian Church were not
monks. They were persons who raised themselves above
the common level of religious life by exercises in fasting,
prayer, study, alms-giving, celibacy, bodily privations of
all kinds. These habits obtained for them great admiration and reverence. Such persons are frequently designated by writers of the first three centuries as 'an ascetic,'
'a follower of the religious ascetics.' [1] But they did not
form a class distinctly marked off by dress and habitation

[1] Cyril. Catech. x. n. 19. Athanas. Synopsis.

from the rest of the world, like the monks or even the
anchorites of later time. They lived in the cities or
wherever their home might be, and were not subject
to any rules beyond those of their own private making.
Eusebius calls them σπουδαῖοι, 'earnest persons;' and
Clemens Alexandrinus ἐκλεκτῶν ἐκλεκτότεροι 'more elect
than the elect.'[1] Midway between the primitive ascetic
and the fully-developed monk must be placed the anchorite or hermit, who made a step in the direction of
monasticism by withdrawing altogether from the city or
populous places into the solitudes of mountain or desert.
Persecution assisted the impulse of religious fervour.
Paul retired to the Egyptian Thebaid during the persecution of Decius in A.D. 251, and Antony during that of
Maximin in A.D. 312. They are justly named the fathers
or founders of the anchorites, because, though not actually
the first, they were the most distinguished; and the
fame of their sanctity, their austerities, their miracles,
produced a tribe of followers. The farther Antony retired into the depths of the wilderness, the more numerous became his disciples. They grouped their cells
around the habitation of the saintly father, and out of the
clusters grew in process of time the monastery. A
number of cells ranged in lines like an encampment, not
incorporated in one building, was called a 'Laura' or
street.[2] This was the earliest and simplest kind of
monastic establishment. It was a community, though
without much system or cohesion.

The real founder of the Coenobia or monasteries in the
East, was the Egyptian Pachomius; he was the Benedict
of the East. His rule was that most generally adopted,
not only in Egypt but throughout the oriental portions

---

[1] Euseb. l. vi. c. 11. Clemens
Alex. Hom. Quis Dives salvetur?

[2] Vide Epiphan. 69. Hæres. n. i.,

whence it appears that Laura, or Labra,
was the name of an ecclesiastical dis-
trict in Alexandria.

of the empire.   He and Antony had now been dead about twenty years, and Hilarius, the pupil and imitator of Antony, had lately introduced monasticism on the Pacho-mian model into Syria.   In about fifty years more, the nomadic Saracens will gaze with veneration and awe at the spectacle of Simeon on his pillar, forty miles from Antioch.   Thousands will come to receive baptism at his hands; his image will have been placed over the entrance of the shops in Rome.[1]   The spirit had been already caught in the West.   The feelings of abhorrence with which the Italians first beheld the wild-looking Egyptian monks who accompanied Athanasius to Rome had soon been exchanged for veneration.   The example of Mar-cellina, and the exhortations of her brother Ambrose of Milan, had converted multitudes of women to take vows of celibacy.[2]   Most of the little islands on the coasts of the Adriatic could boast of their monasteries or cells.[3]   St. Martin built his religious houses near Poitiers and Tours, and was followed to his grave by two thousand brethren.[4]   But St. Jerome, perhaps, more than anyone else, promoted the advance of monasticism in the West. Born on the borders of East and West,[5] he mingled with the Eastern Church at Antioch and Constantinople, and in the desert of Chalcis had inured himself to the most severe forms of oriental asceticism, and returned to Rome eager and able to impart to others a kindred spirit of enthusiasm for the ascetic life.   A little later, early in the fifth century, John Cassianus, president of a religious establishment in Marseilles, propagated monastic insti-tutions of an oriental type in the south of France, and made men conversant with the system by his work on the

---

[1] Theod. Lector. II. 1. c. col. 102–104.

[2] Jerome, Ep. 77, 5; Ambrose de Virgin. i. 10, 11.

[3] Baron. 398, 49–52; Giesel, I. ii. 251.

[4] Sozom. III. 14; Sulp. Severus.

[5] At Stridon, on the frontiers of Pannonia and Dalmatia.

rules of the cloister. These were the scattered forces which in the West awaited the master mind and strong hand of Benedict to mould and discipline them into a mighty system. The nearest approach in the West to the Egyptian system of Pachomius was among the Benedictines of Camaldoli.

There is every reason to suppose on general grounds, and the supposition is corroborated by notices in the writings of Chrysostom, that the monasteries near Antioch, like the rest of the Syrian monasteries, were based on the Pachomian model. Pachomius was a native of the Thebaid, born in A.D. 292. He began to practise asceticism as a hermit, but, according to the legend, was visited by an angel, who commanded him to promote the salvation of other men's souls besides his own, and presented him with a brazen tablet, on which were inscribed the rules of the Order which he was to found. He established his first community on Tabennæ, an island in the Nile, which became the parent of a numerous offspring. Pachomius had the satisfaction in his lifetime of seeing eight monasteries, containing in all 3,000 monks, acknowledging his rule; and after his death, in the first half of the fifth century, their numbers had swelled to 50,000.[1] Chrysostom exulted with Christian joy and pride over the spectacle of ' Egypt, that land which had been the mother of pagan literature and art, which had invented and propagated every species of witchcraft, now despising all her ancient customs, and holding up the Cross, in the desert no less if not more than in the cities : . . . for the sky was not more beautiful, spangled with its hosts of stars, than the desert of Egypt studded in all directions with the habitations of monks.'[2]

By the Pachomian rule no one was admitted as a full

---

[1] Sozom. iii. 14. Palladius, Hist. Lausiaca. 38.   [2] In Matt. Hom. 8, p. 87.

monk till after three years of probation, during which period he was tested by the most severe exercises. If willing, after that period, to continue the same exercises, he was admitted without further ceremony beyond making a solemn declaration that he would adhere to the rules of the monastery. That no irrevocable vow was taken by the members of the monastery near Antioch which Chrysostom joined, seems proved by his return to the city after a residence in the monastery of several years' duration. According to Sozomen, the several parts of the dress worn by Pachomian monks had a symbolical meaning. The tunic (a linen garment reaching as far as the knees) had short sleeves, to remind the wearers that they should be prompt to do such honest work only as needed no concealment. The hood was typical of the innocence and purity of infants, who wore the same kind of covering; the girdle and scarf, folded about the back, shoulders, and arms, were to admonish them that they should be perpetually ready to do active service for God. Each cell was inhabited by three monks. They took their chief meal in a refectory, and ate in silence,[1] with a veil so arranged over the face that they could see only what was on the table. No strangers were admitted, except travellers, to whom they were bound, by the rule of their Order, to show hospitality. The common meal or supper took place at 3 o'clock,[2] up to which time they usually fasted. When it was concluded, a hymn was sung, of which Chrysostom gives us a specimen, though not in metrical form.[3] 'Blessed be God, who nourisheth me from my youth up, who giveth food to all flesh: fill our hearts with joy and gladness, that we, having all sufficiency at all times, may abound unto every good work, through Jesus Christ our

---

[1] The custom of one monk reading the Scriptures aloud during dinner was first adopted, according to Cassian, in the Cappadocian monasteries.—

Cass. l. iv. c. 17; Sozom. iii. 14; Jerome's translation of the rule.

[2] But sometimes later, vide p. 63.

[3] Hom. in Matt. 55, vol. vii. p. 545.

Lord, with Whom be glory, and honour, and power to Thee, together with the Holy Ghost, for ever and ever, Amen. Glory to Thee, O Lord! Glory to Thee, Holy One! Glory to Thee, King, who hast given us food to make us glad! Fill us with the Holy Spirit, that we may be found well pleasing in thy sight, and not ashamed when Thou rewardest every man according to his works.'

The whole community in a Pachomian monastery was divided into twenty-four classes, distinguished by the letters of the Greek alphabet; the most ignorant, for instance, under class Iota, the more learned under Xi or Zeta, such letters being in shape respectively the simplest and the most complicated in the alphabet. Those hours which were not devoted to services or study were occupied by manual labour, partly to supply themselves with the necessaries of life, partly to guard against the incursion of evil thoughts. There was a proverbial saying attributed to some of the old Egyptian fathers, that 'a labouring monk was assaulted by one devil only, but an idle one by an innumerable legion.' They wove baskets and mats, agriculture was not neglected, nor even, among the Egyptian monks, ship-building. Palladius, who visited the Egyptian monasteries about the close of the fourth century, found, in the monastery of Panopolis, which contained 300 members, 15 tailors, 7 smiths, 4 carpenters, 12 camel-drivers, 15 tanners. Each monastery in Egypt had its steward, and a chief steward stationed at the principal settlement had the supervision of all the rest. All the products of monkish labour were shipped under his inspection on the Nile for Alexandria. With the proceeds of their sale, stores were purchased for the monasteries, and the surplus was distributed amongst the sick and poor.[1]

A monastery founded on this model might be fairly

---

[1] Sozom. iii. 14, 15; Cassian de Coenob. Instit. iv. x. 22.

described as a kind of village containing an industrial and
religious population; and had the Eastern monks adhered
to this simple and innocent way of life, such communities
might have become more and more schools of learning,
centres of civilisation, and homes of piety. But they
were increasingly forgetful of the wholesome saying of
Antony, that a monk in the city was like 'a fish out of
water.' Instead of attending exclusively to their pious
and industrial exercises, they mixed themselves up with
the theological and political contests which too often convulsed the cities of the Eastern Empire. Their influence
or interference was frequently the reverse of peace-making,
judicious, or Christian. They would rush with fanatical
fury into the city, to rescue the orthodox, or with equal
violence to attack those whom they considered heretical.
The evil had grown to such a height by the reign of
Arcadius, that a law was passed by which monks were
strictly forbidden to make such outrages on civil order,
and bishops were commanded to prosecute the authors of
such attempts.[1] Eastern monasticism, in fact, partook of
the character which distinguished the Eastern Church as
a whole, and which we may regard as one principal cause
of its corruption and decay. A certain stability, sobriety,
self-control, a law-making and law-respecting spirit, as
it is the peculiar merit of the Western, so the want of
it is the peculiar defect of the Oriental temperament.
Hence a curious co-existence of extremes; the passions,
unnaturally repressed at one outlet by intense asceticism,
burst forth with increased fury at another. He who had
subdued his body in the wilderness or on the mountains
by fastings and macerations, entertained the most implacable animosity towards pagans and heretics, and fought
them like a ruffian (the word is not too strong for truth),
when some tumult in an adjacent city afforded him an

[1] Cod. Theod. ix. 40, 16.

opportunity for this robust mode of displaying and defending his orthodoxy. Western monasticism, on the other hand, is distinguished by more gravity, more of the old Roman quality, a love of stern discipline. It did not run to such lengths of fanatical asceticism, and consequently was exempt from such disastrous reactions. It never produced such a caricature of the anchorite as Simeon Stylites, or such savage zealots as the monkish bands who dealt their sturdy blows in the religious riots of Constantinople and Alexandria. From the notices scattered up and down Chrysostom's writings of the monasteries in the neighbourhood of Antioch, it appears that they conformed in all essential respects to the Pachomian model. We might anticipate, indeed, that where such a man as Diodorus was president or visitor, they would be conducted on a simple and rational system.

South of Antioch were the mountainous heights of Silpius and Casius, whence rose the springs which in a variety of channels found their way into the city, provided it with a constant and abundant supply of the purest water, and irrigated the gardens for which it was celebrated.[1] In this mountain region dwelt the communities of monks, in separate huts or cells (καλύβαι[2]), but subject to an abbot, and a common rule. Chrysostom has in more passages than one furnished us with a description of their ordinary costume, fare, and way of life. He is fond of depicting their simple, frugal, and pious habits, in contrast to the artificial and luxurious manners of the gay and worldly people of the city. They were clad in coarse garments of goat's hair or camel's hair, sometimes of skins, over their linen tunics, which were worn both by night and day.[3] Before the first rays of sunlight, the

[1] Vide Müller de Antiq. Antioch. c. 3.

[2] Chrysost. in Matt. Hom. 69, p. 652.

[3] In Matt. Hom. 68, c. 3. When they received the Eucharist, which they did twice a week, on Sundays

abbot went round, and struck those monks who were still
sleeping with his foot, to wake them.   When all had
risen,—fresh, healthy, fasting, they sang together, under
the precentorship of their abbot, a hymn of praise to God.
The hymn being ended, a common prayer was offered up
(again under the leadership of their abbot), and then
each at sunrise went to his allotted task, some to read,
others to write, others to manual labour, by which they
made a good deal to supply the necessities of the poor.
Four hours in the day, the third, the sixth, the ninth,
and some time in the evening, were appointed for prayers
and psalms.   When the daily work was concluded, they
sat down, or rather reclined, on strewn grass, to their
common meal, which was sometimes eaten out of doors by
moonlight, and consisted of bread and water only, with
occasionally, for invalids, a little vegetable food and oil.
This frugal repast was followed by hymns, after which
they betook themselves to their straw couches, and slept,
as Chrysostom observes, free from those anxieties and
apprehensions which beset the worldly man.   There was
no need of bolts and bars, for there was no fear of robbers.
The monk had no possession but his body and soul, and if
his life was taken he would regard it as an advantage, for
he could say that to live was Christ, and to die was gain.[1]
Those words 'mine and thine,' those fertile causes of innumerable strifes, were unknown.[2]   No lamentations were
to be heard when any of the brethren died.   They did not
say, such a one is dead, but, he has been perfected (τετε-
λείωται), and he was carried forth to burial amidst hymns
of praise, thanksgiving for his release, and the prayers of
his companions that they too might soon see the end of
their labours and struggles, and be permitted to behold

and Saturdays, they threw off their
coats of skins and loosened their
girdles.—Sozom. iii. 14.

[1] In Matt. Hom. 68, c. 3; 69, c. 3;
in 1 Tim. Hom. 14, c. 4, 5.
[2] In Matt. Hom. 72, vol. vii. p. 671.

Jesus Christ.[1] Such was the simple and industrial kind of monastic body to which Chrysostom for a time united himself; and to the end of his life he regarded such communities with the greatest admiration and sympathy. But he never failed to maintain also the duty of work against those who represented the perfection of the Christian life to consist in mere contemplation and prayer. Such a doctrine of otiose Christianity he proved to be based on a too exclusive attention to certain passages in the New Testament. If, for instance, our blessed Lord said to Martha, 'Thou art careful and troubled about many things, but one thing is needful'; or again, 'Take no thought for the morrow'; or, 'Labour not for the meat that perisheth'—all such passages were to be balanced and harmonised by others, as, for example, St. Paul's exhortation to the Thessalonians to be 'quiet and to do their own business,' and 'let him that stole steal no more, but labour with his hands that which is good, that he may have to give to him that needeth.' He points out that the words of our Lord do not inculcate total abstinence from work, but only censure an undue anxiety about earthly things, to the exclusion or neglect of spiritual concerns. The contemplative form of monasticism, based on misconception of Holy Scripture, had, he observes, seriously injured the interests of Christianity, causing it to be derided as a source of indolence.[2]

[1] In Ep. 1 Tim. Hom. 14, c. 5.   [2] In Joh. Hom. 44, c. 1.

CHAPTER VI.

SEVERAL treatises were composed by Chrysostom during his monastic life. Among the first must be placed two books addressed to Demetrius and Stelechius. Of these the former was evidently written soon after the commencement of his retreat, for he speaks of having recently determined to take the step, and of the petty anxieties about food and other personal comforts which had at first unsettled his purpose a little. But he had soon conquered these hankerings after the more luxurious life which he had abandoned. It seemed to him a disgrace that one to whom heaven and celestial joys were offered, such as eye had not seen nor ear heard, should be so hesitating and timorous, when those who undertook the management of public affairs did not shrink from dangers and toil, and long journeys, and separation from wife and children, and perhaps unfavourable criticism, but only enquired whether the office was honourable and lucrative.[1]

The scope of the books is to animate torpid characters to a warmer piety, first by drawing a lively picture of the depravity of the times, secondly by a glowing description of the fervent energy of apostles and apostolic saints, and insisting that those lofty heights of Christian holiness were not unattainable by the Christian of his own day, if

---

[1] De Compunct. i. c. 6.

he bent the whole energy of his will, aided by Divine grace, to the attempt.

'So great,' he observes, 'was the depravity of the times, that if a stranger were to compare the precepts of the Gospel with the actual practice of society, he would infer that men were not the disciples, but the enemies of Christ. And the most fatal symptom was their total unconsciousness of this deep corruption. Society was like a body which was outwardly vigorous, but concealed a wasting fever within; or like an insane person who says and does all manner of shocking things, but, instead of being ashamed, glories in the fancied possession of superior wisdom.'[1] Chrysostom applies the test of the principal precepts of morality in the Sermon on the Mount to the existing state of Christian morals. Everyone of them was shamelessly violated. A kind of regard, superstitious or hypocritical, was paid to the command in the letter which was broken in the spirit. Persons, for instance, who scrupled to use the actual expressions 'fool' or 'Raca,' heaped all kinds of opprobrious epithets on their neighbours.[2] So the command to be reconciled with a brother before approaching the altar was really broken though formally kept. Men gave the kiss of peace at the celebration of Holy Communion when admonished by the deacon so to do, but continued to nourish resentful feelings in the heart all the same.[3] Vainglory and ostentation robbed prayer, fasting and almsgiving of their merit; and as for the precept 'Judge not,' a most uncharitable spirit of censoriousness pervaded every class of society, including monks and ecclesiastics.[4] Contrast with this false and hollow religion of the world the condition of one in whom a deep compunction for sin, and a genuine love of Jesus Christ, was awakened. The whole multitude of vain frivolous passions was dispersed like dust before

[1] C. 1.   [2] C. 2.   [3] C. 3.   [4] C. 4, 5.

the wind. So it was with St. Paul. Having once turned
the eye of his soul towards heaven, and being entranced
by the beauty of that other world, he could not stoop to
earth again. As a beggar, in some gloomy hovel, if he
saw a monarch glittering with gold and radiant with
jewels, might altogether for a time forget the squalor of
his dwelling-place in his eagerness to get inside the
palace of the king, so St. Paul forgot and despised the
poverty and hardship of this present world because the
whole energy of his being was directed to the attainment
of that heavenly city.[1] But men objected to the citation
of apostolic examples. Paul and Peter, they said, were
superhuman characters; models beyond our limited powers.
'Nay,' Chrysostom replies, 'these are feeble excuses.
The Apostles were in all essential points like ourselves.
Did they not breathe the same kind of air? eat the same
kind of food? were not some of them married men? did
they not follow mechanical trades? nay more, had not
some of them deeply sinned? Men at the present day
did not indeed receive grace at baptism to work miracles,
but they received enough to enable them to lead a good
and holy Christian life.[2] And the highest blessing of
Christ—his invitation to those who were called "blessed
children" to inherit the kingdom prepared for them—was
addressed, not to those who had wrought miracles, but to
those who had ministered to himself through feeding the
hungry, entertaining the stranger, visiting the sick and
the prisoners, who were his brethren. But grace, though
undoubtedly given by God, required man's own co-
operation to become effectual. Otherwise, since God is
no respecter of persons, it would have resided in equal
measure in all men; whereas we see that with one man
it remains, from another it departs; a third is never
affected by it at all.'[3] The second book on the same

[1] C. 7.   [2] C. 8.   [3] C. 9.

subject, addressed to another friend, named Stelechius, is an expression of more rapturous and highly-wrought feeling, and is more rhetorical in style. His description in the beginning of the blessed freedom of the monk's life from secular vanities and cares, his remarks on David and St. Paul,[1] two of his most favourite characters, and still more his masterly enumeration of the manifold ways in which God manifests his providential care for man,[2] well deserve to be read. They are too long to be translated here in full, and a paraphrase would very inadequately represent such passages of which the peculiar beauty consists in the language more even than in the ideas. One special interest of these books, written immediately after his retirement from the world, is that they put clearly before us what it was which drove him and many another to the monastic life. It was a sense of the glaring and hideous contrast between the Christianity of the Gospel and the Christianity of ordinary society. A kind of implacable warfare,[3] as he expresses it, seemed to be waged in the world against the commands of Christ; and he had therefore determined, by seclusion from the world, to seek that kind of life which he saw exhibited in the Gospels, but nowhere else.[4]

But the largest and most powerful work which Chrysostom produced during this period was occasioned by the decree of the Emperor Valens in A.D. 373—a decree which struck at the roots of monasticism. It directed that monks should be dragged from their retreats, and compelled to discharge their obligations as citizens, either by serving in the army, or performing the functions of any . civil office to which they might be appointed.[5] The edict

---

[1] C. 1, 2, 3.   [2] C. 5.

[3] ἔχθρα ἀκήρυκτος, lib. i. c. 5.

[4] Lib. i. c. 4.

[5] The word in the decree is 'militare,' but this term appears to be applied to civil duties as well as military.

Vide Suicer sub v. στρατεύειν. The Egyptian monks, however, do seem to have been specially forced into the army. De Broglie, v. 303; Gibbon, iv. ; Milman, iii. 47, ' History of Christianity.'

is said to have been enforced with considerable rigour, and in Egypt this seems to have been the case. But it was evidently far from complete or universal in its operation. None of Chrysostom's brethren appear to have been compelled to return to the city; certainly he himself was not. But they were liable, of course, to the persecution which, under the shelter of the decree, all the enemies of their order directed against them. These enemies of monasticism were of several kinds. There were the zealous adherents of the old paganism; men like Libanius, who were opposed to Christianity on principle, and especially to the monastic form of it, as encouraging idleness, and the dereliction of the duties of good citizens. There were also the more worldly-minded Christians, who had adopted Christianity more from impulse or conformity than from conviction, and who disliked the standing protest of monastic life against their own frivolity. They were irritated also by the influence which the monks often acquired over their wives and children, sometimes alluring the latter from that lucrative line of worldly life which their fathers had marked out for them. And lastly, there were those who regretted that some men should have taken up a position of direct antagonism to the world, instead of mingling with it, and infusing good leaven into the mass of evil. The treatise of Chrysostom addressed ' to the assailants of monastic life ' was intended to meet most of these objections.

A friend had brought the terrible tidings to his retreat of the authorised persecution which had just broken out. He heard it with indescribable horror. It was a sacrilege far worse than the destruction of the Jewish Temple. That an Emperor (an Arian, indeed, yet professing himself Christian) should organise the persecution, and that some actually baptised persons should take, as his friend informed him, a part in it, was an intolerable aggravation

of the infliction. He would rather die than witness such
a calamity, and was ready to exclaim with Elijah, 'Now,
O Lord, take away my life!' His friend roused him from
this state of despondency by suggesting that, instead of
giving way to useless lamentations, he should write an
admonitory treatise to the originators and abettors of this
horrible persecution. At first Chrysostom refused, partly
from a feeling of incompetency, partly from a dread of
exposing to the pagans by his writings some of the internal corruptions, dissensions, and weaknesses of the
Church. His friend replies that these were already but
too notorious; and as for the sufferings of the monks, they
formed the topic of public conversation, too often of
public jest. In the market-place and in the doctors'
shops the subject was freely canvassed, and many boasted
of the part which they had taken against the victims. 'I
was the first to lay hands on such a monk,' one would
cry, 'and to give him a blow;' or, 'I was the first to discover his cell;' or, 'I stimulated the judge against him
more than any one.' Such was the spirit of cruelty and
profanity by which even Christians were animated; and,
as for the pagans, they derided both parties. Roused by
these dreadful communications, the indignation of Chrysostom no longer hesitated to set about the task.[1]

His pity, he says, was excited chiefly for the persecu-
tors; they were purchasing eternal misery for themselves,
while the future reward of their victims would be in proportion to the magnitude of their present sufferings, since
'Blessed were those whom men should hate, persecute,
and revile for Christ's sake, and great was to be their
reward in heaven.'[2]

To persecute monks was to hinder that purity of life to
which Christ attached so deep an importance. It might
be objected, Cannot men lead lives uncontaminated at

home? to which Chrysostom replies that he heartily
wishes they could, and that such good order and morality
might be established in cities as to make monasteries unnecessary.   But at present such gross iniquity prevailed
in large towns, that men of pious aspirations were compelled to fly to the mountain or the desert.   The blame
should fall, not on those who escaped from the city, but
on those who made life there intolerable to virtuous men.
He trusted the time might come when these refugees
would be able to return with safety to the world.[1]

If it was objected that on this principle of reasoning
the mass of mankind was condemned, he could only reply,
in the words of Christ himself, ' Narrow is the way which
leadeth unto life, and few there be that find it.'   We
must not honour a multitude before truth.   If all flesh
was once destroyed except eight persons, we cannot be
surprised if the number of men eventually saved shall be
few.   ' I see,' he says, ' a constant perpetration of crimes
which are all condemned by Christ as meriting the
punishment of hell—adultery, fornication, envy, anger,
evil speaking, and many more.   The multitude which is
engaged in this wickedness is unmolested, but the monks
who fly from it themselves, and persuade others to take
flight also, are persecuted without mercy.'   So much for
the Christianity of the world.[2]

In Book II. he expresses his astonishment that fathers
should so little understand what was best for their sons
as to deter them from studying ' the true philosophy.'
But in combatting this error he will put forward all that
can be urged on their side.   He imagines the case of a
pagan father, possessed of great worldly distinction and
wealth.   He has an only son, in whom all his pride and
hopes are centred; one whom he expects to surpass himself in riches and honour.   Suddenly this son becomes

[1] C. 5-7.   [2] C. 8.

converted to monasticism; this rich heir flies to the
mountains, puts on a dress coarser than that of the
meanest servant, toils at the menial occupations of
gardening and drawing water, becomes lean and pale.
All the schemes of his father for the future are frustrated,
all past efforts for his education seem to have been
squandered.   The little vessel which was his pride and
pleasure is wrecked at the very mouth of the harbour
from which it was setting out on the voyage of life.   The
parent has no longer any pleasure in life; he mourns for
his son as for one already dead.[1]

Having thus stated the case on his adversary's side as
strongly as possible, Chrysostom begins his own defence
by asking which would be best, that a man should be
subject to thirst all his life, or wholly exempt from it?
Surely to be exempt from it.   Apply this to the moral
appetites—love, avarice, and the rest.   The monk is
exempt from them; the man of the world is distracted by
them, if not overwhelmed.   Again, if the monk has no
wealth of his own, he exercises a powerful influence in
directing the wealth of others.   Religious men will part
with much of their riches according to his suggestions; if
one refuses, another will give.   The resources, in fact, of
the monk are quite inexhaustible; many will subscribe to
supply his wants or to execute his wishes, as Crito said
that he and his friends would subscribe for Socrates.   It
is impossible to deprive the monk of his wealth or of his
home; if you strip him of everything he has, he rejoices,
and thanks you for helping him to live the life which he
desires; and as for his home, the world is his home; one
place is the same as another to him; he needs nothing but
the pure air of heaven, wholesome streams, and herbs.
As for high place and rank, history suffices to teach us
that the desert does not destroy, and the palace does not

[1] C. 1, 2.

give, true nobility. Plato—planting, watering, and eating olives—was a far nobler personage than Dionysius the Tyrant of Sicily, amidst all the wealth and splendour of a monarch. Socrates—clad in a single garment, with his bare feet and his meagre fare of bread, and dependent upon others for the mere necessaries of life—was a far more illustrious character than Archelaus, who often invited him, but in vain, to court. Real splendour and distinction consisted not in fine raiment, or in positions of dignity and power. but only in excellence of the soul and in philosophy.[1]

He then proceeds to maintain that the influence of the monk was more powerful than that of the man of the world, however distinguished he might be. If he descended from his mountain solitude, and entered the city, the people flocked round him, and pointed him out with reverence and admiration, as if he were a messenger from heaven. His mean dress commanded more respect than the purple robe and diadem of the monarch. If he was required to interfere in matters of public interest, his influence was greater than that of the powerful or wealthy; for he could speak before an emperor with boldness and freedom, and without incurring the suspicion of self-interested or ambitious motives. He was a more effectual comforter of the mourners than any one in a prosperous worldly condition was likely to be. If a father had lost his only son, the sight of other men's domestic happiness only revived his grief; but the society of the monk, who disdained the ties of home and family, and who talked to him of death as only a sleep, soothed his grief. Thus the man who wished his son to possess real honour and power would permit him to become a monk; for monks who were once mere peasants had been visited in their cells and consulted by kings and ministers of state.

[1] C. 2 5.

Chrysostom concludes this book by relating the history of one of his own brethren in the monastery, who, when first he desired to become a monk, had been disowned by his father, a wealthy and distinguished pagan, who threatened him with imprisonment, turned him out of doors, and allowed him almost to perish with hunger. But, finding him inflexible in his purpose, the father at last relented, and, at the time when Chrysostom wrote, honoured, he might say venerated, that son, considering the others, who occupied distinguished positions in the world, scarcely worthy to be his servant.[1]

As the second book was intended to meet the objections of a pagan father, so the third contains admonitions to one who was professedly Christian, but worldly-minded, on the duty of parents in regard to the moral and religious education of their children.

It appeared to him that the fathers of that day gave their sons none but worldly counsel, inculcated none but worldly industry and prudence, and encouraged to the emulation of none but worldly examples.[2] The force of habit was intensely strong, especially when pleasure co-operated with it, and parents, instead of counteracting habits of worldliness, promoted them by their own example. God led the Israelites through the wilderness as a kind of monastic training, to wean them from the luxurious and sensual habits of an Egyptian life; yet even then they hankered after the land of their bondage. How, then, could the children of parents who left them in the midst of the Egypt of vice, escape damnation? If they achieved anything good of themselves, it was speedily crushed by the flood of worldly conversation which issued from the parent. All those things which were condemned by Christ — as wealth, popularity, strife, an evil eye, divorce—were approved by parents of that day, and they threw a veil over the ugliness of these vices, by giving them specious names. Devotion to the hippodrome and theatre was called fashionable refinement; wealth was called freedom; love of glory, high spirit; folly, boldness; prodigality, benevolence; injustice, manliness. Virtues, on the contrary, were depreciated by opprobrious names: temperance was denominated rusticity; equity, cowardice; justice, unmanliness; modesty, meanness; endurance of injury, feebleness. He truly remarks, that nothing contributes so much to deter men from vice as calling vices plainly by their proper names.[1]

'How can children escape moral ruin, when all the labour of their fathers is bestowed on the provision of superfluous things—fine houses, dress, horses, beautiful statues, gilded ceilings—while they take no pains about the soul, which is far more precious than any ornament of gold?' And there were worse evils behind—vice too monstrous and unnatural to be named, but to which he was constrained to allude, because he felt that it was poisoning with deadly venom the very vitals of the social body. 'Well,' but worldly men reply, 'Would you have us all turn philosophers, and let our worldly affairs go to ruin? Nay, says Chrysostom, it is the want of the philosophic spirit and rule which ruins everything now; it is your rich men—with troops of slaves and swarms of parasites, eager for wealth and ambitious of distinction, building fine houses, adding field to field, lending money at a usurious rate of interest—who propagate the strife and litigation, and envy, and murder, and general confusion, by which life is distracted. These are they who bring down the vengeance of Heaven, in the shape of droughts, and famines, and inundations, and earthquakes, and submersion of cities, and pestilences. It is not the simple

---

[1] Compare similar remarks by Thucydides, book iii., in his account of the Corcyræan sedition on the misapplication of names to vices.   [2] C. 6. 7.

monk, or the philosophic Christian, who is contented with
a humble dwelling, a mean dress, a little plot of ground.
These last, shining like bright beacons in a dark place,
hold up the lamp of philosophy on high, and endeavour to
guide those who are tossing on the open sea in a dark
night into the haven of safety and repose.'[1]

'In spite of law, disorder prevailed to such an extent,
that the very idea of God's providence was lost. Men
assigned the course of events to fate, or to the stars, or to
chance, or to spontaneous force. God did, indeed, still
rule; but He was like a pilot in a storm, whose skill in
managing and conducting the vessel in safety was not
perceived or appreciated by the passengers, owing to the
confusion and fright caused by the raging of the elements.
In the monastery, on the other hand, all was tranquillity
and peace, as in a community of angels. He strenuously
combatted the error of supposing that sin was more par-
donable in a man of the world than in a monk. Anger,
uncleanness, swearing, and the like, were equally sinful in
all. Christ made no distinctions, but propounded one
standard of morality for all alike. Nothing had inflicted
more injury on the moral tone of society than the supposition that strictness of life was demanded of the monk
only.'[2] He strongly urges the advantage of sending youths
for education to monasteries, even for so long a period
as ten or twenty years. Men consented, he says, to part
with their children, for the purpose of learning some art
or trade, or even so low an accomplishment as rope-
dancing; but when the object was to train their souls for
Heaven, all kinds of impediments were raised. To object
that few attained through residence in a monastery that
perfection of spiritual life which some expected of them,
was a mere excuse. In the case of worldly things, on
which men's hearts were set, they thought of getting as

[1] C 8, 9.   [2] C 14, 15.

much as they could, not of reaching absolute perfection.
A man did not prevent his son from entering military service because the chances of his becoming a prefect were
small; why, then, hesitate to send your son to a monastery
because all monks do not become angels? [1]

These treatises are remarkable productions, and deserve
to be read, not only because they exhibit Chrysostom's
best power of argument and style, but also because they
throw light upon the character of the man and the times
in which he lived. He pleads his cause with the inge-
nuity, as well as eloquence, of a man who had been trained
for the law courts. We find, indeed, that his opinions on
the advantages of the monastic life were modified as he
grew older; but that bold condemnation of worldliness,
that denunciation of a cold secularised Christianity, as
contrasted with the purity of the Gospel standard, the
deep aspirations after personal holiness, the desire to be
filled with a fervent and overflowing love of Christ, the
firm hold on the idea of a superintending Providence,
amidst social confusion and corruption; these we find, as
here, so always, conspicuous characteristics of the man,
and principal sources of his influence.

From the frightful picture here drawn of social depravity, we perceive the value—we might say, the necessity—of monasteries, as havens of refuge for those who
recoiled in horror from the surrounding pollution. It is
clear also that the influence of the monks was considerable.
Monasteries were recognised places of education, where
pious parents could depend on their children being virtu-
ously brought up. The Christian wife of a pagan or
worldly husband could here find a safe home for her boy,
where he could escape the contamination of his father's
influence or example. Chrysostom relates, in C. 12, how
a Christian lady in Antioch, being afraid of the wrath of

[1] C. 18, 19.

a harsh and worldly-minded husband if she sent away her
son to school at the monastery, induced one of the monks,
a friend of Chrysostom's, to reside for a time in the city,
in the character of pedagogue. The boy, thus subjected
to his training, afterwards joined the society of the monks;
but Chrysostom, fearing the consequences both to the
youth and to the monastic body, should his father detect
his secession, persuaded him to return to the city, where
he led an ascetic life, though not habited in monkish
dress. Out of these monastic schools, after years of
discipline and prayer, and study of the Word, there issued
many a pastor and preacher, well-armed champions of the
truth, strong in the Lord, and in the power of His might;
like Chrysostom himself, instant in season and out of
season; stern denouncers of evil, even in king's courts;
holding out the light of the Gospel in the midst of a dark
and crooked generation.

The foregoing extracts and paraphrases from these
treatises prove also that among zealous Christians the
monastic form of life was regarded as the highest; that
as philosophy was considered the highest flight in the
intellectual culture of the pagan, so was asceticism regarded as the highest attainment in the Christian's life;
it was to the education of the soul what philosophy was
to the education of the mind, and hence it was called by
the same name—'philosophy.' Possessed by this idea,
Chrysostom threw himself at this period of his life into
the system with all the ardour of his nature. If asceticism was good, it was right to carry it as far as nature
could bear it. He adopted the habits of an old member
of the brotherhood, named Syrus, notorious for the severity of his self-inflicted discipline. The day and greater
part of the night were spent in study, fastings, and vigils.
Bread and water were his only habitual food. At the end
of four years he proceeded a step farther. He withdrew

from the community to one of those solitary caves with which the mountains overhanging Antioch on its southern side abounded. In fact, he exchanged the life of a monk for that of an anchorite. His frame endured this additional strain for nearly two years, and then gave way. His health was so much shattered that he was obliged to abandon monastic life, and to return to the greater comfort of his home in Antioch.[1]

Meanwhile a friend of his, Stagirius by name—a person of noble birth, who, in spite of his father's opposition, had embraced monasticism—was reduced to a more deplorable condition. While Chrysostom was confined to his house by illness, a friend common to him and Stagirius brought him the sad intelligence that Stagirius was affected with all the symptoms of demoniacal possession—wringing of the hands, squinting of the eyes, foaming at the mouth, strange inarticulate cries, shiverings, and frightful visions at night.[2] We shall perhaps find little difficulty in accounting for these distressing affections, as the consequence of excessive austerities. The young man, who formerly lived a gay life in the world, and in the midst of affluence, had in the monastery fared on bread and water only, often kept vigil all night long, spent his days in prayer and tears of penitence, preserved an absolute silence, and read so many hours continuously, that his friends and brother monks feared that his brain would become disordered.[3] Very probably it was, and hence his visions and convulsions; but those were not days in which men readily attributed any strange phenomena, mental or bodily, to physical causes. We may believe in the action of a spirit world on the inhabitants of this earth; but we require good evidence that any violent or strange affection of mind or body is due to a

---

[1] Pallad. Dial. c. v.

[2] Ad Stag. a Daem. vex., vol. i.,

lib. i. c. i.

[3] Lib. ii. c. 1.

directly spiritual agency, rather than to the operation of
God according to natural law.   The cases of demoniacs in
the Gospel stand apart.   Our Lord uses language which
amounts to a distinct affirmation that those men were
actually possessed by evil spirits.   To use such expressions as 'come out of him,' 'enter no more into him,'
and the like, if there was no spirit concerned in the case
at all, would have been, to say the least, a mere unmean-
ing piece of acting, of which it would be shocking to
suppose our Lord capable.   But to admit the direct agency
of spirit, when confirmed by such authoritative testimony,
is widely different from the hasty ascription to spiritual
agency by an uncritical and unscientific age, of every
thing which cannot be accounted for by the most super-
ficial knowledge and observation.   Chrysostom, of course,
not being beyond his age in such matters, did not for a
moment dispute the supposition that Stagirius was actually possessed by a demon, but he displays a great deal of
good sense in dealing with the case.   As the state of his
own health did not permit him to pay Stagirius a visit in
person, he wrote his advice instead.   He perceived the
fatal temptation to despair in a man who imagined that
the devil had got a firm hold upon him, and that every evil
inclination proceeded directly from this demoniacal invader.   He will not allow that the suggestion to suicide,
of which Stagirius complained, came direct from the
demon, but rather from his own despondency,[1] with which
the devil had endeavoured to oppress him, that he might
under cover of that, work his own purposes more effectually, just as robbers attack houses in the dark.   But this
was to be shaken off by trust in God; for the devil did
not exercise a compulsory power over the hearts of men;
there must be a co-operation of the man's own will.   Eve
fell partly through her own inclination to sin: 'When
she saw that the tree was good for food, and pleasant to

[1] Lib. ii. c. 1

the eyes, she took of the fruit thereof and did eat;' and
if Adam was so easily persuaded to participate in her sin,
he would have fallen even had no Devil existed.

Chrysostom endeavours also to console his friend by
going through the histories of saints, in all times who
have been afflicted. His sufferings were not to be compared to those of Abraham, Isaac, Jacob, Moses, David,
and St. Paul. 'These afflictions were sent for remedial,
purgatorial purposes—that the soul might be saved in the
day of the Lord. It was not easy to say why such a
person was tried by this or that form of suffering, but if
we knew exactly God's motives, there would be no test of
faith. The indispensable thing was, to be firmly convinced
that whatever God sent was right. Some men were disturbed because the good were often troubled, and the
wicked prosperous; but such inequality in the distribution
of reward and punishment in this life, suggested a future
state, where they would be finally adjusted. The wicked
who had here received his good things, would there
receive his evil.[1] Stagirius had not been attacked by any
demon when he was living in carelessness and worldly
pleasure, but when he had buckled on his armour and
appeared as an antagonist, then the devil descended to the
assault. Hence he had no need to be ashamed of his
affliction; the only thing to be ashamed of was sin, and
it was owing to his renunciation of sin that the devil
assailed him. The real demoniacs were those who were
carried away by the impulses of unregulated passions.'
His summaries of the lives of the Old Testament saints,
which fill the rest of the second book and most of the
third, are very masterly, and display most intimate acquaintance with Holy Scripture in all its parts. A powerful
mind and retentive memory had profited by six years of
retirement largely devoted to study.

[1] Lib. i. c. 5-9.

CHAPTER VII.

ORDINATION AS DEACON—DESCRIPTION OF ANTIOCH—WORKS COMPOSED
DURING HIS DIACONATE. A.D. 381–386.

PROBABLY one of the last acts of Bishop Meletius before
he left Antioch to attend the Council of Constantinople in
381, was to ordain Chrysostom a deacon. The bishop
never returned. He died during the session of the council
of which he was president, leaving both that and the see
of Antioch distracted by the most deplorable factions.
It will be remembered[1] that the Catholics of Antioch had,
ever since the ill-judged mission of Lucifer of Cagliari,
been divided between allegiance to Paulinus, a priest of
the old Eustathian party, who had been consecrated
bishop by Lucifer, and Meletius, bishop of the more
moderate party. With the laudable purpose of healing
this schism, it is said that several of the clergy at Antioch,
who were considered most likely to succeed to a vacancy,
bound themselves under an oath, that in the event of
either bishop dying, they would decline the offer of the see,
if made, and acknowledge the survivor. But on the death
of Meletius, their plan was frustrated. Either the Asiatics,
who generally favoured Meletius, refused to submit to the
authority of Paulinus, because he had been ordained by a
Western prelate, or the Eustathians who acknowledged
Paulinus were unwilling on their side to admit Meletians
into their fold. In any case, the earnest endeavours of
Gregory of Nazianzum, now President of the Council, to

---

[1] See *ante*, Chapter II.

unite the two factions under one prelate were unsuccessful.[1] The Meletians elected Flavian to be their bishop, one of the very priests who had, under oath, renounced their pretensions to the see. This appointment of course exposed Flavian to the imputation of perjury, but we may hope that, like Gregory, he yielded to a pressing necessity only, and to a conviction that the dissension would have been aggravated and protracted if he had obdurately refused.[2] At any rate, as will hereafter appear, his conduct, wherever it comes before us, is worthy of all admiration, and Chrysostom must have filled the office of deacon with happiness under his administration. A greater contrast than the initiation of Chrysostom into clerical life, and that of a young deacon in modern times, can scarcely be imagined. He was in his thirty-seventh year, and had supplemented the good liberal education of his youth by several years of devotion to close study of Scripture, to rigorous mortification of the body, to prayer and meditation, and to every means of promoting the culture of the soul. After this long and careful training, he enters the subordinate ranks of the clergy, not to discharge, like a modern deacon, duties as laborious and often as responsible, as those which pertained to the priest, but such light and irresponsible tasks as were suitable to men who might be young, and were necessarily inexperienced in pastoral work. The deacons were sometimes called the Levites of the Christian Church.[3] It was their office, to take care of the holy table and its furniture, to administer the cup to the laity, but not to a priest or a bishop, and occasionally to read the Gospel.[4] They were

---

[1] See preface to his Orat. 43.

[2] The bishops of Egypt and the West generally adhered to Paulinus, Sozom. vii. 11, till by the united efforts of Chrysostom and Theophilus the universal acknowledgment of Flavian was obtained in A.D. 398.

[3] So Jerome, Ep. xxvii.

[4] Nice Counc. Can. 18.　(Hefele, p. 426.)

in most churches permitted to baptize.[1] But their peculiar duty in the services of the Church was to call the
attention of the people to every fresh movement, to use a
musical expression, in the progress of the service. Thus
at the close of the sermon, the deacon's voice was heard
crying, 'let the hearers (i.e. the second order of catechumens who were permitted to hear the sermon, but not the
conclusion of the Eucharistic service) and the unbelievers
depart!'[2] Then he bid the remaining orders of the
catechumens, i.e. the energumens, the competentes, and
the penitents, to pray for one another, and the people also
to pray for them; ἐκτενῶς δεηθῶμεν, 'let us ardently pray
for them'; such was the form. Again, when they were
dismissed by the command ἀπολύεσθε, 'disperse,' the
faithful were invited by the deacon to pray for the whole
state of Christ's Church.[3] Thus the deacons were the
sacred criers or heralds of the Church; they 'proclaimed
or bid prayer,' they announced each part as it was unfolded in the sacred drama of the Liturgy. The frequent
recurrence in our own Liturgy without much apparent
significance, of the form 'Let us pray,' is a remnant of
these old diaconal invitations. The deacons were not
permitted to preach except by a special direction of the
bishop. Their duty in part corresponded to that of our
churchwardens; they were to reprove any improper behaviour during divine service,[4] to bring cases of poverty
and sickness before the notice of the bishop, to distribute
the alms under his direction, and also to report to him
grave moral offences.[5] They were essentially, as the name
implies, ministers to the bishops and priests, and were
often styled, in symbolical language, 'the bishop's eyes,'
or 'ears,' or 'right hand.' The attitude of respect, which

[1] Tertull. de Bapt. cxvii. Jerome Dial. contr. Lucif.
[2] Chrysost. Hom. ii. in 2 Cor.
[3] Constit. Apost. l. viii. c. 10.
[4] Constit. Apost. lib. ii. c. 57. Chrysost. Hom. xxiv. in Act.
[5] Constit. Apost. lib. ii. c. 31, 32. Cyprian. Ep. xlix.

they were bound to maintain in church towards bishops
and priests, was in keeping with the servatorial character
of their office as a whole. While the priests had their
chairs ranged on either side of the central chair of the
bishop in the choir, the deacons stood humbly by, as if
ready to receive and execute the directions of their supe-
riors.[1] Even the Roman deacons, who rose rather above
the natural lowliness of their office, did not presume to
sit in the church.[2]

The duties of the diaconate must have brought Chrysostom into constant intercourse with the Christian population of Antioch, and especially with the poorer portion of
it. The whole population of the city amounted, according
to Chrysostom's statement, to 200,000,[3] and the Christians
to 100,000,[4] of whom 3,000 were indigent, and mainly
supported by the bounty of the Church.[5] The deacon's
function of searching out and relieving the necessitous by
distribution of alms must have been peculiarly congenial
to him. There is no Christian duty on which he more
constantly and earnestly insists than that of almsgiving,
not only in order to alleviate the sufferings of poverty,
but as a means of counteracting the inordinate avarice
and selfish luxury which were the prevailing vices in the
higher ranks of society, both in Antioch and Constantinople. His hold upon the affections of the common
people, partly no doubt through his sympathy with their
needs, partly by his bold denunciation of the vices of the
wealthy, partly by his affectionate and earnest plain-speaking of Christian truth, was remarkably strong throughout
his life. As during the secluded leisure of his monastic
life he had acquired a profound intimacy with Holy
Scripture, so in the more active labours of his diaconate

---

[1] Conc. Nic. c. 18. Hefele, p. 426.
[2] Jerome, Epist. 85 ad Evang.
[3] Chrysost. vol. ii. p. 591.
[4] Vol. vii. p. 762.
[5] Ibid. p. 629.

he enlarged his knowledge of human nature, and stored up observations on the character and manners of the people among whom he moved; qualifications no less important for the formation of a great and effective preacher.

It may not be uninteresting to take a brief glance at the character of the city and its inhabitants among whom he was destined to labour for the next seventeen years of his life.

Both nature and art combined to make Antioch one of the most delectable and luxurious residences in the world. The advantages of its situation, in some most important respects, could scarcely be exceeded. The river Orontes, connecting it with the sea about three miles distant, was the throat through which the city was fed with merchandise from all parts of the world. The wooded shores of the large lake of Antioch some miles above the city, supplied the inhabitants with fuel, and its waters yielded fish, in great abundance. The hills which impended over the town on the southern side, sent down numerous and copious streams, whose water, unsurpassed in purity, bubbled up through the fountains which stood in the court of every house. Northwards extended a fertile plain between the Orontes and Mount Coryphæus. The northern winds were occasionally keen and searching, but the prevailing western breezes coming up from the sea were so delicately soft yet refreshing, that the citizens delighted in summer to sleep upon the flat roofs of their dwellings. These advantages, however, were in some degree balanced by a liability to inundations and earth-quakes. Those hill-streams, the blessing and delight of the inhabitants in summer, were sometimes swollen in winter by excessive rains into torrents of incontrollable fury, and caused much damage to the buildings which were situated near their course. But far more destructive were the earthquakes. More than once, indeed, especially in the reigns of Caligula, Claudius, and Trajan, the whole city was almost shattered to pieces; but on each occasion, through public and private exertions, it arose from its ruins in new and, if possible, increased magnificence. The peculiar glories of Antioch were its gardens, and baths, and colonnaded streets. As in its population, and religion, and customs, so also in its architecture, it presented, as time went on, a remarkable mixture of Asiatic, Greek, and Roman elements. The aim of each Greek king and Roman emperor was to leave it more beautiful than he had received it from the hands of his predecessor. Each marked his reign by the erection of a temple or basilica, or bath, or aqueduct, or theatre, or column. The church in which Chrysostom officiated, usually called 'the great Church,' to distinguish it from the smaller and older church, called the Church of the Apostles, was commenced by Constantine, and finished by Constantius. In the main principles of structure, we may find some parallel to it in St. Vitale at Ravenna. It stood in the centre of a large court, and was octangular in shape; chambers, some of them subterranean, were clustered round it; the domed roof, of an amazing height, was gilded on the inside; the floor was paved with polished marbles; the walls and columns were adorned with images, and glistened with precious stones; every part, indeed, was richly embellished with bronze and golden ornament.[1] Among the principal wonders of Antioch was the great street constructed by Antiochus Epiphanes, nearly four miles in length, which traversed the city from east to west; the natural inequalities of the ground were filled up, so that the thoroughfare was a perfect level from end to end; the spacious colonnades on either side were paved with red

---

[1] Euseb. Vita Const. iii. 50. Chrysost. vol. iii. p. 160 and vol. xi. p. 78.   Vide also Müller de Antiq. Antioch, p. 103.

granite. From the centre of this magnificent street, where stood a statue of Apollo, another street, similar in character, but much shorter, was drawn at right angles, leading northwards in the direction of the Orontes. Many of the other streets were also colonnaded, so that the inhabitants, as they pursued their errands of business or pleasure, were sheltered alike from the scorching sun of summer, or the rains of winter. Innumerable lanterns at night illuminated the main thoroughfares with a brilliancy which almost rivalled the light of day, and much of the business, as well as the festivity, of the inhabitants was carried on by night.[1]

The character of the inhabitants partook of the various elements—Asiatic, Syrian, Greek, Jewish, Roman—which composed the whole population. But the impulsive oriental temperament, subject at times to fits of gloomy despondency, and to outbursts of wild ferocity, was undoubtedly the most dominant. When not driven under the pressure of excitement to either of these extremes, they abandoned themselves very freely to those voluptuous recreations for which the character of their city and climate afforded every facility and inducement. The bath, the circus, the theatre, were the daily amusements of the citizen; the Olympic games (instituted in the time of Commodus), which were celebrated in the grove of Daphne, and the festivities held at particular seasons in honour of different deities, were the greater occasions to which he looked forward with all the eagerness of a pleasure-loving nature.

These main characteristics of the people are abundantly illustrated in detail, as will be seen hereafter in the homilies of Chrysostom. He is ever, in them, labour-

---

[1] This description of Antioch is mainly collected from Müller's admirable and exhaustive work on the 'Antiquities of Antioch,' or from the authorities referred to therein.

ing with indefatigable industry and earnestness to lift the
Christians above the frivolity and vices of the rest of the
population.   His opportunities for investigating the condition of the Christian community were great during his
diaconate.   He did not as yet preach; but by observations on life and manners, he laid up copious materials
for preaching.   And he was not idle in the use of his
pen, for to this period may be assigned the treatise 'On
Virginity,' a letter addressed to a young widow; a book
on the Martyr Babylas; and, perhaps, though this cannot
.certainly be determined, the six books on the Priesthood.[1]

The letter to a young widow must have been written
soon after the destruction of the Emperor Valens and his
army by the Goths in A.D. 378, since it contains a reference to that event as a recent occurrence,[2] yet it must
have been antecedent to the crushing defeats inflicted on
them by Theodosius in A.D. 382. because the writer implies that at the time of composition the Goths were
overrunning large tracts of the empire with impunity,
and mocking the helplessness and timidity of the imperial troops.[3]   The whole book is penetrated with that
profound sense of the misery and instability of things
human, which the corruption of society and recent calamities of the empire impressed with peculiar force on
the minds of reflecting persons; which produced among
pagans either melancholy or careless indifference, but
made Christians cling with a more earnest and tenacious
trust to the hopes and consolations of the Gospel.

Therasius, the husband of the young widow, had died
after five years of married life.   He is described by
Chrysostom as having been distinguished in rank, in
ability, and above all, in virtue; as having held a high

---

[1] See Socrates vi. 1, and Mont-   [2] Ad vid. jun. c. 5.
fauçon's preface to 'De Sacerdotio.'   [3] C. 4.

position in the army, with a reasonable expectation of
soon becoming a prefect. But these very excellencies
and brilliant prospects, which seemed to aggravate the
sense of his loss, 'ought,' Chrysostom observes, 'to be
regarded as sources of consolation. If death were a final
and total destruction, then, indeed, it would have been
reasonable to lament the extinction of one, so benevolent,
so gentle, so humble, prudent, and devout, as her late
husband. But if death was only the landing of the soul
in a tranquil haven, only a transition from the worse to
better, from earth to Heaven, from men to angels and
archangels, and to Him who is the Lord of angels, then
there was no place left for tears. It was better that he
should depart and be with Christ, his true King, serving
Whom in that other world, he would not be exposed to
the dangers and animosities which attended the service
of an earthly monarch. They were, indeed, separated in
body, but neither length of time nor remoteness of place
could sunder the friendship of the soul. Endure patiently
for a little time, and you will behold again the face of
your desire; perhaps even now in visions, his figure will
be permitted to visit you.[1] If it was the loss of the
prefecture that she specially deplored, let her think from
what dangerous ambitions her husband had been preserved; think of the fate of Theodorus, who was tempted
by his high station to lay a plot against the Emperor,
and suffered capital punishment for his treason.[2] The
loftier a man's ambitions in life, the more probable a
disastrous fall. Look at the tragical fate of the Emperors
in the course of the past fifty years. Two only, out of
nine, had died natural deaths; of the other seven, one had
been killed by a usurper,[3] one in battle,[4] one by a sedition

[1] C. 3.

[2] C. 4. Executed in 371 in the
reign of Valentinian, Valens, and Gratian. Ammian. Marcell. xxix. 1, who

calls him a Gaul, not, as Chrysostom.
a Sicilian.

[3] Constans by Magnentius.

[4] Constantine the younger.

of his domestic guards,[1] one by the man who had invested
him with the purple.[2] Julian had fallen in battle in the
Persian expedition. Valentinian I. died in a fit of rage,
and Valens had been burnt, together with his retinue, in
a house to which the Goths set fire. And of the widows
of these Emperors, some had perished by poison, others
had died of despair and broken hearts. Of those who yet
survived, one was trembling for the safety of an orphan
son,[3] another had with difficulty obtained permission to
return from exile.[4] Of the wives of the present Emperors,
one was racked by constant anxiety on account of the
youth and inexperience of her husband,[5] the other was
subject to no less anxiety for her husband's safety, who
ever since his elevation to the throne had been engaged
in incessant warfare with the Goths.[6] Human ambition
was a hard task-mistress, who employed arrogance and
avarice as her agents; 'do not, then, mourn that your
husband has been emancipated from her tyranny.' Most
of the wisest and noblest characters even of the pagan
world had resisted the allurements of ambition,—Socrates,
Epaminondas, Aristides, Diogenes, Crates. Shall the
Christian then complain, if God takes one away from these
temptations? He who cared least about glory, who was
natural and modest, and unambitious, often acquired most
glory, whereas he who was most eager and anxious to
secure it, often obtained nothing but derision and reproach.
She believed that her husband might have obtained the pre-

---

[1] Jovian.

[2] Gallus Cæsar by Constantius.
The two who died natural deaths
were Constantine the Great and his
son Constantius.

[3] The widow of Jovian, whose son
Varronian was deprived of an eye.
See Gibbon, vol. iv. p. 222.

[4] Doubtful; possibly first wife of
Valentinian I., divorced from him and
sent into exile.

[5] Constantia, wife of Gratian.

[6] Flacilla, wife of Theodosius. Compare this mournful list of tragic deaths
of sovereigns with the splendid passage in Shakespere's Richard II. :—

'For Heaven's sake let's sit upon the ground,
And tell sad stories of the death of kings,' &c.

fecture; it was a reasonable hope, but there is many a slip betwixt the cup and the lip, and he who was king to-day was dead to-morrow. Strive, then, to equal and even surpass your husband in piety and goodness, that you may be admitted into the same home, and reunited to him in a bond far more lovely and enduring than that of earthly wedlock.'

In the long treatise ' De Virginitate,' Chrysostom boldly pronounces his preference for celibacy, but at the same time he exposes and denounces the mischievous error of Marcionites and Manichæans, who condemned marriage altogether as positive sin. ' They were mistaken in supposing that abstinence from marriage would procure them a high place in Heaven, because, even if it were granted that marriage was a positive sin, it must be remembered that not those who abstained from sin, but those who did positive good would receive the highest rewards; not one who abstained from calling his brother ' Raca,' but he who loved his enemies. The celibacy of heretics, such as the Manichæans, was based on the false conception that all created matter was evil, and that the Creator Himself was an inferior being to the Supreme Deity. Hence their celibacy was the work of the devil; they belonged to those mentioned only to be condemned in 1 Tim. iv. 1–3 'as forbidding to marry.'[1] Chastity of body was worthless, if the soul within was depraved; but celibacy rightly cultivated to preserve the purity of the soul towards God was better than marriage, better as Heaven was better than earth, and angels better than men. He confronts the common objection, if all men embrace celibacy, how would the race be propagated? Myriads of angels inhabit Heaven, yet we believe they were not propagated by matrimony, and it was only by the special provision and will of God, that matrimony

[1] Ch. i.–v.

itself produced offspring. Sarah was barren till God
vouchsafed her Isaac. Marriage was the inferior state
to conduct us to the higher; it was to celibacy as the Law
to the Gospel, it was a crutch to support those who would
otherwise fall into sin, but to be dispensed with when
possible. Let those, then, who reproached and derided
celibacy, put a restraint upon their lips, lest like Miriam,
or the children who mocked Elisha, they should be
severely punished for pouring contempt on so holy a
state.'[1]

We are enabled to understand from this work why the
best Christianity in the East was so disparaging of the
married state. The woman had not attained her proper
place in society. She seems to have been ill-educated, to
have been kept, especially before marriage, in a state of
unnatural seclusion, which she broke when she could, and
was too often treated by the husband like a slave, with
severity and distrust. This degrading position was partly
a remnant of the pagan state of society, but partly seems
natural to oriental manners. Christianity perceived the
evil, but had not effected much towards a remedy. Instead of endeavouring to elevate, to soften, and refine the
relation of one sex to the other, it encouraged rather a
total separation. The treatise now under notice presents
curious pictures of domestic life, if such it can be called,
in that age. Matrimonial matches were arranged entirely
by the parents, the attentions of the suitors were paid to
the parents, not to the maiden herself. She suffered an
agony of suspense, while the favourite of yesterday was
supplanted by the superior charms of some rival of to-day,
who in his turn was superseded by a third. Sometimes,
on the very eve of marriage, the suitor whom she herself
preferred was dismissed, and she was finally handed over
to another whom she disliked. The suitors also, on their

[1] C. 14–22.

side, were racked by anxiety; for it was difficult to ascertain what the real character, personal appearance, and manners were of the maiden, who was always kept in the strictest seclusion. Then there was often great difficulty in getting the dowry paid by the father-in-law, which was an annoyance to each of the newly-married pair.[1]

He draws a highly-wrought picture, with some caustic humour, of the miseries of jealous wives and husbands. When a man constantly suspects 'his dearest love,'[2] for whom he would willingly sacrifice life itself, what can console him? By day and night he has no peace, and is irritable to all. Some men have even slain their wives, without succeeding in cooling their own jealous rage. The trials of the wife were more severe; her words, her very looks and sighs were watched by slaves, and reported to her husband, who was too jealous to distinguish false tales from the true. The poor woman was reduced to the wretched alternative of keeping her own apartment, or, if she went out, of rendering an exact account of her proceedings. Untold wealth, sumptuous fare, troops of servants, distinguished birth, amounted to nothing when placed in the balance against such miseries as these. If it was the woman who was jealous, she suffered more than the man, for she could not keep him at home, or set the servants to watch him. If she remonstrated with him, she would be told that she had better hold her tongue, and keep her suspicions to herself. If the husband instituted a suit against the wife, the laws were favourable to him, and he could procure her condemnation, and even death; but if she were the petitioner, he would escape.[3]

It was very natural that the woman, who, before marriage, was cooped up like a child in the parental home, should break out afterwards into extravagance, dissipation, and frivolity, if not worse. An inordinate

<hr/>

[1] C. 57.   [2] τὴν μάλιστα πάντων ἀγαπωμένην. c. 52.   [3] C. 52.

amount of time and money was bestowed upon dress,
though perhaps not more than by the fashionable ladies of
modern times.   Women loaded themselves with ornaments, under the delusion that these added to their
charms, whereas, Chrysostom observes, if the woman was
naturally beautiful, the ornaments only concealed and de-
tracted from her charms. 'If she was ugly, they only set
off her ugliness by the glaring contrast, and the effect on
the spectator was ludicrous or painful.   But the adornment of the virgin who had dedicated herself to God was
altogether spiritual.   She arrayed herself in gentleness,
modesty, poverty, humility, fasting, vigils.   Incorporeal
graces and incorporeal beauty were the objects of her
love and contemplation.   She treated enemies with such
perfect courtesy and forbearance, that even the depraved
were put to shame in her presence.   The goodness of the
soul within overflowed into all her outer actions.'[1]   From
this rapturous description of a highly spiritual kind of
life, Chrysostom passes, with versatile quickness, to a
somewhat ludicrous picture of the petty cares of life in
the world. 'The worldly lady thinks it a fine thing to drive
round the Forum ; how much better to be independent,
and use her feet for the purpose for which God gave
them ! There was always some difficulty about the mules :
she and her husband wanted them at the same time ; one
or both were lame or turned out to grass.   A quiet and
modestly-dressed woman needed no carriage and attendants to protect her in her passage through the streets, but
might walk through the Forum, free from any annoyance.
Some might say it was pleasant to be waited on by a
troop of handmaids ; but, on the contrary, such a charge
was attended with much anxiety.   Not only had the sick
to be taken care of, but the indolent to be chastised,
mischief, quarrels, and all kinds of evil doings to be cor-

[1] C. 62, 63.

rected; and if there happened to be one distinguished by
personal beauty, jealousy was added to all these other
cares, lest the husband should be so captivated by her
charms as to pay more attention to her than to her mistress.[1] If it was replied to all these objections against
married life, that Abraham and other saints in the Old
Testament were all married men, it must be remembered
that a much higher standard was required under the New
Dispensation. There were degrees of perfection. When
Noah was said to be "perfect in his generation," it meant
relatively to that age in which he lived, for what is perfect in relation to one era becomes imperfect for another.
Murder was forbidden by the Old Law, but hatred and
wrath under the New. A larger effusion of the Holy
Spirit rendered Christian men fully grown as compared
with the children of the Old Dispensation. Degrees of
virtue, impossible then, were attainable now, and as the
moral standard under the Old Dispensation was lower, so
the rewards of obedience were less exalted. The Jews
were encouraged to obedience by the promise of an earthly
country, Christians by the prospect of Heaven. The Jews
were deterred from sin by menaces of temporal calamity;
the Christian, of eternal punishment. Let us, therefore,
not spend our care upon money-getting and wives and
luxurious living, else how shall we ever become men
rather than children, and live in the spirit? for when we
have taken our journey to that other world, the time for
contest will have past, then those who have not oil in
their lamps will be unable to borrow it from their neighbours, or he who has a soiled garment to exchange it for
another robe. When the Judge's throne has been placed,
and He is seated upon it, and the fiery stream is "coming
forth from before Him" (Dan. vii. 10), and the scrutiny of
past life has begun: though Noah, Daniel, and Job were

[1] C. 66, 67.

to implore an alteration of the sentence passed upon their own sons and daughters, their intercession would not avail.'[1]

The long treatise ' de S. Babyla contra Julianum et Gentiles,' presents several interesting subjects for consideration. In the history of the grove of Daphne we have a singular instance of the way in which Grecian legend was transplanted into foreign soil. Daphne, the daughter of the Grecian river god Ladon, was, according to the Syrian version of the myth, overtaken by Apollo near Antioch. Here it was, on the banks, not of the Peneus, but of the Orontes, that the maiden prayed to her mother earth to open her arms and shelter her from the pursuit of the amorous god, and that the laurel plant sprang out of the spot where she disappeared from the eyes of her disappointed lover. The horse of Seleucus Nicator, founder of the Syrian monarchy, was said to have struck his hoof upon one of the arrows which Apollo had dropped in the hurry of his chase; in consequence of which the king dedicated the place to the god. A temple was erected in his honour, ample in proportions, and sumptuous in its adornments; the interior walls were resplendent with polished marbles, the lofty ceiling was of cypress wood. The colossal image of the god, enriched with gold and gems, nearly reached the top of the roof; the draped portions were of wood, the nude portions of marble. The fingers of the deity lightly touched the lyre which hung from his shoulders, and in the other hand he held a golden dish, as if about to pour a libation on the earth, ' and supplicate the venerable mother to give to his arms the cold and beauteous Daphne.'[2] The whole grove became consecrated to pleasure, under the guise of festivity in honour of the god. A more beautiful combination of delights cannot well be conceived. The grove

[1] C. 83.   [2] Gibbon iv. p. 111.

was situated five miles to the south-west of Antioch, among the outskirts of the hills, where many of the limpid streams, rushing down towards the valley of the Orontes, mingled their waters. The road which connected the city with this spot was lined on the left hand with large gardens and groves, baths, fountains, and resting-places; on the right were villas with vineyards and rose-gardens irrigated by rivulets. Daphne itself was, according to Strabo,[1] eighty stadia, or about ten miles, in circumference. It contained everything which could gratify and charm the senses; the deep impenetrable shade of cypress trees, the delicious sound and coolness of falling waters, the fragrance of aromatic shrubs. Such a combination of all that was voluptuous told with fatal and enervating effect upon the morals of a people who were at all times disposed to an immoderate indulgence in luxurious pleasures. Roman troops, and even Roman emperors, fell victims to the allurements of the spot.[2] The annual celebration of the Olympian games instituted by Commodus, which took place here, was especially the occasion of shocking excesses of every kind. But by the order of Gallus Cæsar, an attempt was made to introduce a pure association into the spot hitherto contaminated by the licentiousness of pagan rites. The remains of Babylas, the Bishop of Antioch, who had suffered martyrdom in the reign of Decius, were transferred from their resting-place in the city to the grove of Daphne. The chapel or martyry erected over the bones of the Christian saint stood hard by the temple of the pagan deity. Here it confronted the Christian visitor, as a warning to him not to take part in pagan and licentious rites, abhorrent to the faith for which the Bishop had died. But the remains of the martyr were not permitted

---

[1] Strabo, p. 750.

[2] As Verus, Pescennius Niger, Macrinus and Severus Alexander.--Herodian ii. 7. 8. v. 2. vi. 7.

to rest in peace. When Julian visited Antioch, he consulted the oracle of Apollo at Daphne respecting the issue of the expedition which he was about to make into Persia. But the oracle was dumb. At length the god yielded to the importunity of repeated prayers and sacrifices so far as to explain the cause of his silence. He was disturbed by the proximity of a dead body: 'Break open the sepulchres, take up the bones, and remove them hence.' The demand was interpreted as referring to the remains of Babylas, and the wishes of the crestfallen oracle were complied with.[1] But the insult done to the Christian martyr was speedily avenged. Soon after the accomplishment of the impious act, a violent thunderstorm broke over the temple, and the lightning consumed both the roof of the building and the statue of the deity. At the time when Chrysostom wrote, some twenty years after the occurrence, the mournful wreck was yet standing; but the chapel again contained the relics of the saint and martyr, and conferred blessings on the pilgrims who resorted thither in crowds. The ruined and deserted temple, side by side with the carefully-preserved church of the martyr, thronged by devotees, presented a striking emblem of the fate of paganism, crumbling, and vanishing away before the presence of the new faith, blasted by the lightning flash of a mightier force. A great portion of the treatise of Chrysostom is occupied by an analysis of his old master Libanius's elegy over the fate of the stricken shrine of pagan worship. The affected and inflated tone of the sophist's composition deserves the sarcasm and scorn which his pupil unsparingly pours upon it.

[1] C. 14–16.

CHAPTER VIII.

CHRYSOSTOM had used the office of a deacon well. The
lofty tone of Christian piety, the boldness, the ability, the
command of language manifested in his writings, marked
him out as eminently qualified for a preacher. His
treatises, indeed, are distinguished by an eagerness and
energy of style, which belongs more to the fervour of the
orator than to the calmness of the writer. No doubt also
men had not forgotten the talent for speaking which he
had displayed when he began to practise, nearly twenty
years before, as a lawyer. The Bishop Flavian ordained
him a priest in 386, and immediately appointed him to
be one of the most frequent preachers in the church.
The bishop of a see like Antioch at that time more
resembled in his relations to the city, the rector of a large
town parish, than the bishop of modern times. He
resided in Antioch, and discharged the duties of a chief
pastor, assisted by his staff of priests and deacons. Where
the whole Christian population amounted to not more
than 100,000 souls, as in Antioch,[1] that division into
distinct districts, such as were formed in Alexandria,[2]
Rome, and Constantinople, with separate churches, served

---

[1] Hom. in Matt. vol. vii. p. 762.

[2] To the establishment of parochial
divisions with separate pastors in
Alexandria we have the direct testimony of Epiphanius, Hæres. 69,
Arian c. 1. In Rome, however, and

Constantinople, though the Churches
were numerous, the clergy seem to
have been more or less connected with
the mother Church.—Vide Bingham,
chap. viii. 5, book ix.

by members of the central staff in rotation, or by pastors especially appropriated to them, does not seem to have taken place. Chrysostom officiated and preached in the great church, where the bishop also officiated. The less learned and less able priests were appointed to the less responsible duties of visiting the sick and the poor, and administering the sacraments. The vocation of Chrysostom, however, was especially that of a teacher. It will be readily acknowledged how difficult, how delicate an office preaching was, in an age when Christianity and paganism were still existing side by side, and when the opinions of many men were floating in suspense between old forms of faith and the new, and were liable to be distracted from a firm hold upon the truth by Judaism and heresies of every shade.

Either on the occasion of his ordination, or very soon after it, Chrysostom preached an inaugural discourse, in the presence of the bishop. It is distinguished by that flowery and exaggerated kind of rhetoric which he occasionally displays in all its native oriental luxuriance, and which is due to the school in which he was brought up, rather than to the man. On such a public and formal occasion, he appears less as the Christian teacher than as the scholar of Libanius the Rhetorician. His self-disparagement at the opening of his discourse, and his flattering encomiums on Flavian and Meletius at the close, would to modern, certainly at least to English, ears, sound intolerably affected. No doubt, however, they were acceptable to the taste of his audience at Antioch; and, indeed, the whole discourse contains nothing more overstrained or ornate than is to be found in some of the most celebrated performances of the great French preachers in the seventeenth and eighteenth centuries.

A few paraphrases will suffice to illustrate the character of his discourse.

‘ He could scarcely believe what had befallen him, that
he, an insignificant and abject youth,[1] should find himself
elevated to such a height of dignity. The spectacle of so
vast a multitude hanging in expectation on his lips, quite
unnerved him, and would have dried up fountains of
eloquence, had he possessed such. How, then, could he
hope that his little trickling stream of words would not
fail, and that the feeble thoughts which he had put
together with so much labour, would not vanish from his
mind ?

‘ Wherefore he besought them to pray earnestly that he
might be inspired with courage to open his mouth boldly
in this hitherto unattempted work.[2] He wished to offer
the first-fruits of his speech in praise to God. As the
tiller of the ground gave of his wheat, grapes, or olives,
so he would feign make an offering in kind ; he would
“ praise the name of God with a song, and magnify it with
thanksgiving.” But the consciousness of sin made him
shrink from the task, for as in a wreath, not only must
the flowers be clean but also the hands which wove it, so
in sacred hymns not only must the words be holy but also
the soul of him who composed them. The words of the
wise man who said “ praise is not becoming in the mouth
of a sinner,” [3] sealed up his lips, and when David invited
all creation, animate and inanimate, visible and invisible,
to “ praise the Lord of Heaven, to praise him in the
height,” he did not include the sinner in the invitation.
He would rather therefore dilate on the merits of some
of his fellow-men who were worthier than himself. The
mention of their Christian virtues would be an indirect
way, legitimate for a sinner, of paying glory and honour

---

[1] μειρακίσκος εὐτελὴς καὶ ἀπερριμμένος, applied by rather a strong rhetorical licence to a man forty years old.

[2] μηδέπω πρότερον : this seems to prove that he had not preached during his diaconate.

[3] Ecclus. xv. 9.

to God himself. And to whom should he address his praises first but to their bishop, whom he might call the teacher of their country, and through their country of the world at large? To enter fully, however, into his manifold virtues was to dive into so deep a sea that he feared he should lose himself in its profundities. To do justice to the task would require an inspired and apostolic tongue. He must confine himself to a few points. Although reared in the midst of affluence, Flavian had surmounted the difficulties which impeded the entrance of a rich man into the kingdom of heaven. He had been distinguished from youth by perfect temperance and control over the bodily appetites, by contempt of luxury and a costly table. Though untimely deprived of parental care and exposed to the temptations incident to wealth, youth, and good birth, yet had he triumphed over them all. He had assiduously cultivated his mind, and had put the bridle of fasting on his body sufficient to curb excess, without impairing its strength and usefulness; and though he had now glided into the haven of a calm old age, yet he did not relax the severity of this personal discipline. The death of their beloved father Meletius had caused great distress and perplexity to the Church, but the appearance of his successor had dispersed it, as clouds vanished before the sun. When Flavian mounted the episcopal throne, Meletius himself seemed to have risen from his tomb.' All that can be collected from history respecting Flavian's character, confirms and justifies these eulogiums, though English taste would prefer them to have been uttered after his death than in his actual presence.

Chrysostom concludes by saying that he had prolonged his address beyond the bounds which became his position, but the flowery field of praise had tempted him to linger. 'He would conclude his task by asking their prayers; prayers that their common mother the Church might remain undisturbed and stedfast, and that the life of their father teacher, spiritual shepherd and pilot, might be prolonged; prayers finally that he the preacher, might be strengthened to bear the yoke which was laid upon him, might in the great day restore safely the deposit which his master had committed to his trust, and obtain mercy for his sins through the grace and goodness of the Lord Jesus Christ, to whom be glory, and power, and worship for ever and ever.'

We now enter on a period of ten years, during which Chrysostom constantly resided in Antioch, and was occupied in the almost incessant labour of preaching. The main bulk of those voluminous works which have been preserved to our times belongs to this period; yet there can be no doubt that, numerous as are the extant works, they represent but a fraction of the discourses which he actually delivered. For we know on his own authority, that he frequently preached twice, occasionally oftener in the course of a week.[1]

It does not fall within the scope of this essay to determine how many of the homilies which we possess were delivered in each year, or to enter into a critical examination of every set. But an attempt will be made to extract from them whatever seems to throw light upon the life and times of their author, upon events in which he played a conspicuous part, or which were of great public importance; whatever also illustrates the special condition of the Church,—her general practice, her merits and defects, the dangers and difficulties with which, from dissension within, or heresy without, she had at this era to contend.

The field of subjects on which the preacher was called to exercise his powers was varied and extensive. Christianity was imperilled by corruption of morals and cor-

[1] Hom. xi. in Ac. Apost. in fine.

ruption of faith. Not the laity only, but the clergy also,
at least in the great towns, had become deeply infected
by the prevalent follies and vices of the age. Again,
between the orthodox Christian and the Pagan, every
variety of heresy intervened. The Arian, the Manichæan,
the Marcionite, the Sabellian, the Jew,—all were, so to
say, touching and fraying the edge of pure Christianity;
the danger was, lest they should gradually so wear it away
as to injure the very vitals of the faith. Such were the
evils, such the enemies which Chrysostom bent his energies
courageously, perseveringly to redress or repel. He is
alternately the champion of a pure morality and of a
sound faith.

Among the discourses which belong to the first year of
his priesthood, falls one delivered in commemoration of
Bishop Meletius, the predecessor of Flavian.[1] He had
died at Constantinople about the end of May A.D. 381,
and Chrysostom in the commencement of his homily
remarks, that five years had now elapsed since the bishop
had taken his journey to the 'Saviour of his longings.'
The tone of the discourse illustrates a characteristic of
the times; a passionate devotion to the memory of departed saints which was rapidly passing into actual adoration; a subject on which more will be said hereafter.
The shrine which contained the reliques of Meletius was
placed in the sight of the preacher and the congregation,
who swarmed round it like bees.[2] When Chrysostom
looked at the great multitude assembled 'he congratulated
the holy Meletius on enjoying such honour after his death,
and he congratulated the people also on the endurance of
their affection to their late spiritual father. Meletius
was like the sound root which though invisible proved its
strength by the vigour of its fruit. When he had returned from his first banishment the whole Christian popu-

[1] Vol. ii. p. 515.   [2] C. 3.

1

lation had streamed forth to meet him. Happy those who
succeeded in clasping his feet, kissing his hand, hearing
his voice. Others who beheld him only at a distance
felt that they too had obtained a blessing from the mere
sight. A kind of spiritual glory emanated from his holy
person, even as the shadows of St. Peter and St. John
had healed the sick, on whom they fell.' 'Let us all, rulers
and ruled, men and women old and young, free men and
slaves, offer prayer, taking the blessed Meletius into part-
nership with this our prayer (since he has more confidence
now in offering prayer, and entertains a warmer affection towards us), that our love may be increased and that
as now we stand beside his shrine, so one day we may all
be permitted to approach his resting-place in the other
world.'

The discourses of Chrysostom against Arians and Jews,
fall within the first year of his priesthood.[1] They are
among the finest of his productions, and deserve perusal
on account of their intrinsic merit no less than of the important points of doctrine with which they are concerned.
Antioch, indeed, may in some sort, be regarded as the
cradle of Arianism. Paul of Samosata, who was deposed
from the see of Antioch in A.D. 272, advocated doctrines
of a Sabellian character, but that sophistical dialectical
school of thought of which the Arians were the most
conspicuous representatives, may be traced to him. His
original calling had been that of a sophist, and he was
therefore by training more fitted to attack established
doctrines than to build up a definite system of his own.
Hence it is not surprising that, though his own tendency
was to Sabellian opinions, Lucian, his intimate friend and
fellow-countryman, held doctrines diametrically opposite,
or what were afterwards called Arian.[2] Lucian, when

---

[1] See the Monitum to these Homilies, vol. i. p. 699.

[2] See Newman's Arians, chap. i.
sect. i.

presbyter at Antioch, was the teacher of Eusebius, Bishop
of Nicomedia, of Leontius, the Arian Bishop of Antioch,
and perhaps also of Arius himself.[1] Aëtius, and his pupil
Eunomius, originators of the most extreme and undis-
guised form of Arianism, resided in the beginning of
their career at Antioch. Eunomius, in fact, was the
founder of a sect which was called Eunomian after
him; or sometimes Anomœan, because it denied not
only equality but even similarity (ὁμοιότης) between
the Father and the Son in the Holy Trinity. It was
the most materialistic phase which Arianism developed.
Mystery was to be eliminated from revelation as much as
possible, sacramental grace was little recognised, asceticism disparaged. Adherents of this school seem to have
existed still in some force at Antioch. A system marked
by so much of cold intellectual pride was especially repugnant to the fervid and humble faith of Chrysostom. Yet
in his assaults upon it he was neither precipitate nor
harsh. In his first homily 'On the incomprehensible
Nature of God,' he says that having observed several
persons who were infected by this heresy listening to his
discourses, he had abstained from attacking their errors,
wishing to gain a firmer hold upon their interest before
engaging with them in controversy. But having been
invited by them to undertake the contest, he could not
decline it, but would endeavour to conduct it in a spirit
of gentleness and love, since 'the servant of the Lord must
not strive, but be gentle towards' all, as well as 'apt to
teach.' He urges all disputants to remember our Lord's
answer when He was buffetted, 'If I have spoken evil,
bear witness of the evil; but if well, why smitest thou
me?'[2]

He dilates on the arrogance of the Anomœans in pre-

---

[1] Arius, in a letter to Eusebius,
addresses him as συλλουκιανιστά,

'fellow Lucianist,' Theod. i. 5.
[2] I. c. 6, 7.

tending to understand and to define the exact nature of God. 'Professing themselves wise they only discovered their folly. Imperfect knowledge on so profound a subject was an inevitable part of the imperfection of our human state. The condition of our present knowledge was this — we know many things *about* God, but we do not know *how* they are or take place. For example, we may know that He is everywhere and without beginning or end, but *how* He is thus, we know not. We know that he begat the Son, and that the Holy Spirit proceeded from Him, but *how* these things can be we are unable to tell. This is analogous to our knowledge of many things which are called natural. We eat various kinds of food, but *how* they nourish us and are transmuted into the several humours of the body we do not understand.'[1]

'Again, if the wisest and holiest men have confessed themselves incompetent to fathom the *purposes* and *dispensations* of God, how far more inscrutable must his *essence* be! If David exclaims 'such knowledge is too wonderful and excellent for me, I cannot attain unto it;' and St. Paul, 'Oh the depth of the riches and wisdom of God, how unsearchable are his judgments, how untraceable his ways;' if the very angels do not presume to discuss the nature of God, but humbly adore Him with veiled faces, crying ' Holy, Holy, Holy,' how monstrous is the conceit and irreverence of those who curiously investigate and pretend to define the exact nature of the Godhead.'[2]

He proceeds to dwell upon the littleness and feebleness of man, as contrasted with the amazing and boundless power of God. The Eunomians maintained that man could know the nature of God as much as God Himself knew it. 'What mad presumption was this! the Prophets exhaust all available metaphors to express the insignifi-

[1] C. 3.   [2] I. c. 4.

cance of man, as compared with God. Men are "dust and
ashes," "grass," and the "flower of grass," "a vapour,"
"a shadow." Inanimate creation acknowledges the irresistible supremacy of his power; "if He do but touch
the hills they shall smoke," "He shaketh the earth out of
her place, and the pillars thereof tremble" (Job ix. 6).'
'Seest thou not yon sky, how beautiful it is, how vast,
spangled with what a choir of stars? Five thousand
years and more has it stood, yet length of time has left
no mark of old age upon it: like a youthful vigorous body
it retains the beauty with which it was endowed at the
beginning. This beautiful, this vast, this starry, this
ancient firmament, was made by that God into whose
nature you curiously pry, was made with as much ease
as a man might for pastime construct a hovel: "He established the sky like a roof, and stretched it out like a
tent over the earth" (Isa. xl. 22). The solid, durable
earth He made, and all the nations of the world, even as
far as the British isles, are but as a drop in a bucket;
and shall man, who is but an infinitessimal part of this
drop, presume to enquire into the nature of Him who
made all these forces and whom they obey?'[1] 'God dwells
in the light which no man can approach unto. If the
light which surrounds Him be inaccessible, how much
more God Himself who is within it? St. Paul rebukes
those who presume to question the dispensation of God.
'Nay but, O man, who art thou, that repliest against God?
shall the thing formed say unto him that formed it, why
hast thou made me thus?' How much more, then, would
he have reproved dogmatic assumption respecting the
nature of the great Dispenser?[2] The declaration of St.
John that no man had seen God at any time might
appear at variance with the descriptions in the prophets
of visions of the Deity. As: "I saw the Lord sitting on

[1] II. c. 3, 4.   [2] II. c. 4, 5; III. 3, 4, 5, 6.

his throne high and lifted up" (Isa. vi. 1). "I saw the
Lord standing above the altar" (Amos ix. 1). "I beheld
till the thrones were cast down, and the Ancient of days
did sit whose garment was white as snow," &c. (Dan.
vii. 9). But the very variety of forms under which God
is said to have appeared, proves that these manifestations
were merely condescensions to the weakness of human
nature, which requires something that the eye can see and
the ear can hear. They were only manifestations of the
Deity adapted to man's capacity; not the Divine Nature
itself which is simple, incomposite, devoid of shape. So,
also, when it is said of God the Son that He is "in the
bosom of the Father," when He is described as standing,
or sitting on the right hand of God, these expressions
must not be interpreted in too material a sense; they are
expressions accommodated to our understandings, to convey an idea of such an intimate union and equality
between the two Persons as is in itself incomprehensible.'[1]

And this leads him on to consider the second error of
the Arians—their denial of absolute equality between the
three Persons in the Godhead. His arguments are based,
as usual, entirely on an appeal to Holy Scripture. He
makes a skilful selection and combination of texts to
prove his point, that the titles 'God' and 'Lord' are
common to the first two Persons in the Trinity—the
names Father and Son being added merely to distinguish
the Personality. Had the Father alone been God, then it
would have been superfluous to add the name Father at
all: 'there is one God' would have been sufficient. But,
as it was, the titles 'God' and 'Lord' were applied to
both Persons to prove their equality in respect of Godhead. That the appellation of Lord no way indicated
inferiority was plain, because it was frequently applied to
the Father. 'The Lord our God is one Lord,' Exod.

[1] IV. 4.

xx. 2. 'Great is our Lord and great is his power,' Psa.
cxlvii. 5. On the other hand, Christ is frequently entitled
God, e.g. 'Immanuel—*God* with us.' 'Christ according to
the flesh, who is over all, *God* blessed for ever.' In some
instances the Father and the Son are both called Lord, or
both God in the *same* passage; as, for example, 'The
Lord said unto my Lord' . . . . 'thy throne, O God (the
Son), is for ever and ever' . . . . 'wherefore God (the
Father), even thy God, hath anointed thee with the oil
of gladness,' &c.[1]

'The reason why Christ sometimes acted and spoke in a
manner which implied human infirmity, and inferiority to
the Father, was twofold. First, that men might be convinced that He did really, substantially exist in the truth
of our human nature; that He was not a mere phantom
—the error of Marcion, Manes, and Valentinus—an error
which would have been still more prevalent had He not
so clearly manifested the reality of his humanity. On
the other hand, He was reserved and cautious in declaring the highest mystery—his divine union and equality
with the Father—out of condescension to the weakness of
man's intellect, which recoiled from the more recondite
mysteries. When He told them that "Abraham rejoiced
to see his day," that "before Abraham was He was," "that
the bread from heaven was his flesh, which He would give
for the life of the world," that "hereafter they should see
the Son of Man coming in the clouds," they were invariably offended. But, on the contrary, He was chiefly
accepted when He spoke words implying more humiliation
—for example, "I can of my own self do nothing, but as
my Father taught me, even so I speak." "As He spake
these words," we are told, "many believed on Him."[2]

'Two other reasons might be assigned for this language
of self-abasement. One was, that He came to teach us

---

[1] V. 2, 3.   [2] VII. c. 3. 4.

humility,—"learn of me, for I am meek and lowly of
heart." He "came not to be ministered unto but to
minister." He who bids others be lowly must first and
pre-eminently be lowly Himself. Therefore He performed
such acts as washing his disciples' feet; and the Incarnation itself was no sign, as the Arian maintained,
of inferiority, but only the highest expression of that
great principle of self-sacrificing love which He came to
teach. Lastly, by such language He directs our minds
to the apprehension of a clear distinction between the
Persons in the Godhead. If his sayings about Himself
had all resembled such as "I and my Father are one," the
Sabellian error of confounding the Persons would have
become yet more prevalent than it was. Thus, we find
throughout our Lord's life, in his acts and language, a
careful mixture and variation of character in order to
present the two elements—the human and divine—in
equal proportions. He predicts his own sufferings and
death, yet quickly afterwards He prays the Father that
He might be, if possible, spared undergoing them. In
the first act is pure divinity; in the second humanity
shrinking from that pain which is abhorrent to human
nature.'[1]

This very fact, however, of our Lord's praying, was
laid hold of by the Arians to prove the inferiority of his
nature. This argument Chrysostom meets in Homilies IX. and X. The raising of Lazarus had been read
in the gospel for the day. 'I perceive,' he says, 'that
many of the Jews and heretics will find an excuse in the
prayer offered by Christ before performing this miracle, to
impugn his power, and say He could not have done it
without the Father's assistance.' But this fell to the
ground, because on most other occasions our Lord
wrought his miracles without any prayer at all. To the

[1] VII. c. 6, 7.

dead maiden he simply said, 'Talitha Cumi,' and she
arose; the woman with an issue of blood was healed
without any word or touch from Him. In the case of
Lazarus He prayed, as He Himself declared, for the sake
of the people, that they might perceive that God heard
his prayers—that there was a perfect unanimity between
the Father and the Son. Martha, in fact, had asked for
a prayer, 'I know whatsoever thou shalt ask of God God
will give it thee,' therefore He prayed; just as when the
centurion said, 'Speak the word only,' He spake the word
and the servant was healed. If He had needed help He
would have invoked it before all his miracles. In fact
there was no kind of sovereign power which He hesitated
to exercise. 'Son, be of good cheer, thy sins be forgiven
thee;' . . . . 'the Son of Man hath power on earth to
forgive sins;'—to an evil spirit, '*I* charge thee come out
of him, and enter no more into him;' . . . 'to them of
old it was said, Thou shalt not kill, but *I* say, whosoever is
angry with his brother without a cause,' &c. He represents Himself as saying on the final day, 'Come, ye
blessed;' or 'Depart, ye cursed.' Thus He claims authority
to absolve, to judge, to legislate.

Homilies XI. and XII. against the Anomœans were delivered some ten years later at Constantinople, but as they
contain no special references to the events of that time the
continuity of this subject may be maintained by extracting
from them the argument there employed to prove the
equality of the Son with the Father. It is based on the passage, 'My Father worketh hitherto, and I work' (St. John
v. 17); by which our Saviour justified Himself from the
accusation of breaking the Sabbath when He healed the
paralytic. The words 'My Father worketh,' Chrysostom
observes, refer to the daily operations of God's providence,
by which He sustains in being those things which He
commanded into existence.

This upholding energy, our Lord declares, is active at all
times and on all days alike; and if it were not, the fabric
of the universe would fall to pieces. He claims a similar
right to providential rule, which implies equality with the
Father. 'My Father worketh, *and I* work.' If the Son
had been inferior, such a method of justifying Himself
would only have added force to the charges of his enemies.
If a subject of the Emperor were to put on the imperial
diadem and purple, it would be no excuse to say that he
wore them *because* the Emperor wore them—' the Emperor
wears them and I wear them;'—on the contrary, it would
augment the offensiveness of his presumption and arrogance. If Christ were not equal with the Father, it was
the height of presumption to use those words, ' My Father
worketh hitherto, and I work.'

In dealing with such lengthy homilies, it has been
impossible to do more than give specimens in a very
condensed form of the main lines of argument which Chrysostom adopts. They vary greatly in value; but two points
cannot fail to arrest the notice of anyone who reads
these homilies through. First, the profound acquaintance
of their author with Holy Scripture; extending apparently
with equal force to every part of the sacred volume. Old
and New Testament and Apocrypha, are almost equally
employed for argument, illustration, adornment: he is at
home everywhere. Secondly, upon Scripture all his arguments are based: in none of his controversial homilies
does Chrysostom take his stand upon the platform of
existing tradition, or rely on the authority of the Church
alone; ' to the law and to the testimony' is always the
way with him. And this was a test at that time universally accepted. The dispute with the most rationalistic
and critical Arians seems never to have turned on the
authority, but only on the *interpretation* of Scripture.
Scripture is appealed to as the supreme court for trying

all their differences; the only question was, as to the exact meaning of its decisions.

Again, we cannot fail to be struck by the ease and rapidity with which he glances off from the most controversial and theological parts of his discourse to practical reproof and exhortation. Nothing provoked him more than to see the bulk of that large concourse of people who had been listening with profound attention to his address leave the church just as the celebration of the Eucharist was about to commence. 'Deeply do I groan to perceive that when your fellow-servant is speaking, great is your earnestness, strained your attention, you crowd one upon another, and stay till the very end, but that when Christ is about to appear in the holy mysteries the church is empty and deserted. . . . If my words had been laid up in your hearts they would have kept you here, and brought you to the celebration of these most solemn mysteries with greater piety; but as it is, my speech seems as fruitless as the performance of a lute-player, for as soon as I have finished you depart. Away with the frigid excuse of many, I can say prayers at home, but I cannot at home hear homilies and doctrine. Thou deceivest thyself, O man; you may, indeed, pray at home, but it is impossible to pray *in the same manner* as at church, where there is so large an assembly of your spiritual fathers, and the cry of the worshippers is sent up with one accord; where there is unanimity and concert in prayer; and where the priests preside, that the weaker supplications of the multitude being supported by theirs, which are more powerful, may ascend together with these to heaven. First prayer, then discourse; so say the Apostles. 'But we will give ourselves to *prayer and* to the ministry of the word.'[1]

Again, as frequently in other discourses, he reproves the

[1] III. c. 6.

congregation for testifying their admiration of his words
by applause. 'You praise what I have said, you receive
my exhortation with tumults of applause : but show your
approbation by obedience : that is the praise which I seek,
the applause which comes through deeds.'[1]

His hearers, in fact, were so closely packed, and so
much absorbed in listening to his discourse, that pickpockets often practised on them with some success.
Chrysostom advises them, therefore, to bring no money
or ornaments about their persons to church. It was a
device of the devil, who hoped by means of this annoyance to chill their zeal in attending the services, just as
he stripped Job of everything, not merely to make him
poor but to rob him if possible of his piety.[2]

But the most inveterate enemy with which Chrysostom
had to contend was the circus. Against this he declaims
with all the vehemence of Evangelical invectives against
horse-racing in modern times. The indomitable passion
for the chariot-races, and the silly eagerness displayed
about them by the inhabitants of Rome, Constantinople,
and Antioch, are among the most remarkable symptoms
of the debased and vitiated character of society, under the
later Empire. The whole populace was divided into factions
distinguished by the different colours adopted by the charioteers, of which green and blue were the two chief
favourites. The animosity, the sanguinary tumults, the
superstitions,[3] folly, violence of every kind, which were
mixed up with these popular amusements, well deserved
the unsparing severity with which they were lashed by
the great preacher.

A few specimens shall be collected here from other

---

[1] III. c. 6, in fine.
[2] IV. in fine.
[3] The colours represented the sea- sons, and according as one or other was victorious a plentiful harvest or pros- perous navigation was indicated.

homilies, as well as from those immediately under consideration.

' Again we have the horse-races; again our assembly is thinned. But he cared not so much for the loss of the leaves, the scum in fact, of the congregation, provided that the sound and genuine portion of it remained.[1] Sometimes, however, the church was deserted by those of whom he had expected more fidelity. He felt disheartened, like a sower who had scattered good seed plentifully, but with no adequate result. Gladly and eagerly would he continue his exertions could he see any fruit of his labours; but when, forgetful of all his exhortations and warnings, and solemn remindings of the terrible doom, the unquenchable fire, the undying worm, they again abandoned themselves to the diabolical exhibitions of the race-course, with what heart could he return to the unthankful task? They manifested, indeed, by applause, the pleasure with which they heard his words, and then they hurried off to the circus, and, sitting side by side with Jew or Pagan, they applauded, with a kind of frenzied eagerness, the efforts of the several charioteers; they rushed tumultuously along, jostling one another, and shouting, "that horse didn't run fairly," "that was tripped up, and fell," and the like.[2] Various excuses were pleaded for absence from church — the exigencies of business, poverty, ill health, lameness; but these impediments never prevented attendance at the Hippodrome. In the church the chief places even were not always all occupied, but *there* old and young, rich and poor, crowded every available space for standing or sitting; pushing, and squeezing, and trampling on one another's feet, while the sun poured down on their heads: yet they appeared thoroughly to enjoy themselves, in spite of all these discomforts; while

[1] VII. contra Anom. c. i.   [2] De Laz. vii. c. 1.

in the church the length of the sermon, or the heat, or the crowd were perpetual subjects of complaint.'[1]

Such are a few illustrations of one, but perhaps the most notable, form among many in which the impulsiveness and frivolity of the people of Antioch were displayed. 'The building which the preacher had so laboriously and industriously reared in the hearts of his disciples was thus cruelly dashed down and levelled to the very ground by a few hours of dissolving pleasure and iniquitous frivolity.'[2]

Truly, indeed, might the lamentation of the prophet over the evanescent piety of Ephraim and Judah have been applied to these people: 'Your goodness is as a morning cloud, and as the early dew it goeth away' (Hos. vi. 4).

[1] De Anna iv. 1.　　　　[2] De Laz. vii. c. 1.

CHAPTER IX.

In dealing with the Arians, the contest mainly turned, as
has been pointed out in the previous chapter, on the interpretation of Scripture, but in doing battle with Pagans
and Jews, with the former especially, Chrysostom had of
course to take up a different attitude. The method which
he adopts towards the Jew is to demonstrate the fulfilment of Old Testament prophecy in the person and work
of Jesus Christ, and to insist on the consequent abrogation of the Jewish dispensation. The ground on which
he mainly relies against the Pagan is the miraculous
establishment and progress of Christianity in the face of
unprecedented opposition, as an evidence of its divine
origin.

The treatise addressed to Jews and Gentiles combined,
exhibits a powerful application of both these methods.[1]
'He would first of all enter the lists against the Pagan.
And here caution was requisite. He would not say, when
the Pagan asked how the divinity of Christ was to be
proved, that Christ created the world, raised the dead,
healed the sick, expelled demons, promised a resurrection
and a heavenly kingdom, because these were the very

---

[1] It is a treatise, because too long
for a homily, though mutilated of its
proper conclusion. It must belong to
the first two years of his priesthood,
because it promises a more ample
discussion of several points, which
promise we find redeemed in the homilies against the Jews, and these homilies, again, can be proved, by internal
evidence, to have been delivered not
later than A.D. 387. See Montfauçon's
'Monitum,' vol. i. pp. 811 and 839.

questions upon which they joined issue. But he would
start from a ground which even the Pagan would accept;
no one would venture to deny that the Christian religion
was founded by Jesus Christ, and from this simple fact
he would undertake to prove that Christ could be no
less than God. No mere man could, in so short a time,
with such feeble instruments, and in the face of such
opposition arising from inveterate custom and forms of
faith, have subdued so many and such various races of
mankind.[1] How contrary to the common course of events,
that He who was despised, weak, and put to an ignominious death, should now be honoured and adored in all
regions of the earth! Emperors who have made laws,
altered the constitution of states, who have ruled nations
by their nod, in whose hands was the power of life and
death, pass away, their images are in time destroyed, their
actions forgotten, their adherents despised, their very
names buried in oblivion:—present grandeur is succeeded
by nothingness. In the case of Jesus Christ, all is re-
versed. During his lifetime, all seemed failure and degradation, but a career of glory and triumph succeeded his
death.[2] Before his death Judas betrayed Him, St. Peter
denied Him; after his death, St. Peter and the rest of
the Apostles traversed the world to bear witness to his
truth, and thousands of people have died, rather than
utter what the chief of the Apostles once uttered from
fear of a maid servant's taunts. "His rest shall be
glorious:"—this was true, not only of the Master but also
of his disciples. In that most royal city of Rome
monarchs, prefects, generals, flocked to the sepulchres of
the fisherman and the tent-maker; and in Constantinople
they who wore the diadem were content to lay their bones

[1] C. 1.
[2] See a singular parallel to this
thought in the Emperor Napoleon I.'s
remarks on Christianity : ' Table Talk
and Opinions of Napoleon I.'

in the porch of the Apostle's Church, and to become as it were the door-keepers of humble fishermen.[1] Christ had made the most ignominious death, and the instrument of it, glorious. It was written, " cursed is he that hangeth on a tree," yet the cross had become the object of desire and love; it was more honourable than the whole world, for the imperial crown itself was not such an ornament to the head: princes and subjects, men and women, bond and free, all delighted to wear it imprinted on the brow. It was conspicuous on the Holy Table, and in the ceremony of ordaining priests; in houses, in market-places, by the wayside, and on mountain sides, on couches and on garments, on ships, on drinking vessels, in mural decorations, the cross was depicted. Whence all this extraordinary honour to a piece of wood, unless the power of Him who died upon it was divine ?"[2]

Christ had declared that the gates of hell should not prevail against his Rock-founded Church. How far had this prediction been verified? In a short space of time Christianity had abolished ancestral customs, plucked up deeply-rooted habits, overturned altars and temples, caused unclean rites and festivals to vanish away. Christian altars had been erected in Italy, in Persia, in Scythia, in Africa. ' What say I? even the British Isles, which lie outside the boundaries of our world and our sea, in the midst of the ocean itself, have experienced the power of the Word, for even there churches and altars have been set up.' Thus the world had been, so to say, cleared of thorns, and purified to receive the seed of godliness. What a proof of superhuman power! The progress of the Church had been encountered by customs which were not only venerated but pleasant; yet these traditions, handed down through long lines of ancestors, were abandoned for a religion far more severe and laborious, a

[1] C. 9.   [2] Ibid.

K

religion which substituted fasting for enjoyment, poverty
for money-getting, temperance for lasciviousness, meekness for wrath, benevolence for ill-will. Men who had
long been enervated by luxury, and accustomed to the
broad way, had been converted into the narrow rugged
path, not by tens or twenties, but by multitudes under
the whole heaven. By whose agency had these mighty
results been wrought? By a few unlearned obscure men,
without illustrious ancestors, without money, without
eloquence.[1] And all this in the teeth of opposition of the
most varied kind. For where the new doctrine penetrated
it excited divisions and strife; children were set at
variance with parents, brother with brother, husband with
wife, master with servant. Yet, in spite of persecution
and disruption of social ties, the new faith grew and
flourished. How could such unprecedented marvels have
come to pass but through the divine power, and in
obedience to that Word of God which is creative of actual
results? Just as, when He said, 'Let the earth bring
forth grass' the wilderness became a garden, so when the
expression of his purpose had gone forth, 'I will build
my Church,' straightway the process began, and though
tyrants and people, sophists and orators, custom and religion, had been arrayed against it, yet the Word going
forth like fire, consumed the thorns, and scattered the
good seed over the purified soil.[2]

In attempting to convince the Jews of the divinity of
Jesus Christ by proving the exact fulfilment of Old Testament prophecy in his person and work, Chrysostom
displays that intimate familiarity with every part of
Scripture which is his eminent characteristic.

The passages are, on the whole, most judiciously
selected; some corresponding passage from the New
Testament being placed, if possible, against each, with

[1] C. 12.   [2] C. 13.

a careful attention even to verbal parallelism. For instance, against the passage in Isaiah, 'The spirit of the Lord shall *rest* upon him,' he places the verse from St. John i. 32, 'I beheld the spirit descending like a dove, and it *abode* upon him.'[1] He refers each event in Christ's life, His Incarnation, His rejection by the Jews, His betrayal, crucifixion, burial, resurrection, the descent of the Holy Ghost, and the beginning of the Apostolic labours to some corresponding prediction.[2] He sometimes, however, falls into the error, less common in him than in other patristic interpreters, of seeing direct references to the Messiah and the Messianic kingdom, to the almost total exclusion of any other meaning. For instance, such passages as 'Their sound is gone out into all lands,' 'That thou mayest make princes in all lands,' are cited as if exclusively predictive of the propagation of Christianity. In such words as, 'The virgins that be her fellows shall bear her company,' he sees a distinct foreshadowing of the honour to be paid to virginity under Christianity.[3] In other passages, again, he is misled by ignorance of the Hebrew, and a too literal adherence to the Septuagint translation. In the passage, 'I will make thy officers peace,' thine 'exactors' being rendered in the Septuagint bishops or overseers, he extracts from this word a direct reference to the Christian priesthood.[4] 'He shall descend like rain into a fleece of wool' is interpreted as significant of the extreme secrecy of Christ's birth, and the noiseless gentleness with which his kingdom was founded.[5] Whereas the strict translation being 'like rain upon new-mown grass,' it is rather illustrative of the fruitful results of Christ's advent, if indeed, a Messianic reference is to be admitted at all.[6]

Such occasional defects, however, will not prevent us

---

[1] C. 2.	[4] C. 2–5.	[3] C. 6.	[4] C. 7.	[5] C. 3.
[6] See Perowne, vol. i. in loco. Ps. lxxii. 6, and Delitzsch in Isai. lx. 17.

from according the praise due to the great skill with which, on the whole, he has worked out this method of argument, and the noble vindication of Christianity in this treatise has seldom if ever been surpassed by Chrysostom elsewhere. The several parts of his argument are unfolded in orderly procession, and expressed with an eloquence at once luminous and earnest, and which, though at times copious and ornate, does not degenerate into the mere redundancy, still less into the affectations and flowery artifices of rhetoric; he is always real and earnest, he is sometimes sublime.

Closely connected with this treatise in subject, and not far distant in time of composition, are the Homilies directed against Jews and Judaising Christians. The Jews, ever since the time of Antiochus the Great, were a considerable body in Antioch, and over the Christian population exerted a seriously pernicious influence. Their position, indeed, in the Empire at large, had been increasingly favourable from the reign of Hadrian to Constantine. Though they were not permitted to approach Jerusalem, yet the worship in their synagogues was freely tolerated; they were permitted to circumcise their own children though not the children of proselytes; and their religious organisation in the Empire was held together under the sway of the Patriarch of Tiberias.[1] After the recognition of Christianity by the Empire, the Jews, as a natural consequence, were less favourably treated. The statutes of Constantine and Constantius were severe. Those Jews who attempted the life of a Christian were to be burned. No Christians were to become Jews, under pain of punishment. Jews were forbidden to marry Christian women or to possess Christian slaves. The national character of the Jew seems to have deteriorated, as the race became more widely dispersed, and as their

[1] Milman's 'History of the Jews,' vol. ii. book xix.

wealth and importance increased. They were no longer indeed so morosely and sullenly proud as when they gloried in the possession of a holy city and distinct religious ordinances and a geographical position which isolated them from the rest of mankind, but neither were their faith or morals so pure. Self-indulgence, sensualism, and low cunning, corrupted their life, a superstitious and material cast of thought depraved their faith. Their habits harmonised too well with that propensity to luxury and licentiousness which was the besetting vice of the people of Antioch; their materialism worked hand in hand with the prevailing Arianism, if, indeed, Arianism may not be regarded as in some sort its product. Certainly, whenever popular insurrections caused by religious dissensions occurred either in Antioch or in Alexandria, the Jews ranged themselves on the Arian side, as if, though not identical in faith, the spirit and character of the Arian sect, were the most congenial to their own,[1] among the conflicting parties.

Allowing for some exaggerations in the preacher, carried away by the impulse of the moment, the invectives of Chrysostom must be permitted to prove that the Jewish residents in Antioch were of a low and vicious order. They seem to have been regarded by the common people with a mixture of dislike and awe; the age was superstitious, and the Jews availed themselves of superstitious terrors to make a livelihood, especially through a kind of quackery in medicine. Their quarters are denominated by Chrysostom as dens of robbers and habitations of demons.[2] 'A whole day would not suffice to tell the tale of their extortions, their thefts, their deceptions, their base methods of traffic, such as the sale of amulets and

---

[1] Basnage's 'Hist. des Juifs,' vi. 41. Newman's 'Arians,' ch. i. sect. i.

[2] V. in fine; robbers may possibly be used in a figurative sense.

charms.[1] Their priests were no better than counterfeits, because they had not gone through all the elaborate rites of consecration. They had no sacred ephod, no Urim and Thummim, no altar, no sacrifice, no prophecy.'

'The Festival of Trumpets was a scene of great debauchery, more iniquitous than the proceedings in the theatre. Any catechumen who was detected attending that festival was to be excluded from the porch of the church ; any communicant so detected was to be denied access to the Holy Table. The booths erected at the Feast of Tabernacles were like taverns, crowded with flute-players and ill-conditioned women. The synagogues were frequented by the most abandoned characters of both sexes, and dancers, actors, and charioteers were largely drawn from the Jewish population. In spite of this, many Christians were seduced to attend the Jewish festivals and fasts, and even to swear Jewish oaths in the synagogues, under the superstitious impression that such were more solemn and binding than any Christian forms. He had himself, only three days ago, rescued a woman being dragged off, against her will, to take an oath of this kind, by a man who professed himself a Christian.' On stopping to rebuke him in the sternest language, Chrysostom was shocked to learn that the practice was extremely common among Christians. He passionately exhorts the faithful to reclaim their deluded brethren from these pernicious ways : ' If twelve Apostles had converted the larger part of the world, it would be a shame that the Christians, who were the majority in the population of Antioch, should fail to allay the plague of Judaism. What treason ! what inconsistency, that they,

---

[1] I. c. 7. They seem early to have claimed medical skill. When Simon Ben Jochai went to Rome as ambassador, in the reign of Antoninus Pius, to obtain the abrogation of persecuting edicts, he won the favour of the Emperor by curing his sick daughter. — Milman, ii. 443.

who worshipped the Crucified One, should associate with
the race which crucified Him.'[1] The synagogue ought
not to be an object of reverence because it contained the
Books of the Law and the Prophets, but rather of abhorrence, because those who possessed the Prophets refused
to recognise Him of whom their writings spoke. Was the
temple of Serapis holy because it contained the Septuagint, deposited there by Ptolemy Philadelphus?[2]

Christians seem to have attended Jewish services much
in that spirit of curiosity with which Protestants sometimes go to Roman Catholic churches, to be entertained
by music, incense, and a grand ritual. They maintained
that the effect was solemnising; but, observes Chrysostom,
the value of the offering to God depends not on the nature
of the offering, but on the heart of the offerers. The
worshippers sanctify the temple, not the temple the
worshippers. You would not touch or address the murderer
of your own son, and will you court the society of those
who slew the Son of God?[3] Let them consider that
cry uttered by the deacon from time to time in the celebration of the holy mysteries, 'discern one another.'[4] So
let them do. 'If you discern anyone Judaising, hold him
fast and expose him, that you may not yourself participate in the danger.'

'In military camps, if any soldier be detected sympa-
thising with the barbarian or the Persian, not only does
he himself run a risk of his life, but also any of his com-
rades who were conscious of his defection, but did not
represent it to the general. Since, then, you are the
army of Christ, search diligently whether any stranger

---

[1] II. 3; vii. in initio; i. c. 3, 4.

[2] I. c. 6.

[3] I. c. 7. So the idle youth of
Rome turned for amusement into the
Synagogue. Horace, Sat. ix. l. 69.

[4] ἐπιγινώσκετε ἀλλήλους. I. 4. This
admonition 'discern one another' was
uttered just at the close of the Missa
Catechumenorum, when all but the
baptized had to depart.

has intruded into your camp, and expose him, not that
we may put him to death, but that we may punish him,
deliver him from his error and impiety, and render him
wholly our own; but if you willingly conceal him, be well
assured that you will sustain the same punishment with
him.' This homily is concluded by a solemn adjura-
tion: 'In the words of Moses, I call Heaven and earth
to record against you this day, that if any of you now
present or absent, attend the Feast of Trumpets, or enter
a synagogue, or observe a fast, or a sabbath, or any
Jewish rite whatever, I am guiltless of your blood. These
discourses will rise up for both of us in the great day of
our Lord: if you shall have obeyed them, they will give
you confidence; but if otherwise, they will stand as severe
accusers against you.' Therefore he implored them to
institute the most rigorous search after the Judaising
brethren. 'When their mother the Church had lost a child,
it was criminal to conceal either the captor or the captured; let the men seek out the men, the women the
women, the slave his fellow-servant, and present the
culprit to him before the next assembly.'

Another Judaising practice, which he condemns in the
severest language, was the custom of keeping Easter on
the 14th day of the month, according to Jewish calculation,
irrespective of the week day on which it might fall; thus
sometimes feasting when the rest of the Church was fasting, or fasting when the rest was feasting. The existence
of such a practice at this time was a remarkable instance
of the increasing influence of the Jews in Antioch and the
neighbouring regions. For up to the year A.D. 276, the
Antiochene patriarchate had observed Easter in conformity with the Catholic usage; the adoption of the
Jewish calculation was made after that date, when most
of the rest of Christendom had dropped it, and was
therefore the subject of special condemnation at the

Council of Nice.[1] Such a discrepancy in practice was
regarded as a most serious rent in the unity of the Church.
Chrysostom denounces it especially as a contumacious
disregard of the Council of Nice, which had distinctly
ordained by the mouths of 300 bishops, that Easter should
be kept at one and the same time throughout Christendom. He implores the Judaisers to desist from the idle
enquiry into the exact dates of seasons; to follow the
Church, and to place harmony and charitable peace before
all things. It was impossible, in fact, to hit the actual
day on which Christ rose; therefore let them observe that
day which the Church through her bishops had prescribed.
It was a less offence to fast on the wrong day than to rend
the unity of the Church. 'How long halt ye between two
opinions;' if Judaism be true, embrace it altogether, and
'cease to annoy the Church; if Christianity be true, abide
in it, and follow it.'[2]

The Jews themselves could not, in Chrysostom's opinion, legally perform sacrifices, or observe festivals of any
kind. Jerusalem was the only place in which such observances were commanded; and Jerusalem being destroyed, they became void.[3] They had been suspended
during the Captivity, to be resumed when the people
returned to the holy soil. If the Jews of the present day
also expected restoration, let them likewise suspend their
rites; but, in fact, this never would occur. The Temple
never would be rebuilt, and restoration was a vain hope.
Jerusalem was to be trodden down of Gentiles till the
times of the Gentiles were fulfilled; and by the fulfilment
of those times Chrysostom understood the end of the

[1] Newman's 'Arians,' ch. i. p. 16.
Hefele, pp. 305, 306.

[2] In Jud. iii. 6, iv. 4.

[3] According to Theod. iii. 20. The
Jews had ceased to offer sacrifices by
the reign of Julian, and when he enquired the reason, said, because it was
unlawful except on the site of the
Temple; and this was one chief reason
why Julian commanded the Temple to
be restored.

world.[1] All four Captivities of the Jews—their subjection
to the Egyptians, Babylonians, Antiochus, and Romans—
had been distinctly foretold. To each of the *first three*
prophecy had assigned a *limit*; but to the last *none*—it
reached into all time ; there was no sign or intimation of
any probable cessation.[2] The revolt of the Jews under
Hadrian, and under Constantine,[3] had ignominiously
failed; the attempt of Julian to rebuild the Temple had
been frustrated by portents : fire issuing from the founda-
tions had consumed some of the workmen, and scared the
spectators ; the naked substructions left just as they were
when the work was abandoned, presented a visible monument of the divinely arrested work.[4]

The eager exhortation reiterated in his last homily, that
the faithful would seek out their brethren who had been
caught in the Jewish snare, is a powerful rush of indignant eloquence, and a wholesome admonition on the responsibility of all for the spiritual welfare of their fellow
men. ' Say not within thyself, I am a man of the world ;
I have a wife and children ; these matters belong to the
priests and the monks. The Samaritan in the parable did
not say, Where are the priests ? where are the Pharisees ?
where are the Jewish authorities ? but seized the opportunity of doing a good deed, as if it was a great advantage.
In like manner, when you see anyone requiring bodily
or spiritual care, say not within thyself, Why did not this
or that man attend to him ?—but deliver him from his infirmity. If you find a piece of gold in your path, you do
not say, Why did not some other person pick it up ? but
you eagerly anticipate others by seizing it yourself. Even
so, in the case of your fallen brethren, consider that you
have found a treasure in the attention necessary for their

[1] V. 1.

[2] V. c. 4–7.

[3] Who punished the captives by
cutting off their ears. It is singular
that there is no record of this rebellion in history.

[4] For a full relation of this singular
event, see Milman's 'Jews,' book xx.

wants.' He besought them not to proclaim the calamity
of the Church by idly gossiping about the numbers of
those who had observed some Jewish custom, but to
search them out; and, if necessary, to enter their houses,
tax them with their guilt, and solemnly warn them
against the iniquity of consorting with the enemies of
Jesus Christ. ' Listen not to any excuses which they may
plead on the ground of cures effected by the Jews; expose
their impostures, their incantations, their amulets, their
charms, their drugs.' ' Even if they really effected cures,
it would be better to die and save the soul, than resort to
the enemies of Christ to heal the body. Let them rather
appeal to the assistance of the martyrs and saints who
were His friends, and had great confidence in addressing
Him.' ' Why did the Son of Man Himself enter the
world? Was it not to seek and to save wandering sheep?
This do thou, according to thy ability. I will not cease to
speak, whether you hear or whether you forbear. If you
heed not, I shall do it, but with grief; if you listen and
obey, I shall do it, but with joy.' [1]

It is difficult for us, in our altered position towards Jews
and heretics of all kinds to sympathise with the vehemence of Chrysostom's feelings and language. Yet there
can be no doubt that such dabbling, if the word may be
used, in the customs, the observances, the ritual of an
obsolete dispensation, and a debased people, did seriously
imperil purity of faith and morals, and unity of discipline,
in the Christian Church. It was beheld by the staunch
Catholic with somewhat of the same dismay and horror
with which the moderate Anglican witnesses any recurrence to mediæval and pre-reformation ceremonial and
dogma.

Towards dissentient Christians, not infected by Judaism,
Chrysostom adopts a milder tone, and indeed restrains

[1] Hom. viii. 4, and in fine.

the immoderation of party feeling in others with wholesome censure. He laments[1] the distracted state of the
Church in Antioch, which was now divided into the three
sections of Meletians, Eustathians, and Arians; but he
denounces the practice of anathematising. It was uncharitable and presumptuous. St. Paul anathematised
once only; the casting off of a heretic ought to be as
painful as plucking out an eye or cutting off a limb. A
holy man before their times, one of the successors of the
Apostles, and judged worthy of the honour of martyrdom,
used to say, that to assume the right to anathematise was
as great a usurpation of Christ's authority as for a subject
to put on the Imperial purple. In dealing with erring
brethren, the Christian should 'in meekness instruct those
that oppose themselves, if God, peradventure, will give
them repentance to the acknowledging of the truth.' 'If
a man accepts your counsel and confesses his error, you
have saved him, and delivered your own soul also; but if
he will not, do you nevertheless continue to testify with
longsuffering and kindness, that the Judge may not require his soul at thy hand. Hate him not; turn not from
him; persecute him not, but catch him in the net of sincere and genuine charity. The person whom you anathematise is either living or dead; if living, you do wrong to
cut off one who may still be converted; if dead, much
more you do wrong; " to his own Master he standeth or
falleth;" and "who hath known the mind of the Lord,
or who hath been his counsellor?" You may anathematise heretical dogmas, but towards the persons who hold
them show the greatest possible forbearance, and pray for
their salvation.'

In the winter of 386, Chrysostom preached a sermon
on Christmas Day, which, though not distinguished by

[1] Hom. de Anathemate, delivered soon after the discourses against the
Anomæans. See Monitum. vol. i. 914.

any unusual merit, possesses an interest of its own. We
learn from it, that this festival was not originally celebrated in the Eastern Church ; it had been adopted from
the West, and, in Antioch at least, less than ten years
before the year of Chrysostom's discourse. It had gradually increased in popularity, and this year Chrysostom
rejoiced to observe that the church was crowded to overflowing. Rome had fixed the observance of the 25th of
December, and this was the day kept throughout Christendom from Thrace to Gades ; but the propriety of the
date was much debated in the Eastern Churches, and the
observance of the festival at all was considered by some
as a questionable innovation. Chrysostom energetically
vindicates the dignity of the festival and the correctness
of the date.[1] It was the metropolis, so to say, of all other
festivals, and as such it was the most solemn and awful.
For the incarnation of Christ was the necessary condition
of all the succeeding events of his career on earth, and in
the profundity of its mystery it exceeded them all. That
Christ should die was a natural consequence of human
nature once assumed ; but that He, being God, should
have stooped so low as to assume that nature, was a
mystery unfathomable to the mind of man! 'Wherefore
I specially welcome and belove this day, and desire to
make you partakers in my affection. I pray and implore
you all to come with zeal and alacrity, every man first
purging his own house, to behold our Lord wrapped in
swaddling clothes and lying in a manger ; for if we come
with faith we shall, indeed, behold Him lying in the
manger ; for this Table supplies the place of the manger,
and here also the body of the Lord will lie, not wrapped
in swaddling clothes, but invested on all sides by the
Holy Spirit. The initiated (or the baptized) understand

---

[1] The former chiefly in the Hom.
de Philog. vol. i. 752; the latter in
the Hom. in Nat. Diem Christi, vol. ii.
p. 552.

what I mean.'[1]   But he warns his hearers against crowd-
ing in a tumultuous and disorderly manner to partake of
the holy feast. 'Approach with fear and trembling, with
fasting and prayer, not making an uproar, hustling and
jostling one another: consider, O man, what kind of
sacrifice thou art about to handle; consider that thou,
who art dust and ashes, dost receive the body and blood
of Christ.'[2] This irreverent conduct at the reception of
the Eucharist frequently provoked the indignation and
censure of Chrysostom. It occurred especially at the
greater festivals, because on those days multitudes received the Eucharist who did not enter the church at
other times. 'How,' he cries in the homily on the Epiphany, 'shall we teach you what is necessary concerning
your soul, immortality, the kingdom of heaven, the longsuffering and mercy of God, and a future judgment,
when you come to us only once or twice in the year?'
Many of those who pushed and kicked one another in
the eagerness of each to get foremost to the holy Table,
withdrew from the church before the final thanksgiving.
'What,' Chrysostom cries, 'when Christ is present, and
the angels are standing by, and this awe-inspiring Table
is spread before you, and your brethren are still partaking
of the mysteries, will you hurry away?' Too often they
who thronged the church on these great occasions led
worldly and even vicious lives; they hurried away before the
sacred feast was ended, like Judas to do the devil's work.[3]
Such is one among many examples which may be elicited
from Chrysostom's works of that pagan grossness and
superstition which was mingled with the faith and the
most solemn observances of Christianity. The vitality of
superstitious customs, the subtlety with which they have
grafted themselves upon and become mixed up with Chris-

[1] De Beato Philog. vol. i. p. 753.   [2] In Nat. Christi, vol. ii. p. 360.
[3] De Bapt. Christi, c. 4.

tianity, or the tenacity with which they have clung to
men in spite of it late into modern times, is indeed extraordinary; but for centuries their existence and influence were not appreciably if at all affected by Christianity. A half Oriental, half Greek, partly Jewish
population, like that of Antioch, whose purer feelings and
nobler reason were seriously impaired by habits of licentiousness and luxury, was naturally liable to superstitious
terrors, and addicted to superstitious practices of all
kinds. Chrysostom is frequently reproving his people for
being anxious and afraid where there was no cause, while
they abandoned themselves to vice, the only worthy cause
for fear, without scruple or alarm. If Christmas Day was
observed as a Christian festival, though without becoming
reverence, New Year's day was given up to riotous festivity, thoroughly Pagan in character. The houses were
festooned with flowers, the inns were scenes of the most
disgraceful intemperance; men and women drinking un-
diluted wine there from an early hour in the morning;
auguries and omens were consulted by which the horo-
scope of the year was cast. Good luck in the coming
year was supposed to depend (how is not clearly stated)
on the manner in which the first day was spent. This is
the theme of the preacher's righteous indignation : 'The
real happiness of the year was determined not by the
observation of particular feasts, but by the amount of
goodness which we put into it. Sin was the only real evil,
virtue the only real good; therefore, if a man practised
justice, almsgiving, and prayer, his year could not fail to
be propitious; for he who had a clean conscience, carried
about with him a perpetual holy day, and without this,
the most brilliant and joyous festival was obscured by
darkness.' 'When thou seest the year completed, thank
God that He has brought thee safely to the conclusion of
the cycle: prick thine heart, reckon up the time of thy

life, and say to thyself, The days are hurrying along, the years are being fulfilled, I have advanced far on the road, the judgment is at the doors, my life is pressing on towards old age: well! what good have I done? shall I depart hence destitute and empty of all righteousness?'[1]

There is a fuller notice in some of his homilies on the Epistle to the Ephesians of the many gross and senseless forms of superstition which prevailed even among the communicants in the Christian Church. He laments the decay of discipline by which a more rigorous scrutiny was once instituted into the characters of those who came to the holy feast. 'If you were to examine the lives of all those who partake of the mysteries on Easter Day, you would find amongst them persons who consulted auguries, who used drugs, and omens, and incantations; even the adulterer, curser, and drunkard, dared to partake. Iniquitous men had crept into the Church, the highest places of command were bought and sold, till the pure livers had betaken themselves to the mountain tops to escape from the contamination.'[2] Some of the vulgar superstitions of the day were ludicrously puerile. 'This or that man was the first to meet me as I walked out; consequently innumerable ills will certainly befall me: that confounded servant of mine, in giving me my shoes, handed me the left shoe first; this indicates dire calamities and insults: as I stepped out, I started with the left foot foremost; this too is a sign of misfortune: my right eye twitched upwards as I went out; this portends tears.'[3] To strike the woof with the comb in a particular way, the braying of a donkey, the crowing of a cock, a sudden sneeze,—all these were indications of something or other. 'They suspect everything, and are more in bondage than if they were slaves many times over. But

---

[1] In Kalend. c. 2.
[2] In Ephes. hom. vi. c. 4.
[3] Perhaps that convulsive twitching which we call 'quick-blood.'

let not us, brethren, fear such things, but laughing them
to scorn as men who live in the light, and whose citizenship is in Heaven, and who have nothing in common with
this earth, let us regard one thing only as terrible,
namely, to sin and offend God.' [1]

[1] In Ephes. hom. xii. c. 3. In hom.
viii. and xii. on 1 Cor. he rebukes the
heathenish ceremonies performed at
the birth of a child. One was, to give
it that name which was attached to
the candle that burned longest out of
a row of candles.

CHAPTER X.

SURVEY OF THE FIRST DECADE OF THE REIGN OF THEODOSIUS — HIS
CHARACTER—HIS EFFORTS FOR THE EXTIRPATION OF PAGANISM AND
HERESY — THE APOLOGIES OF SYMMACHUS AND LIBANIUS. A.D.
379–389.

BEFORE Chrysostom had laboured two full years in 'confirming the souls of the disciples' at Antioch, that city
became the scene of events memorable in history; and
events in which the great preacher played an honourable
and distinguished part.

The foremost man of the age, not only by position but
also to a great extent in character, was Theodosius the
Emperor; Theodosius the Great, deservedly so called in
spite of one prevailing defect in character, and a few glaring misdeeds which tarnish his reputation. The military
exploits of his father, Theodosius the elder, had provoked
the jealousy of the court [1] and cost him his life, and the son,
who had manifested ability almost equal, in serving under
him both by land and sea against Scots and Saxons,
Moors and Goths, was glad to escape a similar ungrateful
return for his services, by retiring to the obscurity of
his native village in Spain. He was disgraced when the
Empire had been liberated from danger by the exertions
of his father and himself; but in the hour of its utmost
jeopardy, and direst distress, he was recalled to more
than his former position. The total defeat and death of
Valens, and the almost extermination of his army before
Hadrianople in A.D. 378, placed the Empire at the mercy
of victorious barbarians within, and on the edge of the

---

[1] He was executed at Carthage in A.D. 376.

horizon more storm clouds of Gothic or Hunnish invasion were lowering.   There was but one person to whom
the mind of Gratian, the young Emperor of the West,
and his advisers, overwhelmed by the prospect of impending calamity, instinctively turned as capable of saving the
state in this crisis.   For three years, Theodosius had
been occupied with the cultivation of his farm between
Valladolid and Segovia, when he was summoned to accept
the title of Augustus, together with all the responsibilities
and perils which attended the possessor, at such a time,
of that venerable name.   He was equal to the situation;
handsome with a manly beauty, courageous and determined of purpose, just and politic in intention if not
always in act, he was endowed with some of the noblest
qualities of a soldier and a statesman, by which to rescue
and reorganise a panic-stricken and crumbling state.
This is not the place to narrate the military achievements
of Theodosius.   The original materials for information
respecting them are scanty; but they have been collected
and arranged by that historian whose indefatigable industry brings order out of confusion, and whose luminous
style lights up with interest even the darkest and most
meagre annals.[1]   It is sufficient to remind the reader of
Gibbon, that Theodosius subdued the Goths, not in any
one or two great battles, but by frequent and skilfully
contrived engagements on a smaller scale.   He thus
gradually revived the drooping courage and discipline of
the imperial troops, and wore out the enemy.   The several
tribes, on their submission, were settled in the waste tracts
of country, which they were to occupy free of taxation, on
the wise condition that they kept the land in a state of
cultivation.   So a numerous colony of Visigoths was
established in Thrace, of Ostrogoths in Phrygia and Lydia.
The ability of Theodosius is demonstrated more by the

[1] See Gibbon, ch. xxvi. xxvii.

results of his energy than by anything that we know of
the manner in which he accomplished them. He not only
vanquished the Goths, but arrested the progress of the
usurper Maximus in the West, who was leading his victorious legions to Italy, flushed with success after the ignominious flight and assassination of Gratian. Theodosius
was not in a position, surrounded as he was by half-
vanquished barbarians, to dispute the passage of the conqueror; but by assuming a firm tone in negotiations,
he secured for Valentinian, Gratian's brother and successor, the sovereignty of Italy, Africa, and Western
Illyricum, surrendering for the present to the usurper the
regions north of the Alps.

Theodosius was a Christian; as a Spaniard he was a
Trinitarian, and as a soldier he was anxious to establish
one uniform type of religious faith and ecclesiastical discipline throughout the Empire. But such a task proved
more impracticable than the reduction of military foes.
Neither Paganism nor Arianism could be extinguished in a
few years by suppressive edicts. Theodosius himself had
been baptized in the first year of his reign, A.D. 380, when
his life was threatened by a severe illness, and he had
then announced his will and pleasure that his own
solemn declaration of faith should be accepted as that of
his subjects also. That faith which was 'professed by the
Pontiff Damasus and Peter, Bishop of Alexandria,' was to
be the faith of the Empire. 'Let us believe the sole deity
of the Father, the Son, and the Holy Ghost, under an equal
majesty and a pious Trinity. We authorise the followers
of this doctrine to assume the title of Catholic Christians,
and as we judge that all others are extravagant madmen,
we brand them with the infamous name of heretics.'[1]
Their places of assembly were not to enjoy the title of
churches, and they themselves were to expect severe civil

---

[1] Cod. Theod. xvi. 1, 2.

penalties as well as the Divine condemnation. Damophilus, the Arian Bishop of Constantinople, preferred exile to signing the creed of Nice; and Gregory of Nazianzum was conducted by the Emperor in person through the streets of Constantinople (though not without a strong guard) to occupy the episcopal throne. A project for another general council (after the Council of Constantinople, A.D. 381,) was entertained but abandoned, for the factious demeanour of the several prelates and their partisans on their arrival did not augur a very successful settlement of differences by that method. The Emperor fell back, for the accomplishment of his object, on his own authority. On July 25, A.D. 383, an edict was posted in Constantinople, prohibiting all the heretics therein named, Arians, Eunomians, Macedonians, and Manichæans, from holding any kind of assembly, public or private, either in the cities or in the country. Any ground or building used for such illegal purpose was to be confiscated to the state; and the penalty of banishment was pronounced against those who allowed themselves to be ordained priests or bishops of the heretical sects. Historians concur in the opinion that few of these penalties were actually enforced. The heretical sects were not animated by a spirit of martyrdom; the intimidation was generally sufficient.[1] The hypocrite or the indifferent conformed, the more conscientious retired into obscurity. There seem to have been few if any Arian prelates of great and commanding ability. All the leading ecclesiastics of the day—Chrysostom, Jerome, Basil, the two Gregories, and Ambrose—were by conviction on the side of the Emperor, and added all the weight of their influence to his decrees.

When measures had been taken for the suppression of

[1] Sozom. vii. c. 12 ; Gibbon, ch. xxvii.; De Broglie, 'L'Église et L'Empire,' vi. p. 93.

heresy, it was the Pagan's turn to suffer. The spectacle of temples standing open for worship side by side with Christian churches, was a painful incongruity in the eyes of Theodosius, with his soldier-like ideas of uniformity and discipline. The first blow was directed against those disloyal sons of the Church who had seceded to Paganism. They were deprived of the power to make wills or to receive bequests.[1] The second step was absolutely to prohibit all sacrifices in those temples which were still open. Nearly twenty years before, the sacrifice of animals had been forbidden by Valentinian and Valens, owing to their connection with arts of divination, which were used for political purposes. As long as such sacrifices were permitted, the priests could not refrain from consulting the entrails of the victims, and pretending to read therein future events : the death of this Emperor, the elevation of that, the success or failure of expeditions, and the like, were intimated to the people, always eager to know what is beyond the limits of human knowledge. Such divinations encouraged a restless spirit in the subjects, and often disaffected them towards the ruling power. That these laws of Valentinian were renewed by Theodosius in 381, and again in A.D. 385, proves that they had been imperfectly obeyed.[2]

They were followed up by a yet more decisive step in A.D. 392. Cynegius, the Prætorian Prefect of the East, the Counts Jovinus and Gaudentius in the West, were commissioned to shut up the temples, to destroy their contents, images, and vessels, and to confiscate their property. In many instances the executors of the edict, aided by the fanatical fury of monks, seem to have exceeded their instructions. The great temple of Jupiter, at Apamea, in

---

[1] Cod. Theod. xvi. v. 7, l. 1, 2.
[2] Cod. Theod. xvi. v. 10, l. 7, 9. Sozomen informs us (vii. 22) that

Eugenius, the usurper, after the death of Valentinian II., was persuaded by divinations to take up arms.

Syria, of which the roof was supported on sixty massive columns, fell, but not unavenged; for the Bishop Marcellus, who headed the assailants, fell a victim to the rage of the exasperated rustics who defended it.[1] The safety of the universe was represented by Pagans to depend on the preservation of the colossal gold and silver image of Serapis, at Alexandria.   Even Christians beheld with some trepidation an audacious soldier deal a blow with a battle-axe on the cheek of this awful deity; but as the only result of the gash was the issue of a swarm of rats who had harboured in the sacred head, instead of the avenging thunders which had been expected, a revulsion of feeling was experienced.   The huge idol was hewn to pieces, the limbs were dragged through the streets, and the remains of the carcase burned in the amphitheatre, amidst the derision of the populace.

These were shattering blows to Paganism. But the religion of sentiment and custom long survives the extinction of more solid if not reasonable convictions. Chrysostom's homily on New Year's day is only one among many illustrations of the way in which Pagan rites and superstitions lingered, especially in connection with public festivals.   All the Pagan concomitants of these festivals in the country districts—hymns, libations, garlands, incense, lights—were strictly prohibited, under heavy penalties, by Theodosius in A.D. 392, but, in the West especially, the extirpation was very incomplete. The Bishops of Verona and of Brescia protested, but in vain, against the proprietors of land indulging their tenantry in these practices. Sicily, Corsica, and Sardinia, were strongholds of Paganism as late as A.D. 600. Sacrifices were offered to Apollo on Monte Casino till the establishment of St. Benedict's monastery in A.D. 529.

The riotous populace of towns, and the simple country

---

[1] Sozomen vii. 15. Theod. v. 21.

folk attached to old customs, thus evinced some spirit in
their resistance to repressive enactments. But the hold
which Paganism retained upon intellectual people was
feeble indeed. Two apologists only, with any pretensions
to ability, stepped forward to plead for the sinking cause :
Symmachus [1] in the West, and Libanius in the East ; and
their intercessions are addressed to sentiments of affection
for antiquity, and compassion for oppressed weakness,
rather than to the reason. Symmachus, as is well known,
pleaded twice for the retention of the altar and statue of
Victory in the senate house at Rome. Eloquent and
touching, his appeal is directed to patriotic feeling and a
sense of political expediency, not to religious conviction.
He does not profess to *believe* in the Pagan deities, but
regards with a philosophic eye the various kinds of faith
in the world as so many forms of homage to the great
unknown Being who presides over the universe. ' It is
right to recognise that what all adore can be at bottom
but one Being only. We contemplate the same stars ;
the same sky covers us ; the same universe incloses us.
What matters it by what reasonings each seeks the truth ?
a single path cannot conduct us to the grand secret of
nature. As an individual, a man may be a worshipper of
Mithras, or of Christ, but as a citizen it is his duty to
conform to that worship which is bound up with the history and glory of his country ; to part from it is heartless
and disloyal.' [2]

The memorial of Symmachus got into the hands of
Ambrose, and was rather rudely treated by him. He
subjects it to a stern test of facts. ' Had the national
gods indeed protected the Romans from disaster ? It was
maintained that by their aid the conquest of Italy by

---

[1] The most distinguished scholar
and orator, and one of the most upright statesmen of his time—quæs-
tor, prætor, and proconsul of Africa.

[2] Fragments of his speeches preserved in Mai's collection, vol. i.

Hannibal had been averted. Why then did they permit
the invader to inflict such ravages as he had done?
Would not the Gauls also have captured the Capitol, but
for the timely cry of the goose? Where was Jupiter
then? but perhaps he was speaking through the goose.
The Carthaginians worshipped some of the same deities
as the Romans. If then the gods conquered with the
Romans they yielded with the Carthaginians. Paganism
declined, notwithstanding support; the Church flourished,
in spite of opposition. As to the abandonment of ancient
customs, was not progress the law of improvement? The
glimmering dawn gradually brightened into the full and
perfect day; the riches of harvest and vintage came in
the maturity of the year; even so the faith of Christ had
gradually planted itself on the ruins of a worn-out creed,
and was now reaping an abundant harvest among all
nations of the earth.'[1] The whole reply of Ambrose is
pitched in the positive, confident, authoritative tone of
one who speaks from a conviction that he stands on the
platform of absolute truth, and that his cause is therefore
inevitably destined to win.

If the appeal of Symmachus was addressed to the sentiment of reverence for *national* antiquity, that of Libanius
was directed to a sentiment of attachment to *classical* antiquity. The citizen mourns over the suppression of a
worship which was bound up with the history and the
glory of his country; the scholar sighs over the degradation of that which was connected with what was most
beautiful in the literature and life of the olden time—with
the poetry of Homer and the tragedians—with the festive
song and dance—with the hills, and fountains, and groves
of Greece. He clings to the past with the love of the
antiquarian. Though his actual belief in the myths of the
classical era may not have been very deep or earnest,

[1] Ambrose Op. vol. ii. Ep. 18.

there is no doubt that he entertained a genuine animosity towards the new faith which was usurping their place. A flowery description of the origin and antiquity of the honour paid to the gods, is followed by a vehement invective against the monks, ' those black-robed creatures, more voracious than elephants, who rush upon the temples, armed with stones, wood, and fire ; who break up the roofs, destroy the walls, throw down the statues, raze the altars.' ' They glaringly exceeded the edicts of the Emperor, which had forbidden the offering of sacrifice in the temples, not the actual destruction of the buildings.' [1] There is real feeling also in his description of the distress caused in country districts by the demolition of the temples. ' They were the centres round which human habitations and civilisation grew; in them the labourer placed all his hopes; to them he commended his wife, his children, his plantation, his crops. Deprived of the gods, from whom he expected the rewards of toil, he felt as if henceforth his labours would be vain. Sometimes the very land was wrested from them on the pretext that it had been consecrated to gods ; if the poor despoiled owners sought redress from the pastor (i.e. the bishop) of the neighbouring town (falsely called pastor, since there was no gentleness in his nature), he praised the robber and dismissed the complainers.' No doubt to a great extent this was a true picture, and such harshness and injustice must have retarded (as is ever the case when the attempt is made to coerce opinion) the cause of Christianity, which the law was intended to promote.

Theodosius, however, was in principle far too upright to treat the Church with a blind partiality. Cynegius, the Prefect, was ordered to enforce the law at Alexandria with full rigour against those despicable beings who sought to

---

[1] Liban. pro templis non exscind. The oration was certainly not spoken before the Emperor, and probably not even sent to him.

make traffic by informing against Pagans. Constantine
had exempted the clergy from serving in curial offices;
Theodosius compelled them to pay for substitutes, and
renounce their claims to patrimony. They were to enjoy
immunity from torture when brought to trial, but if detected in falsehood were to be visited with penalties of
peculiar severity, because they had abused the shelter of
the law which favoured them.[1]

Such was Theodosius—a prudent and skilful general,
a firm and upright ruler; a sincere and simple-minded
believer in Christianity, who did his best, as head at once
of the army, the civil government, and the Church, to
consolidate the fabric of the Empire. The barbarians
were repelled, or held down, taxes were collected with
honest exactitude; some of the most burdensome were
taken off; Paganism and heresy languished, however far
from being extinguished, and the Emperor fondly hoped
that uniformity in faith and discipline would soon be
established throughout Christendom.

The good genius of his life was the Empress Flacilla;
she was a Christian of a pure and noble type; imperial
state had not corrupted the simplicity or hardened the
kindliness of her disposition. She was accustomed to
visit the hospitals in Constantinople not attended by a
single slave or waiting-woman; administered food and
medicine to the patients, and dressed their wounds with
her own hands. She was wont to remind her husband of
the great change in their worldly position, as a motive to
humility and gratitude to God. ' It behoves thee to consider what thou wert and what thou hast become; by
constantly reflecting on this thou wilt not be ungrateful
to thy benefactor, but wilt guide the kingdom which thou
hast received with a due regard to law, and by so doing
wilt pay homage to Him who gave it thee.'

[1] Cod. Theod. xii. 104-115.

She, we may well believe, restrained the impulses of that choleric temper which was the principal defect in the Emperor's character, and which occasionally after her death burst forth into acts of deplorable violence. This wise and pious monitress was taken from him in A.D. 385. She died at a watering-place in Thrace, whither she had gone to recover her health after the shock caused by the death of the infant Princess Pulcheria. Her body was brought back to Constantinople on a melancholy day in autumn, when the skies poured down a gentle rain, as if mingling their tears with those of the disconsolate people.[1]

This condensed survey of the character and work of Theodosius, during the first ten years of his reign, will assist us in forming a proper estimate of his conduct in that memorable occurrence which brings his life into connection with the life of Chrysostom.

[1] Theodor. v. 19. A funeral oration on her and the infant was pronounced by Gregory Nyssen. Greg. Nyss. Op. vol. iii. pp. 513, 527, 533.

CHAPTER XI.

THE wise counsel and softening influence of the Empress
were removed from her husband at an inopportune season.
Political storms were approaching, and the passionate
temper of Theodosius was soon to be subjected to a most
severe trial.

The year 388 would have completed the first decade
of his reign. The year 387 was the fifth of the reign of
his son Arcadius, whom he had nominally associated with
himself in the government. The celebration of these two
events Theodosius, from motives of prudent economy and
convenience, resolved to combine. The army on such occasions claimed a liberal donative, five gold pieces to each
man. It was obviously desirable, therefore, to avoid, if
possible, the repetition of such a donative within a
short space of time. It was always a strain on the royal
treasury, and at the present juncture, the strain was
increased, for the Goths were assuming a menacing attitude on the Danubian frontier. It was necessary to mass
troops in that direction, and with a view to provide for
these expenses, it was proposed to raise a special subsidy
from the opulent cities of the Eastern empire. But the
inhabitants of Alexandria and Antioch were loth to part
with any of the wealth which they had accumulated during
nearly ten years of peace, and exemption from onerous
taxation. Large meetings were held by the citizens of
Alexandria in the theatres and other public places; inflam-

matory and seditious speeches were made. ' If we are to
be treated thus,' they cried, ' a simple remedy is open, we
will appeal to Maximus in the West; he knows how to
shake off a troublesome tyrant.' Fortunately the Prefect
Cynegius was a man of firmness and promptitude ; he
made some arrests of the most conspicuous leaders of the
mutinous faction, and enforced an immediate payment of
the tribute, and by these decisive measures public order
was restored. Either the people of Antioch were more
deeply disaffected, or no such energetic officer was in that
city to suppress the spirit of rebellion in the bud. It is
said that the inhabitants entertained a grudge against
the Emperor, because he had never visited their city,
which had been frequently graced by the royal presence in
previous reigns.[1]

The edict which enjoined the levying of the tribute was
proclaimed by a herald on February 26. Large numbers
of the people assembled on the spot, collected chiefly into
groups, amongst which were some persons of distinction,
senators and other civic functionaries, noble ladies, and
retired soldiers. An ominous silence succeeded the announcement of the edict. The crowd then dispersed, but
reassembled about the prætorium, where the governor
resided.[2] There they stood in gloomy silence, save that
the women, from time to time, raised a wailing lamentation, crying that the ruin of the city was determined, and
that since the Emperor had abandoned them, God alone
from henceforth could come to their succour. At last a
little band detached itself from the mass, shouting that
they must go and seek the Bishop Flavian, and constrain
him to intercede with the Emperor on their behalf.
Flavian, by accident or design, was absent from the epis-

---

[1] Libanius Or. 12. pp. 391–395.
[2] Probably the prætorium built in
the reign of Constantine for the Count
of the East, who from that time resided in Antioch. V. Müller 'Antiq.
Antioch,' ii. 16.

copal residence, and the mob returned to the prætorium,
crying that the governor must do them justice. The
people appear to have been excited to violence chiefly by
those turbulent foreign adventurers who abounded in
Antioch, sordid venal creatures, often hired by actors to
get up applause in the theatres, or by great men not over
popular to raise cheers when they appeared in public
places. But however stimulated, the passions of the mob
were thoroughly roused, and their fury vented itself in a
tumultuous rush into one of the great public baths, where
they soon tore everything to pieces. Having completed
this work of destruction, they hurried back once more to
the hall of the unfortunate governor. Here they were
kept at bay by a guard for a sufficient time to enable the
governor to escape by a back door, and when they at last
succeeded in bursting in, the vacancy of the place aggravated their rage. The governor was not seated in the
judicial chair, but they found themselves face to face with
the statues of the imperial family, which as emblems of
authority were ranged above it. They paused for a few
moments; highly excited as they were, imperial majesty,
even so represented, had some deterrent influence over
their passions.

But, unfortunately, there were boys in the crowd; the
love of stone-throwing without respect of persons was as
ardent in boy nature fifteen hundred years ago as it is
now. A stone was cast by one of these juvenile hands,
which hit one of the sacred statues. The momentary
feelings of reverence which had arrested the people were
dissipated. The images were mutilated, almost battered
to pieces, and the fragments dragged through the streets.
Other images of the imperial family with which the city
was adorned were treated in the same manner; the
equestrian statue of Count Theodosius, father of the
Emperor, was dislodged from its pedestal and hacked

about, amidst derisive shouts of 'Defend thyself, grand cavalier !'[1]

The unrestrained fury of the people was inflamed by success; they began to bring up torches and actually set fire to one of the principal buildings of the city, when the governor, who had escaped their hands, returned at the head of a company of archers. As usual with disorderly mobs, however furious, they were unable to face the discipline of military force; the soldiers were no sooner drawn up and preparing to fix their weapons than rage turned to panic, and the mob, lately so formidable, melted away.

The whole tumult had not lasted more than three hours; before noon, every one had returned to his home, the streets and squares were empty, and a death-like stillness pervaded the city. Remorse was mingled with great terror respecting the consequences of the outrage which had been perpetrated. The Emperor, indeed, was humane and forgiving of wrongs which concerned himself alone, but how would he brook the insults done to the memory of his father and his tenderly beloved Empress? One hope remained : Flavian, the bishop, was a favourite at court, his intercessions might avail; the people besought him with tears to stand their friend in this distress. From Antioch to Constantinople was a long and perilous journey of 800 miles, and the winter was not yet ended. Flavian was old, his only sister was seriously ill, and the approaching season of Lent required his presence at Antioch, but a sense of the emergency prevailed over all these obstacles. Animated by the spirit of the Good Shepherd who was ready to lay down his life for his flock, the intrepid old man set out upon his errand of mercy, with all possible speed, in the hope of overtaking the messengers who had started before him, but had

[1] Liban. Or. 12, p. 395 and 21, p. 527. Theod. vii. 20. Sozom. vii. 23. Zos. iv. 41.

been detained at the foot of Mount Taurus by a fall of snow.[1]

During the absence of Flavian all the powers of Chrysostom as an orator, pastor, and a citizen, were called forth in attempting to calm the fears and revive the deeply-dejected spirits of the people. Perseveringly did he discharge this anxious and laborious task; almost every day for twenty-two days, that small figure was to be seen either sitting in the Ambo, from which he sometimes preached, on account of his diminutive stature, or standing on the steps of the altar, the preacher's usual place;[2] and day after day, the crowds increased which came to listen to the stream of golden eloquence which he poured forth. With all the versatility of a consummate artist, he moves from point to point. Sometimes a picture of the city's agony melts his hearers to tears, and then again he strikes the note of encouragement and revives their spirits by bidding them take comfort from the well-known clemency of the Emperor, the probable success of the mission of Flavian, and above all, from trust in God.

'The gay and noisy city, where once the busy people hummed like bees around their hive, was petrified by fear into the most dismal silence and desolation; the wealthier inhabitants had fled into the country, those who remained shut themselves up in their houses, as if the town had been in a state of siege. If anyone ventured into the market-place, where once the multitude poured along like the stream of a mighty river, the pitiable sight of two or three cowering, dejected creatures in the midst of solitude soon drove him home again. The sun itself seemed to

---

[1] Chrys. Hom. de Stat. III. i. xxi. i. Zosimus (iv. 41), sends Libanius also to Constantinople, but this is a palpable error. There is no trace of his having gone, either in his own orations or in any other historian.

[2] Socrat. vi. 5. The most common practice was for the preacher to sit, the people to stand.

veil its rays as if in mourning. The words of the prophet were fulfilled, "Their sun shall go down at noon, and their earth shall be darkened in a clear day" (Amos viii. 9). Now they might cry, "Send to the mourning women, and let them come, and send for cunning women that they may come" (Jer. ix. 17). Ye hills and mountains take up a wailing, let us invite all creation to commiserate our woes, for this great city, this capital of Eastern cities, is in danger of being destroyed out of the midst of the earth, and there is no man to help her, for the Emperor, who has no equal among men, has been insulted; therefore let us take refuge with the King who is above, and summon Him to our aid.'[1]

The chief reason of the people's extreme dejection was, that the governor and magistrates, probably to disarm any suspicion at court of their own complicity in the sedition, were daily seizing real or supposed culprits, and punishing them with the utmost rigour. Even those who might have been pardoned on account of their tender age, were mercilessly handed over to the executioner. Chrysostom speaks of some even having been burnt, and others thrown to wild beasts. 'The weeping parents followed their unhappy offspring at a distance, powerless to help but fearing to plead, like men on shore beholding with grief shipwrecked sailors struggling in the water, but unable to rescue them.'[2]

But the object of Chrysostom was, not to rest in ineffectual lamentations, but partly to rouse the people from their profound dejection, partly to print, if possible, on their hearts, humbled and softened by distress, deep and lasting impressions of good. He told them that there was everything to be hoped for from the embassy of Flavian. 'The Emperor was pious, the bishop courageous, yet prudent and adroit; God would not suffer his errand to

[1] Hom. II. 2.   [2] III. c. 6.

be fruitless. The very sight of that venerable man would dispose the royal mind to clemency. Flavian would not fail to urge how especially suitable an act of forgiveness was to that holy season, in which was commemorated the Death of Christ for the sins of the whole world. He would remind the Emperor of the parable of the two debtors, and warn him not to incur the risk of being one day addressed by the words, "Thou wicked servant, I forgave thee all that debt, shouldest not thou also have had compassion on thy fellow-servants?" He would represent that the outrages had not been committed by the whole community, but chiefly by some lawless strangers. He would plead that the inhabitants, even had they all offended, had already undergone sufficient punishment in the anxiety and alarm which they endured. It would be unreasonable to visit the crime of a few by the extirpation of a whole city, a city which was the most populous capital of the East, and dear to Christians as the place where they had first received that sweet and lovely name.'[1]

Meanwhile he earnestly calls upon the people to improve this season of humiliation by a thorough repentance and reformation in respect of the prevailing vices and follies. The words of St. Paul in writing to the Philippians, 'to write the same things to you, to me, indeed, is not grievous, and for you, it is safe,' might be aptly applied to Chrysostom. He is never tired of denouncing special sins and exhorting to the renunciation of them in every variety of language. Ostentatious luxury, sordid avarice, religious formalism, a profane custom of taking rash oaths, were the fashionable sins against which he waged an incessant and implacable warfare.

His exhortations are generally based on some passage read in the lesson of the day. 'What have we heard today? "Charge them that are rich in this world, that they

---

[1] III. c. 1, 2.

be not high-minded." He who says " the rich in this
world," proves there by that there are others rich in
regard to a future world, like Lazarus in the parable.'
'Wealth of this world was a thankless runaway slave,
which, if bound with thousands of fetters, made off, fetters
and all. Not that he would quarrel with wealth; it was
good in itself, but became evil when inordinately desired
and paraded, just as the evil of intoxication lay not in
wine itself, but in the abuse of it. The Apostle did not
charge those who were rich to become poor, but only not
to be high-minded. Let us adorn our own souls before we
embellish our houses. Is it not disgraceful to overlay our
walls with marbles and to neglect Christ, Who is going
about unclothed? What profit is there, O man, in thy
house? Wilt thou carry it away with thee? Nay, thou
must leave thy *house*; but thy *soul* thou wilt certainly
take with thee. Lo! how great the danger which has
now overtaken us: let our houses, then, be our defenders;
let them rescue us from the impending peril;—but they
will not be able. Be those witnesses to my words who
have now deserted their houses, and hurried away to the
wilderness as if afraid of nets and snares. Do you wish
to build large and splendid houses? I forbid you not,
only build them not upon the earth; build yourselves
tabernacles in heaven—tabernacles which never decay.
Nothing is more slippery than wealth, which to-day is
with thee and to-morrow is against thee ; which sharpens
the eyes of the envious on all sides; which is a foe in
your own camp, an enemy in your own household.
Wealth makes the present danger more intolerable; you
see the poor man unencumbered and prepared for whatever may happen, but the rich in a state of great embarrassment, and going about seeking some place in which
to bury his gold, or some person with whom to deposit it.
Why seek thy fellow-servants, O man? Christ stands

ready to receive and guard thy deposits—yea, not only to
guard, but also to multiply and to return with rich interest.   No man plucks out of his hand; men, when they
receive a deposit from another, deem that they have conferred a favour upon him; but Christ, on the contrary,
declares that He receives a favour, and instead of demanding a reward, bestows one upon you.'[1]

He entreated them to make the present Lent a season
of spiritual renovation.   'Lent fell in the spring, when
the stream of industry which the winter had frozen began
to flow again.   The sailor launched his vessel, the soldier
furbished his sword, the farmer whetted his scythe, the
traveller set out confidently on his long journey, the athlete
stripped for the contest.'   'Even so let this fast be to us a
spiritual spring-tide; let us polish our spiritual armour,
let us breast the waves of evil passions, set out like travellers on our journey heavenwards, and prepare like athletes
for the combat.   For the Christian is both husbandman,
and pilot, and soldier, and athlete, and traveller.   Hast
thou seen the athlete? hast thou seen the soldier? if thou
art an athlete thou must strip to enter the lists; if thou
art a soldier thou must put on armour before taking thy
place in the ranks.   How then to the same man can both
these things be possible?'   'How, dost thou ask?   I will
tell thee.   Strip thyself of thy worldly business and thou
hast become an athlete; clothe thyself with spiritual
armour and thou hast become a soldier.   Strip thyself, for
it is a season of wrestling; clothe thyself, for we are engaged in a fierce warfare with devils.   Till thy soul, and
cut away the thorns; sow the seed of piety, plant the
good plants of philosophy, and tend them with much care,
and thou hast become a husbandman, and St. Paul will say
to thee "the husbandman which laboureth must first be a
partaker of the fruits."   Whet thy sickle which thou hast

[1] II. 5.

blunted by surfeiting; sharpen it, I say, by fasting. Enter
on the road which leads to heaven, the rugged and narrow
road, and travel along it. And how shalt thou be able to
set out and travel? By buffeting thy body and bringing
it into subjection; for where the road is narrow, obesity,
which comes from surfeiting, is a great impediment.
Repress the waves of foolish passions, repulse the storm of
wicked imaginations, preserve the vessel, display all thy
skill, and thou hast become a pilot.'[1] The originator and
instructor of all these arts was abstinence; not the vulgar
kind of abstinence, not abstinence from food only, but also
from sins. 'If thou fastest, show me the results by thy
deeds. What deeds, do you ask? If you see a poor man
have pity on him, if an enemy be reconciled, if a friend in
good reputation, regard him without envy. Fast not only
by thy mouth, but with thine eyes, thine ears, thy hands,
thy feet; avert thine eyes from unlawful sights, restrain
thy hands from deeds of violence, keep thy feet from
entering places of pernicious amusement, bridle thy mouth
from uttering and stop thine ears from listening to tales
of slander.' 'This kind of fast would be acceptable to
God, only it should be co-extensive with life. To spend a
few days in penance and then to relapse into the former
course of life, was only an idle mockery.'[2] He disparaged
that rigorous kind of fasting which some had carried to
the extent of taking no food but bread and water. 'Many
boasted of the number of weeks they had fasted; this excessive abstinence was likely to be followed by a reaction.
Let them seek rather to subdue evil passions and habits;
let one week be devoted to the suppression of swearing,
another of anger, a third of slander, and so gradually
advancing they might at last attain the consummation of
virtue, and propitiate the displeasure of God.'[3] 'Let us not
do now what we have so often done, for frequently when

[1] III. 3.   [2] III. 4. 5.   [3] XVI. 6.

earthquakes, or famine, or drought have overtaken us, we
have become temperate for three or four days and then
have returned to our former ways of life. But, if never
before, now at least let us remain stedfast in the same
state of piety, that we may not again require to be chastised by another scourge.'[1]

Almost all the homilies are concluded by an admonition
against the sin of swearing, and the greater portion of
some is devoted to this topic. The passionate impetuous
people of Antioch seem to have been constantly betrayed
into the folly of binding themselves by rash oaths. The
master, for instance, would take an oath to deprive his
slave of food, or the tutor his scholar, till a certain task
was accomplished, a threat which it was of course often
impossible to enforce. Hence perjury on the part of the
superior and loss of respect on the side of the subordinate.
Chrysostom himself had often dined at a house where the
mistress swore that she would beat a slave who had made
some mistake, while the husband would with another oath
forbid the punishment. Thus one of the two would be
inevitably involved in perjury.[2] He frequently exhorted
his hearers to form a kind of Christian club amongst themselves for the suppression of this vice. In one place he
suggests a stern remedy: 'When you detect your wife or
any of your household yielding to this evil habit, order
them supperless to bed, and if you are guilty impose the
same penalty on yourself.'[3] Near the close of Lent he
declares that he will repel from the holy Table at Easter
those whom he detects still addicted to this vice.[4]

---

[1] III. 7.   [2] XIV. 1.
[3] V. 7.
[4] XX. 9. A passage in another
homily on this subject is curious, as
proving that just the same juggler's
feats were performed in Antioch in
the fourth century as at the fairs and
races of the present day. 'Persons

pretended it was next to impossible
to conquer an inveterate habit: this
was a paltry excuse, perseverance
could conquer any difficulty. To un-
learn a habit of swearing could not
be more impossible than to acquire
the art of throwing up swords, and
catching them by the handle, or bal-

On the whole the eager and earnest pastor may be said
to have rejoiced at the grand opportunity afforded by the
humiliation of the city, to effect a reformation in the moral
life of the people. He observed with great satisfaction,
that if the forum was deserted the church was thronged,
just as in stormy weather the harbour is crowded with
vessels.[1] Many an intemperate man had been sobered,
the headstrong softened, or the indolent quickened into
zeal. Many who once assiduously frequented the theatre
now spent their day in the church. Meanwhile they must
abide God's pleasure for the removal of their affliction.
He had sent it for the purpose of purifying and chastening
them; He was waiting till He saw a genuine an un-
shakeable repentance, like a refiner watching a piece of
precious metal in a crucible, and waiting the proper moment for taking it out.[2] As for those who said what they
feared was not so much death as *ignominious* death by the
hand of the executioner, he protested that the only
' death really miserable was a death in sin. Abel was murdered and was happy, Cain lived and was miserable. John
the Baptist was beheaded, St. Stephen was stoned, yet
their deaths were happy. To the Christian there was
nothing formidable in death itself. To dread death but
not to be afraid of sin was to act like children who are
frightened by masks whilst they were not afraid of fire.
What, I pray you, is death? It is like the putting off of
a garment, for the soul is invested with a body[3] as it were
with a garment, and this we shall put off for a little while
by death, only to receive it again in a more brilliant form.'
' What, I pray you, is death? It is but to go a journey for
a season, or to take a longer sleep than usual.' Death was but

---

uncing a pole on the forehead with
two boys at the top of it, or dancing
on a tight rope.'—Hom. in Dom.
Serv.

[1] IV. 1.

[2] IV. 2.

[3] V. 3. τὸ σῶμα τῇ ψυχῇ περίκειται
καθάπερ ἱμάτιον. Compare Shakspere:
' When we have shuffled off this mortal
coil.'

a release from toil, a tranquil haven. Mourn not over him who dies, but him who living in sin is dead while he liveth.'[1]

Chrysostom's own calmness, and his skill in diverting the thoughts of his flock from present alarm, are manifested by the power and ease with which he dilates on such grand topics as the creation, Divine Providence, the nature of man, and his place in the scale of created beings. His best thoughts, expressed in his best style on these subjects, are to be found in the homilies now under consideration.

'The size and beauty of the universe, but still more the perfect regularity with which the system worked, proclaimed a designing power. The succession of day and night, the series of the seasons, like a band of maidens dancing in a circle, the four elements of which the world was composed, mingling in such exquisite proportions that they exactly balanced one another, the sun tempering the action of water, the water that of the sun, the sea unable to break its bounds or reduce the earth to a mass of clay; who could contemplate all these forces at work and suppose that they moved spontaneously, instead of adoring Him who had arranged them all with a wisdom commensurate with the results? As the health of the body depended on the due balance of those humours of which it was composed, if the bile increased fever was produced, or if the phlegmatic element prevailed many diseases were engendered, so was it in the case of the universe; each element observed its proper limits, restrained, as it were, with a bridle by the will of the Maker; and the struggle between these elements was the source of peace for the whole system. As the body failed, languished, died, in proportion as the soul was withdrawn from it, so if the regulating and life-giving power of God's providence were removed from the earth, all would go to rack and ruin, like a vessel deserted by her pilot.'[2]

[1] V. 3.   [2] IX. 3, 4.

In treating this subject, he manifests a keen appreciation of natural beauties. 'The infinite varieties of flowers and herbs, trees, animals, insects, and birds—the flowery fields below, the starry fields above—the never-failing fountains—the sea receiving countless streams into its bosom, yet never overflowing,—all proclaimed a Creator and an Upholder, and drew from man the exclamation, "How manifold are Thy works; in wisdom hast Thou made them all!" Yet, lest they should be worshipped instead of the Maker, conditions of change, as decay or death, were imposed upon all.'[1] His observation of nature appears in some of his similes. The poor female relatives hovering about the courts of justice, when the culprits of the outrage on the statues were being tried, he compares to parent birds, which wildly flutter round the hunter who has stolen the young from their nest, in an agony of grief, but impotent from weakness and fear.[2] He perceives in some of the lower animals characteristics to be imitated or avoided, and describes them with a kind of humour. 'The bee especially was a pattern for imitation, not merely because it was industrious, but because it toiled with an unconscious kind of self-sacrifice for the benefit of others as well as itself. It was the most honourable of insects; the spider, on the contrary, was the most ignoble, because it spread its fine web for its own selfish gratification only. The innocence of the dove, the docility of the ox, the light-heartedness of birds, were all examples for imitation. The ferocity, or the cunning of other animals or insects, were examples for avoidance. The good which brutes had by nature man might acquire by force of moral purpose; and the sovereign of the lower animals ought to comprise in his nature all the best qualities of his subjects.[3] The plumage of the peacock excelling in variety and beauty all

---

[1] X. 2, 4.   [2] XIII. 2.   [3] XII. 2.

possible art of the dyer, evinced the superhuman power of the Maker of all things.'[1]

His ethical doctrine bears singular resemblance to that of Butler. God has bestowed on man a faculty of discerning right from wrong; He has impressed upon him a natural law, the law of conscience. Hence some commands are delivered without explanation; for instance, the prohibition to kill, or to commit adultery, because these merely enjoin what is already evident by the light of the natural law. On the other hand, for the command to observe the Sabbath, a reason is assigned, because this was a special and temporary enactment. The obligation of the law of conscience was universal and eternal. As soon as Adam had sinned, he hid himself, a clear evidence of his consciousness of guilt, although no written law existed at that time.

The Greeks might attempt to deny the universality of this inherent law, but to what other origin could they ascribe the laws which had been made by their own ancestors concerning respect for life, the marriage bond, covenants, trusts, and the like? They had indeed been handed down from generation to generation; but whence did the first promulgators derive the idea of them, if not from this moral sense? To the law of conscience was added the energy of a moral purpose, προαίρεσις, which enabled man to practise what conscience prescribed: conscience informs man that temperance is right; moral purpose enables him to become temperate. God had also endowed man with some natural virtues: indignation at injustice, compassion for the injured, sympathy with the joys and sorrows of our fellow men.[2] At the same time

---

[1] X. 3.

[2] XII. 2-4. XIII. 3. Comp. Aristotle's distinction between natural and conventional law or justice, Eth.v. 7, 1. ' φυσικόν' and νομικόν δίκαιον. Compare also his description of προαίρεσις as the ἀρχὴ κινήσεως in b. iii., and of φρόνησις (nearly = Butler's 'Conscience,') in b. vi.

Chrysostom fully allows the value of training and teaching as supplementary to and co-operating with all these natural gifts.[1] If conscience grew languid, the admonition of parent and friend, and, in the case of public offences, the law, stepped in, to effect what conscience failed to do; and frequently God sent afflictions for the same remedial purpose.[2]

Thus, day after day the indefatigable preacher sounded the note of encouragement, or warning, or instruction. He not only held the Christian flock together, but largely increased its numbers. His eloquence frequently excited rapturous applause, which was invariably repressed with sternness. On one occasion the congregation yielded to a panic; a false rumour was circulated that a body of troops was entering the city, to take vengeance on the inhabitants. The Prefect entered the church to allay the fears of the affrighted people who had fled thither, but Chrysostom was overwhelmed with shame, and sharply upbraided them that a Christian congregation should owe the restoration of calmness to a Pagan, whom they ought to have impressed, like Paul before Agrippa, by a display of Christian firmness and fortitude.[3]

About the middle of Lent, two commissioners, Hellebicus and Cæsarius, arrived at Antioch, invested with full powers to enquire into the late outrage. Their authority was backed by a considerable military force. They were men not only of intelligence and humanity, but Christians in faith; and they had many friends in Antioch. They entered the city, surrounded by a large multitude, who turned weeping faces and held out supplicating hands towards them. The commissioners were moved, and in deep silence entered the lodging provided for them; but it was neces-

---

[1] Comp. again what Aristotle says of the necessity of *training* to improve the *natural* gifts, b. x. 9, and of the formation of *habits* by repeated *acts*.

Comp. Chrys. hom. xiii. 3, with Arist. Eth. ii. 4, 5.

[2] XIII. 4.

[3] XVI. 1.

sary for them to perform their duty, which was in the first
place to announce that Antioch was degraded from the
rank of capital of Syria, and its metropolitan honours
were transferred to the neighbouring city of Laodicea.
Secondly, all the public baths, circuses, theatres, and other
places of recreation, were to be closed for an indefinite
time. Thirdly, the commissioners were to revise the trials
already held by the local governor, and to inflict rigorous
sentences upon all the guilty, especially any persons of
distinction. These judicial proceedings were to begin on
the following day.

The scene at the entrance of the court was a melancholy
spectacle; the wives and daughters of the accused hung
around it in mean garments sprinkled with ashes, and in
attitudes of supplication or despair.

There were no lawyers to plead for the prisoners; they
had run away or concealed themselves, to evade the perilous duty. Libanius alone, towards evening, crept timidly
into the court. Cæsarius, to whom he was known, observed him, beckoned him to approach, and placed him
by his side. In a low voice he bade him take courage,
himself and colleague would endeavour as much as possible to spare life. Libanius earnestly thanked him, and
promised if he kept his word to immortalise him by an
oration in his honour.[1]

An appeal, however, more effectual, was made to the
mercy of the commissioners, by persons widely different
from Libanius. As they were riding in state to the hall
of justice on the second day, they saw amongst the people
a group of strange half-wild-looking beings, in rough
coarse garments, with long unkempt hair. These were
hermits, who had descended from their solitudes in the
neighbouring mountains—some who for years had not been
seen in the streets of the city, but now appeared to plead

[1] Liban. Or. 21, in Helleb. and 20, 517.

on behalf of the offending people.   An old man, diminutive
in stature, whose clothing was in tatters, started forward
from the group as the commissioners passed by, seized the
bridle of one, and commanded them in a tone of authority, to dismount.   'Who is this mad fellow?' enquired the
commissioners.   They were informed that he was the
revered hermit Macedonius, surnamed Crithophagus, or
the barley-eater, because barley was his only sustenance.
Hellebicus and Cæsarius immediately alighted, and, falling
on their knees before him, craved his pardon for having
received him so rudely.   'My friends,' replied the solitary,
'go to the Emperor and say, "You are an emperor, but
also a man, and you rule over beings who are of like
nature with yourself.   Man was created after a Divine
image and likeness; do not, then, mercilessly command
the image of God to be destroyed, for you will provoke
the Maker if you punish his image.   For, consider that
you are doing this from displeasure at the injury inflicted
on a statue of bronze; and how far does a living rational
creature exceed the value of such an inanimate object!
Let him consider that it is easy to manufacture many
statues in the place of those destroyed, but it is wholly
impossible for him to make a single hair again of those
men who have been put to death."'[1]   The other hermits
declared that they were all prepared to shed their blood
and lay down their lives for the culprits; that they would
not withdraw from the city until they were sent as ambassadors to the Emperor, or until the city itself had
been acquitted.   The joy of Chrysostom at the courage
displayed by these hermits was extreme; their noble
conduct compensated for the sad pusillanimity lately
exhibited by the congregation in the church.   He tri-
umphantly contrasts them with the so-called philosophers
of Antioch, who appear to have displayed anything but

[1] Theodor. v. 20.

philosophic calmness in the hour of danger. 'Where now are those long-bearded, cloak-wearing, staff-bearing fellows—cynic refuse, more degraded than dogs licking up the crumbs under the table, doing everything for their belly? Why, they have all hurried out of the city and hidden themselves in caves and dens, whilst those who inhabited the caves have entered the city, and boldly walk about the forum as if no calamity had happened. Their conduct illustrates what I have never ceased to maintain, that even the furnace cannot injure one who lives in virtue. Such is the power of philosophy introduced to man by Christ.'[1] The result of this singular intercession was, that the commissioners consented to suspend the execution of their sentence on those pronounced guilty, until an appeal had been made to the Emperor. Meanwhile the prisoners were to remain in confinement, and their property to be held by the State.

The hermits were anxious to repair to the court of Theodosius, but the commissioners wisely refused, making the length of the journey an objection, but perhaps really because they feared such excitable zealots might frustrate the object of their embassy by imprudent behaviour. It was finally decided that Hellebicus should remain to preserve order in Antioch, while his colleague went to Constantinople, carrying with him an intercessory letter signed by the hermits, and declaring that they were ready to give their own lives in ransom for the city.

Cæsarius departed amidst the blessings and acclamations of the people.[2]

What had the energetic preacher, who had sustained the spirits of the people so long, been doing, since the arrival of the Emperor's legates? It had been, indeed, a relief to find that the city was not to be surrendered to

---

[1] Hom. xvii. 1, 2.
[2] Liban. Orat. 20.   De Broglie, vi. 150, 151.   Chrys. hom. xvii. 2.

the sword; but, to a proud and luxurious people the loss of metropolitan rank, and the closing of the public baths, theatres, and public places of amusement, were severe blows. Loud and general was the lamentation over their fallen grandeur and their lost enjoyments. Chrysostom expostulated with them on their discontent. 'The real dignity of a city did not consist in pre-eminence of rank or vastness of population, but in the virtue of its citizens. What constituted the noblest reputation of Antioch ?— the fact that the disciples there were the first to be called Christians—that they had sent relief to the distressed brethren in Judea in the time of the famine (Acts xi. 28, 29)—that they had sent Paul and Barnabas to that Council at Jerusalem which had emancipated the Gentile Christians from Judaic bondage. These were honourable distinctions, which no other city, not even Rome itself, could rival. They enabled Antioch to look the whole Christian world in the face, for they proved how great had been her Christian courage and her Christian love. These were her true metropolitan honours; and, if these were in aught diminished, not by the size or beauty of her buildings, not by her airy colonnades or her spacious porticoes and promenades,[1] not by the sacred Grove of Daphne, not by the number and loftiness of her cypresses, not by her fountains or her multitudinous population, or her genial climate, making walks in the depth of evening pleasant and secure,—not by these could she recover her tarnished reputation, but by equity, almsgiving, vigils, prayers, temperance. External size and beauty did not constitute real greatness. David was little of stature, yet he prostrated by a single blow a very tower of flesh. Away with these womanish complaints! I have heard many in the forum saying,

[1] XVII. 2. The colonnades, especially of the great street which ran through the city from east to west, the περίπατοι or promenades, were lined by colonnades with seats.—V. Müller, Antiq. Ant. ii. 12.

"Woe to thee, Antioch, what has become of thee, how art thou dishonoured!" and when I heard I laughed at the childish understanding of those who say such things. It behoves you not to speak thus, now; but, when you see dancing, and drunkenness, and singing, and blaspheming, and swearing, then utter the cry, Woe to thee, O city! what has become of thee? but when you see only a few equitable, temperate, and moderate men in the forum, then call the city happy.'[1]

He remonstrates indignantly with them for their querulous complaints of the prohibition to use the public baths. Bathing, indeed, was a luxury so indispensable to the bodily health and comfort of the people, that they now resorted to the river in large numbers, with very little regard to decency. He reminds those who murmured over this deprivation of their favourite indulgence, that a short time ago, when they were daily expecting an incursion of soldiers, and were flying to the desert and mountains, they would have been too thankful to escape with so cheap a penalty. He urges the duty of reconciliation with enemies as specially incumbent on them when such great efforts were being made to obtain mercy for themselves. They should have one enemy alone, the devil, with whom they should wage an implacable warfare.[2]

Thus the prophet, ever vigilant for the true welfare and honour of his people, ceased not to lift up his voice.

Cæsarius travelled day and night, and in the course of a week accomplished the eight hundred miles which separated Antioch from Constantinople. But his arrival and his errand had been anticipated. Flavian had reached the court a week before, and the pardon of Antioch was already obtained. The aged bishop returned to Antioch just in time to celebrate Easter, and to augment the natural joy-

---

[1] XVII. 2.   [2] XX. 5, and XVIII. in fine.

fulness of the festival by the tidings which he brought.
He had, however, been preceded a few days by an express
courier, who delivered the imperial rescript to Hellebicus.
When the contents were publicly proclaimed, the pent-up
feelings of the people burst forth into demonstrations of
almost frantic joy.   Hellebicus was received with ovation
wherever he went.   Libanius walked by his side, reciting
passages from his orations, in honour of Theodosius and
praise of the two commissioners.[1]   On Holy Saturday,
Flavian himself entered the city, partly attended, partly
borne along by vast crowds of grateful people.   On that
night the forum was decorated with garlands and illuminated by lanterns.   On the next morning, Easter-day,
a vast concourse thronged the church, and once more the
well-known voice, which had exhorted and encouraged and
warned, during the days of their gloom, now poured forth
in the sunshine of their joy a pœan of thanksgiving and
praise.

‘ Blessed be God, who hath vouchsafed us to celebrate
this holy feast with great joy and gladness, who has restored
the Head to the body, the Shepherd to the sheep, the
Master to his disciples, the Pontiff to the priests.   Blessed
be God, who hath done exceeding abundantly above all
that we ask or think, for it seemed to us sufficient to be
for a time released from the impending calamities ; but
the merciful God, ever exceeding in his gifts our petitions,
has restored to us our father sooner than all our expectation.’   ‘ Not only had their beloved prelate escaped all the
perils incident to so long a journey in the winter season,
but had found his sister, whom he had left on the point
of death, still living to welcome his return.’[2]

He then proceeds to describe the interview of Flavian
with Theodosius, as it had been related to him by an eye-
witness.   The bishop, when introduced into the royal

[1] Liban. Or. xxi. p. 536.   [2] XXI. 1.

presence, stood at a distance, silently weeping, bending
low, and covering his face, as if he himself had been the
author of all the late offences. By this attitude he hoped
to expel emotions of anger, and introduce the emotion of
pity into the Emperor's breast, before he undertook the
actual defence of the city.

Theodosius was moved; he advanced to the bishop, and
used no harsh or indignant language, but only mildly reproached with ingratitude a city which he had always
treated with lenity, and had long desired and intended to
visit. Even had the people been able to accuse him of any
injury done to them, they might at least have respected
the dead, who could do them no harm (alluding to the
destruction of his wife's and father's images).

The aged prelate no longer remained silent. With a
fresh flood of tears, he poured forth his pathetic appeal to
the Christian clemency and forbearance of the Emperor.
' He would not attempt to extenuate the offence, the sense
of their ingratitude caused them the deepest distress, and
they frankly confessed that it deserved the severest chastisement which could be inflicted. Yet the noblest kind
of revenge which he could take was freely to forgive the
insult; thereby he would defeat the malice of those demons
who had tried to work the ruin of the people by seducing
them from their allegiance. In like manner, the devil had
tried to compass the death of the human race, but his
malevolence had been frustrated by God, who offered even
heaven to those who had been excluded from Paradise. A
free pardon would secure for him a station in the hearts of
all his subjects, far more enduring than those statues which
had been broken down. He reminded him, how once his
great predecessor, Constantine, when urged to revenge
some insult done to one of his statues, passed his hand
over his face, and observed, with a quiet smile, that he did

not feel the blow; a saying which had endeared him to
his people more than his military exploits. But why need
he refer to Constantine? Theodosius himself, on a previous
Easter, had commanded a general release of prisoners, and
had nobly exclaimed, " Would that it were possible also for
me to recall the dead to life !" [1]   Now he might in some
sort realise that wish, by restoring to security a whole
city, which lay, as it were, dead under remorse and fear.
Such an act of clemency would both strengthen his own
throne and the cause of Christianity. Greeks, Jews, and
barbarians were waiting to hear his decision. If it was
on the side of mercy, all would applaud it, saying,
" Heavens ! how mighty is the power of Christianity,
which has restrained the wrath of a monarch who has not
his peer in the world." How noble a tale for posterity to
hear, that what the governor and magistrates of a great
city dared not ask, had been granted to the prayer of an
old man, because he was the priest of God, and from
reverence to the Divine laws. He would solemnly remind
him of the words, " If ye forgive not men their trespasses,
neither will your Father which is in heaven forgive you
your trespasses." He begged him to remember that there
was a day coming in which all men would render an account of their actions, and to imitate the example of God,
who, though daily sustaining insults from man, did not
cease to bestow blessings upon him. He concluded by
declaring that he would never return to Antioch unless
he could take back the imperial pardon, but would enrol
himself in another city.' [2]

[1] It was the custom to signalise the
great festivals by acts of mercy. ' The
oil of mercy glistens on the Festivals
of the Church,' says Ambrose, Serm.
14, on Ps. cxviii. 7. Leo the Great,
also, Serm. 39, alludes to the custom.
But, to prevent any abuse of the
practice, it was enacted by Theodosius
in A.D. 384–385, that it should apply
only to those accused of petty offences :
the grosser crimes of robbery, adultery,
magic, murder, sacrilege, were to be
excepted from claims to this indulgence.

[2] Hom. xxi. 1–4.

If Flavian's intercession was thrown into the form of an oration at all, it is clear that Chrysostom's version of it, which has been here greatly condensed from the original, must be his own, rather than the speech actually delivered. If it had been only half as long, it could not have been accurately related to him from memory, or faithfully rehearsed by him afterwards. The excitement of addressing so large an audience on so great an occasion, would naturally stimulate him to amplify and embellish.

There is, however, no reason to doubt that Chrysostom has furnished us with an accurate description of Flavian's conduct in the interview, and given us the main substance of his arguments. The whole narrative of the occurrence illustrates the difference between the Eastern and Western character. Compare the demeanour of Ambrose and of Flavian. The first speaks in a tone of majestic authority, which brooks no disputing; the other, though far from deficient in courage, approaches the Emperor with that deferential and submissive manner which the oriental is accustomed to adopt in the presence of a potentate. His tone is that of an appeal, though based upon the highest grounds; not of a command. There is something of the courtier in Flavian; in Ambrose there is more of the pope.

To conclude Chrysostom's account: the Emperor was deeply affected, though, like Joseph, he refrained himself in the presence of spectators. He declared his intention of granting a free pardon, in language eminently Christian. 'If the Lord of the earth, who became a servant for our sakes, and was crucified by those whom He came to benefit, prayed for the pardon of his crucifiers, what wonder was it that a man should forgive his fellow-servants?' He begged Flavian to return with all expedition, that he might release the people from the agony of their suspense. The bishop entreated that the young

prince Arcadius might accompany him as a pledge of
imperial favour to the city.   But Theodosius said that
he designed to confer on Antioch a greater honour.   He
requested the bishop to offer up prayers for the termination of the present war, that he might ratify his pardon
by a visit to the city in person.   The express courier was
then despatched, while Flavian followed at a pace more
suitable to his dignity and advanced age.

Chrysostom concludes his discourse by a moral exhortation suggested by those festive demonstrations of joy
already described.   ' Let the lanterns and the chaplets be
to them emblems of spiritual things.   Let them not cease
to be crowned with virtue or to light up a lamp in their
soul by the diligent practice of good works ; let them
rejoice with holy joy and thank God not only for rescuing
them from destruction, but for sending them so wholesome a chastisement, the salutary effects of which would,
he trusted, extend to many generations.' [1]

Thus terminated the celebrated sedition of Antioch.
It is a singular and instructive picture of the times : the
impulsive character of the people, in the great Eastern
cities of the Empire, alternating between frantic rage and
abject despondency ; the expectation of violent imperial
vengeance, nothing less than the extermination of the
city ; the remarkable veneration paid to monks,—these
are points which stand out in vivid colours.   But still
more remarkably this event supplies an example of the
softening, humanising influence of Christianity, in a fierce
and heartless age.   The issue reflects the greatest honour
on those who brought it to pass ; and they were *all Christians* : the intrepid old bishop, sacrificing comfort and
risking life to intercede, the generous Emperor who
yielded to the persuasion of his Christian arguments ; the
humane commissioners ; and last but not least, the pastor

[1] XXI. 4.

and preacher, who, with unwearied patience, invincible
courage, unfailing eloquence, sustained the fainting spirits
of his flock, and endeavoured to convert their calamity into
an occasion of lasting good.

One great and happy result of the recent trouble was
a large accession of Pagans to the ranks of the Church.
When the city lay under ban, the baths, theatres, circus,
were closed, and the panic-stricken people had no heart
to pursue their ordinary business. But one place had
been constantly open. All knew that in the church
prayer was being offered up day by day; and to the first
portion of the service up to the end of the sermon, there
was free admission for all without respect of creed.
Curiosity alone, if not any deeper feeling, would lead
many Pagans to turn into the church, to hear what consolations, what encouragements the Christian preacher
had to offer in this season of general distress and painful
suspense. And what had they heard? An unsparing
exposure and denunciation of the follies and vices which
prevailed in that great and dissolute city, a trumpet call
to repentance and reformation; the fleeting nature of
earthly honour and earthly riches, their impotence to
satisfy the heart or to save the life in the time of danger
and distress had been vividly contrasted with the Christian's aim of laying up treasure which should not fail in
a world which would not be destroyed, with the Christian's faith that righteousness was the only permanent
good, as sin was the only real evil, that to a good man
death was only the transition to a more blessed life, and
that affliction was useful in purifying and elevating the
soul. They had heard the proofs of a Creator, and of His
providential care for the things which He had made as
evinced by the majesty, beauty, and organisation of the
universe, by the conscience and moral faculties of man,
as well as by the more direct testimony of the written

word.[1]   There is no evidence as to the number of converts reclaimed from Paganism.   Chrysostom only informs us [2] that he was occupied for some time after the return of Flavian with confirming in the faith those who 'in consequence of the calamity had come to better mind and deserted from the side of Gentile error.'

The sermons themselves are lost.

[1] Hom. i. de Anna, vol. iv. c. 1, where he recapitulates the arguments which he had used in the Homilies on the Statues.

[2] Hom. de Anna, i. c. 1.

CHAPTER XII.

VERY probably the physical labour and mental strain which Chrysostom had undergone during the events recorded in the previous chapter may have brought on the illness to which he alludes in the homily preached on the Sunday before Ascension Day.[1] He was prevented by this attack from taking part in the services which were held some time after Easter under the conduct of Bishop Flavian at the chapels built over the remains of martyrs and saints.[2] A variety of homilies delivered by Chrysostom at such 'martyries' on other occasions are extant, and it may be as well to introduce here such indications as can be collected from them of the general feeling of the Church, as well as of himself, with regard to saints, and such kindred subjects as pilgrimages and reliques.

Churches had in most instances been erected to commemorate the death of a martyr, or to mark the spot where he died. Tertullian's saying that 'the blood of martyrs was the seed' of the Church, thus became verified in a literal, material sense. Socrates (iv. 23) even speaks of the churches of St. Paul and St. Peter at Rome as

---

[1] Called κυριακὴ τῆς ἐπισωζομένης, this last word being the name of Ascension Day among the Cappadocians, possibly because Christ's work on earth for man's redemption was completed by his return into heaven. (v. Leo Allatius, quoted in Suicer Thesaur. sub verbo 'Episozomene,' and Bingham, Antiq. b. xx. sect. 5.)

[2] Hom. de Stat. 19, i. vol. ii.

their 'martyries,' as Eusebius [1] also calls the church which
Constantine built on Golgotha the 'martyry' of our
Saviour. By the age of Chrysostom the festivals of martyrs
and saints had grown so numerous that frequently more
than one occurred in the same week.[2]   Good Friday and
Ascension Day, and the Sunday after Whitsun Day (not
observed as Trinity Sunday till much later), were especially dedicated to the commemoration of saints.[3]   The
congregation kept a vigil the night before, or very early
before dawn on the Saints' day itself.   The vigil consisted of psalms, hymns, and prayers, and was followed
early in the day by a full service, when, in addition to the
ordinary lessons of the day, the acts or passions of the
saint or martyr were read.   St. Augustine permitted his
people to sit during the reading of them because they
were often of great length.   Pope Gelasius forbad them
to be read because they were so seldom authentic.[4]   The
martyries were generally outside the city walls, not always
built over the grave of the saint, but close to it; in which
case the congregation assembled at the grave first, and
walked in procession from it to the church, singing hymns
as they went.   There can be no doubt that Chrysostom
believed in the intercessory power of departed saints, and
encouraged the invocation of their intercession.   'They
were nearer to the Divine ear, and by virtue of their
glorious deaths had justly obtained more confidence in
making their requests to God than had the inhabitants
of earth.'   He implores Christians not to resort for medical
assistance to Jews, who were the enemies of Christ, but
to seek aid from His friends the saints and martyrs, who

---

[1] Euseb. de Vitâ Constant. l. iv.

[2] Chrys. hom. xl. in Juvent.

[3] Hom. de Cœmet. et Cruce, vol. ii.
c. i. in Ascens. Christi, vol. ii., and de
Sanct. Martyr. vol. ii. p. 705. The
Sunday corresponding to the present
Trinity Sunday was kept as a kind of

All Saints' Day. See Bingham, b. xx.
c. 7, sect. 14.

[4] Aug. hom. xxvi. Gelas. Decret.
in Grab. vol. i. The word 'legend'
is perhaps derived from these Acts of
the Saints, which were to be read,
'legenda.'

had much confidence in addressing God.[1] At the close
of his homily on the festival of two soldiers who had been
beheaded by Julian for obstinate adherence to Christianity, he says : ' Let us constantly visit them, touch
their shrine, and with faith embrace their reliques, that we
may derive some blessing therefrom ; for like soldiers who
converse freely with their sovereign when they display
their wounds, so these, bearing their heads in their hands,
are easily able to effect what they desire at the court of
the King of Heaven.'[2] So, again, in the homily on Ber-
nice and Prosdoke : ' let us fall down before their reliques
. . . . let us embrace their shrines : not only on their
festival, but at other times, let us resort to them and
invoke them to become our protectors ; for they can use
much boldness of speech when dead, more, indeed, than
when they were alive, for now they bear in their bodies
the marks of Jesus Christ . . . . let us therefore procure
for ourselves, through them, favour from God.'[3] Thus
the saint is to be appealed to as a kind of friend at court,
who will present petitions, and use his influence to obtain a favourable answer from the Monarch ; but the
further step of invoking saints as the *direct* dispensers
of spiritual and other benefits had not yet been taken.
The feeling of the Church of Smyrna towards their beloved martyr and Bishop Polycarp, as expressed in A.D.
160 to the Church of Philomelium, still represented the
general state of feeling in the Church.[4] The Jews and
other malignants had suggested, when the remains of
Polycarp had been earnestly asked for, that the Christians
intended to worship him ; and ' this they said, being
ignorant that we should never be able to desert Christ,
or worship any other Being. For Him, being the Son of

[1] Adv. Judæos viii. c. 7.

[2] Hom. in Juvent. et Maxim. vol. ii.
p. 576.

[3] De Bern. et Prosd. vol. ii. p. 640.

[4] See the letter in Euseb. l. iv. c. 15

God, we adore, but the martyrs, as the disciples and imitators of the Lord, we love with a deserved affection; desiring to become partners and fellow disciples with them.' The language of St. Augustine and St. Chrysostom thoroughly corresponds to that in the passage just cited. 'Our religion,' says Augustine, 'consists not in the worship of dead men; because if they lived piously they are not considered likely to desire that kind of honour; but would wish Him to be worshipped by us through whose illumination they rejoice to have us partners with them in their merit. They are therefore to be honoured for the sake of imitation, not to be worshipped as a religious act.' [1]   And in another place: 'Christian people celebrate the memory of martyrs with religious solemnity, to stimulate imitation, to become partners in their merits, and to be assisted by their prayers; but in doing this we never offer sacrifice to a martyr, but only to Him who is the God of martyrs.' [2] A multitude of passages might be cited from Chrysostom's homilies on Saints' Festivals, in which he passionately exhorts to the imitation and emulation of their noble lives and glorious deaths, and dwells on the great advantages to the Church arising from these solemn commemorations. 'The very memory of the martyrs wrought upon the minds of men in confirming them against the assaults of wicked spirits, and delivering them from impure and unseemly thoughts;' . . . 'the death of the martyrs was the exhortation of the faithful, the confidence of Churches, the confirmation of Christianity, . . . the reproach of devils, the condemnation of Satan, a consolation in affliction, a motive to patience, encouragement to fortitude, the root, fountain, mother of all which is good.' [3]

[1] Aug. de Vera Relig. c. 55.   [2] Aug. cont. Faustum, l. xx. c. 21.
[3] De Droside, vol. ii. p. 685.

But if no inculcations to direct worship of saints are to be found in Chrysostom, it is evident that no small virtue was ascribed by popular faith (and, in his opinion, justly) to their remains.[1] Miracles of healing were wrought, or supposed to be wrought, at their tombs; demons were expelled by the application of their ashes to the persons possessed. It is obvious that, where such a belief has taken possession of the popular mind, prayer will very soon be addressed to the saint for the direct bestowal of those advantages which are supposed to be derivable from his reliques. Pilgrimages were fashionable in all parts of Christendom. Prefects and generals, when they visited Rome, hastened to pay their devotion at the tombs of the tentmaker and fisherman; journeys were made into Arabia to visit the supposed site of Job's dunghill.[2]

Two different causes seem to have led on the mind of the Church to an increasing veneration of martyrs. First, the Church owed to them a real debt; the heroic stedfastness of their deaths contributed much to promote and establish Christianity. Chrysostom observes how the sight of the aged Ignatius going to die at Rome for his faith — going not only with calmness, but even with alacrity — mightily confirmed the souls of the disciples in the several cities through which he passed.[3] 'As irrigation made gardens fruitful, so the blood of martyrs gave drink to the Churches.'[4] Honour, affection, veneration, easily pass into actual adoration.

Secondly, there is a natural desire to bridge over the chasm which divides the human nature from the Divine,

---

[1] Flavian caused the remains of some much-revered saints who were buried beneath the pavement of the church to be taken up, and placed in another separate grave, because the people were distressed that the reliques of such venerated personages should repose in the same vaults with the remains of less saintly, if not heretical, characters.—Hom. in Ascen.

[2] De S. Babyla. c. 12. De Stat. i. 2, and viii. 2. Quod Christus sit Deus, c. 7. De Stat. v. 1.

[3] In S. Ignat. Mart. c. 4.

[4] In Juvent. et Maxim. c. 1.

and earth from heaven, by enlisting the agency of some intermediate being. In its earliest conflicts with heresy, theology was chiefly engaged in zealously defending the pure divinity of Christ—his co-equal, co-eternal power and majesty with the Father. The more He was withdrawn into a less accessible region of exalted deity, the more this need of the half-deified human interpositor was felt, and worked itself out at last into a distinct article of faith.

Some of those abuses of saints' days, which we are apt to associate more especially with mediæval times, were far from uncommon in the days of Chrysostom. The day which had begun in fasting, and was preceded by a vigil, too often terminated in a very carnal kind of revelry. 'Ye have turned night into day by your holy vigils: do not turn day into night by drunkenness, surfeiting, and lascivious songs; let not anyone see you misbehaving in an inn on your return home.'[1] A custom prevailed of holding a 'love-feast' at or near the tomb of the saint, which was furnished by the oblations of the wealthier devotees. Chrysostom on one occasion urges his congregation to attend such a sacred banquet when they dispersed after service, instead of hurrying off to the diabolical entertainments at Daphne: 'the sight of the martyr, standing as it were near their table, would prevent their pleasure from running to excess.'[2] But there is abundant evidence in other contemporary writers that these meetings too often did degenerate into scenes of mere conviviality and intemperance. Augustine speaks of those who 'made themselves drunk at the commemoration of martyrs.'[3] Ambrose prohibited all such feasts in the churches of Milan; and Augustine cited his example to obtain a similar prohibition from Aurelius, the Primate

---

[1] Hom. in Martyres, vol. ii. p. 663.   [3] Aug. cont. Faustum, l. xx. c. 21.
[2] In Sanct. Jul. vol. ii. p. 673.

of Carthage.[1] Basil reprobates a growing custom of
trading near the martyries on festival days, under pretence of making a better provision for the feasts, to which
we may fairly, perhaps, attribute the universal custom in
Christendom of holding fairs on saints' days.[2] As they
were in mediæval times, so in Roman Catholic countries
at the present day, the booths of the fair are in close con-
tiguity with the walls of the church, and they who attend
mass in the morning, as well as those who do not attend
it at all, may disgrace themselves by drunkenness and all
kinds of folly in the evening. Such abuses are an inevitable consequence of keeping up the observance of days
after the real enthusiasm for the person or cause which
they commemorate has begun to grow, or has altogether
grown, cold. Little may ever have been really known
about the saint whose memory is celebrated, and that
little ceases to speak with any meaning to the minds of
later generations. The service, which was once a living
reality, becomes a cold and empty form, or the place of
religious enthusiasm is supplied by some form of sensual
excitement. Crowds of peasants will not fail to be attracted to a church which blazes with thousands of
candles arranged in fantastic patterns, and which rings
with noisy sensational music: they probably place a
superstitious faith in the tutelary power of their patron:
but how different is all this from the hearty, genuine,
reasonable devotion of more enlightened worshippers to
the Lord Himself, and the less strong but more real
respect and honour paid by such to his day! It is
surely one among many proofs of the deep and lasting
hold of Christ's character upon the mind of men, of the
applicability of its influence to all times and places, and
of its Divine superiority to that of all His followers, how-

---

[1] Aug. Confess. l. vi. 2. Epist. 64, ad Aurel. Conc. Carth. iii. c. 30.
[2] Basil Regul. Major. quæst. 40.

ever exalted, that abuses which have accompanied the
commemorations of saints have never extended in the
same degree to His day.[1]

As already remarked, Chrysostom was prevented this
year by illness from attending the festivals of saints and
martyrs, which fell very thickly between Easter and
Whitsun Day. He commences his homily preached on
the Sunday before Ascension Day with an allusion to his
recent sickness, and tells his congregation 'that, though
absent in body from their sacred festivities, he had been
present and rejoiced with them in spirit; and now, though
he had not fully recovered his health, he could not refrain
from meeting his beloved and much-longed-for flock
again. He was the more anxious also to occupy his
accustomed place on that day, because large numbers of
the rustic population from the neighbouring country had
flocked into the city and attended the services of the
church. They spoke a different dialect, but they were
one with the Christian inhabitants of the town in the
soundness of their faith; and their habits of simple piety,
pure morality, and honourable industry, put to shame the
dissolute manners and indolence which prevailed in the
city. Their peasant clergy were a noble race of men;
they might be seen one while yoking their oxen to the
plough, and marking out furrows in the soil; another
while mounting the pulpit and ploughing the hearts of
their flock; now cutting away thorns from the ground
with a sickle, now cleansing men's minds from sin by
their discourse: for they were not ashamed of hard work,
like the people of the city, but of idleness, knowing that
it was idleness which taught men vice, and had been from
the beginning to those who loved it the schoolmaster of
all iniquity. Though little skilled, by training, in reasoning or rhetoric, they proved more than a match for those

---

[1] See Dr. Hessey's 'Bampton Lectures on Sunday.'

counterfeit philosophers who paraded themselves about
the streets with their professional cloak, staff, and beard,
but who could not give any satisfactory information on
the subjects upon which they expended such a heap of
words,—as the immortality of the soul, the creation of the
world, Divine Providence, a future world and judgment.
The rustic pastor, being simply and firmly persuaded of
the truth of these things, could instruct men with clear-
ness and decision about them; he could give solid matter,
the others only polished language, like a man who should
have a sword with a silver ornamented hilt, but a weak
blade.   Their wives were not luxurious creatures, covering
themselves with unguents, paints, and dyes, but simple,
sober, quiet matrons; which increased the influence of
the pastor over the people committed to his charge, and
caused the precept of St. Paul, " having food and raiment,
let us be therewith content," to be strictly observed [1]
among them.

[1] Whether it was a regular custom for the rustic population to visit Antioch on this day, or whether it was the first great influx for trade and legal business after the recent suspension of all business, does not appear.

CHAPTER XIII.

SOME account has now been given of the most remarkable
among the homilies delivered by Chrysostom during the
first year of his priesthood; not only because to follow
the course of the Christian seasons through the cycle of
one year seemed the most convenient method of giving
specimens of his ordinary style of preaching, but also
because these first efforts were seldom if ever surpassed
in power and beauty by his later productions. A more
extensive survey of his theology, under its several heads,
is reserved for the concluding chapter; and the remainder
of the ten years during which he resided at Antioch being
uneventful as regards his life, it will be profitable to fill
up the gap by taking a glance at the world outside his
present sphere. Some knowledge of contemporary events
and men is indeed necessary to a just appreciation of his
position and conduct, when he is summoned to occupy a
more public and exalted station.

It is a melancholy scene which meets the eye. The
mighty fabric of the Empire crumbles, perhaps, more
rapidly in this decade than in any previous period of equal
length; like an old man whose constitution is thoroughly
broken.

Effeminate luxury in the civilised population is matched
by the coarse ferocity of the barbarians who hem it in or
mingle with it, and the new barbarian patch agrees ill

with the old garment, which is not strong enough to bear
it.   The historians' records are full of tales of murder,
massacre, treachery, venality, corruption, everywhere and
of all kinds.   There is no national greatness, but great
men move across the stage : Theodosius himself, generous,
just though passionate, vigorous when roused to a sense
of emergency; the last Emperor who deserved the name of
'great;' Ambrose, the intrepid advocate of religious duty
to God and man, the champion of the rights of Church
and hierarchy; Stilicho, the skilful commander of armies
and able guardian of the Empire after the death of Theodosius; Alaric, the very type of Gothic force; Rufinus and
Eutropius, the clever, scheming adventurers, destitute of
all nobility, who in a degenerate court contrive to raise
themselves to the pinnacle of power, and are suddenly
toppled headlong from it.

The most commanding public character in the West at
this time was, and for some years had been, Ambrose,
Archbishop of Milan.   Disliked but feared by the Arian
court, respected and beloved by the people, he fought in
some respects a similar battle to that in which Chrysostom
was afterwards engaged in the East, and amidst many
differences there are also many parallels in the character
and history of the two men : the same fearless courage to
speak what they believed to be God's truth in the face of
royalty itself animated both; in both cases was it rewarded by virulent persecution ; both had to contend with
an imperious, passionate woman ; both were protected from
her fury by the populace keeping guard night and day
before the walls of the church.   In A.D. 384, Ambrose had
been summoned before a royal council, and in the presence
of the young Emperor Valentinian II. and the Queen-
mother Justina, had been commanded to surrender the
Portian Basilica for the use of the Arians.   But Ambrose
had replied undauntedly, that not one inch of ground which

had been consecrated to truth would he concede to error.[1]
For more than two years Ambrose maintained his ground
against all the stratagems of his adversaries. On one
occasion they seized the Portian Basilica, but dared not
hold it in the face of the infuriated people. Messengers
from court endeavoured to maintain before the archbishop
that the Emperor had a right to dispose of the churches as
he pleased, but the argument was contemptuously dismissed as a base sophistry. 'What!' he cried; 'the
Emperor has no right to violate the house of a private
individual, and think you that he may do violence to the
house of God? No! let him take all that is mine—my
land, my money, though these belong to the poor; if he
seeks my patrimony, let him seize it; if my person, I will
present it to him : but the church it is not lawful for me
to surrender or for him to accept.'[2] Force was not more
successful than argument. Soldiers were sent to dislodge
him and his congregation from one of the basilicas, but
instead of drawing their swords they fell on their knees,
and declared that they came not to attack the archbishop
but to pray with him. The effect of an edict was tried in
A.D. 386,[3] which permitted free worship to all who professed the creed of Rimini (an Arian creed), and rendered
liable to capital punishment any who should impede the
action of the edict, as offenders against the imperial
majesty. Under shelter of this edict, the Portian Basilica
was again demanded, but Ambrose refused to recognise
such an edict, which militated against his sense of duty
to a higher power. 'God forbid that I should yield the
heritage of Jesus Christ. Naboth would not part with
the vineyard of his fathers to Ahab, and should I surrender the house of God? the heritage of Dionysius, who
died in exile for the faith; of Eustorgius the confessor; of

[1] Ambr. Ep. xx.   [2] Ibid. p. 854.
[3] Sozomen, vii. 13.   Ruf. ii. 16.

Miroclus, and all the faithful bishops which were before
me ?'[1]   But though Ambrose disobeyed, the penalties of
the edict were not enforced upon him.   An order of
banishment was served upon him, expressed in vague
terms : ' depart from the city, and go where you please.'
But Ambrose did not please to go anywhere, and remained
where he was, moving up and down the city, and officiating as usual in the churches, using in his sermons the
same Scripture parallels to indicate the Queen-mother,
' Herodias,' and ' Jezebel,' which Chrysostom afterwards
applied to the Empress Eudoxia.   He preaches day after
day, guarded by his faithful flock, who during passion-tide
suffered him not to quit the cathedral for fear of violence
to his person.   Amongst that crowd, touched by the spell
of the chants and hymns which Ambrose taught the
people [2] to beguile the tediousness of their watch, and impressed by his pungent and decisive doctrine, are two
remarkable persons, mother and son, Monica and St. Augustine.   Monica is among the most faithful in watching,
the most earnest in praying for the welfare of the bishop
and the church.   Augustine is about thirty-two years old; he
has been in many places and passed through many phases
of thought.   He has subdued the vices and follies which
stained his youth; he has shaken off the errors of Mani-
cheism which for a time enthralled him; he has been a
teacher of rhetoric at Tagaste, at Carthage, at Rome, and
Symmachus has now obtained for him a professional chair
at Milan.   But Pagan literature is losing its hold upon
him.   Plato no longer fascinates him equally with Holy
Scripture.   He is gravitating steadily towards Christianity,

[1] Ambr. Ep. xxi. Sermo cont. Aux.
p. 868.

[2] Ignatius is said to have first introduced antiphonal singing at Antioch,
Flavian and Diodorus to have established it there.   Socr. v. 8.   Theod.

ii. 19.   Basil refers to it as a common
practice, but Ambrose is generally
allowed to have introduced it to the
Western Church, and on this occasion
v. Suicer.

and in another year, April 387, just about the time that
Chrysostom is delivering his homilies on the Statues, he
will crown his mother's hopes by making a public confession of his faith, and receiving baptism at the hands of
Ambrose.[1]

One more effort was made to win the contest, this
time through diplomacy. The court proposed that the
question under dispute should be settled by arbitration,
the judges to be selected by Ambrose and Auxentius the
Arian bishop. But Ambrose would not accept the arbi-
trators nominated by Auxentius, four of whom were
Pagans and one a catechumen. In the name of himself
and the clergy of his province he denied the validity of
the tribunal. In an address to the people the same lofty
tone of independence was maintained. 'He would pay
deference to the Emperor, but never yield in things
unlawful: the Emperor was "in the Church, not above
it."'[2] So he remained master of the field. The unfinished
basilica, which had been the prize contended for, was consecrated by Ambrose with great pomp, and the joy of the
people was completed by the discovery of the martyrs'
skeletons beneath the pavement, pronounced to be those
of Gervasius and Protasius, who had suffered in the persecution of Diocletian. When demoniacs shuddered on
being placed in proximity to these reliques, and a blind
man was cured by the application to his eyes of a hand-
kerchief previously in contact with these same reliques,
the crown was put on the triumph of Ambrose; the
people were more firmly convinced than ever that his
cause was the cause of God.[3]

He was so indisputably the ablest man of the time in the
West, that, when danger impended over the state, the
very court which persecuted him turned to him to rescue
the country. Threatening messages came from the court

---

[1] Aug. Conf. ix. 7, and preceding
books.
[2] Ambr. Ep. xxi.
[3] Ambr. Ep. xxii. Aug. Conf. ix. 7.

of Maximus at Treves. Ambrose was the ambassador selected to go and pacify or intimidate the tyrant. Maximus was a Catholic, and a ruthless persecutor of those whom he deemed heretics, especially Priscillianists; yet Ambrose did not hesitate to denounce his cruelty to brethren who were Christians, however erring, as well as his disloyal attitude towards Valentinian. The embassy was unsuccessful, but the dignity of the ambassador and of the court which he represented was fully maintained. The artifices by which another ambassador, the Syrian Domninus, was blinded to the preparations of Maximus for the invasion of Italy; the passage of the Alps by the usurper, the flight of Justina and her son to Thessalonica; the prompt march of Theodosius to the succour of Italy, and his complete victory over Maximus, near Aquileia,—belong to the secular historian; but the connection between Theodosius and Ambrose will be related here more in detail.

There is no account of the first meeting between the two great characters of the day—the Emperor and the archbishop. That Ambrose immediately exercised influence over the imperial mind is inferable from the mildness of the measures by which the embers of the late revolution were extinguished. No bloody executions took place; no rigorous search for rebels was made; the mother and daughter of Maximus, who had been himself beheaded, were provided with a maintenance. Ambrose, in one of his letters, thanks the Emperor for granting liberty, at his request, to several exiles and prisoners, and for remitting the sentence of death to others.

Theodosius could be generous to enemies, and was the zealous friend of catholic Christianity, but he was a strict punisher of any violations of civil order, even when the offenders were Christian. The people of Callinicum in Osrhoene, instigated by the bishop and some fanatical monks, had set fire to a Jewish synagogue, and to

a church of the sect of Valentinians. The Emperor
directed the Count of the East to punish the offenders,
and commanded the bishop to restore the buildings at
the expense of the Church. But the extension of such
favour to heretics was in the sight of Ambrose intolerable. It might, indeed, have been wrong to disturb
civil order, but it was far more wrong to reinstate error:
to order Christians to rebuild a place of worship for those
who set Christ at nought was, in his eyes, simple profanity. He expressed his opinion to the Emperor in a
letter. It is the first great instance of the Church distinctly claiming a pre-eminence of authority superseding
that of civil law. 'If I am not worthy to be listened to
by you, how can I be worthy to transmit, as your priest,
your vows and prayers to God?' Basing on this ground
his right to speak out his mind, he declares that 'if the
Bishop of Callinicum obeyed the imperial command, he
would be guilty of culpable weakness, and the Emperor
would be responsible for it. If he refused to obey, the
Emperor could execute his will by force of arms only; the
labarum, perhaps the standard of Christ, would be employed to rebuild a temple where Christ would be denied.
What a monstrous inconsistency!' The last words which
it contained were, 'I have endeavoured to make myself
heard in the palace; do not place me under the necessity
of making myself heard in the church:' but, the letter
was unanswered, and so Ambrose put his threat into execution. He preached in Milan in the presence of the
Emperor; 'he compared the Christian priest to the
prophets of the Old Testament, whose duty it was to
proclaim God's message to the king himself, as Nathan did
to David. As the Israelites were warned not to say when
they entered the land of Canaan, "My virtue has deserved
these good things, but the Lord God has given them,"
so the Emperor should remember that he was what he was

by the mercy of God. Therefore, he ought to love the
body of Christ, the Church—to wash, kiss, and anoint her
feet, that all the dwelling where Christ reposes, might be
filled with the odour; that is, he ought to honour his
least disciples, and pardon their faults; every one of the
members of the Christian body was necessary to it, and
ought to receive his protection.'

Having uttered such words, he descended from the altar
steps. Theodosius perceived that the archbishop had taken
up his parable against him, and as Ambrose was going
out of the church he stopped him, saying, 'Is it I whom
you have made the subject of your discourse?' 'I have
said that which I deemed useful for you,' Ambrose replied.
'I perceive it is of the synagogue that you would speak,'
rejoined Theodosius. 'I own that my commands have
been a little severe, but I have already softened them, and
these monks are troublesome men.' 'I am going to offer
the sacrifice,' said Ambrose, 'enable me to do so without
fear for you; deliver me from the load which oppresses
my spirit.' 'It shall be so,' responded the Emperor;
'my orders shall be mitigated; I give you my promise.'
But Ambrose was not satisfied with so vague an assurance.
'Suppress the whole matter,' he said; 'swear it to me,
and, on your sworn promise, I proceed to offer the sacrifice.' The Emperor swore; Ambrose celebrated mass;
'and never,' said he, in a letter written the day after to his
sister, 'did I experience such sensible marks of the presence
of God in prayer.'[1]

In the spring of A.D. 389, Theodosius made his triumphal
entry into Rome, accompanied by Valentinian and his own
son Honorius, a boy of ten. His arrival was preceded by
two popular enactments; one a decree, renouncing for
himself and family all bequests made by codicils—striking
a blow at a vicious custom which had long prevailed, of

---

[1] Ambr. Ep. xl. and xli.

bribing imperial favour for particular families, by be-
queathing large legacies to the reigning sovereign. By
heathen emperors these bequests had been sought with
great cupidity; sick or old men were sometimes threatened
with an acceleration of death, unless they satisfied the
royal expectations in this way. The other, no less popular decree was, to abolish the custom by which royal
couriers, when conveying news of victory, exacted donations from the villages through which they passed. The
victory of Theodosius over Maximus was the first which
had been gratuitously proclaimed along the route to
Rome; and the people greeted the Emperor as he made
his progress to the capital with all the warmer welcome
in consequence.[1]

Rome had at this period scarcely recovered from the
ferment into which society had been thrown by the three
years' residence of Jerome, A.D. 382–385. His denunciations of clerical luxury; his cutting satires on the vices
and follies of the laity; his allurement to monastic life of
some of the wealthiest and noblest of the Roman ladies,
had stirred up a tumult of feeling for the most part adverse to him. But Theodosius prudently abstained from
interfering with the religious debates of Rome. In Constantinople he was the absolute sovereign; in Rome he
desired to appear simply as the successful general and the
foremost citizen. He assumed no imperial or Asiatic splendour; he exhibited no fastidious abhorrence of statues,
temples, and other remnants of Paganism. Symmachus,
the most eminent Pagan citizen, was cordially received,
and gratified by the promise of consulship. The result of
this amiable and moderate conduct was that some of the
most powerful Roman families embraced the faith of the
Emperor.

A.D. 390. But the generosity which Theodosius had

---

[1] Cod. Theod. iv. v. 4, l. 2. De Broglie, vol. vi. p. 257.

manifested towards the people of Antioch, his moderation
after the defeat of Maximus, and during his triumphal
residence in Rome, was presently stained by one of those
paroxysms of anger to which he was occasionally subject.
The intercession of Flavian had averted any practical
expression of such emotion in the case of the sedition of
Antioch; the authority of Ambrose, too late to prevent
the crime, was exercised to exact penance for the cruel
vengeance executed on the people of Thessalonica.

Botheric, the governor of Thessalonica, had imprisoned
a favourite charioteer for attempting to commit a disgust-
ing crime. The people, passionately attached to the races
of the circus, demanded his release on a certain day to
take part in the contest. The governor refused, and the
people then broke out into rebellion; the tumult was with
difficulty quelled by the troops, and not before Botheric
had been mortally wounded, several other officers torn
to pieces, and their mangled remains dragged through
the streets. The irritation of the Emperor, on hearing of
this barbarous violence, was extreme; and all the more so,
that of Thessalonica he could have expected better things.
It did not contain, like Antioch, Rome, or Alexandria, a
large mixed population, but one almost exclusively Christian, and for the most part even Catholic. The city was
the scene of his early triumphs and frequently honoured
by his visits. It is possible that Ambrose may have
pushed his exhortations to clemency too far in the first
glow of the Emperor's resentment. At any rate, the
counsel of those rivals or enemies of Ambrose, who represented that the affair belonged purely to civil government, and should be decided independently of all
clerical interference, prevailed. Rufinus, the flattering,
heartless courtier, persuaded Theodosius that a public
offence of such magnitude deserved the most merciless
punishment which could be inflicted. Orders were issued

to the officials at Thessalonica to assemble the populace, as
if for a fête, in the circus, and then to let in the troops upon
them. This barbarous mandate was too faithfully executed.
The unsuspecting victims crowded into their favourite
place of amusement; at a given signal the soldiers rushed
in, and in the course of two or three hours the ground was
strewn with some 7,000 corpses of men, women, and children.[1] The horror of the people of Milan was only equalled
by their astonishment. Was it possible that he who had
displayed such magnanimity and Christian moderation
could be guilty of an act which savoured of the most
heathen treachery and ferocity? When the Emperor
returned from Rome, Ambrose withdrew from Milan into
the country, and thence wrote to him a letter expressing
his horror at the recent massacre; exhorting him to the
deepest repentance and humiliation as the only hope of
obtaining mercy from God, and declaring that he could
not celebrate mass again in his presence. The mode by
which the Emperor was to expiate his guilt is not indicated in this epistle, and he presented himself soon afterwards at the doors of the cathedral church with his usual
royal retinue. But he was confronted by Ambrose in his
pontifical robes, who with flashing eyes expressed his
astonishment at such audacity, and barred the entrance
with his person. 'I see, Emperor, you are ignorant of
the flagrancy of the murder which you have perpetrated.
Perhaps your unlimited power blinds you to your guilt,
and obscures your reason. Yet consider your frail and
mortal nature; think of the dust from which you were
formed, and to which you will return, and beneath the
splendid veil of your purple recognise the infirmity of the
flesh which it covers. You rule over men who are your
brethren by nature, and by service to a common King, the
Creator of all things. How then will you dare to plant

---

[1] Soz. vii. 25. Theod. v. 17. Ambr. Ep. li. De Broglie, vi. 302, &c.

your feet in His sanctuary, and elevate your hands towards Him, all dripping as they are with the blood of men unjustly slain? How will you take into your hands the sacred body of the Lord, or dare to put His precious blood to those lips, which by a word of anger have spilt the blood of so many innocent victims? Withdraw, then, and add not a fresh crime to those with which you are already burdened.' The Emperor returned, conscience-stricken and weeping, to his palace. For eight months no intercourse took place between him and Ambrose. Christmas approached; exclusion from the church at such a season seemed insupportable to the Emperor. Rufinus found him one day dissolved in tears. 'The church of God,' he cried, 'is open to the slave and the beggar, but to me it is closed, and with it the gates of heaven; for I remember the words of the Lord, "Whatsoever ye shall bind on earth shall be bound in heaven."' Rufinus sought to console him : 'I will hasten to Ambrose, and force him to release you from this bond.' 'No,' said the Emperor, 'you will not persuade Ambrose to violate divine law from any fear of imperial power.' Rufinus, however, sought an interview with the archbishop; but Ambrose spurned him indignantly from him, as being the chief counsellor of the late massacre. Rufinus informed him that the Emperor was approaching. 'If he comes,' said the prelate, 'I will repel him from the vestibule of the church.' The minister returned to the Emperor discomfited, and advised him to abstain from visiting the church; but Theodosius had subdued all pride, and replied that he would now go and submit to any humiliation which Ambrose might see proper to impose. He advanced to the church. Perceiving the archbishop in the exterior court or atrium, he cried, 'I have come; deliver me from my sins.' 'What madness,' replied Ambrose, 'has prompted you to violate the sanctuary, and to trample on divine law?' 'I ask for my deliverance,' said the humbled monarch; 'shut not the door which God has opened to all penitents.' 'And where is your penitence?' said the bishop; 'show me your remedies for healing your wounds.' 'It is for *you* to show them to *me*,' Theodosius replied; 'for me to accept them.' Once more Ambrose had gained the day. He could prescribe his own terms. First, he required that the recurrence of a similar crime should be guarded against by a decree which should interpose a delay of thirty days between a sentence of confiscation or death and the execution of it. At the expiration of this period the sentence was to be presented to the Emperor for final reconsideration. Theodosius consented, ordered the law to be drawn up, and subscribed it with his own hand. He was then admitted within the walls, but in deeply penitential guise; stripped of imperial ornaments, prostrate on the pavement, beating his breast, tearing his hair, and crying aloud, 'My soul cleaveth unto the dust, quicken thou me according to thy word.' So he remained during the first portion of the Liturgy. When the offertory began, he rose, advanced within the choir to present his offering, and was about to resume the place which at Constantinople he usually occupied—a seat in the midst of the clergy, in the more elevated portion of the choir. But Ambrose determined, by taking advantage of the Emperor's present humiliation, to put a stop to this custom. An archdeacon stepped up to Theodosius, and informed him that no layman might remain in the choir during the celebration. The submissive Emperor withdrew outside the rails. When he had returned to Constantinople, he was invited by Nectarius, the archbishop, to occupy his accustomed chair in the choir. 'No!' replied Theodosius, with a sigh; 'I have learned at Milan the insignificance of an Emperor in the Church, and the difference between him and a bishop. But no one here tells me the truth. I know not

any bishop save Ambrose who deserves the name.'[1] He
had hit the truth. The difference between the conduct of
Ambrose and of Nectarius symbolised the difference between the character of the Western and Eastern Church
generally; the one stern, commanding, jealous of any
encroachment of the civil power; the other, subservient,
submissive, courtier-like; the one aspiring and advancing,
the other receding and decadent. Chrysostom would have
told him the truth; but Chrysostom, in his uncompromising and fearless honesty of purpose and speech is such a
grand exception among the patriarchs of Constantinople,
that he proves the general rule. Even Flavian had only
supplicated mercy from the Emperor; Ambrose *commanded* it.

On one subject, the deference of Theodosius for the
opinion of Ambrose caused him some embarrassment.
Ambrose, in common with the other Western prelates, had
recognised Paulinus as Bishop of Antioch—the priest of
the Eustathian party who had been consecrated by Lucifer
of Cagliari; and he now acknowledged Evagrius, his successor. Theodosius was distracted between his friendship
for Flavian, the rival of Evagrius, and for Ambrose.
Flavian was summoned to court. The Emperor implored
him to go to Rome and justify his claims before the Pope;
but Flavian refused. At the suggestion of Ambrose, the
Western Bishops assembled in council at Capua, and there
delegated the decision to Theophilus, Patriarch of Alexandria. Once more Flavian was summoned to court, and
advised to submit to the arbitration of Theophilus; but
he was still intractable. 'Take my bishopric at once, and
give it to whom you please; but I will submit neither my
honour nor my faith to the judgment of my equals.' Nearly
eighteen months were consumed in these negotiations.
The West grew impatient. The letters of Ambrose took

[1] Theod. v. 18. De Broglie, vol. vi. 302 et seq.

a severer tone : ' Flavian has something to fear; that is
why he avoids examination. Will he place himself outside the Church, the communion of Rome, and intercourse
with his brethren ?' The strife was mercifully broken off
by the sudden death of Evagrius, before he had time to
designate a successor; and the wound was salved, though
not healed. That final good work was destined to be
accomplished by Chrysostom.[1]

A.D. 392. Only a few years more of life remained for
Theodosius, and his reign was occupied at the end as at
the beginning, by quelling rebellion in the West. When
he returned to the East, in A.D. 391, after the defeat of
Maximus, he had generously left the youthful Valentinian
in full possession of all his hereditary dominions, which
he had rescued for him from the usurper. Arbogastes, a
Gaul, was appointed general of the forces; Ambrose was
a kind of general counsellor. But Arbogastes was bold,
ambitious, unscrupulous. He possessed much power; he
determined to acquire the whole. He obeyed the commands of his young sovereign or not, as suited his pleasure and purposes, and surrounded him with creatures of
his own, who, under the semblance of courtiers, acted as
spies and gaolers. Valentinian's residence at Vienne, in
Gaul, became his prison rather than his palace. The sequel
belongs to secular history, and is well known. An open
rupture took place. Arbogastes threw off the mask.
Valentinian was found strangled, too late to receive baptism at the hands of Ambrose, whose coming he had
awaited with great eagerness, as soon as he knew that his
life was in danger.[2] Once more Italy became the prey of
a usurper; once more the veteran Emperor of the East
roused himself from his well-earned repose, collected a
huge force, consulted John, the hermit of the Thebaid, on

---

[1] Sozom. vii. 15. Socr. v. 15. Ambr. Ep. lvi. Theod. v. 23.
[2] Ambr. de ob. Val.

the issue of the war, solicited the favour of Heaven by visiting the principal places of devotion in the city, and kneeling on flint before the tombs of martyrs and apostles, then set out on his march, and by the summer of A.D. 394 again looked down from the Alps on the plains of Venetia, near the scene of his former victory over one usurper, and now covered with the tents belonging to the army of another. He prosecuted the campaign in the same religious spirit in which he had undertaken it. The first assault made on the 5th of September against the enemy was repulsed. Theodosius rallied and harangued the troops, lifted up his eyes to heaven, and cried, 'O Lord, Thou knowest that I have undertaken this war only for the honour of thy Son, and not to leave crime unpunished; stretch forth, I pray Thee, thy hand over thy servants, that the heathen say not of us " where is their God?"' The second assault was more successful; the night was spent by the Emperor in prayer, who was rewarded towards dawn by a vision of two horsemen, clothed in white, who bade him be of good cheer, for that they were the apostles St. Philip and St. John, and would not fail to come to his succour on the following day. The issue of that day was decisive; the overthrow of Arbogastes complete; his army routed; himself slain.[1]

The conqueror was received by Ambrose, at Milan, with transports of joy. The victory was nobly signalised by a display of Christian clemency. Free pardon was proclaimed in the church (whither the offenders had fled for refuge) to all those Milanese who had joined the side of the usurper. Among them were the children of Arbogastes, and of the puppet king which he had set up, Eugenius. They were made to expiate the crimes of their pagan fathers by submitting to baptism.[2]

[1] Theod. v. 24. Socr. v. 25. Sozom. vii. 24. De Broglie, vi. c. 8.
[2] Ambr. Ep. lxi. lxii.

P

But there was an increasing shade of gloom which overcast the general sunshine of joy. The health of Theodosius, long undermined by a disease, was now manifestly fast giving way. He was sensible of his danger, and despatched a message to Constantinople, desiring that his younger son, Honorius, should be sent to join him at Milan. The young prince, accompanied by his cousin Serena (the wife of Stilicho) and his little sister Placidia, set off without delay. They reached Milan early in the year A.D. 395. Some shocks of earthquake, and terrific storms, which coincided with their arrival, were regarded as portents of future evil. The malady of Theodosius, a dropsical disorder, was rapidly gaining ground. He revived a little at the sight of his son, and received the Eucharist from the hands of Ambrose, which he had hitherto refused, as having too recently been engaged in the sanguinary scenes of war. He gave audience to a deputation of western bishops, who came to pay him homage, and besought them to heal the schism of Antioch by acknowledging Flavian. He besought the Pagan members of the senate of Rome to embrace the Christian faith, adding the somewhat potent argument, that Pagan worship must no longer expect any pecuniary aid from the State. He appeared for a few times at the circus, where races were held in honour of his victory and the arrival of the young prince; but one day, while dining, he was taken suddenly worse, and expired early the next morning, Jan. 17th, A.D. 395, in the fiftieth year of his age, and the sixteenth of his reign. Those who watched by his bedside thought they detected the name of Ambrose faintly murmured by his dying lips.[1]

So passed away the last great Emperor of the Roman world.[2] He had persistently kept in view a single and

[1] Socr. v. 26. Sozom. vii. 29. Ambrosii Vita a Paul. scripta, de Obit. Theod.

[2] Of course I do not forget that the idea and name of Roman Emperor and Roman Empire lived on for centuries more, but the elevation of Charlemagne was a revolt against the

noble aim—the consolidation of the Empire. He had repelled invasion, crushed rebellion, laboured to convert
heathenism, to suppress heresy, to reconcile opposing factions in the Church; and the work seemed advancing
when he was called away, and years ensued of misrule
and disorder, Gothic devastation, and internal corruption
and decadence.

The history of the Empire under Arcadius and Honorius
presents a pitiable picture of imbecility on the part of the
sovereigns; of infidelity and unscrupulous ambition on the
part of their ministers. Theodosius himself, as he lay on
his death-bed, was perhaps conscious of impending troubles. The words supposed by Claudian to be spoken by
the shade of Theodosius to his son Arcadius, ' Res incom-
positas fateor tumidasque reliqui,' [1] express at any rate
the true condition of affairs. To Stilicho he commended
his younger son, Honorius, and the interests of the Western
Empire, but added a request that he would not neglect
Arcadius and the Eastern portion of the Empire also. The
legal guardian, however, of Arcadius was not a man who
would tamely submit to any supervision, or to any encroachment, fancied or real, upon the rights of his office.
He was as jealous of Stilicho as Constantinople was of
Rome. Discernment of character cannot be reckoned
among the great qualities of Theodosius; otherwise he
would not have entrusted his two sons to the guardianship of two men dissimilar in all respects but one—an
insatiable love of power. He had placed the two weak
princes in the hands of deadly rivals.

Rufinus, the guardian of Arcadius and regent of the
East, was an Aquitanian Gaul, born at Elusa, the modern
Eause, at the foot of the Pyrenees. [2] He was the very
model of an accomplished adventurer. Sprung from

old order of things. He can hardly   successor of Augustus.
be regarded as a successor of Theo-   [1] Claud. de Bello Gild. 293.
dosius so truly as Theodosius was a   [2] Claud. in Ruf. i. v. 137.

poverty and obscurity, he was gifted by nature with a handsome figure, a noble demeanour, a ready tongue, an inventive, versatile wit.[1] He made his way, after residing in Milan and Rome, to the court of Constantinople ; and found in Theodosius a patron who could appreciate his talents without detecting his vices. He rapidly rose till he had attained the high distinction of 'Master of the Offices,' in A.D. 390, of consul, in connection with Arcadius, in A.D. 392, and, in A.D. 394, prætorian prefect in presenti, a position second only to that of the Emperor himself.[2] He affected the warmest zeal for the Catholic faith, and threw himself heartily into the schemes of Theodosius for the suppression of heresy, no less than into those for the consolidation of the social and political fabric.

But underneath this appearance of patriotic enthusiasm he indulged what Claudian terms an ' accursed thirst' for gain.[3] By unjust law-suits he wrested patrimonies from the poor, and manœuvred to unite the daughters and widows of the wealthy in marriage with his own favourites, in order that he might reap their legacies and gifts. If any exposure of these iniquities was threatened, he stopped the mouths of accusers by large bribes, and compensated his extortions from towns by making presents to their churches or enlarging their public buildings.

When Theodosius departed for the Italian war, Rufinus, being left as guardian of Arcadius, began to conceive the project of elevating himself to the imperial throne. He made a magnificent display of his piety. Hard by his villa, or rather palace, in the suburb of Chalcedon, called the Oak, a spot which will presently acquire a melancholy notoriety in the history of Chrysostom, he had built a

[1] Philostorg. xi. 3. For much assistance in his notices of Rufinus and Eutropius, the writer must pay his acknowledgments to the admirable work by M. Amédée Thierry, ' Les trois ministres des fils de Théodose.' Rufin, Eutrope, Stilicon.

[2] Gibbon, iii. 67. Zozim. iv. 51.

[3] Claud. in Ruf. i. v. 220.

church, and a monastery attached to it. This church he now determined to dedicate with great pomp, and at the same time to be baptized himself. For this purpose he assembled nineteen eastern bishops, chiefly metropolitans, and a number of Egyptian hermits; strange-looking figures, who, with their raiment of skins, their flowing beards and long hair, excited much superstitious reverence. In the midst of this august assembly, the depredator of the East descended into the baptismal waters, arrayed in the white robes typical of innocence. The celebrated Egyptian solitary, Ammonius (who will come before us again), administered the Sacrament, and Gregory of Nyssa delivered a discourse.[1] Rufinus now surrounded himself with a powerful party of followers; Arcadius was too stupid to see, or too timid to oppose, the dangerous ambition of his so-called protector.

But the death of Theodosius and the elevation of Stilicho to the guardianship of the West brought the intriguer face to face with an able and determined soldier, who united some of the ferocity of the barbarian with the stedfast patriotism of an old Roman. This last, indeed, was the character which Stilicho, a Vandal by birth, but educated at Rome, more especially emulated. It was his ambition to be compared to Fabricius, Curtius, Camillus.[2] Great was his delight when Claudius, himself called a second Virgil, likened him in his verses to Scipio.[3] The poet declared that Theodosius had never fought without Stilicho, though Stilicho had fought without Theodosius. He was made not only the guardian, but father-in-law of Honorius, who was betrothed to his eldest daughter beside the deathbed of Theodosius; the father dying in the happy assurance that, by creating this parental tie, he had secured the fidelity of his minister. The boy and

---

[1] See references in Thierry, p. 19.
[2] De Laud. Stil. ii. v. 379.
[3] 'Noster Scipiades Stilicho.' De Consulat. Stilic. præf. v. 21.

girl were brought into the sick room, exchanged rings, and repeated the words which were dictated to them.[1]

The regent of the East naturally became profoundly jealous of the regent of the West, and in point of royal connection determined to be even with him.   He humoured Arcadius into a consent to marry his own daughter; and his scheme seemed on the point of completion when an inopportune matter of business took him away to Antioch, and his enemy, the Chamberlain Eutropius, took advantage of his absence to frustrate the plan.   A Frankish general, called Bautho, who had been elevated to the consulship, but had prematurely died, left a daughter of rare beauty, named Eudoxia.   The orphan girl was brought up by a friend of Bautho, the son of Promotus, a magister militum, whom Rufinus, in revenge for an insult, had caused to be assassinated.   Eutropius introduced a portrait of the young beauty to the notice of Arcadius.   Curiosity, and soon a tenderer sentiment, were excited in the young Emperor's breast; the cunning chamberlain fanned the flame, till he was able to persuade the royal youth that Eudoxia was a more eligible bride than the daughter of the low-born Gaul.[2]   The intrigue was conducted with such secrecy, that Rufinus, on his return from Antioch, remained unsuspicious, and his boastful remarks on the approaching nuptials excited the indignation of the public.   The wedding-day was fixed for April 25, A.D. 395.   Eutropius selected from the imperial wardrobe some of the costliest female robes and jewels which it contained.   They were placed on litters, which, escorted by a large train of splendidly apparelled serving-men, paraded the streets on the way, as was supposed, to the house of Rufinus.   What was the astonishment of the populace when the procession suddenly turned in another direction, and presently stopped in

---

[1] Claud. de Nupt. Honor. et Mariæ.   [2] Zosim. v. 3.

front of the house of Promotus! A loud shout of joy
burst from the lips of the multitude, and proclaimed to
Rufinus the unpopularity of his project, and the general
satisfaction at its defeat. The bride thus cunningly substituted was destined to play a conspicuous part in the
later scenes of Chrysostom's career. She inherited the
fair beauty, the energetic spirit, the impulsive, sometimes
fierce temper of the race from which she sprang. Her
father had remained firmly attached to the pagan religion
of his ancestors, but, in deference to Theodosius, his
patron, he had allowed his daughter to be baptized and
educated in the Christian faith.[1] Impatient of control,
she resolved to possess herself of her husband's confidence
in order to govern through him, and gradually to dis-
engage herself from the management alike of Rufinus and
Eutropius.

Rufinus had been thoroughly outwitted in his matrimonial scheme, but his resources were far from being
exhausted. The sequel of his life belongs too exclusively
to secular history to be more than glanced at here. He
played a subtle and desperate game, seldom, if ever, surpassed in villany. Some Hunnish tribes, encouraged by
him, made incursions into Armenia, Pontus, Cappadocia,
and even as far as the vicinity of Antioch.[2] The court
was in the extremity of alarm, for the main forces of the
army and treasury had been drained to the West when
Theodosius marched against Arbogastes, and remained in
the hands of Stilicho. Worse still, the formidable chieftain Alaric, of the royal race of the Visigoths, who had
lately distinguished himself in the Italian wars under
Theodosius, began to complain of unrequited services, and
with a motley force of Huns, Alani, Sarmatians, and

[1] Symmach. Ep. iv. 15 and 16.
[2] Possibly alluded to by Chrysostom
in hom. iv. de Penitentiâ, c. 2, where
he mentions 'incursions of enemies'
among other recent calamities. These
homilies were probably delivered in
A.D. 395.

Goths, descended into Thrace, and ravaged the country up to the walls of Constantinople. The inhabitants were convulsed with panic; all except the artful intriguer, who had already struck his bargain with the invaders. He rode out of Constantinople accoutred as a Gothic warrior, went through the farce of an interview with Alaric, and returned with the joyful intelligence that his intercessions had saved the city, and that the Gothic prince had consented to withdraw his troops. And so he did; not, however, to retire to the Gothic settlements in the north, but to pour southwards in a devastating flood over Greece. This was the plot of Rufinus. The possession of the Illyrian provinces was disputed between the courts of East and West. Alaric occupied these. Stilicho, with extraordinary energy, collected a large army, advanced against the devastator, who was supposed to be the common enemy of the whole Empire; but when on the point of attacking him, he was arrested by a message from Constantinople, which commanded him to abstain from any hostilities against the ravager of Greece. 'He was the good friend of Arcadius: he occupied the province of Illyria as his ally, which Stilicho was to evacuate immediately, and to restore the troops and treasure which belonged to the East.' The troops were sent back by Stilicho under the command of Gaïnas, but with the secret understanding that he should compass the death of Rufinus. The result is well known. Rufinus fell just as he was placing his foot on the topmost round of his ladder of ambition. He was standing on the tribune, where Arcadius was to proclaim him Cæsar, in the presence of a vast multitude; he was making a flowery harangue to the troops, complimenting them on their exploits, congratulating them on their restoration to their homes, when those very troops closed in upon him, plunged their swords into his body, and presently hacked it to pieces. A soldier who got hold of his right arm, and having crooked the fingers of the hand, went about the town, holding it in front of him, and crying, 'An obol, an obol for him who never had enough,' collected a large sum by his grim and savage jest.[1]

Arcadius was quite incapable of handling the reins of government himself, and the downfall of one all-powerful minister would in any case have been quickly followed by the rise of another; but, as it happened, there was one ready to step immediately into the vacant place. The fortunes of this person, the eunuch Eutropius, ran a strange career. Born a slave, somewhere in the region of the Euphrates, and condemned in infancy to the most degraded condition possible even to slavery, he passed in boyhood and youth through the hands of many owners. He performed the most menial offices as a household slave, cutting wood, drawing water, or whisking the flies from his mistress's face with a large fan. Arinthus, an old magister militum, who had become possessed of him, presented him to his daughter on her marriage; and, in the words of Claudian, 'the future consul of the East was made over as part of a marriage dowry.'[2] But the young lady grew tired of the slave, who was getting elderly and wrinkled, and, without attempting to sell him, simply turned him out of doors.[3] He lived for a time, picking up a precarious livelihood, and often in great want, till an officer about court at Constantinople took pity on him, and with some difficulty obtained for him a situation in the lowest ranks of the imperial chamberlains.[4] This was the beginning of his rise. By the diligence and precision with which he discharged his ordinary duties, by occasional witty sayings, and the semblance of a fervent piety,

---

[1] Thierry, pp. 35-78. Claud. in Ruf. bk. ii.

[2] In Eutrop. i. v. 104. 105.

[3] 'Contemptu jam liber erat.'— Claud. in Eutrop. i. v. 132.

[4] Ibid. v. 148, 149.

he attracted the notice of the Emperor Theodosius, and
gradually acquired his confidence so as to be employed
on difficult and delicate missions. He it was whom the
Emperor sent to consult the hermit John in Egypt before
undertaking the Italian campaign in A.D. 394.[1]

On the death of Theodosius he became, in the capacity
of grand chamberlain, the intimate adviser and constant
attendant of Arcadius; and, when Rufinus was removed,
the government was practically in his hands, though he
was careful to avoid the error of his late rival, and was
content with the reality without the display of power.
He continued to execute all the household duties which
fell to his lot as chamberlain with humble assiduity, and
sought no other title than what he possessed.[2] But it was
soon apparent, to the amusement of the East and the
indignation of the West, that the eunuch slave was really
master of the Emperor of half the Roman world. He
gradually removed by his arts the friends of Theodosius
from the principal posts of trust, and replaced them by
creatures of his own. By surrounding his royal charge
with a crowd of frivolous companions; by dissipating his
thoughts amidst a perpetual round of amusement, public
spectacles, chariot races, and the like; by taking him
every spring to Ancyra in Phrygia, where he was subjected
to the soft enchantments of a delicious climate and luxurious manner of life, he made the naturally feeble mind
of Arcadius more feeble still, and withdrew it from the
influence of every superior intellect but his own.[3]

Whilst the effeminate monarch languished in inglorious
ease in Phrygia, the fairest and most renowned portions
of his Empire were overrun by the barbarian forces of
Alaric. The sacred pass of Thermopylæ was violated by
the Gothic prince, and the ravager spread his devasta-

---

[1] Sozom. vii. 22.   [3] Claud. in Eutrop. i. 427, &c.; ii.
[2] Philostorg. xi. 5.   97, &c.

tions over Peloponnesus. Once more Stilicho hastened
to the rescue; once more his hand was stayed by the
astonishing announcement that Alaric was rewarded for
his career of spoliation by being made commander-in-
chief of the forces of the East. Thus the invader was
turned into the position of friend, and the defender into
the position of rebel, who had to withdraw with feelings
of shame, disappointment, and rage. To such base arts
did the court of Arcadius, under the direction of Eutropius, stoop to protect itself in its pitiful jealousy of its
rival in the West.[1]

Eutropius mounted to the summit of power by the
simple process of putting all dangerous competitors out
of the way, under various pretexts, as treasonable or
otherwise public offenders.[2] He deprived them of their
last hope of escape, by abolishing the right of the Church
to afford asylum to fugitives.[3] He sold the chief functions
of the State, and the command of the provinces, to the
highest bidders. He was ambitious even of military
glory; and, to the amusement of the enemy, as well as of
the imperial army, appeared in military costume at the
head of the troops, to repel an incursion of Huns. He
succeeded, however, more in his negotiations by which he
bought off the enemy, than in his martial exploits, and
returned mortified by the ridicule which had attended his
attempts in war.[4]

From the pettiest detail of domestic life to the most
serious affairs of state, the minister was supreme. Arcadius was little more than a magnificently dressed puppet.
The descriptions of his palace read like accounts in
fairy tales: it swarmed with slaves of every conceivable
variety of race, profession, and costume; the floors of the

---

[1] Thierry, pp. 97–126. Zosim. v. 5.
Claud. in Eutrop. ii.
[2] Zosim. v. 8, 9, 12.
[3] Sozom. viii. 7.
[4] Claud. in Eutrop. i. 235, &c.

imperial apartments were sprinkled with gold dust, in the carriage of which from Asia a special service of vessels and waggons was constantly engaged.[1]   The great annual public spectacle was the departure of the Emperor for his summer sojourn in Phrygia.   From an early hour the streets were thronged with people eagerly waiting for the pageant.   At length, from the portals of the palace there issued a gorgeous procession; soldiers in white uniform, with gold-brocaded ensigns; then the body guard, called domestics, with their tribunes and generals arrayed in robes flashing with gold, mounted on horses with golden caparisons; each rider bore a gilded lance in the right hand, and in the left a gilded shield studded with precious stones.   In the rear, surrounded by a grand cortege of state officials, came the imperial car, drawn by milk-white mules, clothed in purple housings, which were tricked out with gold and jewels.   The sides of the car also were gilded, and flashed out rays of golden light as it moved along towards the harbour, where rode a fleet of barges richly decorated, waiting to convey the royal traveller to the opposite shore of the Bosphorus.   In strange contrast to all this splendour appeared in the centre of the car the dull and somnolent countenance of the young Arcadius and the wrinkled visage of his old minister.   The multitude, ever greedy of show, would eagerly strain forward their necks to catch a glimpse, if it were only of the imperial ear-rings, or the circlet of his diadem, or the strings of pearls upon his robe.   With such empty exhibitions of their puppet king did the wily minister seek to amuse the frivolous inhabitants of the capital, while he himself enjoyed the exercise of real power.[2]

---

[1] Synes. de Regno, p. 16.
[2] Claud. in Eutrop. ii. 95.   Thierry, p. 162, &c.

CHAPTER XIV.

SUCH was the political and social condition of the Empire in the year A.D. 397. In September of that year died Nectarius, Archbishop of Constantinople, a man of an easy, amiable disposition, who, not taking a very elevated or severe view of the duties of his position, had administered the see for sixteen years, without annoyance, but without distinction.[1] A conscientious discharge, indeed, of episcopal duties was at this epoch beset by no small difficulties in the great cities of the Empire. Bishops of important sees now occupied a high social rank.[2] This had to be assumed (in Constantinople at least) in the midst of an intriguing, factious court, a corrupt, frivolous people, and a demoralised, or at least secularised, clergy. 'Nothing,' said St. Augustine, 'can in this life, and especially at this time, be easier or more agreeable than the office of bishop, presbyter, or deacon, if discharged in a perfunctory and adulatory manner; nothing can in this life, and especially at this time, be more laborious and perilous than such an office, if discharged as our heavenly Commander bids us.'[3] And the testimony of Chrysostom's friend, Isidore, Abbot of Pelusium, is to the same effect: 'True freedom and independence are not to be found in these

[1] Socr. vi. 2.
[2] See Chrysostom's own remarks in De Sacerdotis, b. iii., cited above in

c. iv. and in Act. Apost. hom. iii. 5.
[3] Epist. xxi. ad Valerium.

distinguished positions : it is so difficult to rule some, and to submit to others ; to direct some, and to be directed by others ; to be complaisant to some and severe to others.' Into this difficult and delicate position the pious, single-minded, unworldly, but courageous preacher of Antioch was to be suddenly transplanted, and that in a city where the difficulties incident to such a position existed in peculiar force.

At the time of the decease of Nectarius, several bishops happened to be sojourning in Constantinople on business, and as tidings of the vacancy of the see got abroad, the number of episcopal visitors largely increased ; some coming as candidates, others by the invitation of the Emperor, who wished to make the ceremony of consecration as dignified and august as possible.[1] Constantinople became convulsed by all those factious disputes and dissensions which usually attended the election of a bishop to an important see, and which Chrysostom has so vividly described in his treatise on the priesthood.[2] From dawn of day the places of public resort were occupied by the candidates and their partisans paying court, or paying bribes to the common people ; canvassing the nobles and the wealthy not without the potent aid of rich and costly gifts, some statue from Greece or silk from India, or perfumes from Arabia.[3] One of the most conspicuous candidates was Isidore, a presbyter of Alexandria. His claims were eagerly pushed by Theophilus, Archbishop of Alexandria, who had a strong personal interest in securing his success. For Isidore was the depositary of a rather awkward secret in the past history of Theophilus himself. When the war between Theodosius and the usurper Maximus was impending, Isidore had been despatched by the Archbishop to Italy

---

with letters of congratulation to be presented to him who
should prove the conqueror. Isidore waited till victory
had declared itself in favour of Theodosius; presented
the humble felicitations of the patriarch, and returned to
Alexandria. But he was unable on his return to produce
the other letter, designed for Maximus had he proved
the victor. According to his own account, it had been
abstracted by the reader who had accompanied him on
the journey. Theophilus, however, suspected the fidelity
of Isidore himself, and that some ugly stories which
began to circulate respecting the affair had emanated
from him. The see of Constantinople, if secured through
his interest, would be an effectual means, he thought, of
stopping the mouth of Isidore.[1] But he was doomed to
disappointment. While the several candidates and their
patrons were exhausting all their arts on the spot to
obtain the favour of the electors, the clergy and people,
distracted by conflicting bribes and arguments, unani-
mously decided to summon a man from a distance who
had not come forward at all. They submitted the name
of Chrysostom to the Emperor, who immediately approved their choice.[2] In fact, the election of Chrysostom
was in all probability the suggestion of Eutropius.
During a recent visit on public business to Antioch he
had heard and recognised the eloquence of the great
preacher. Even if the heart of the man was not touched
by the pungent warnings, or warmed by the kindling
exhortations of Chrysostom, he had plenty of astuteness to
perceive, if only such an eloquence could be employed in
the service of the Government, what a powerful engine
it would be.[3] The appointment, at any rate, was certain
to be welcomed by the people, and of popularity Eutropius
stood greatly in need. By the people of Antioch indeed

---

[1] Socr. vi. 2. Sozom. viii. 2. Pallad.
Dial.

[2] Socr. vi. 2.   Sozom. viii. 2.

[3] Pallad. Dial. c. 5.

Chrysostom was so deeply and ardently beloved, that the question was how to remove him without causing a disturbance of the public peace. The excitable feelings of the populace at Antioch were at all times a very powder train which needed but the application of a spark to cause a serious explosion of tumult. The difficulty was solved by a mixture of force and fraud highly characteristic of the chief designer and executor of the project. Eutropius addressed a letter to Asterius, the Count of the East, who resided in Antioch, and who promptly acted on his instructions. He proposed to the unsuspecting Chrysostom that they should pay a visit together to one of the martyries outside the city walls. Well pleased to make this pious pilgrimage, the saintly preacher accompanied his captor through the Roman gate, and turned his back on his beloved native city, which he was destined never to revisit. At the martyry he was seized by some Government officials, and carried on to Pagræ, the first station on the high road for Constantinople. Here a chariot and horses awaited them, together with one of the imperial chamberlains, a 'magister militum,' and an escort of soldiers. The bewildered Chrysostom was hurried into the chariot, without any attention being paid to his remonstrances or enquiries; the horses were put into a smart gallop and the pace well kept up to the next stage, where a similar equipage was in waiting. Such was the rapid, but, considering all the circumstances, undignified approach of the future archbishop to take possession of his see.[1]

Great was the joy of the people on his arrival, great the mortification and consternation of the rival candidates. Theophilus loudly declared that he would take no part in the ordination. 'You will ordain him,' said Eutropius, 'or take your trial on the charges contained in these

[1] Sozom. viii. 2. Pallad. Dial. 5.

documents;' and thereupon produced certain papers of
accusations brought against him from various quarters,
at the sight of which Theophilus turned pale.   His opposition was effectually silenced, though he nourished his
revenge for a future day.[1]   And we may presume that he
took the lead, by virtue of his rank, in the ceremony of
consecration—that is, that he pronounced the consecration
prayer and blessing, while two other bishops held the
gospels over the head, and the other prelates who were
present laid their hands on the head of the recipient of
consecration.[2]   The ceremony took place on February 26,
A.D. 398, in the presence of a vast concourse of people,
who came, no doubt, not only to witness the spectacle,
but to hear from the lips of one so famed for eloquence
the ' Sermo enthronisticus,' or homily on the lesson for
the day, which was delivered by the new Patriarch[3]
after he had been conducted to his throne, and which was
regarded as a test of his powers.   This discourse has not
been preserved, but Chrysostom alludes to it in the
homily numbered xi. against the Anomœans, which was
the second discourse he delivered as archbishop.   He
there reminds his hearers how in his first discourse he
had promised, in his warfare with heretics, to trust, not
in the carnal weapons of human dialectic, but in the
spiritual armour of Holy Scripture, even as David had
confronted and prevailed over the Philistine with weapons
which the warrior despised, but which were crowned with
success because blessed by God.[4]   In the review already
taken of his discourses against Arians and other heretics,

[1] Socr. vi. 2.

[2] Bingham, b. ii. c. 11, sec. 8.

[3] The title Patriarch is occasionally
used in the following pages, although
it does not appear to have been a formally recognised title till fifty years
later.   Socrates (A.D. 440 about) uses
it (vide c. 8), but the first occurrence
of it in any public document is in the
acts of the Council of Chalcedon, A.D.
451, where it is applied especially to
Leo I. of Rome.—Can. 28.   Labbé,
vol. iv.

[4] Hom. xi. in Anom. vol. i. p. 795.

it has been seen how faithfully he adhered to this principle.

The disadvantages of a monastic, secluded training, in one who was called upon to occupy a large and important see, have been pointed out by no one better than Chrysostom himself,[1] and he now experienced the truth of his own observations. His genius was not of that practical order which displays itself in great discernment of character, and tact in the management of men; and his virtues were of that austere kind, the virtues of the monk rather than of the Christian citizen, joined to a certain irritability of temper and inflexibility of will, which were ill calculated to first conciliate and then delicately lead on to a purer way of life the undisciplined flock committed to his care.[2] If Nectarius had been too much the man of the world, his successor was, for the position in which he was placed, too much the saint of the cloister. The new wine burst the old bottles. He began immediately to reform with an unsparing hand—first of all within the limits of his own palace. The costly store of silken and gold-embroidered robes, the rich marbles, ornaments, and vessels of various kinds which his courtly predecessor had accumulated, were sold in exchange for homelier articles, and the surplus was applied to the aid of hospitals and the relief of the destitute.[3] The bishop, and many of the clergy of Constantinople, had been accustomed to entertain and be entertained by the wealthy and the great. Ammianus Marcellinus contrasts the luxurious style of living affected by the bishops of great cities, who 'rode about in their carriages, elaborately dressed, and gave princely banquets,' with the frugal fare, the cheap clothing, the modest deportment of the provincial bishops.[4] The admonition of Jerome also to an

---

[1] De Sacerd. b. vi. c. 6–8, quoted above, c. iv.

[2] Sec. vi. 3. Sozom. viii. 9.

[3] Pallad. Dial. c. v. p. 20.

[4] Lib. xxvii. c. 3.

episcopal friend demonstrates the tendency at this period
to an immoderate and worldly hospitality on the part of
the clergy. 'Avoid,' he says, 'giving great entertainments to the laity, and especially to those who occupy
high stations; for it is not very reputable to see the
lictors and guards of a consul waiting outside the doors of
a priest of Jesus Christ, nor that the judge of a province
should dine more sumptuously with you than in the
palace. If it be pretended that you do this only to be
able to intercede with him for poor criminals, there is no
judge who will not pay greater respect to a frugal priest
than to a rich one, and show more deference to your piety
than to your wealth.'[1] Chrysostom, like Jerome, was an
uncompromising ascetic in his views on clerical life. He
ate in solitude the spare and simple diet of a monk, and
declared that he would never set foot at Court except on
pressing affairs concerning the welfare of the Church.
When one considers what the character of that Court
was, it must be confessed that the resolution highly
became a Christian bishop.[2] His own seclusion might
have been easily tolerated if he had not exacted the same
severe simplicity of life in his clergy. He denounced
their parasitical flatteries, and their propensity to seek
entertainments at the tables of the wealthy, and insisted
that their stipends must be quite sufficient to supply them
with the necessaries of life. He suspended many from
their cures on account of worldly or immoral conduct, and
repelled others from the Eucharist. Several of these
became the most active organisers of hostile cabals.

But there was another cause of the Archbishop's unpopularity with his clergy, which arose from his vigorous
assaults upon a deep and apparently most prevalent evil.

Celibacy appears never to have been made obligatory
on the clergy of the Eastern Church. The Synod of

---

[1] Epist. ii. ad Nepotianum.   [2] Pallad. Dial. c. v. and xii.

Elvira, which enjoins celibacy, was a purely Spanish synod;[1] and the decree of Pope Siricius to the same effect, in A.D. 385, could not affect any countries beyond Italy, Spain, and perhaps Southern Gaul.   That decree is a remarkable instance of the law-giving spirit of the Western Church, which hardened tendencies into binding statutes.   But sentiment and opinion were quite as strong in favour of clerical celibacy in the East as in the West.   It was proposed at the Council of Nice that a canon should be passed enforcing it upon every order of the clergy; a proposal which was defeated only by the influence of the aged Egyptian monk Paphuntius, who, though he had never been married and had always lived an ascetic life, earnestly deprecated the imposition of a burden upon all men which some men only were able to bear.   The result was that the clergy were permitted to retain their wives whom they had married before ordination, but were forbidden to marry after ordination.   And this is called 'the ancient tradition of the Church.'[2]   There can be no doubt, however, that a profound conviction possessed the minds of all the most earnest Christians in Eastern Christendom that the unmarried life was inherently better than the married; and, consequently, clerical celibacy was honoured and encouraged, though marriage was allowable.   On the other hand, there grew up, side by side with the practice of celibacy, a custom which broke it in the spirit while it was preserved in the letter.   The same Council of Nice which by one canon freely granted to the clergy the society of their lawful wives, by another prohibits unmarried clergy of every rank to have any woman dwelling under the same roof who was not their mother, sister, or aunt.[3]   It was the transgression of this canon which

---

[1] See Hefele, p. 131, and on the date of this synod.

[2] Stanley East. Church, lecture v. Soc. i. 11.   Sozom. i. 23.   The truth of the story has been disputed, but apparently on insufficient grounds. Vide Hefele, p. 436.

[3] Can. 3.   Hefele, p. 379.

was indignantly complained of by several writers[1] and councils[2] in or near the time of Chrysostom as well as by Chrysostom himself.   Under the name of spiritual sisters, young women, often consecrated virgins of the Church, lived, as they maintained, in all innocent and sisterly affection with unmarried priests.   But the risk to the morals of both was imminent, and the scandal which it brought upon the clergy in the eyes of the world was certain. Chrysostom denounces the custom on both these grounds. Whether two treatises, one addressed to the men, the other to the women, were composed at Constantinople, or, as Socrates says, during his diaconate, they embody his views on the whole subject, and afford a curious insight into clerical life in the great cities at this epoch.[3]

He places the offenders on the horns of a dilemma.   'If you are weak, the temptation to evil is so great, that for your own sake you ought to avoid it; if you are strong, you ought to abandon the practice for the sake of those who are weak.'   They brought a great scandal on the Church and opened the mouths of adversaries.   An isolated sin would be less severely visited than one which, though comparatively small in itself, caused others also to offend. They should imitate the wisdom of St. Paul, who would not do a thing in itself desirable or harmless, if the evil resulting to some exceeded any possible advantage to others.[4]   A pretext for the reception of these unmarried women was made on the ground that they were orphans who had no protectors.   But this became a great snare both to the women and the clergy: they were occupied with the management of property instead of devoting themselves to spiritual concerns.   It would be far better that a maiden should marry than, by abstaining from

---

[1] Jerome, Ep. xxii. ad Eustoch. Epiphan. Hær. 63.

[2] See refer. in Bingham, b. vi. c. ii. 13.

[3] Contra eos, etc., vol. i. p. 495.

[4] Ibid. c. 3, 4.

marriage, involve herself and others in worldly business, who ought to be free from it. If poor, it was better she should remain poor and friendless, than be received into a home where the danger incurred by the soul would far exceed the advantages procured for the body. There were many aged women who were poor, friendless, maimed, or diseased; the city was full of them. These were the most deserving objects of clerical charity, and on them it could be exercised without fear of reproach.[1] These 'spiritual sisters' appear from Chrysostom's account to have often lived very much like fine ladies of fashion. 'How incongruous and ludicrous,' he says, 'when you enter the house of one who calls himself a single man, to see articles of female dress and instruments of female occupation lying about—girdles, head gear, wool baskets, spindles, distaffs!' In the elaboration of their dress these companions often surpassed actresses; they were gossips and match-makers. The man who ought to have renounced all worldly calls, might be seen enquiring at the silver-smith's if his lady's mirror was ready, her casket finished, her flask returned; from the silversmith's he hurried to the perfumer's to see about her scents; from the perfumer to the linen-draper, and so on upon a round of shopping. All this business and worldly worry made them harsh to the servants, who retaliated by secretly abusing their master and mistress.[2] This was bad enough, but the clergy were not ashamed to display their servile attach-ment to these women even in the churches. They re-ceived them at the doors, forced others to make way for them, and walked in front of them with a proud air, when they ought not to have been able to lift up their heads for shame.[3]

Chrysostom implores the clergy as a suppliant to liber-ate themselves from these disgraceful and degrading connections. 'Christ would have them be strenuous soldiers and combatants. He did not arm them with spiritual weapons to help women sew and weave, but to engage with the invisible powers, to put to flight the forces of Satan, and to lead captive the rulers of spiritual darkness. If a soldier who was fully equipped were to run in-doors and sit down with the women just at the moment of the enemy's attack, when the trumpet sounded everyone to the combat, would you not run your sword through the craven on the spot? How much more would God be offended with the Christian soldier who evaded the combat with the spiritual enemy?' [1]

The rigour with which Chrysostom pressed reformation upon the clergy in these and many other points, not being tempered by a conciliatory manner or genial way of life, excited a vehement spirit of opposition. He was encouraged in his severity by his Archdeacon Serapion, who on one occasion had said, in the hearing of a large body of clergy, 'You will never subdue these mutinous priests, my Lord Bishop, till you drive them all before you as with a single rod.' [2] In fact, a large body of the more worldly clergy seem to have regarded the Archbishop and his deacon with much the same mingled feelings of fear and aversion which unruly schoolboys entertain towards an austere master.

The rigorous discipline exacted from the clergy was probably by no means distasteful to the people or the Court, and by the eloquence of their new bishop they were entranced so long as his declamations were poured forth against the vices and follies of society in general. The Empress and Archbishop stood for a time high in each other's favour. She conducted with him a vast torchlight procession in which the reliques of some martyrs were conveyed to the martyry of St. Thomas in Drypia,

[1] Contra eos, etc., c. 10.   [2] Soc. vi. 4.

a considerable distance outside the city. A rapturous homily was delivered by Chrysostom when they reached the chapel at dawn of day. ' What shall I say? I am verily mad with joy ; yet such a madness is better than even wisdom itself. Of what shall I most discourse ?—the virtue of the martyrs, the alacrity of the city, the zeal of the Empress, the concourse of the nobles, the worsting of the demons ? ' . . ' Women, more delicate than wax, leaving their comfortable homes, emulated the stoutest men in the eagerness with which they made this long pilgrimage on foot. Nobles, leaving their chariots, their lictors, their attendants, mingled in the common crowd. And why speak of them when she who wears the diadem, and is arrayed in purple, has not consented along the whole route to be separated from the rest even by a little space, but has followed the saints like their handmaid, with her finger on the shrine and upon the veil covering it—she, visible to the whole multitude, whom not even all the chamberlains of the palace are usually permitted to see ?' The mixture of populations in Constantinople is indicated in one passage, where, comparing the Empress to Miriam leading the chorus of triumphant Israelites, he says, ' *she*, indeed, led forth a people of one language only, but *thou* innumerable bands, chanting the Psalms of David, some in the Roman, some in the Syrian, some in a barbarian, some in the Greek tongue.' The procession moved along like a stream of fire, or continuous golden chain ; the moon shone down upon the crowd of the faithful, and in the midst the Empress, more brilliant than the moon itself ; for what was the moon compared to a soul adorned with such faith? He called her blessed, for the ends of the earth would hear of and extol this glorious act of piety. ' If the deed of the poor sinful woman in the Gospel, who anointed our Lord's feet, was to be proclaimed throughout the world, how much more that of a modest, dignified, chaste woman, who displayed much piety in the midst of imperial state.' And there is much more to the same effect; all singularly oriental, rhapsodical, almost dervish-like in the ecstasy of its style.[1]

The Emperor made a pilgrimage on the following day to the shrine, accompanied by all the great officials of the Court; and another discourse, similar in tone though not quite so extravagantly rapturous, was delivered by the Archbishop.

As in Antioch, so also and with still greater vehemence in Constantinople the voice of Chrysostom was incessantly lifted up against those vices which specially beset a large mixed population living under a corrupt despotism. Here as there the avarice and luxury of the wealthy are the themes of his indignant invective; the wrongs and pitiable poverty of the poor the occasions of his pathetic appeal. One day lamenting the paucity of worshippers, he exclaims, ' O tyranny of money which drives the greater part of our brethren from the fold! for it is nothing but that grievous disease, that never quenched furnace, which drives them hence; this mistress, more ferocious than any barbarian or wild beast, fiercer than the very demons, taking her slaves with her, is now conducting them round the Forum, inflicting upon them her oppressive commands, nor suffers them to take a little breath from their destructive labours.' . . . ' May you derive great good from the zeal with which you listen to these words, for your groaning and the smitings of your foreheads prove that the seed which I have sown is already bearing fruit.'[2]

A signal instance of the passionate attachment of the people to the Circensian and theatrical exhibitions occurred about the close of the first year of his episcopate.[3]

---

[1] Vol. xii. p. 468.
[2] Ibid. p. 485.
[3] Contra Lud. et Theat. vol. vi. p. 269, in fine.

A violent rain had half inundated the fields and almost
destroyed the growing crops; solemn processional litanies
were made to the churches of the Apostles on both sides
of the Bosphorus; yet two days later the majority of that
multitude, which had just been invoking the intercession
of saints and supplicating the mercy of God, poured into
the circus, and might be seen wildly applauding and
cheering on the chariots; and from that they hastened
to witness with eager eyes the indecent performances of
the theatre: 'while I,' said the Archbishop, 'sitting at
home and hearing your shouts, suffered worse agonies
than those who are tossed by storms at sea.'[1] . . . 'What
defence will you be able to make when you have to render
an account of that day's work? For thee the sun rose, the
moon lit up the night, choirs of stars spangled the sky;
for thee the winds blew, and rivers ran, seeds germinated,
plants grew, and the whole course of nature kept its
proper order: but thou, when Creation is ministering to
thy needs, thou fulfillest the pleasure of the devil.'[2] . . .
'Say not that few have wandered from the fold; though
it were but five or two or one, the loss would be great.
The shepherd in the Gospel left the ninety and nine, and
hastened after the one, nor did he return till he had made
up the complete number of the flock by its restoration.
Though it be only one, yet it is a soul for which this
visible world was created, for which laws and statutes
and the diverse operations of God have been put in motion,
yea, for whose sake God spared not his only Son.' . . .
'Therefore I loudly declare that if anyone after this admonition shall desert the fold for the pestilent vice of the
theatre, I will not admit him inside these rails.[3] I will
not administer to him the holy mysteries or allow him to

---

[1] Contra Lud. et Theat. c. 1.

[2] Ibid. c. 2.

[3] From this and what follows it
would appear that communicants went
within the rails to receive, and close

to the altar. This was the most primitive custom. Sometimes the recipients stood: vide passages cited in
Bingham, b. viii. ch. 6. sec. 7.

touch the holy table, but expel him as shepherds drive out the diseased sheep from the fold lest they should contaminate the rest.'

The iniquity of the people's defection had been aggravated on this occasion by the fact that the days on which they had rushed in such crowds to the circus and theatre were Good Friday and Holy Saturday. On the Sunday following Easter Day the church was fully thronged. An aged Galatian bishop, being present, was requested, according to a polite custom of that time, to preach. But the congregation expressed their disapproval by shouts of dissent, and by withdrawing in large numbers. They wanted to hear what more their eloquent castigator had to say on the subject on which he had so vehemently declaimed on Easter Day. Chrysostom was so much gratified and encouraged by the alacrity which the people had thus manifested to listen to his objurgations that his censure of the chariot races, the next time he preached, were milder than usual. He contents himself with observing that the shocking accident of the day before, when a young man about to be married had been run over in the course and cut to pieces by the chariot wheels, was a damning proof of the wild folly and wickedness of these spectacles. Nor does he rebuke them very sharply for their discourtesy to the Galatian prelate.[1] They always resented the preaching of a stranger; on several occasions Chrysostom had to appeal to their feelings of respect for the custom of the Church, or enlarge on the reverence due to the preacher, either on account of his age or his great virtues, before they would listen patiently.

It is impossible to determine in every case whether a homily or set of homilies was delivered at Antioch or Constantinople, but the character of society seems to have been in its main features so similar in the two cities that

[1] Vol. xii. Hom. ix.

it may be allowable to collect into one place notices on
various social subjects scattered up and down his works.
The extremes of wealth and poverty, barbaric splendour
and abject beggary, existed side by side in hideous and
glaring contrast.

The passion for the use of the precious metals was
amazing. Vessels for the meanest purposes were made
of silver; superfluous display without regard to utility
prevailed everywhere. ‘ If it were in their power, I verily
believe that some men would have the ground they walk
on,[1] the walls of their houses, and perhaps even the sky
and air, made of gold.’ Clothes were in the opinion of
Chrysostom a memorial of man’s fall from that state of
innocence in which they had been unnecessary, and were
therefore to be made of as little consequence as possible.
‘ Say, ye who indulge in such grandeur as to discard all
woollen garments and array yourselves in silk only, and
have even advanced to such a height of madness as to
weave gold into your robes (for most women do this), to
what purpose do you deck out your persons in these things,
not perceiving that the covering of dress was devised for
us after the transgression in the place of a severe punishment?’[2]

The particular make of shoes worn by the fashionable
young ladies and gentlemen of the day seems to have
excited his special indignation. ‘ To put silk threads into
your boots, how disgraceful, how ridiculous!’[3] Ships are
built, sailors hired, pilots appointed, the sails are spread,
the sea crossed, wife, children, and home left behind, the

---

[1] In Coloss. Hom. vii. vol. xi.
p. 350.

[2] Hom. xviii. in Genes. vol. iv. p. 150.

[3] The use of silk seems from its
first introduction into the Empire to
have been regarded as the ne plus
ultra of luxury. It was condemned by
Pliny, vi. 20, xi. 21. Elagabulus was

the first man as well as the first Emperor who ventured to wear a material
hitherto confined to female dress. See
Gibbon, vol. vii. c. 40, and his interesting account of the introduction
of silk-worms from China to Constantinople by some Persian monks in the
reign of Justinian.

country of the barbarian entered, and the life of the merchant exposed to a thousand perils, in order that after it all you may trick out the leather of your boots with these silken threads: what form of madness can be worse?' . . . . 'He who ought to bend his thoughts and eyes heavenwards casts them down upon his shoes instead. His chief care, as he walks delicately through the Forum, is to avoid soiling his boots with mire or dust. Will you let your soul grovel in the mire while you are taking care of your boots? Boots were made to be soiled; if you cannot bear this, take them off and wear them on your head instead of on your feet. You laugh when I say these words, but I rather weep for your folly.'[1] Again, 'you may see one sitting in his chariot with haughty brow, touching as it were the clouds in the senseless pride of his heart; but think him not really lofty, for it is not the sitting up in a chariot drawn by mules, but only virtue mounting to the vault of Heaven which really elevates a man. Or if you see another on horseback, attended by a troop of lictors driving the multitude out of his way in the Forum, call him not happy on that account. How ridiculous! why, prithee, do you drive your fellow creatures before you? Were you made a wolf or a lion? Your Lord Jesus Christ raised man to Heaven; you do not condescend to share even the market-place with him. When you put a gold bit on your horse, a gold bracelet on your slave's arm, when your clothes even to your shoes are gilded, you are feeding that most ferocious of monsters, avarice; you are robbing the orphan, denuding the widow, and acting as the common enemy of all. When your body is committed to the ground the sight of your houses will not permit the memory of your ambition to be buried with you, but each passer-by, as he contemplates the height and size of your grand mansions,

[1] In Matt. Hom. xlix. vol. vii. p. 501.

will say to himself or his neighbour, "How many tears did it cost to build that house! how many orphans were left naked! how many widows wronged! how many persons deprived of wages!" Thus the exact contrary of what you expected comes to pass : you desired to obtain glory during your life, and lo! even after death you are not delivered from accusers.'[1]

Such are the natural expressions of indignation on the part of one trained in a monkish school of piety and austere simplicity of life, when brought into practical contact with a corrupt civilisation. Every denunciation of inordinate luxury is coupled with an exhortation to the relief of distress. Almsgiving is represented as the one certain method of laying up treasure in Heaven, and the true riches are increased in proportion as this world's goods are given away.   He lived in the days when social science and political economy did not exist; he only perceived the moral wrong of profuse luxury and extreme destitution side by side, and the only method which he could suggest for rectifying the evil was to impress on the wealthy the duty of almsgiving on a large scale. Beggars swarmed in the streets, and thronged the entrances of the churches and public baths;[2] and he is for ever exhorting his congregations to relieve these unfortunate people. All honour to his simple Christian charity! though of course he could not have given worse advice with a view to curing the evil which he deplored. The man who wore shoes inwoven with silk or gold threads may have been a ridiculous fop, and yet have done more good by buying his finery, the produce of honest labour, than did the pious member of Chrysostom's congregation, who flung his money to the beggars congregated at the church doors.

The luxurious habits and extravagant dress of the ladies were especial objects of Chrysostom's attack ; but he draws

[1] In Psalm xlviii. vol. v. p. 514.   [2] Hom. i. de Lazaro, c. 8.

a charming picture on the other side of the influence
which good Christian wives might, and which many did,
exercise upon their husbands. The close of the exhortation
in our own 'Marriage Service' seems almost as if suggested
by a passage in which he quotes Sarah the wife of
Abraham as a pattern of dutiful obedience to her husband,
as adorned with virtue, instead of the outward adorning
of 'plaiting the hair and putting on of apparel.'[1] 'The
good wife, as she remains more at home than the man, and
has more leisure for "pious contemplation" ($\phi\iota\lambda o\sigma o\phi\iota\alpha$).
can calm and soothe the husband when he returns ha-
rassed by business, cut off his superfluous cares, and so
send him back free of the troubles contracted in the
Forum, and carrying with him the good lessons which he has
learned at home.' . . . 'No influence is more potent than
that of a careful and discreet wife to harmonise and mould
the soul of a man.' . . . 'I could mention many hard, intractable men who have been softened in this manner.'
And this influence would be in proportion to the Christian
purity and simplicity of her own life. 'When thy husband
shall see thee modest, not a lover of ornament, not demanding an unnecessary allowance, then he will listen to
thy counsel. When you seek not gold or pearls, or costly
array, but modesty, temperance, and benevolence, in proportion as you manifest these virtues yourself, you may
demand them of him; these are the ornaments which
never fail to attract; this is the adornment which old age
does not dissolve or disease destroy.' . . . . 'When your
husband sees you laying aside luxury, he will lay aside the
love of gain, and will be more inclined to deeds of charity.
With what face, O ye wives, can you exhort your husbands
to almsgiving, when you consume the largest portion of
his means on the decoration of your own persons?'[2]

---

[1] In Gen., Hom. xli. p. 382.
[2] In Joan. Hom. lxii. p. 340, and Hom. lxix. p. 380.

He urgently represents to the wealthy proprietors of land in the country the solemn duty incumbent on them of providing for the spiritual welfare of the people on their estate, by building a church and maintaining a pastor among them. 'There are many who possess farms and fields, but all their anxiety is to make a bath-house to their mansion, to build entrance courts and servants' offices; but how the souls of their dependants are cultivated they care not.' . . . 'If you see thorns in a field, you cut them down and burn them; but when you see the souls of your labourers beset with thorns and cut them not down, tell me, do you not fear when you reflect on the account which will be exacted from you for these things? Ought not every Christian estate-holder to build a church and to make it his aim before all things else that his people should be Christian?' . . . 'Therefore I exhort, I supplicate as a favour, or rather I affirm it as a principle, that no one should be seen in possession of an estate which is not provided with a church.' He concludes by drawing a pleasing picture of the benefit derived from the residence of a pastor in the quiet country village; the softening, humanising, civilising effect of his presence; the relief given to the needy, the comfort to the sick and dying; the pleasant repose which the proprietor may enjoy when he withdraws for a time from the turmoil of city life, and worships among his grateful people in the church which he has founded, and where his name will be blessed for many future generations. 'And think of the reward in Heaven; Christ said, "If thou lovest me feed my sheep." If you were to see any of the royal sheep or horses destitute of shelter and exposed to attack, and were to house them, provide stabling for them, and appoint some one to tend them, with how great a gift would the sovereign requite you. And think you that if you fold Christ's flock and set a shepherd over them, He will not do some great thing for you?'[1]

The responsibility indeed of *every* Christian man to promote the spiritual welfare of his brethren is one of the topics on which Chrysostom most constantly and earnestly dilates. ' Nothing can be more chilling than the sight of a Christian who makes no efforts to save others. Neither poverty, nor humble station, nor bodily infirmity can exempt men and women from the obligation of this great duty. To hide our Christian light, under pretence of weakness, is as great an insult to God as if we were to say that He could not make his sun to shine.'[2]

The practice of taking deep oaths on trivial matters appears to have been as prevalent at Constantinople as at Antioch, and equally to have excited the indignation of the Archbishop. 'He would not cease to denounce this devilish habit, and that vehemently, lest he should incur the condemnation pronounced on Eli, who rebuked, but not with sufficient severity. He would unsparingly repel from the threshold of the Church any who persisted in this pernicious vice, were he emperor or prince. Men might deride his vehemence, but they forgot that he was only the servant of Jesus Christ; their mockery fell on the

[1] In Act. Apost. p. 147 et seq.

[2] Hom. xx. in Act. Apost. p. 162. This set of fifty-five Homilies on the Acts of the Apostles, of which much use is made in this chapter, was delivered in A.D. 400, between Easter and Whitsuntide, in which interval it was customary to read through the Acts in the Lessons for the day: vide Bingham, vol. iv. These homilies are among the least polished of Chrysostom's productions. Erasmus, who translated them into Latin, was thoroughly disappointed and out of humour with them, and even doubts their authenticity. In a letter to Tonstal, Bp. of Durham, he declares that he could have written better matter himself even when ' ebrius ac stertens.' But most persons familiar with Chrysostom's productions will agree with Montfaucon and Savile that these homilies could have flowed only from that golden vein, though the ore is not so much refined as usual, and that some passages are in his very best style. None of his homilies, except those on the Statues and St. Matthew, contain more curious revelations of the manners and customs of the age.

Master rather than the minister. Let them laugh and
jest as much as they would; he was placed there to suffer
it. "Obey my voice or depose me from this my office. I
cannot consent to mount this throne unless I accomplish
something great. If I cannot do this, it were better for
me to stand below. As long as I sit here I cannot refrain,
not so much out of fear of punishment to myself as on
account of your salvation, which I earnestly desire."[1]

Immoderate addiction to the pleasures of the table is a
frequently recurring subject of censure. He depicts in
lively terms the freshness, activity, and good health of the
temperate man; the lethargy, the headaches, the cramps,
the gout, the sickness of the glutton. Here is his portrait
of a fat gourmand:—'To whom is not the man disagreeable
who makes obesity his study, and has to be dragged about
like a seal? I speak not of those who are such by nature,
but of those who, naturally graceful, have brought their
bodies into this condition through luxurious living. The
sun has risen, he has darted everywhere his brilliant rays,
he has roused everyone to his work: the tiller has taken
his hoe, the smith his hammer, each workman his proper
tool; the woman sets to work to spin or weave; while he
like a hog goes forth to the occupation of filling his
stomach, seeking how to provide for a costly table. When
the sun has filled the market-place, and other men have
already tired themselves with work, he rises from his bed,
stretching himself like a fatting pig. Then he sits a long
time on his couch to shake off the drunkenness of the
previous evening, after which he adorns himself and walks
out a spectacle of ugliness, not so much like a man as a
man-shaped beast.' . . . 'Who might not justly say, "this
fellow is a burden to the earth; he has come into the
world in vain; nay, not in vain, alas! but to the damage
of himself, as well as to the injury of others?"'[2]

[1] In Act. Apost. pp. 71 and 98.   [2] Ibid. p. 256.

Such passages as these prove that the power of Chrysostom to captivate his hearers consisted not always in eloquence or ornate rhetoric, but in a kind of bold and rough plain-speaking, which dragged out into broad daylight the most flagrant evils of the time, and painted them in strong coarse colours, to excite derision or disgust. But the fickleness and impulsiveness of the people were fatal obstacles to the retention of fixed and durable impressions. The population upon whom Chrysostom poured forth his streams of exhortation or invective was even more debased than that to which Savonarola preached; not so earnest, not so homogeneous, not so much animated by a sentiment of citizenship, not under the refining influence of a taste for literature and art.[1] It was a vast, disorderly medley of elements, without coherence, destitute of those political privileges, and of that industrial commercial spirit, which inspire the character with manly energy and independence. A passionate, invincible love of pleasure, an abandoned devotion to public amusements of a quality which in no way appealed to the intellect, and were calculated to debase and relax the finer moral feelings, these were insuperable bars to the substantial success of the Christian reformer. A large proportion of his hearers seem to have listened to his discourses as pleasant exhibitions of bold satire and eloquent declamation; they applauded, they laughed, they wept, they were smitten with something like compunction; and Chrysostom confesses that at the moment he could not repress a natural feeling of gratification at the effect produced; but that when he went home, and reflected that the benefit which his hearers should have derived generally evaporated in empty applause, instead of manifesting itself in some solid improvement, he wept and groaned from vexation. What men learned in the church was undone in the theatre: 'his work was

[1] See Villari's Life of Savonarola, b. i. c. 3.

like that of a man who attempted to clean a piece of
ground into which a muddy stream was constantly
flowing.' [1]

His letters to individuals, and the eulogia which he passes
at the beginning of some of his homilies on the zeal, piety,
and attention of his flock, prove that there were bright
exceptions, but the mass of the people remained irre-
claimable. On grand festivals, such as Easter Day, vast
crowds attended the church; the very precincts were
thronged, and the multitude surged backwards and forwards like the waves of the sea. A large portion was composed of the fashionable and rich; but Chrysostom greatly
preferred those smaller congregations, consisting chiefly
of poor, who attended regularly, and on whose attachment
to the Church he could depend. He enjoyed these quiet
services, free from the bustle and disturbance of large
crowds. [2] The wealthy and the gay spared little time for
the services of the Church, though they never pleaded
business as an excuse to avoid attendance at the theatre.
If they came now and then, they did so as a kind of condescension and favour shown to God and his priest. They
lazily slumbered, or idly gossipped during the service;
yet they boasted of their attendance afterwards. [3]

After the account in previous chapters of Chrysostom's
method of dealing with the prevalent heresies of the day
at Antioch, there is no occasion to say much more. The
same forms of error had to be encountered at Constantinople by much the same arguments. Only one, Novatian-
ism, appears to have been more prominent in this city
than at Antioch. The exclusive pretensions to purity of
doctrine and moral life made by the Novatians, excited
his special indignation. 'What arrogance! what boastfulness is this! Can you, being a man, call yourself clean?

---

[1] In Act. Apost. p. 191.   initio.
[2] Hom. in Inscrip. Altaris, i. in   [3] In Act. Apost. pp. 189, 190.

Nay, what madness is it? As well call the sea free from
waves; for as waves never cease to move on the sea, so do
sins never cease to work in us.'[1] The harshness of the
Novatians, in refusing the re-admission of apostates on
repentance, was peculiarly offensive to his merciful and
hopeful view of human nature. Sicinnius, the Novatian
bishop in Constantinople, wrote a book against him, in
which he makes capital of particular expressions in Chrysostom's homilies detached from their context; such as,
'Repent a thousand times, and enter the Church;' . . .
'let the unclean person, the adulterer, the thief, enter;'
but omitting the words which follow: 'that he may learn
to do these things no more. I draw all, I throw my net
over all, desiring to catch not those only who are sound,
but those who are sick.'[2] A hopefulness and love, which
never despaired of the sinner, are eminently characteristic
of Chrysostom; and the strong words of encouragement
and comfort which he used were of course susceptible of a
construction injurious to him, by those who prided themselves on enforcing a very rigid standard of moral and
ecclesiastical discipline.

Twenty years had elapsed since Gregory of Nazianzum,
with much reluctance and trembling, had accepted the See
of Constantinople. The city was at that time a very strong-
hold of Arianism. Arians had held the see for nearly
forty years. The services of the orthodox were held in a
private house, and were at first exposed to violent disturbance from the populace, which, hounded on by the
Arian clergy, shouted and threw stones. But the eloquence, combined with the holiness, of Gregory had
smoothed down this violent opposition. The ranks of the
orthodox were swelled, and the little house was enlarged

---

[1] Vol. xii. Hom. vi. adv. Cath.
pp. 143 and 491.
[2] Vol. xii. Hom. i., 'Quod fre-
quenter,' etc. Socrates, vi. 22. If we
may estimate the man from the account by Socrates, his admirer, who
relates a number of his so-called wit-
ticisms, the book is no great loss.

into a noble church, under the name of Anastasia, as
significant of the revival of the true faith.[1]   Imperial
authority completed the work which Gregory had begun.
The Arians and other sectaries were prohibited by various
enactments from assembling for worship within the city
walls.[2]   In the time of Chrysostom they began again to
molest the peace of the faithful.   On Saturdays and Sundays they made a practice of assembling in colonnades
and public places, and there loudly singing Arian songs—
songs, that is, embodying Arian doctrine, like the Thalia
composed by Arius ; abstract statements of theology, very
unpoetical in form, very incapable, as we should have
supposed, of exciting popular feeling.   This noisy singing
went on during the greater part of the night ; at dawn they
marched through the streets singing antiphonally, and
then held assemblies for worship outside the gates.   Chrysostom, with more of zeal perhaps than wisdom, organised antagonistic processions of antiphonal singers ; the
Empress supplied them with tapers mounted on silver
crosses.   Street frays were the inevitable consequence
of these counter demonstrations ; the Arians took to
their old practice of stone throwing ; Briso, one of the
Emperor's chamberlains, was wounded by a stone in
the forehead, and several persons killed on both sides,
after which the Arian assemblies were suppressed by
royal order.[3]

The practical energy of Chrysostom was not confined
within the limits of his own diocese.   He did not forget
his native city, but laboured, and laboured successfully, to
heal the schism by which the Church of Antioch had been
so long distracted.   Theophilus, Patriarch of Alexandria,

[1] Greg. De Vitâ suâ, pp. 585–1097.
Orat. xxii., xxvii., xxxii.
[2] Vide Gibbon, v. p. 30.
[3] Socrates, vi. 8. Vide Stanley, East.
Church, pp. 131, 132, for specimens of
these Thalia ; e. g. one commences,
' Where are those who say that the
Three are but one power?'

consented at his earnest request to join with him in the despatch of an embassy to Rome, to supplicate the recognition
of Flavian as sole bishop. Acacius, Bishop of Berœa, and
Isidore, for whom Theophilus had striven to obtain the
See of Constantinople, were selected to carry the petition,
and they returned with a favourable answer from the
Bishops of the West. It is a satisfaction to find Chrysostom united in this charitable work with those who afterwards became his most malignant enemies.[1]

His missionary efforts extended northwards to the
Danube, and southwards to Phœnicia, Syria, and Palestine.
He sought out men of apostolic zeal to evangelise some
Scythian tribes on the banks of the Danube, and appointed a Gothic bishop, Unilas, who accomplished great
things, but died in A.D. 404, when Chrysostom was in
exile, and unable to appoint a successor.[2] A novel spectacle was witnessed one day in the Church of St. Paul. A
large number of Goths being present, Chrysostom ordered
some portions of the Bible to be read in Gothic, and caused
a Gothic presbyter to address his countrymen in their
native tongue. The Archbishop, who preached afterwards,
rejoiced in the occurrence as a visible illustration of the
diffusion of the Gospel among all nations and languages,
a triumph before their very eyes over Jews and Pagans,
and a fulfilment of such prophecy as, ' Their sound is
gone out into all lands ; ' ' the wolf and the lamb shall
feed together, and the lion shall eat straw like the ox.'
' Where is the philosophy of Plato and Pythagoras ? Extinguished. Where is the teaching of the tent-maker
and the fisherman ? Not only in Judæa, but also among
the barbarians, as ye have this day perceived, it shines more
brilliantly than the sun itself. Scythians, and Thracians,
Samaritans, Moors and Indians, and those who inhabit the

---

[1] Sozom. viii. c. 3. Socrat. v. 15. [2] Epist. xiv. vol. iii.

extremities of the world, possess this teaching translated
into their own language; they possess such philosophy as
was never dreamed of by those who wear a beard and
thrust passengers aside with their staff in the Forum, and
shake their wise locks, looking more like lions than men.'
. . . . 'Nay! our world has not sufficed for these evangelists; they have betaken themselves even to the ocean,
and enclosed barbarian regions and the British Isles in
their net.'[1] Chrysostom assigned a church in Constantinople for the use of the Scythian inhabitants (probably
Gothic, for the Greek historians used the word Scythian
very vaguely), ordained native readers, deacons, and
presbyters, and frequently preached there himself through
the medium of an interpreter.[2] Some of his letters when
in exile are addressed to Gothic monks, who occupied the
house where Promotus had lived.[3] They were staunch
friends to him during his exile, and the monastic body
established in this house existed in the seventh century.

Porphyry, Bishop of Gaza, wrote a letter to Chrysostom
in A.D. 398, urging him to obtain an order from the
Emperor for the destruction of Pagan temples in that city.
Chrysostom did not cease to solicit Eutropius till he had
procured an edict, not indeed for the destruction, but for
the closing of the temples, and the demolition of the idols
which they contained. In the following year, however,
A.D. 399, an edict was issued addressed to Eutychianus,
Prefect of the East, directing that the temples should be
demolished throughout the country. This appears to
have been obtained chiefly through the influence of Chrysostom; and large bodies of monks were sent by him into
Phœnicia, where especially Paganism prevailed, who were
to use every effort to extirpate it, both by assisting in the

[1] Vol. xii. Hom. viii.　　　[2] Theod. v. 30.
[3] Epist. xiv. and xvii.

destruction of temples, and by the propagation of Christian truth. The money required for this missionary expedition was supplied by the liberality of some ladies in Constantinople, rich not only in faith, but also in the wealth of this world. The welfare of these missionary projects continued, as will hereafter be seen, to engage his most solicitous attention throughout his exile to the very close of his life.[1]

[1] Theod. v. 29. Tillemont, xi. p. 155.

CHAPTER XV.

THE Empress Eudoxia had rejoiced to discover that the
new Archbishop, although he mainly owed his promotion
to the supreme minister of the Court, was by no means
disposed to be ruled by him. If, indeed, Eutropius had
expected to be rewarded for the elevation of Chrysostom
by finding in him a complaisant servant, he sustained a
severe disappointment. Some little pretences which the
minister made of assisting the Church, by patronising
Chrysostom's missionary projects, could not disguise the
iniquitous venality of his administration, or protect him
from the solemn warnings and severe censure of one who
was no respecter of persons. In fact, when the Archbishop declaimed against the cupidity, injustice, and extortions of the rich, it was obvious to all that Eutropius
was the most signal example of those vices. Eudoxia
was anxiously aiming to compass the fall of the detested
minister; detested by her more especially, not only because he thwarted her influence with Arcadius generally,
but had also persuaded him to withhold from her the
title of Augusta until she should present a male heir to
the throne. She spared no pains therefore to conciliate
the Archbishop, who might prove a valuable ally to her
cause. It has been seen with what an appearance at

least of humble piety she took part in the nocturnal
procession which conducted some sacred reliques to their
resting-place outside Constantinople.

Her chamberlain, Amantius (himself distinguished for
unaffected Christian piety), was the frequent bearer to the
Archbishop of her liberal contributions to the support of
churches, or the relief of the poor. With her own hands,
it is said, she traced designs for basilicas to be erected at
her expense in some of the country districts.[1] Chrysostom
was always ready to welcome as genuine any manifestations of religious feeling. Such practical proofs of her
attachment to the Church completely overcame him, and
for the present his rich vocabulary could hardly furnish
language adequate to express his admiration and gratitude.[2]

Meanwhile, the poor doomed minister, not content to
remain as he began, enjoying the reality of power without
the name, prepared the way for his own destruction by
inducing the Emperor to bestow on him the titles of
Patrician and Consul. The acquisition of these venerated
and venerable names by the eunuch slave caused a profound emotion of indignation and shame throughout the
Empire, but especially in the Western capital, where they
were bound up with all the most noble and glorious
memories in the history of the nation. It is true the consulship was now an empty honour, destitute of all the great
duties and responsibilities which formerly were attached
to it. But the year was still named after the consul,
and the character of the man was by a superstitious
feeling projected on to the year which he inaugurated.
The name of the odious Eutropius, eunuch and slave, if

---

[1] Marc. Diac. ap. Baron. an. 401, 49.
[2] Vol. xii. 471. The titles 'mother
of churches,' 'nurse of monks,' 'staff of
the poor,' etc. were not bestowed till
after his return from his first exile,
vol. iii. p. 446. M. Thierry has erroneously introduced them into this
earlier stage of his life.

prefixed to the year, would seem to overshadow it with a kind of ominous and baleful blight, and to be in itself a portent of incalculable disaster. In short, after their indignation had vented itself in much bitter sarcasm, the Romans resolved that the consulship of Eutropius should never be inscribed at the Capitol. A solemn deputation from the people and senate waited on Honorius and Stilicho at Milan, to submit their decision, and to implore the imperial assent. Their spokesman recounted the glorious exploits of Theodosius and (by a flattering courtesy) of his son. The Saxon by the ocean, defeated, Britain delivered from the Picts, Gaul protected from the menaces of Germany! 'Through thee Rome beholds the Frank humbled at her feet, the Suevian discomfited, and the Rhine, submissive to thy rule, salutes thee under the name of Germanicus. But the East, alas! envies us our prosperity; abominable conspiracies are fermenting there which tend to break up our unity' . . . . the revolt of Gildo, the destruction of African towns, the famine of Rome, all these calamities were the work of Eutropius, and for these he was rewarded with the consulship! The East, accustomed to stoop under the sceptre of women, might accept the rule of an eunuch slave; but that to which the Orontes and the Halys submitted as ordinary custom would be a foul stain on the waters of the Tiber. The image of Eutropius should never be placed in the same rank with those of Æmilius, of Decius, of Camillus, the saviours and supporters of their country, the champions of Roman freedom! . . . 'Rise from your tombs, ancient Romans, pride of Latium; behold, an unknown colleague on your curule chairs; rise and avenge the majesty of the Roman name!'[1]

---

[1] Claud. in Eutrop. lib. i. The pathetic appeal is by Claudian put into the mouth of an allegorical impersonation of the city. Claudian was the intimate friend and companion of Stilico, and may not improbably have

Honorius, prompted no doubt by Stilicho, accorded a favourable reply to the supplication of the Roman people. Mallius Theodorus, prætorian prefect of Italy, a man eminent in virtue and ability as lawyer, soldier, and writer, and not less popular than distinguished, was nominated Consul by Honorius amidst general approbation, and his name appears in the Fasti of the West without a colleague.[1]

No doubt some of the virtuous indignation of the Romans is to be attributed to the jealousy which now ran high between East and West, but we may also not fancifully discern genuine sparks of the independent spirit of their forefathers. Amidst the general declension and degeneracy of the whole Empire, the West did not descend, could not have descended, to such depths of servile adulation as did the Byzantines on the occasion of the inauguration of Eutropius as Consul. When, arrayed in an ample Roman robe, he assumed his seat in the palace of the Cæsars, the doors were thrown open to an eager crowd of flatterers. The senate, the generals, all the high functionaries of the state, poured in to offer their homage to the great personage; emulated each other in the honour of kissing his hand, and even his wrinkled visage. They saluted him as the bulwark of the laws, and the parent of the Emperor. Statues of bronze or marble were placed in various parts of the city, representing him in the costume of warrior or judge, and the inscriptions on their pedestals styled him third founder of the city after Byzas and Constantine.

No wonder that Claudian declaimed with bitter sarcasm against 'a Byzantine nobility and Greek Quirites,' and even invokes Neptune by a stroke of his trident to unseat

---

assisted at this audience. He is a valuable guide to the history of this period, and especially as an indicator of public opinion on the great events of his day.

[1] Gibbon, vol. v. p. 361. Claudian, De Consul. Mall. Theod.

and submerge the degenerate city which had inflicted such a deep disgrace upon the Empire.[1]

And in truth a blow of no mean force, though directed not by the hand of a mythic deity, but of a stout barbarian, was about to descend on the Eastern capital. The consequences of it were averted only by the sacrifice of the new consul who had chiefly provoked it; upon him it came with crushing effect: he fell never to rise again. In the final scene of this curious drama the Archbishop plays a conspicuous part, and therefore it must be unfolded from the beginning. But, independently of this, it throws light upon the condition of the Eastern Empire at that period.

Tribigild, a Gothic soldier of distinction, had been, according to a usage now prevalent, promoted to the rank of Tribune, and placed in command of a military colony of Gruthongi (a large branch of the Ostrogoths), established in the region of Phrygia, near the town of Nacolea. The recent elevation of Alaric to the rank of Commander-in-chief of the Roman forces in the East had encouraged the pretensions and raised the expectations of all barbarian commanders. In the February or March next after the appointment of Eutropius to the consulship, Tribigild appeared at court to solicit promotion for himself and a higher rate of pay for his martial colonists, who, too ignorant or too proud to maintain themselves by cultivating the soil, were perishing of hunger in the midst of the most productive regions of Asia Minor. His suit was one among many of similar applications at that time constantly brought before the Court, and it was coldly dismissed by the Emperor's minister. Tribigild was not one to return home and brood in sullen and ineffective silence over his repulse. Gaïnas, the Gothic leader, to whom it will be remembered Stilicho had confided the task of

[1] In Eutrop. ii. 39, 156.

putting Rufinus to death, was still in Constantinople; and he was a relation of Tribigild, who found in him a sympathiser to inflame rather than soothe his sense of wrong. In this irritated frame of mind, like a train of powder only needing the application of a match to produce an explosion, he returned to Phrygia. According to Claudian, that match was applied by his wife. He dramatically describes her welcome of the returning husband: 'she flies to meet him, embraces him with her snow-white arms, and eagerly inquires what honours or rewards he brings back from the generous prince.' When the chieftain relates his ineffectual errand, and the cold disdain with which he had been treated by Eutropius, the chieftainess tears her face with her nails, and bids her husband with bitter irony sheathe his sword and attend to his plough or his vine. She contrasts her own condition with the happy wives and sisters of other warriors; they enjoyed rich spoils in the shape of adornments or of beautiful Grecian handmaids. 'Alaric, who broke treaties, was rewarded for it, but those who observed them remained poor. Alaric invaded and pillaged Epirus, and was made commander of the forces; *you* go humbly to solicit your due and are repulsed. Enrich yourself with booty, and you will be a Roman citizen as soon as you please.'[1] No doubt this scene, whether wholly imaginary or not, faithfully represents the feelings which, since the fatal promotion of Alaric, must have encouraged treasonable designs on the part of many barbarian chiefs. At any rate, whether the resentment of Tribigild was inflamed or not by the irony of his wife, he resolved to cast off allegiance to the Empire. He mustered his forces, which gladly abandoned their feeble attempts at husbandry to return to the more congenial pursuit of war and plunder. The rich country of Phrygia was rapidly over-

Claud. in Eutrop. ii. 187 et seq.

run, and some of the fortified towns, owing partly to the
decay of their walls, were captured. All Asia Minor was
convulsed with apprehension, and appealed to Constantinople for protection.

Eutropius affected to treat the rebellion as a petty insurrection, the suppression of which belonged rather to
the judge armed with instruments of torture than to a
military force. He declined the proffered assistance of
Gaïnas, but secretly negotiated with Tribigild, in the hope
of subduing him by means of promotion or of a bribe
in money. The Goth, proud to have turned the tables
upon the minister who had recently treated him with
scorn, stedfastly declined to accept any satisfaction but
one—the head of Eutropius himself. Thus war was inevitable; but who was to conduct it? Eutropius dared
not trust Gaïnas to act against his own countryman and
kinsman. He retained him therefore at Constantinople in
command of the city troops, and committed the management of the legions to one of his favourites, Leo, described by Claudian as a man ‘ abounding in flesh, but
scant of brains ;’[1] once a wool-carder, but, under the administration of the eunuch, a military commander. His
obesity made him an object of derision to the army, and,
joined to his natural incapacity and ignorance, rendered
him the most unfit man to conduct an expedition against
the subtle and active barbarian. Leo crossed the Bosphorus with a large, ill-disciplined army, whose approach
was welcomed by the devastated provinces, which vainly
rejoiced at the prospect of speedy deliverance from the
ravager. The enemy, meanwhile, had retreated southwards through Pisidia, and after a narrow escape from
destruction in the defiles of Mount Taurus, where the
inhabitants made a fierce stand, he emerged into Pam-
phylia, and awaited Leo in the vast plain of the Eury-

[1] In Eutrop. ii. 377.

medon and Melas, which extends between the chain of
Taurus and the sea. The doughty commander of the
imperial forces eagerly pursued the Goths, and flattered
himself, as the artful chieftain pretended to retreat in
alarm, that he had cooped him up by the sea. In the
confident anticipation of success, the discipline, such as it
was, of Leo's camp became still more relaxed. Little or
no watch was kept; festivity, drunkenness, and disorder
of all kinds prevailed; while the general had allowed
himself to be drawn into a fatal position between a wary
enemy in front and an impassable morass in his rear. In
the depth of a dark night, the Goth swooped down upon
his prey: all were asleep in the camp, the slumbers of
many deepened by drunkenness. Those who were not
killed on the spot fled in wild confusion, but only to
flounder in the marsh, in the oozy bed of which large
numbers were absorbed. A few scattered remnants reached
the Bosphorus by devious routes, to carry tidings of the
disaster to Constantinople. Leo himself had plunged on
horseback into the morass; the animal soon sank under
the weight of his bulky rider, who, after vain struggles to
extricate himself, was finally sucked beneath the quag.
To such a bathos have the annals of Roman warfare
descended! A Roman general drowned in mud![1]

The news of this overthrow struck panic into the population and Court of Constantinople. There was but one
who rejoiced, for he perceived himself to be master of the
situation. This was Gaïnas; he was the only man
at hand capable of confronting Tribigild, and he was
despatched across the Bosphorus with his barbarian
auxiliaries. But he did nothing to check the enemy, who
had resumed his career of pillage. He represented that
the forces opposed to him were insuperable, but expressed

---

[1] The above account is taken from Zosimus, lib. v. Claudian in Eutrop. ii.
Thierry, 'Tʀois Ministres, Eutrope.'

a firm conviction that Tribigild would become as loyal a servant as himself on one condition—the surrender of the minister Eutropius, the principal author of all the evils of the State.[1]

Arcadius was placed in a state of cruel perplexity. We need not suppose that he was attached to Eutropius, but his weak and indolent nature shrunk from losing that exemption from responsibility and labour which he enjoyed through the industry of his ambitious minister. Now, however, from all quarters the truth was forced upon him, that if he would save his throne, he must part with his newly made consul. Ugly rumours were prevalent that Stilicho was meditating a march to the East, and at the same time a new king, hostile to the Empire, had ascended the throne in Persia.[2] But a nearer and more persuasive enemy of Eutropius was at hand to give the finishing impulse to his fall. The profound jealousy of his power entertained by Euxdoxia has been already intimated. Not only had the title of Augusta been withheld from her through his influence, but he had even carried his arrogance so far at this time as to declare that his hand which had elevated her, could also depose her from her present position altogether. The proud Frankish blood of the Empress could ill brook such words from the lips of an upstart menial, consul though he now was. With a passionate gesture she dismissed him from her presence, hastened to her two young children, Flaccilla and Pulcheria, and with them made her way into the apartment of Arcadius. To his enquiries as to the purpose of her sudden appearance she made at first no reply save by a flood of tears, in which the children, from natural sympathy, joined; but presently, in language broken by sobs, she related a tale of insults received at the hands of Eutropius, and the crowning insult of the whole series.

---

[1] Zosim. v. 17.   [2] Claud. in Eutr. ii. 474 and 584, etc.

This was the blow which was completely to fell the tottering minister. He was summoned to the imperial presence, and having been informed that he was deprived of
his official dignity, and his property confiscated, he was
commanded instantly to quit the palace under pain of
death.[1]

The poor wretch, who had mounted from the lowest
dregs of society to the grandest position a subject could
occupy, was thus by a single blow suddenly reduced to
the position from which he had started ; and even worse,
for death stared him in the face. The bows and smiles
with which most courtiers had greeted him that morning,
when he was still the royal favourite, concealed, he well
knew, a hatred and a scorn which were not confined to
them, but animated the whole population, and only needed
opportunity to declare themselves. That opportunity had
come. He had no friends : whither should he fly ? There
was but one place to which he could in his extremity
naturally turn—the sanctuary of the Church; but here,
by the cruel irony of his fate, a law emanating from himself barred his entrance.

The right of asylum, which was once possessed by many
of the Pagan temples, passed over, by a natural transition
about the time of Constantine, to Christian churches.
However useful in ages of great rudeness and ferocity this
right may be, either to shelter the innocent from lawless
violence, or to give offenders protection from vindictive
rage till the time of equitable trial, it inevitably becomes
eventually an intolerable interference with the natural
course of law and justice. Tiberius had found it expedient to restrict or abolish such rights attached to many
of the Greek and Asiatic temples. Their suppression was
resisted partly from feelings of pride, partly of mercenary
interest, partly of respect for the sanctity of the places,

[1] Philostorg. xi. 6. Zosim. v. 18.

as in the case in our own country of the sanctuary of
Westminster.[1] In the reign of Theodosius I. a law was
passed which excepted gross criminals and public debtors,
and another in the reign of Arcadius, which excepted
Jewish debtors who pretended to be Christians from the
privileges of asylum ; [2] but by a law of September, A.D. 397,
suggested by Eutropius, clergy and monks, in whose
churches or convents fugitives might shelter, were obliged
to surrender them to the officers of justice, though they
might appeal to the Court in their favour.[3] The special
object of Eutropius had been to cut off all retreat from
the victims of his jealous ambition or avarice ; and now
he was one of the first to want the protection which he
had himself abolished. But he knew, no one better, that
the law had excited much resentment and resistance on
the part of the Church ; and it might well be that the
Archbishop would gladly connive at the violation of the
obnoxious measure by the very person who had framed it.
He resolved to make the attempt. In the humblest guise
of a suppliant, tears streaming down his puckered cheeks,
his scant grey hairs smeared with dust, he crept into the
cathedral, pushed aside the curtain which divided the
chancel or sanctuary from the nave, and, clinging closely
to the holy table,[4] awaited the approach of the Archbishop or any of the clergy.[5] The enemy was on his
track. As he lay quaking with terror, he could hear on
the other side of the thin partition the trampling of feet,
mingled with the clattering of arms and voices raised in
threatening tones by soldiers on the search. At this
crisis he was found by the Archbishop, in a state of
pitiable and abject terror; his cheek blanched with a
death-like pallor, his teeth chattering, his whole frame

---

[1] Stanley, Appendix, ' Memorials
of Westminster.'

[2] Cod. Theod. lib. ix. tit. 45.

[3] Ibid.

[4] The altar was sometimes called
ἄσυλος τράπεζα, Synesius, Ep. lviii.

[5] Claud. Prolog. in Eutrop. ii. 25.
Chrysost. in Eutrop. 3. vol. iii.

quivering, as with faltering lips he craved the asylum of the Church.[1]

He was not repulsed as the destroyer of that shelter which he now sought. Chrysostom rejoiced in the opportunity afforded to the Church of exhibiting at once her clemency and power, by taking a noble revenge upon her former adversary. The clamour of the soldiers on the other side of the veil increased. Chrysostom led the unhappy fugitive to the sacristy; and having concealed him there, he confronted his pursuers, asserted the inviolability of the Church's sanctuary, and refused to surrender the refugee. 'None shall penetrate the sanctuary save over my body; the Church is the Bride of Jesus Christ, who has entrusted her honour to me, and I will never betray it.' The soldiers threatened to lay violent hands on the Archbishop; but he freely presented himself to them, and only desired to be conducted to the Emperor, that the whole affair might be submitted to his judgment. He was accordingly placed between two rows of spearmen, and marched like a prisoner from the cathedral to the palace.[2]

The populace meanwhile had heard of the wonderful event of the day. The news of the detested minister's degradation had circulated through the Hippodrome, where a grand performance had attracted large multitudes. The spectators rose in a mass, lifted a shout of exultation, and with loud vociferations demanded the head of the arch offender.[3]

Chrysostom meanwhile maintained before the Emperor his lofty tone of authority in vindication of the Church's right of asylum. 'Human laws could not weigh in the balance against divine; the very man who had assailed the Church's divine right was now forced, in his day of

---

[1] Chrysost. in Eutrop. c. 2.   [2] De Capto Eutrop. vol. iii.
[3] In Eutrop. i.

distress, to plead in favour of it.' The Emperor was
moved, as he always was by any one who possessed some
of that force of character which he himself lacked. Some
feelings of compassion also for his late minister's humiliation may have mingled themselves with superstitious
dread of incurring Divine wrath. He promised to respect
the retreat of Eutropius. But, on learning his decision,
the troops which were in the city became indignant, and
furious in their demands that the culprit should be surrendered to justice. The Emperor made an address to
them, entreating them even with tears to remember that
they had received benefits as well as wrongs from the
object of their present rage, and, above all things, imploring them to respect the sanctity of the holy table, to
which the suppliant was clinging. By such words he
restrained them with difficulty from the commission of any
immediate violence.[1]

The following day was Sunday; but the places of public
amusement and resort were deserted, and such a vast concourse of men and women thronged the cathedral as was
rarely seen except on Easter Day.[2] All were in a flutter
of expectation to hear what the 'golden mouth' would
utter, the mouth of him who had dared, in defence of the
Church's right, to defy the arm of the law, and to stem
the tide of popular feeling. But few perhaps were prepared to witness such a dramatic scene as was actually
presented, and which gave additional force and effect to
the words of the preacher. It was a common practice
with the Archbishop, on account partly of his diminutive
stature and some feebleness of voice, to preach from the
'ambo,' or high reading-desk, which stood a little west-
ward of the chancel, and therefore brought him into closer
proximity with the people.[3] On the present occasion, he
had just taken his seat in the ambo, and a sea of upturned

[1] De Capto Eutrop. c. 4.   [2] In Eutrop. c. 3.   [3] Socrat. vi. 5.

faces was directed towards his thin pale countenance in
expectation of the stream of golden eloquence, when the
curtain which separated the nave from the chancel was
partially drawn aside, and disclosed to the view of the
multitude the cowering form of the unhappy Eutropius,
clinging to one of the columns which supported the holy
table.   Many a time had the Archbishop preached to
light minds and unheeding ears on the vain and fleeting
character of worldly honour, prosperity, luxury, wealth;
now he would enforce attention, and drive his lesson home
to the hearts of a vast audience, by pointing to a visible example of fallen grandeur in the poor unhappy
creature who lay grovelling behind him.   Presently he
burst forth: ' " ματαιότης ματαιοτήτων!—O vanity of vanities ! "' words how seasonable at all times, how pre-eminently seasonable now. ' Where now are the pomp and
circumstance of yonder man's consulship? where his
torch-lit festivities ? where the applause which once
greeted him ? where his banquets and garlands ? Where is
the stir that once attended his appearance in the streets,
the flattering compliments addressed to him in the amphitheatre ?   They are gone, they are all gone; one rude
blast has shattered all the leaves, and shows us the tree
stripped quite bare, and shaken to its very roots.' . . . .
' These things were but as visions of the night, which fade
at dawn; or vernal flowers, which wither when the spring
is past; as shadows which flitted away, as bubbles which
burst, as cobwebs which rent.' . . . ' Therefore we chant
continuously this heavenly strain: ματαιότης ματαιοτήτων
καὶ πάντα ματαιότης. For these are words which should
be inscribed on our walls and on our garments, in the
market-place, by the wayside, on our doors, but, above
all, in the conscience of each should they be written, and
constantly meditated.' Then, turning towards the pitiable
figure by the holy table : ' Did I not continually warn

thee that wealth was a runaway slave, a thankless servant?
but thou wouldst not heed, thou wouldst not be persuaded.   Lo! now experience has proved to thee that it
is not only fugitive and thankless, but murderous also;
for this it is which has caused thee to tremble now with
fear.   Did not I declare, when you rebuked me for telling
you the truth, "I love thee better than thy flatterers; I
who reprove thee care for thee more than thy complaisant
friends?"   Did I not add that the wounds inflicted by a
friend were to be valued more than the kisses given by an
enemy?   If thou hadst endured my wounds, the kisses
of thy enemies would not have wrought thee this destruction.' . . . . 'We act not like thy false friends, who have
fled from thee, and are procuring their own safety through
thy distress; the Church, which you treated as an enemy,
has opened her bosom to receive thee; the theatre, which
you favoured, has betrayed thee, and whetted the sword
against thee.'[1] 'He thus depicted,' he said, 'the abject
condition of the minister, not from any desire to insult the
prostrate, not to drown one who was tossed on the billows
of misfortune; but to warn those who were still sailing
with a fair wind, lest they should be hurried into the same
abyss.' 'Who had been more exalted than this man?
Had he not surpassed all in wealth? had he not climbed
to the very pinnacle of grandeur? yet now he had become
more miserable than a prisoner, more pitiable than a
slave.' . . . . 'It was the glory of the Church to have
afforded shelter to an enemy; the suppliant was the ornament of the altar.   "What!" you say, "is this iniquitous,
rapacious creature an ornament to the altar?" Hush! the
sinful woman was permitted to touch the feet of Jesus Christ
Himself, a permission which excites not our reproach, but
our admiration and praise.' . . . . The degradation of
Eutropius was a wholesome example both to the rich and

[1] In Eutrop. c. 1.

poor. ' Let some rich man enter the church, and he will
derive much advantage from what he sees. The spectacle
of one, lately at the pinnacle of power, now crouching
with fear like a hare or a frog, chained to yonder pillar not
by fetters, but by fright, will repress arrogance, and
subdue pride, and will teach him the truth of the Scripture
precept : " All flesh is grass, and all the glory of man as
the flower of grass." On the other hand, let a poor man
enter, and he will learn not to be discontented, or to
deplore his lot; but will be grateful to his poverty, which
is to him as a most secure asylum, a most tranquil haven,
a most impenetrable fortress.'[1] The Archbishop concluded by exhorting the people to mercy and forgiveness,
following the example of their Emperor. ' How else could
they with a clear conscience join in the Holy Mysteries
about to be celebrated, or join in the prayer : " Forgive
us our trespasses, as we forgive them that trespass against
us ? " He did not deny that the offender had committed
great crimes, but the present was a season not for judgment but for mercy. If they would enjoy the favour of
God, who had declared, " I will have mercy and not sacrifice," they would intercede with the Emperor for the life
of their enemy. So would they obtain the mercy of God
for themselves, and remission of their own sins ; so would
they shed glory on their Church, and win the praise of
their humane sovereign, while their own clemency would
be extolled to the ends of the earth.'

The people probably thought that sufficient mercy had
already been exercised by respecting the asylum of the
Church as against the law, and no further effort, so far as
is known, was made on behalf of the fallen minister. He
remained for several days more in sanctuary, and then
secretly and suddenly quitted it. Whether he fled de-
signedly, mistrusting the security of his retreat, perhaps

[1] In Eutrop. cc. 2–4.

even, with the suspiciousness natural to a deceitful person, mistrusting the fidelity of his protectors, and hoping to make his escape from Constantinople in disguise; or whether he surrendered himself on the condition that exile should be substituted for capital punishment, cannot with perfect certainty be determined. It is implied by one writer[1] that he was seized and forcibly removed from the sanctuary. Chrysostom, on the other hand, declares that he would never have been given up, had he not abandoned the Church.[2] However and wherever he may have been captured, some promise appears to have been made that his life at least should be spared. He was put on board a vessel which conveyed him to Cyprus, that island being designed, it was said, to be the place of his banishment for the remainder of his life.[3] But his enemies had determined that this life should be brief. A suit was instituted against him at Constantinople on a variety of charges, under the presidency of Aurelian, Prætorian Prefect. Over and above all his other crimes, he was found guilty of mingling with the ordinary costume of the consul certain ornaments or badges which belonged exclusively to the Emperors, and even of harnessing to his chariot animals of the imperial colour and breed. These were found to be treasonable offences, on the strength of which, in spite of some misgivings and hesitation on the part of Arcadius, which were overruled by Eudoxia and Gainas, the miserable culprit was recalled from Cyprus to Chalcedon, and there beheaded. As he entered that city, he might have seen affixed to the walls the imperial sentence, by the terms of which his property was declared confiscated to the State, his acts as consul were cancelled, the title of the year was changed, the world invited to rejoice at the purification of the consulship,

---

[1] Zosimus, v. 18, ἁρπάσαντες.   [2] De Cap. Eutrop. c. 1.
[3] Zosim. v. 18.

and to cease to groan over the sight of the monstrosity
which had disgraced and disfigured the divine honour of
that sacred office. Finally, it was commanded that all
statues or representations whatever of Eutropius in public
places should be thrown down and broken to pieces.[1]

Thus the earnest desire of Eudoxia was accomplished :
she remained mistress of the field, mistress, as she fondly
hoped, of the Empire. The government for the present
passed from the hands of an eunuch and slave into the
hands of a woman. The possible rivals to her supremacy
were the Gothic commander Gaïnas and the Archbishop.
In what manner she was brought into hostile collision
with these two very different personages remains now to
be related. The Goth was determined in the ambitious
pursuit of power, the Archbishop equally determined in
the conscientious discharge of duty. The collision of the
ruling powers with him was yet to come, but the contest
with Gaïnas immediately succeeded the fall of Eutropius.

The Empress procured the elevation of Aurelian, Prae-
torian Prefect, to the consulship, and of her favourite
(some said her criminal lover [2]), Count John, to the office of
Comptroller of the Royal Treasury, or sacred largesses.
The public affairs of the Empire were discussed and settled
in a sort of cabinet council by her and her friends, of whom
three wealthy but avaricious ladies, Castricia, Eugraphia,
and Marcia, were the most influential. The haughty and
manly spirit of the Gothic warrior naturally disdained to
be directed by a coterie of women. He united his army
with that of Tribigild, and the two forces assumed a
menacing attitude in the vicinity of Constantinople, on
the Asiatic side of the Bosphorus. Gaïnas opened negotiations with the Emperor, refusing to communicate with
any lesser power, complained that his services had been

[1] Zosim. v. 18. Cod. Theod. ix. 40, 17. Philostorg. xi. 6.
[2] Zosim. v. 18.

inadequately requited, and demanded, as a preliminary
to any further correspondence, the surrender of three principal favourites at Court—Aurelian the Consul, Saturninus
the husband of Castricia, and the Count John.   The embarrassment of the Court was extreme; but the three
ministers, in a genuine spirit, to all appearance, of Roman
courage and self-sacrifice for the good of the State, crossed
the Bosphorus, and sent word to the camp of Gaïnas that
they had come to surrender themselves into his hands.
The chieftain subjected them to a grim practical jest.
He caused them to be loaded with chains, and received
them in his tent in the presence of an executioner.   After
all manner of insults had been heaped upon them, the
executioner approached, and swung his sword over them
with a furious countenance as if on the point of decapi-
tating, but, checking the impending blow, only made a
slight scratch on their necks so as just to draw blood.
This savage farce having been performed, the three were
simply detained in the camp without suffering further
violence.[1]

Chrysostom appears to have laboured diligently to
mitigate the demands of Gaïnas.   His language, in a
homily delivered just after the surrender of the three
captives, implies that some degree of success had attended
his efforts, but it manifests also a feeling of great depression, caused by the unsettled, indeed anarchical, state
of public affairs.

'After a long interval of silence, I return to you, my
beloved disciples—a silence occasioned, not by any indifference or indolence, but by my absence spent in earnest
endeavours to allay a tempest, and to bring into a haven
those who were beginning to drown.' . . . 'For this purpose I have withdrawn from you for a time, going backwards and forwards ' (sc. across the Bosphorus), ' exhorting,

[1] Zosim. v. 18.   Socrat. vi. 6.   Sozom. viii. 4.

beseeching, supplicating, so as to avert the calamity which
was impending over the higher powers. But now that
these dismal matters have been concluded I return to
you.' . . . . He had gone to rescue those who were
falling and tempest-tossed; he came back to confirm
those who were still standing and at rest, lest they should
become victims of some calamity. 'For there is nothing
secure, nothing stable in human affairs; they are like a
raging sea, every day producing strange and fearful shipwrecks. The world is full of tumult and confusion;
everywhere are cliffs and precipices, rocks and reefs,
fearfulness and trembling, peril and suspicion. No one
trusts anyone; each man is afraid of his neighbour.
The time is at hand which the prophet depicted in those
words: "Trust not in a friend, put not confidence in a
guide" (Micah vii. 5); civil strife prevails everywhere,
not honest open warfare, but veiled under ten thousand
masks. Many are the fleeces beneath which are concealed innumerable wolves; so that one might live more
safely among enemies than among those who appear to
be friends.'[1]

It is possible that the intercessions of Chrysostom may
have saved the lives of the three captives, or averted any
immediate assault of the Gothic army; but Gaïnas was
in a position to dictate any terms he pleased, and his
army was like a great swelling wave, threatening at any
moment to break and expend its force upon the capital.
An interview with the Emperor, protected from any insidious attack by the solemn oath of each party, took
place in the church of St. Euphemia, situated on a lofty
eminence over the city of Chalcedon. The Gothic leader
no longer pretended to disguise his ambitious designs.
He demanded to be made Consul and Commander-in-
chief of the Imperial army, cavalry and infantry, Roman

[1] Hom. cum Saturn. et Aurel. vol. iii.

as well as barbarian troops; in short, he aspired to be
in position the Stilicho of the East.   The Emperor
yielded to these ignominious terms, which in effect placed
his capital at the mercy of a foreign invader.   The troops
were rapidly transported from the Asiatic side of the
Bosphorus and occupied Constantinople.   They waited
but the word of their commander to fly upon the booty
with which the wealthy and luxurious city teemed, and
which they beheld with hungry eyes; but for a time the
signal was not given.[1]

Gaïnas, either from sincere attachment to the Arian
form of faith, or possibly from ambition to display his
power to his countrymen, who were mainly of the Arian
persuasion, demanded the abolition of that law of Theodosius by which Arians were prohibited from public
worship inside the city walls.   He represented that it
was specially indecorous for the Commander-in-chief of
the Imperial forces to go outside the city to pay his
public devotions.   Arcadius, intimidated and as usual on
the point of yielding, referred the matter to the Archbishop.   Chrysostom earnestly and indignantly deprecated any concession; 'to give up one of the Catholic
churches to the Arians would be to cast things holy to
the dogs, and to reward the impious at the expense of
the reverend worshippers of Jesus Christ.'   He begged
the Emperor to allow the whole matter to be discussed
between himself and Gaïnas in the royal presence, when
he trusted that, by the help of God, he should succeed in
silencing the Gothic heretic, and in repressing any repetition of his profane demand.[2]   Gaïnas was not averse
from the interview; he rather prided himself on his skill
in theological debate, and boasted of having vanquished
the monk Nilus on the question of the identity, or

---

[1] Socr. vi. 6.   Sozom. viii. 4.   Theod. v. 31.
[2] Sozom. viii. 4.   Theod. v. 32.

similarity, of substance in the first two Persons of the
Holy Trinity.[1] The Emperor was well satisfied to act
the part of a quiet, irresponsible auditor. Accordingly,
on the following day, Chrysostom appeared at the palace,
accompanied by all those bishops who were in Constantinople at the time. Gaïnas put forward his demand.
The Archbishop replied that it was impossible for a
prince who laid claim to piety to take any step adverse
to the interests of the Catholic faith. If Gaïnas wished
to worship inside the walls, all the churches in the city
were open to him. When the Goth claimed a right to
possess one for his own sect, in consideration of his great
services to the State, Chrysostom repelled the demand
with indignant scorn. ‘You have already rewards far
exceeding your deserts; you are Commander-in-chief and
Consul. Consider what once you were, and what now
you are; consider your former destitution and your present abundance. Look at the magnificence of your con-
sular robes, and remember the rags in which you crossed
the Danube. Speak not then of ingratitude on the part
of those who have laden you with honours. Remember
the oaths by which you swore fidelity to the great Theodosius and to his children.’ He then cited the prohibitory
law issued by Theodosius in A.D. 381, called upon the
Emperor to enforce it, and on the Gothic commander to
observe it. The ecclesiastical historians concur in affirming that the Goth was completely vanquished by the
authoritative demeanour and eloquence of the Archbishop, and for the time at least desisted from pressing
his demand; but it appears that Arcadius was obliged to
satisfy his rapacity by melting the plate of the Apostles’
Church.[2]

Possibly, indeed, extortion of money had been the

[1] Nili Mon. Epist. i. 70, 79, 114,
116, 205, 206, 286.   [2] Sozom. viii. 4. Socr. vi. 6. Theod.
v. 32.

object of Gaïnas from the beginning in making his demand
for an Arian church. The plunder-loving spirit of his
army was aroused, and the gold and silver visible on the
counters of money-changers, and in the shops of wealthy
jewellers, was a temptation constantly dangling before
their eyes, till a rumour of violent intentions, or perhaps
common prudence, caused the owners to remove these
dangerous possessions into secret places of safety. If
the enemy had entertained any design upon the shops, it
was transferred from them to the palace, upon which they
made a nocturnal assault. According to some accounts,
it was repulsed by the vigorous courage of the citizens,
who fell with arms upon the assailants; according to
others, Gaïnas was scared in several attempts by a vision
of an angelic host planted in bright array around the
walls of the palace.[1] The materials for the history of
these occurrences are so meagre that it is impossible
to ascertain details, but, from whatever cause, Gaïnas
resolved to escape from the city. Fearing that if he
attempted to quit it openly with his troops, he might be
forcibly stopped or impeded in his departure, he pretended to be under the influence of a demon, and that he
desired to offer up prayers for relief from his affliction at
the martyry of St. John at Hebdomon, seven miles outside
Constantinople.

As he was going out, however, by one of the gates on
this pretext, the guards stationed at the gate perceived
that his followers were taking with them a quantity of
arms which they endeavoured to conceal. The guards
refused to let them pass; a fray ensued in which the
guards were killed. The inhabitants were seized with
mingled rage and terror. Gaïnas was declared by royal
decree a public enemy. He himself was outside the
walls, and the city gates were now all closed to cut off

---

[1] Sozom. viii. 4.   Socr. vi. 6.   Zosim. v. 19.

him, and such forces as were with him, from those who were left inside Constantinople. A large number of these assembled in and around the church of the Goths. Here they were attacked by the infuriated populace, which set fire to the building. The Goths perished wholesale in the flames or by the sword. Gaïnas, with the remainder of his followers, betook himself to a life of plunder in the Thracian Chersonese. But he found the inhabitants generally prepared to offer a stout resistance to his pillaging bands, which were soon reduced to great straits for subsistence. Meanwhile, a countryman of his in Constantinople was organising measures for his destruction. Fravitta was one of those Goths, of whom no doubt there were many, who had become assimilated to the people among whom they lived. He had married a Roman lady, and was eminent alike for refinement of manners, for valour in arms, and for honest fidelity to the government which he served.[1] He offered to lead out such forces as could be placed at his disposal, pledged himself to clear the Chersonesus of the rebels, and drive them, if necessary, beyond the Danube. The offer was accepted with joy, and Fravitta defeated the enemy in several engagements. Gaïnas attempted to cross the Hellespont, and throw his troops again into the fertile regions of Asia Minor; but his flimsy fleet of hastily constructed rafts, being attacked by a well-managed body of galleys in the middle of the passage, was dispersed or broken in pieces, and a large part of his army was drowned. Gaïnas then determined, with the remnant of his followers, to beat a hasty retreat in the direction of the Danube, where he hoped to be joined by some of his own countrymen, and renew the offensive. The accounts of his march are not quite harmonious, and somewhat obscure. According to Zosimus,[2] he was hotly pursued by Fravitta from place to

---

[1] Eunap. Sard. Fragm. 60. Sozom. viii. 4.   [2] Vide c. 21.

T

place, across the range of Hæmus up to the shores of the
Danube, into the waters of which he plunged on horseback, and with a scanty band of followers gained the
opposite bank, intending thence to make his way to the
settlements of his forefathers on the banks of the Pruth or
Borysthenes. But his design was frustrated by an unex-
pected enemy. The Huns occupied at that time the
region immediately north of the Danube, and their king,
Uldes or Uldin, was disposed to enter into friendly relations with the Roman Empire. He took up the pursuit
which Fravitta had abandoned at the river frontier,
chased the unhappy Goth like a wild beast from one
hiding-place to another, till at last the prey was caught
and killed. His head was carried on the point of a lance
to Constantinople, as a visible pledge of the good-will of
the Hunnish chief. Sozomen and Socrates,[1] on the other
hand, represent him to have been overtaken, routed, and
slain by Roman troops in Thrace.[2]

Theodoret has a vague story of his own, that when
Gaïnas was ravaging Thrace, neither warrior nor ambassador could be found courageous enough to encounter
him but Chrysostom, who, yielding to the public appeal,
set forth to intercede, and was most respectfully received
by the barbarian, who placed the right hand of the Archbishop on his own eyes, and brought his children to his
knees, it may be presumed to receive his blessing.
Theodoret does not venture to affirm that the mission
availed to induce the Goth to lay down his arms, and the
whole story has an unreal and romantic character.[3]

Three aspirants to the absolute control of the Eastern
Empire, widely different in race, character, and original

---

[1] Sozom. viii. 4. Socr. vi. 6.

[2] The Alexandrian Chronicle is
precise in fixing Dec. 23, A.D. 400, as
the date of his defeat on the Hellespont, and Jan. 3, A.D. 401, as the day
on which his head was brought into
Constantinople. This certainly leaves
a very insufficient interval for the
events recorded in Zosimus.

[3] Vide c. 33.

condition of life—Rufinus, Eutropius, Gaïnas—had alike perished by a violent death. Fravitta was made consul, but he was too loyal or too unambitious to go beyond the line of his legitimate power. Eudoxia now stood without a rival in the management of the Emperor and the kingdom. Her influence over her husband was enhanced by the birth of a male heir to the throne, the prince afterwards Theodosius II.; and thus the final obstacle was removed to her being solemnly proclaimed Empress under the venerable title of Augusta.

CHAPTER XVI.

CHRYSOSTOM'S VISIT TO ASIA—DEPOSITION OF SIX SIMONIACAL BISHOPS
—LEGITIMATE EXTENT OF HIS JURISDICTION—RETURN TO CONSTAN-
TINOPLE—RUPTURE AND RECONCILIATION WITH SEVERIAN BISHOP
OF GABALA—CHRYSOSTOM'S INCREASING UNPOPULARITY WITH THE
CLERGY AND WEALTHY LAITY—HIS FRIENDS—OLYMPIAS THE DEA-
CONESS—FORMATION OF HOSTILE FACTIONS, WHICH INVITE THE
AID OF THEOPHILUS, PATRIARCH OF ALEXANDRIA. A.D. 400, 401.

Up to this point the episcopal career of Chrysostom may
be pronounced eminently successful. He had distinguished
himself not only as a vigorous reformer of ecclesiastical
discipline, an eloquent master of pure Christian doctrine,
and preacher of lofty Christian morality, but he had done
good service to the State; and even while he upheld with
inflexible firmness the full rights of the Church, he had
not by overbearing or haughty independence forfeited
the good-will, respect, and admiration of the Emperor
and Eudoxia. But now the horizon gradually darkens.
We have to begin unravelling a long roll of troubles, to
trace a series of subtle intrigues, against which the single-
minded honesty of Chrysostom was ill-matched, ultimately bringing about his degradation, exile, and death.
We are fortunate in possessing, to guide us among these
complicated proceedings, the narrative of one who was
not only an eye-witness, but an actor in many of the
scenes which he relates.[1]

In the Spring of the year A.D. 400, during the military

---

[1] Palladius, author of the Dialogue
prefixed to Migné's edition of Chrysostom's works. On the debated
question whether this Palladius was
the same Bishop of Hellenopolis who
wrote the Lausiaca, vide Tillemont, xi.
'Vie de Pallade.'

usurpation of Gaïnas, twenty-two prelates had assembled
in Constantinople to confer with the Archbishop on ecclesiastical business.[1] Palladius has mentioned the names of
a few, Theotimus from Scythia, Ammon an Egyptian
from Thrace, Arabianus from Galatia. One Sunday
when the conclave was sitting, Eusebius, Bishop of Valen-
tinopolis in Asia, apparently not himself a member of the
synod, entered the place of assembly, and presented a
document addressed to the Archbishop as President, which
contained seven grave charges against Antoninus, Bishop
of Ephesus: 'He had melted down some of the sacred
vessels to make plate for his son; he had transferred
some of the marble at the entrance of the baptistry to his
own bath; he had placed some fallen columns which
belonged to the church in his own dining-room; he had
retained in his employment a servant who had committed
murder; he had taken possession of some property in
land which had been left to the Church by Basilina, the
mother of Julian; he had resumed intercourse with his
wife, and had children born to him after his ordination;
lastly, the worst offence of all, he had instituted a regular
system of selling bishoprics on a scale proportioned to the
revenue of the sees.' Chrysostom probably perceived, or
suspected from the eagerness of the accuser, that he
entertained some personal animosity towards the accused. He replied with calmness and caution: 'Brother
Eusebius, since accusations made under the influence of
distressed feelings are often not easy to prove, let me
beseech you to withdraw the written accusation, while we
endeavour to correct the causes of your annoyance.'
Eusebius waxed hot, and repeated his tale of charges
with much vehemence and acrimony of tone. The hour

---

[1] There was in fact what might be
called a floating synod of this kind
always in existence in Constantinople;
the Patriarch being ex officio President.—Tillemont, xv. 703, 704.

of service was approaching; Chrysostom committed to
Paul, Bishop of Heraclea, who appeared friendly to Antoninus, the task of attempting to conciliate Eusebius,
and passed with the remainder of the prelates into the
cathedral.

The opening salutation, 'Peace be with you,' was pronounced by the Archbishop as he took his seat in the
centre of the other bishops, ranged, according to custom,
on either side of him round the wall of the choir or
tribune. The service was proceeding, when, to the
amazement alike of the clergy and the congregation,
Eusebius abruptly entered the choir, hurried up to the
Archbishop, and again presented the document of charges,
adjuring him by the life of the Emperor and other tremendous oaths to attend to its contents. From the agitation of his manner, the people imagined that he must be
a suppliant entreating the Archbishop to intercede with
the Emperor for his life. To avoid a disturbance in the
face of the congregation, Chrysostom received the paper
of charges, but when the lessons for the day had been
read, and the Liturgy of the Faithful (Missa Fidelium)
was about to commence, he desired Pansophius, Bishop of
Pissida, to 'offer the gifts,' and, with the rest of the
prelates, quitted the church. His serenity of mind was
ruffled by the impetuous behaviour of Eusebius, and he
dreaded the possibility of infringing our Lord's command
to abstain from bringing a gift to the altar when 'thy
brother hath aught against thee.' After the conclusion
of the service, he took his seat with the other bishops in
the baptistry, and summoned Eusebius into the presence
of the conclave. Once more the accuser was warned not
to advance charges which he might not be able to substantiate, and was reminded that when once the indictment had been formally lodged, he could not, being a
bishop, retract the prosecution. Eusebius, however, in-

timated his willingness to accept all the responsibility of
persevering with the accusation. The list of charges was
then formally read. The bishops concurred in pronouncing
each of the alleged offences to be a gross violation of
ecclesiastical law, but recommended that Antoninus should
be tried upon the cardinal crime of simony, since this
transcended, and in a manner comprehended, all the rest.
'Love of money was the root of all evil;' and he who
would basely sell for money the highest spiritual office,
would not scruple to dispose of sacred vessels, marbles, or
land belonging to the Church. The Archbishop then
turned to the accused. 'What say you, Brother Antoninus,
to these things?' The Bishop of Ephesus replied by a
flat denial of the charges. A similar question being addressed to some of the bishops there present, described as
purchasers of their sees, was answered by a similar denial.
An examination of such witnesses as could be procured
lasted till 2 o'clock in the day, when, owing to the lack of
further evidence, the proceedings were adjourned. Considering the gravity of the affair, and the inconvenience
of collecting the witnesses from Asia, the Archbishop
announced his intention of paying a visit to Asia Minor
in person. Antoninus, conscious of guilt, and aware of the
rigorous scrutiny to which his conduct would be subjected,
was now thoroughly alarmed. He made interest with a
nobleman at court, whose estates he managed (contrary to
ecclesiastical law) in Asia, and besought him to prevent
the visit of the Archbishop, pledging himself to present
the necessary witnesses at Constantinople. The Archbishop, accordingly, found his intended departure opposed
by the Court. It was represented that the absence of the
chief pastor from the capital, undesirable at all times,
might be especially inconvenient at a crisis when tumults
were apprehended from the movements of Gaïnas; and it
was unnecessary, as the appearance of witnesses from Asia

in due time was guaranteed.[1]   Any delay was an immediate relief to the accused; and there was a further hope
that, by bribery or intimidation, the ultimate production
of the witnesses might be prevented.   But he was disappointed; for though the Archbishop consented to defer
his own visit to Asia, he appointed, with the sanction of
the synod, three delegates to proceed thither immediately
and institute an enquiry into the case of Antoninus.

The delegates were instructed to hold their court at
Hypœpœ, a town not far from Ephesus, in conjunction
with the bishops of the province; and the Archbishop
and his synod further determined, that if either the accuser
or accused failed to appear there within two months, he
should be excommunicated.   One of the delegates, Hesy-
chius, Bishop of Parium, on the Hellespont, was a friend
of Antoninus, and withdrew from the mission under the
pretence of illness; the other two, Syncletius, Bishop of
Trajanopolis in Thrace, and Palladius, Bishop of Hellenopolis in Bithynia, proceeded to Smyrna, announced their
arrival to the accuser and defendant by letter, and summoned them to appear at Hypœpœ within the appointed
time.   The summons was obeyed, but the appearance of
the two was only for the purpose of playing off a farce
before the commissioners.   Strange to relate, a reconciliation had taken place between Antoninus and his apparently
implacable accuser.   Eusebius had yielded to the temptation to commit the very crime which he had so vehemently
denounced.   A bribe of money had quelled his righteous
indignation; plaintiff and defendant were now accom-
plices, whose one interest was to conceal their joint
iniquities.   They professed great willingness to produce
their witnesses, but pleaded the difficulty of collecting
persons who lived in different and distant places, and were

---

[1] We are in the summer of A.D. 400, and the capture and death of Gaïnas
occurred in Jan. A.D. 401.

engaged in various occupations. The commissioners requested the accuser to name a period within which he
could guarantee the appearance of his witnesses. Eusebius
required forty days. As this space of time covered the
hottest part of the summer, it was hoped that the patience
or health of the commissioners would be too much exhausted at the expiration of it to prosecute the enquiry.
Eusebius then departed, ostensibly to search for witnesses ;
but, in fact, he quietly sneaked away to Constantinople,
and concealed himself in some obscure corner in that
great city. The forty days expired, and, Eusebius not
appearing, the two delegates wrote to the bishops of Asia,
pronouncing him excommunicated for contumacy. They
lingered a whole month longer in Asia, and then returned
to Constantinople. Here they chanced to light upon
Eusebius, and upbraided him with his faithless conduct.
He affected to have been ill, and renewed his promises
to produce witnesses. During these prolonged delays
Antoninus died ; and Chrysostom now received earnest
solicitations from the clergy of Ephesus, and from the
neighbouring bishops, to apply a healing hand to the
wounds and diseases of the Asiatic Church. ' We beseech
your Dignity[1] to come down and stamp a divine impress
on the Church of Ephesus, which has long been distressed,
partly by the adherents of Arius, partly by those who, in
the midst of their avarice and arrogance, pretend to be on
our side ; for very many are they who lie in wait like
grievous wolves, eager to seize the episcopal throne by
money.'[2]

The death of Gaïnas in January, A.D. 401, set Chrysostom
free to comply with this earnest appeal to his authority
and aid. It was the depth of the winter season ; his
health was infirm and impaired by the strain of the past

---

[1] σοῦ τὴν τιμιότητα; sometimes we have ὁσιότητα, 'your Holiness.'
[2] Pallad. Dial. cc. 14 and 15.

year's anxiety and toil; but the zeal of the Archbishop disregarded these impediments. He embarked at Constantinople without delay, leaving Severian, Bishop of Gabala, to act as deputy bishop in his absence. Such a violent north wind sprang up soon after starting that the crew of the vessel, afraid of being driven on Proconnesus, lay at anchor for two days under shelter of the promontory of Trito. On the third day they took advantage of a southerly breeze to land near Apamea in Bithynia, where Chrysostom was joined by three bishops, Paul of Heraclea, Cyrinus of Chalcedon, and Palladius of Hellenopolis. With these companions he proceeded by land to Ephesus. There he was received with hearty welcome by the clergy and by seventy bishops.

The first business to which the Archbishop and this council of prelates addressed themselves was the election of a new bishop to the See of Ephesus. As usual, there were many rival candidates, and factions supporting each with equal vehemence. Chrysostom fell back on the expedient of putting forward a candidate regarded with indifference by all parties. The plan succeeded, and Heracleides was elected. He was a deacon of three years' standing, ordained by Chrysostom, and in immediate attendance on him; a native of Cyprus, who had received an ascetic training in the desert of Scetis, a man of ability and learning. He comes before us again as a fellow sufferer with the Archbishop, to whom he had owed his elevation.

Not long after the arrival of Chrysostom, Eusebius, the original persecutor of Antoninus and of the simoniacal bishops, appeared, and requested to be re-admitted to communion with his brethren. The request was not immediately granted; but it was determined to proceed with the trial of the accused bishops, to prove whose guilt Eusebius affirmed that he could produce abundant evi-

dence. The witnesses were examined, and the crime being
considered fully proven in the case of six bishops, the
offenders were summoned into the presence of the council.
At first they stoutly denied their guilt, but finally gave
way before the minute and circumstantial depositions of
lay, clerical, and even female witnesses as to the place,
time, and quality of the sales which they had transacted.
They pleaded partly the prevalence of the custom in
excuse for their crime, and partly their anxiety to be
exempted from the burden of discharging curial duties;
that is, from serving on the common and municipal
council of their city. Every estate holder to the amount
of twenty-five acres of land was bound to serve in the
curia of his city. Many of the functions incident to that
office, such as the assessment and collection of imposts,
were (especially under an ill-administered despotism) in-
vidious and onerous. Constantine had exempted the
clergy from curial office, and the consequence was that
many men got themselves ordained simply to evade the
disagreeable duty; and this becoming detrimental both to
the Church and State, the law of Constantine underwent
modifications by his successors. The Church passed
canons forbidding those who were curiales to be ordained,
the effect of which was to diminish the number of wealthy
men who entered the ranks of the clergy.[1] The Asiatic
bishops, therefore, if curiales when ordained, had acted
against the laws of the Church, and could not legally
have claimed exemption from curial duties on the ground
of their orders. They sued for mercy to the council;
they entreated that, if deprived of their sees, the money
which they had paid to obtain them might be returned.
In many cases it had been procured with much difficulty;
some had even parted with the furniture of their wives to

---

[1] See, on this whole subject, Bing-   187 and 318, and the authorities there
ham, viii. 13, 6; and Robertson, i. pp.   cited.

raise the requisite amount. The Archbishop undertook to intercede with the Emperor for their exemption from curial duty; the ecclesiastical question he submitted to the council. The decision of the prelates, under the influence of their president, was temperate and wise. The six bishops were to be deprived of their sees, but allowed to receive the Eucharist inside the altar rails with the clergy, and the heirs of Antoninus were required to restore their purchase money to them. The deposed prelates were superseded by the appointment of six men, unmarried, eminent for learning and purity of life.[1]

On his return through Bithynia the Archbishop was detained by a not less difficult and delicate piece of business. Gerontius, Archbishop of Nicomedia, the metropolitan of Bithynia, was a singular specimen of an ecclesiastical adventurer. He had been a deacon at Milan, but was expelled by Ambrose for misconduct. He made his way to Constantinople, where, by general cleverness, and by some real or pretended skill in medicine, he became a favourite with people of rank, and through the interest of some influential friends obtained the See of Nicomedia. He was consecrated by Helladius, Bishop of Heraclea, for whose son Gerontius had managed to procure a high appointment in the army. The new Bishop of Nicomedia gained the attachment of his people, again it is said, through his skill in curing diseases of the body rather than of the soul. Ambrose incessantly demanded of Nectarius, then Patriarch of Constantinople, that he should be deposed; but Nectarius did not venture to incur the displeasure of the Nicomedians. The bolder spirit and more scrupulous conscience of Chrysostom did not hesitate to strike the blow which his more worldly

---

[1] Pallad. Dial. cc. 14, 15. Sozomen (viii. 6) says that Chrysostom deposed thirteen bishops of Asia, Lycia, and Phrygia. This is possible, as the synod may have inquired into other simoniacal cases beyond the original six.

and courtly predecessor had shrunk from striking. Gerontius was deposed, whether by the sole authority of
the Archbishop, or by the decree of a council acting
under his influence, is not stated. Pansophius, formerly
tutor to the Empress, a man of piety, wisdom, and gentleness, was promoted to the see. But the Nicomedians
bewailed the loss of their favourite; they went about the
streets in procession, singing litanies, as if in the time
of some great national calamity.[1] Before quitting Asia,
Chrysostom is said to have taken active measures for the
suppression of the worship of Midas at Ephesus, and of
Cybele in Phrygia.[2]

All these proceedings are worth recording, not only as
of some ecclesiastical interest in themselves, but also
because they were all remembered and made capital of
by his enemies. It has been much debated whether Chrysostom, by his acts in Asia, overstrained his legal powers,
or rather, whether he exceeded the legal boundaries of
his jurisdiction as Patriarch of Constantinople. The fact
seems to be that the importance of his see was in that
growing state which enabled the possessor of it, if a man
of energy and ability, to go great lengths without any
exception being taken to his authority, unless and until
a hostile feeling was provoked against him. By the
Council of Constantinople, A.D. 381, the Patriarch of that
city was restricted in his jurisdiction to the Diocese of
Thrace.[3] His authority over the Dioceses of Asia Minor
and Pontus was not established till the Council of Chalcedon, A.D. 451, when there was a long discussion on the

---

[1] Sozom. viii. 6.

[2] Tillemont, xi. p. 170.

[3] Labbé, ii. p. 947. It must always
be borne in mind that Diocese was
the name of the largest *civil* division of
the Roman Empire. Each diocese contained several provinces, e.g. Thrace,
six; Asia, ten; Pontus, eleven. The

whole Empire was divided into thirteen dioceses, and about one hundred
and twenty provinces. The Ecclesiastical divisions followed more or less
the plan of the civil. An archbishop
was bishop of the metropolis of a
Province, a Patriarch of one or more
Dioceses.

subject, and the papal legates especially resisted any claim to such an extension; but it was affirmed that the Patriarchs had *long enjoyed* the privilege of ordaining metropolitans to the provinces of those dioceses, and so it was finally conveyed to them by that council; and the additional right was granted them of hearing appeals from these metropolitans.[1] Theodoret (vide c. 28) simply observes that the jurisdiction of Chrysostom extended not only over the six provinces of Thrace, but also over Asia and Pontus. The Council of Constantinople gave the bishop of that see the first rank after the Bishop of Rome, because Constantinople was νέα Ῥώμη. The Council of Chalcedon declared him for the same reason to be invested with *equal* privileges.

Chrysostom was welcomed, on his return to Constantinople, with hearty demonstrations of joy. On the following day he was at his post in the cathedral, and once more addressing his beloved flock. In somewhat rapturous language he expresses his thankfulness at learning that their fidelity to the Church, and their attachment to their spiritual father, had not been impaired by his absence, which had lasted more than a hundred days. They were disappointed that he had not returned in time to celebrate Easter with them. But he consoles them by representing that every participation of the Eucharist was a kind of Easter. 'As *often* as ye eat this bread, ye do show forth the Lord's death till He come.' 'They were not tied to time and place like the Jew. Wherever and whenever the Christian celebrated that holy feast with joy and love, there was the true Paschal Festival.'[2] They regretted also that so many had been baptized by other hands than his. 'What then? that does not impair the gift of God; I was not

---

[1] Can. xxviii.; and Can. ix. Chalced. in Labbé, iv. pp. 769 and 798.

[2] Comp. Keble, Christian Year for Easter day.

'Sundays by thee more glorious break,
An Easter Day in every week.'

present when they were baptized, but Christ was present.'
'In a document signed by the Emperor, the only question
of importance was the autograph; the quality of the ink
and paper mattered not.   Even so in baptism the tongue
and the hand of the priest are but as the paper and pen:
the hand which writes is the Holy Spirit Himself.'[1]

The thankfulness and joy of Chrysostom at the affectionate reception with which he was greeted by the
people were probably felt and expressed the more warmly,
owing to some unpleasant accounts which had been for-
warded to him by his deacon Serapion, that Severian,
Bishop of Gabala, had been endeavouring to undermine
his influence in his absence.   It will be remembered
that to Severian Chrysostom had entrusted his episcopal
duties during his visitation journey in Asia.   The circumstance of a bishop of Syria residing for so long a
time in Constantinople is worth considering, and affords
a curious insight into the character of the times.   Antiochus, Bishop of Ptolemais in Phœnicia, had a reputation
as a learned and eloquent man; he paid a visit to Constantinople, and excited much admiration by his discourses.   Severian, hearing of his success, was animated
by a spirit of emulation, if not envy, which could not be
satisfied till he had exhibited his powers on the same
theatre.   He carefully composed a large stock of sermons,
and set out to try his fortune in the capital.   The unsuspicious and generous Archbishop received him cordially, and frequently invited him to preach.   Severian
possessed some powers of speaking, though he had a
harsh provincial accent, and he exerted all his eloquence
in the church, and all his arts of flattery out of it, to win
the confidence and admiration, not only of the Archbishop,
but also of the chief personages at court, and even the Emperor and Empress.   It was with their full approval that

[1] Vol. iii. p. 421.

he remained as deputy of the Archbishop during his sojourn
in Asia.   But he found himself narrowly and suspiciously
watched by the Archdeacon Serapion, who opposed some
of his proceedings as arbitrary, and made no concealment
of his dislike.   One day after the return of Chrysostom,
Severian passed through an apartment of the episcopal
palace where Serapion was sitting.   Serapion rose not to
make the customary salutation of respect.   Severian,
irritated by his discourtesy, exclaimed in a loud voice:
'If Serapion dies a Christian, then Jesus Christ was not
incarnate.'   The last clause only of the sentence was
repeated by Serapion to Chrysostom.   It was corroborated
by witnesses; the indignation of the Archbishop was excited.   Severian was peremptorily commanded to quit the
city.   The Empress resented the expulsion of a favourite
preacher, and commanded the Archbishop to recall him.
Chrysostom yielded so far, but was inflexible in his refusal
to admit the offender to communion, till Eudoxia came in
person to the Church of the Apostles, placed her infant
son Theodosius on his knees, and conjured him by solemn
oaths to listen to her request.   The Archbishop then,
but with some reluctance, consented.[1]   He was, however,
thoroughly honest in doing that to which he had once
made up his mind.   Fearing that his congregation, in their
zealous attachment to him, might disapprove of the reconciliation, he delivered a short address on the subject.
'He was their spiritual father, and he trusted therefore
they would extend to him the respect and obedience of
affectionate and dutiful children.   He came to them with
the most appropriate message that could be delivered by
the mouth of a bishop—a message of peace and love.
There was also a further duty incumbent on all—respectful submission to the civil powers.   If the Apostle
Paul said, "Be subject to principalities and powers"

---

[1] Socrat. vi. 11. Sozom. viii. 10.

(Tit. iii. 1), how especially was this precept incumbent
on the subjects of a religious sovereign who laboured for
the good of the Church. He besought them to receive
Severian with a full heart and with open arms.' The
request was received by the congregation with expressions
of approbation. He thanked them for their obedience,
and concluded with a prayer that God would grant a
fixed and lasting peace to his Church.

Severian addressed them the next day in a rhetorical
and artificial discourse on the beauty and blessings of
peace—a subject painfully incongruous with the subsequent conduct of the speaker; for this misunderstanding
with the Bishop of Gabala was the first muttering of the
storm which was soon to burst over the head of the
doomed Archbishop.[1]

The inevitable fate of one who attempts to reform a
deeply corrupt society, and a secularised clergy, on an
ascetic model befell Chrysostom. He lashed with almost equal severity the most unpardonable crimes and
the more venial foibles and follies. His denunciations of
heartless rapacity, sensuality, luxury, addiction to de-
basing and immoral amusements, might have been borne,
but he presumed—an intolerable offence!—to censure the
fashionable ladies for setting off their complexions with
paint, and surmounting their heads with piles of false
hair. The clergy, too, might have tolerated his condemnation of the grosser offences, such as simony or
concubinage, but they resented his restraint of their
indulgence in the pleasures of society, and of their propensity to frequent the entertainments of the noble and
wealthy. He was, as Palladius expresses it, 'like a lamp
burning before sore eyes,' for what he bade others be,
that he was pre-eminently himself.[2] None could say that
he was one man in the pulpit and another out of it. To

[1] Vol. iii. p. 424 et seq.   [2] Pall. Dial. c. 18, pp. 62 and 67.

set an example to his worldly clergy, and to avoid contamination, he gave up his episcopal income, save what sufficed to supply his simple daily wants. He resolutely abstained from mingling in general society, and ate his frugal meals in the seclusion of his own apartment. Thus, with the exception of a few deeply attached friends, who measured practical Christianity by the same standard as himself, he became deeply unpopular among the upper ranks of society. With the poor it was otherwise; they regarded him as a kind of champion, because he denounced the oppressions and extortions of the rich, and the tyranny of masters over slaves; because he was ever inculcating the duty of almsgiving. In the eyes of his friends he was the saint, pure in life, severe in discipline, sublime in doctrine; in the eyes of his enemies he was the sacerdotal tyrant, odious to the clergy as an inexorable maintainer of a rule of life intolerably rigid, odious to clergy and laity as an inhospitable, if not haughty recluse; a vigilant and merciless censor who rode roughshod over established customs. Individuals at last, among clergy and laity, who conceived that they themselves, or at any rate the section of society to which they belonged, were the butts at which more especially the Archbishop aimed his shafts, began to discuss with one another their grievances, till their conferences gradually assumed the shape of positive organised hostility against the disturber of their peace. But before entering on the troublous history of his enemies' machinations, it may be well to take a glance at the most conspicuous of Chrysostom's friends.

The list of those who are known to us by more than their mere names is soon exhausted. Among the clergy may be reckoned Heraclides, made Bishop of Ephesus in the place of Antoninus; Proclus, afterwards (in A.D. 434) Patriarch of Constantinople, at present the receiver of those who demanded audiences with the Patriarch; Cassianus, founder of the Monastery of St. Victor at Marseilles, and his friend and companion Germanus ;—Helladius, the priest of the palace, probably equivalent to private chaplain ; Serapion, the deacon [1] or archdeacon,[2] afterwards made Bishop of Heraclea in Thrace, from which see he was expelled in the persecution which befell Chrysostom's followers. With most of these men he maintained a constant and affectionate intercourse or correspondence during his exile to the close of his life. With such intimate companions and friends the austerity and reserve of manner which he assumed towards those outside this circle vanished. All the natural amiability and playful humour of his disposition shone out when he was in their company ; he called some of them by nicknames of his own invention, especially those who practised such ascetic exercises as he specially approved of.[3]

Three ladies are distinguished as among his most faithful friends. Salvina was the daughter of the African rebel Gildo, and had been married by Theodosius to Nebridius, nephew of his Empress, in the hope—a vain one as it proved—that this tie would attach Gildo to the Empire. Her husband died young; she vowed perpetual widowhood, and became the patroness and protectress at the Court of Arcadius of Oriental churches and ecclesiastics.

Pentadia was wife of the consul Timasius ; and when her husband was banished by Eutropius to the Oasis of Egypt, she had been persecuted by the merciless tyrant, and fled for refuge to the Church, where she was protected in sanctuary by the Archbishop in spite of the opposition of her persecutor.

But by far the most eminent of Chrysostom's female friends was the deaconess Olympias. She sprang from a

[1] Socr. vi. 4.   [2] Sozom. viii. c. 9.   [3] Pall. Dial. c. 19.

noble but pagan family. Her grandfather, Ablavius, was
a prætorian prefect, highly esteemed and trusted by Constantine the Great, and her father, Seleucus, had attained
the rank of count. She was early left an orphan, endowed
with great personal beauty, and heiress to a vast fortune.
Her uncle and guardian, Procopius, was a man of probity and piety, a friend and correspondent of Gregory
Nazianzen. Her instructress also, Theodosia, sister of
St. Amphilocius, was a woman of piety; one whom
Gregory recommended Olympias to imitate as a very
model of excellence in speech and conduct. Under this
happy training, the girl grew up to emulate and surpass
her preceptress in goodness. Gregory delighted to call
her ' his own Olympias,' and to be called ' father ' by her.[1]
There could be no difficulty in finding a suitor for a lady
possessed of every attraction. The anxiety of Procopius was
to secure a worthy one. Nebridius was selected, a young
man, but high in official rank; Count or Intendant of the
Domain in A.D. 382, Prefect of Constantinople in A.D. 386.
They were wedded in A.D. 384. Many bishops assisted
at the ceremony, but Gregory was prevented from attending by the state of his health. He wrote a letter to Procopius, saying that in spirit, nevertheless, he would join
their hands to one another and to God. Part of the letter
is written in a vein of sprightly humour. ' It would have
been very unbecoming for a gouty old fellow like himself
to be seen hobbling about among the dancers and merry-
makers at the nuptials.'[2] He also addressed a poem to
Olympias, in which he gives her advice how she ought to
conduct herself as a married woman. She did not long
need his counsel. Nebridius died about two years after
their marriage. Olympias regarded this early dissolution
of the marriage bond as an intimation of the Divine will
that she should henceforth live free from the worldly

[1] Greg. Naz. Epp. lvii. lviii.   [2] Ep. lvii.

entanglements and cares incident to married life. The
Emperor Theodosius desired to unite her to a Spaniard
named Elpidius, a kinsman of his own; but she stedfastly
refused. The Emperor acted in that despotic manner
which occasionally marred his usually generous character.
He ordered the property of Olympias to be confiscated till
she should be thirty years of age; she was even denied
freedom of intercourse with her episcopal friends, and of
access to the Church. But she only thanked the Emperor
for those deprivations which were intended to make her
hanker after worldly life. 'You have exercised towards
your humble handmaiden a virtue becoming a monarch
and suitable even to a bishop; you have directed what
was to me a heavy burden, and the distribution of it an
anxiety, to be kept in safe custody. You could not have
conferred a greater blessing upon me, unless you had
ordered it to be bestowed upon the churches and the
poor.' The Emperor was softened; at any rate, he perceived the uselessness, if not the injustice, of his treatment.
He cancelled the order for the confiscation of her property, and left her in the undisturbed enjoyment of single
life and of her possessions. Henceforward her life and
wealth were devoted to the interests of the Church. She
was the friend, entertainer, adviser of many of the most
eminent ecclesiastics of the day; the liberal patroness
of their works in Greece, Asia, Syria, not only by donations of money but even of landed property. We may not
admire, what was regarded in those days as among the
most admirable traits of saintliness, a total disregard to
personal neatness and cleanliness, but we can admire her
frugal living, and entire devotion of her time to ministering to the wants of the sick, the needy, and the ignorant.
Her too indiscriminate liberality was restrained by Chrysostom, who represented to her that, as her wealth was a
trust committed to her by God, she ought to be prudent

in the distribution of it. This salutary advice procured for him the ill-will of many avaricious bishops and clergy, who had profited, or hoped to profit, by her wealth.[1] She, on her side, repaid the Archbishop for his spiritual care by many little feminine attentions to his bodily wants, especially by seeing that he was supplied with wholesome food, and did not overstrain his feeble constitution by a too rigid abstinence.[2]

The leaders of the faction hostile to Chrysostom among the clergy were the two bishops already mentioned—Severian of Gabala, and Antiochus of Ptolemais. To these was added a third in the person of Acacius, Bishop of Berœa. He had in A.D. 401 or A.D. 402 paid a visit to Constantinople, and, in a fit of rage at what he considered the mean lodging and inhospitable entertainment of the Archbishop, had coarsely exclaimed, in the hearing of some of the clergy, 'I'll season a dainty dish for him.'[3] The ladies who acquired a melancholy pre-eminence among the enemies of the Archbishop were the intimate friends of the Empress, already mentioned—Marsa, widow of Promotus, the consul whom Rufinus murdered; Castricia, wife of the consul Saturninus; and Eugraphia, a wealthy widow—all rich women 'who used *for* evil the wealth which their husbands had *through* evil obtained.' Proud, intriguing, licentious, they were all exasperated against the Archbishop for the censure which he had not spared to pronounce upon their moral conduct, as well as their vain and extravagant display in dress. The house of Eugraphia became the rendezvous of all clergy and monks, as well as laity, who were disaffected to him. Among the clergy was Atticus, who was obtruded on the

---

[1] Theophilus is said to have fallen down before her and kissed her knees, an obeisance prompted by avaricious hopes on his part, and repelled by genuine humility on hers.

[2] Pall. Dial. cc. 16 and 17. Sozom. viii. 9.

[3] Pall. Dial. c. 6. Tillemont, xiv. p. 219 seq.: ἐγὼ αὐτῷ ἀρτύω χύτραν.

see as Archbishop after the banishment of Chrysostom. This worthy cabal collected, and disseminated with praiseworthy industry, whatever tales could damage the character and influence of the Archbishop. His real failings were exaggerated and others were invented, and his language misrepresented. ' He was irascible, inhospitable, uncourteous, parsimonious; he had unmercifully assailed Eutropius with harsh language when he fled for refuge to the Church; he had behaved disrespectfully to Gaïnas when he was ' magister militum ;' but, worse than all, he had audaciously attacked the Augusta herself, and had insulted her sacred majesty by indicating her under the name of Jezebel. This is scarcely credible in itself, and is distinctly contradicted by the most trustworthy authorities; but it is stated that he had reproved the Empress for appropriating with harshness if not violence a piece of land; and of course the blows which he directed against inordinate luxury, unseemly parade of dress and the like, fell heavily upon the most prominent leader in these follies. She was probably mortified also to find that her display of religious zeal, her pious attendance on the services of the Church, her pilgrimages, her really liberal donations to good works, did not protect her from censure in other things. Chrysostom was not one of those who would connive at evil for the benefit, as some might have represented it, of the Church. He would not sacrifice what he believed to be the interests of morality, for the supposed advantage either of himself or of the Church over which he ruled. Wrong was wrong, and must be rebuked though the actor was the Empress herself, though that Empress was inclined to be the benefactress and patroness of the Church, though she might become, as she *did* become, his implacable enemy, and chief director of those who were inimical to him.

The clergy only needed an equally potent leader on

their side, and then the organisation of the hostile forces would be complete. Such a chief was to be found in the Patriarch of Alexandria, Theophilus, who had already displayed a malignant spirit at the ordination of the Archbishop, though intimidated by Eutropius into submission. He was only waiting his opportunity for revenge, which a concurrence of circumstances now put into his hands.

After making the most of such charges as gossip, aided by malice, could manufacture at Constantinople, the enemy employed one of the party, a despicable Syrian monk named Isaac, to make a scrutinising enquiry at Antioch into the previous life of Chrysostom. A youth passed in such a licentious and voluptuous city could not fail, they thought, to betray some stains if submitted to a rigorous inspection. But their malevolent expectations were disappointed, for their miserable spy could bring back nothing but unmixed praise of an immaculate youth and a pious manhood.[1]

At this juncture the intriguers applied to Theophilus, and they could not have secured a more willing and able director of their plans. The character of this prelate, and his prominent position in the final events of Chrysostom's career, demand some notice. Of his family and early life little is known. He had a sister who sympathised with him in his ambitious schemes; and Cyril, who succeeded him in the patriarchate, and too largely inherited his spirit, was his nephew. He spent a portion of his younger manhood as a recluse in the Nitrian desert, where he became familiar with the most eminent anchorites of that period, Elurion, Ammon, Isidore, and Macarius. He was secretary to Athanasius, and a presbyter of Alexandria under Peter, his successor; and, on the death of Timothy in A.D. 385, who succeeded Peter, he was elevated to the see. All historians concur in admitting

[1] Pall. Dial. ce. 5, 6, 18, 19.

that he possessed great ability; that he was capable of conceiving great projects, and executing them with courage and address. Jerome has described him as deeply skilled in science, especially mathematics and astrology, and highly praises his eloquence.[1] He had a passion for building, and his episcopate was distinguished equally by the destruction of Pagan temples and the erection of Christian churches. The most splendid of these were the church of St. John the Baptist at Alexandria, and another at Canopus. But to gratify this expensive taste he was grasping of money, too often to the neglect of those indigent people who were dependent on the alms of the Church. He combined his efforts with Chrysostom's, as has been already related, in healing the schism of Antioch in A.D. 399, after which little is known of his history, till he becomes Chrysostom's implacable and too successful foe.[2]

---

[1] Jerome in Ruf. lib. ii. c. 5.   Ep. xxxi. p. 203.
[2] Tillemont, xi. ' Vie de Theoph.'

CHAPTER XVII.

CIRCUMSTANCES WHICH LED TO THE INTERFERENCE OF THEOPHILUS
WITH THE AFFAIRS OF CHRYSOSTOM — CONTROVERSY ABOUT THE
WRITINGS OF ORIGEN—PERSECUTION BY THEOPHILUS OF THE MONKS
CALLED 'THE TALL BRETHREN'—THEIR FLIGHT TO PALESTINE—TO
CONSTANTINOPLE—THEIR RECEPTION BY CHRYSOSTOM—THEOPHILUS
SUMMONED TO CONSTANTINOPLE.   A.D. 395–403.

In tracing to its starting-point the interference of Theophilus with the affairs of Chrysostom, we have to unravel
a curious and tangled skein of controversy. The doctrines
of Origen were as much an occasion of strife a hundred
and fifty years after his death, as he himself had been
during his life.   With one hand holding on to the philosophy of the past, and with the other firmly grasping the
Christianity of the present, he was persecuted by Pagans,
yet never universally accepted and cordially trusted by
the Church.[1]   So with his system of doctrine; it became
a sort of debatable ground for the possession of which
contending parties strove.   The prize was worth the
struggle; for the genius of Origen could not be questioned, but the quantity of his writings being enormous,[2]
and the range of his doctrine wide and many-sided,
narrow-minded partisans, grasping only a part of it, condemned or extolled him unfairly on a single issue.   The
mystical element in his teaching was carried by some of
his admirers to extremes of fanciful, allegorical interpretation of Scripture, such as he himself would never
have devised or approved.   To others of a more prosaic,
material cast of thought this same mystical vein was re-

---

[1] Euseb. Hist. vi. 3, 19.

[2] Jerome declared that Origen had composed more books than most men would find time to copy.—Epist. xxix.

pugnant, and was denounced by them with characteristic
coarseness. Men of larger minds, who had patience to
peruse his voluminous works, and ability to criticise
them, admired his genius, recognised his great services to
Christianity, heartily embraced much of his teaching,
questioned some portions, and rejected others. Such
were Gregory of Nazianzum, Basil, Chrysostom, and
Jerome, who would never have been so great as writers,
or commentators, had they not been students of Origen.
As a general statement, it may be true to say that he
was less acceptable to the colder, more practical, more
realistic mind of the Western Church, than to the lively
imagination and speculative spirit of Oriental churchmen.
The most controverted points, indeed, in his system were
of a kind with which the Western mind did not naturally
occupy itself. The pre-existence of souls ; their entrance
into human bodies after the fall as the punishment of
sin ; their emancipation from the flesh in the resurrection;
the ultimate salvation of all spirits, including Satan himself,—these are questions singularly congenial to Oriental,
singularly alien from Western thought. The Origenistic
controversy fell into abeyance before the engrossing interest and importance of the Arian contest; but when that
wave had spent itself, it revived, and just at this period
all the greatest names of the day became engaged on one
side or the other. As usual, the real questions at issue
were too often forgotten amidst the personal jealousies,
intrigues, angry recriminations to which the discussion of
them gave birth.

In spite of his doubtful orthodoxy, the Egyptian Church
could not fail to be proud of so distinguished a son as
Origen, and Theophilus was at first his earnest defender.
Some of the more illiterate Egyptian monks had recoiled
from Origen's highly spiritual conception of the Deity
into an opposite extreme. Interpreting literally those

passages of Scripture where God is spoken of as if possessing human emotions and corporeal parts, they altogether
humanised his name; they conceived of Him as a Being
not 'without body, parts or passions;' they obtained, in
consequence, the designation of 'Anthropomorphites.'
Against this humanising, material conception Theophilus,
in a paschal·letter, directed argument and reproof.[1]   It
was received by many of the monks with dismay, sorrow,
and resistance.   Serapion, one of the most aged, burst
into tears when informed that the mind of the Eastern
Church concurred, on the whole, with the doctrine of
Theophilus, and exclaimed, 'My God is taken away, and
I know not what to worship.'[2]

Rufinus, a monk of Aquileia, and for a time the ardent
friend of Jerome, was, during a visit to Egypt, initiated
by Theophilus into the doctrines of Origen, conceived a
warm admiration for them, extolled him as the light of
the Gospel next to the Apostles, and imparted some of
his own enthusiasm to John, Bishop of Jerusalem, whom
he soon afterwards visited.   Jerome fully appreciated the
merits of Origen, though his larger mind and more extensive knowledge was not blind to his defects.

Such were the amicable relations between the leading
churchmen of the East in A.D. 395, when a visitor from
the West threw among them the apple of discord.   This
was Aterbius, a pilgrim, who had a reputation as a subtle
theologian, and appears, immediately on his arrival in
Jerusalem, to have applied himself to the business of
detecting heresy.   He entered into friendly intercourse
for a short time with the bishop and Rufinus, and then
suddenly included Jerome with them both in a public

---

[1] The 'Paschal letter' was a circular addressed to clergy and monks
throughout the diocese soon after the
Epiphany; the primary object was to
announce the date of the 1st day of
Lent and of Easter day, whence the
name; but other matters were, as in
the present instance, frequently introduced. See Tillemont, xi. 462.

[2] Socr. vi. 7. Sozom. viii. 11, 12.

denunciation as Origenists, and declared the whole diocese
of Jerusalem to be infected with that heresy. Jerome
immediately and indignantly repudiated the charge from
himself; he declared that he was not an Origenist, for
that he merely read the works of Origen with reservations
as he might those of a heretic.[1] Rufinus would not
condescend to make any defence, oral or written, but shut
himself up in his cloister in sullen silence till Aterbius
had quitted Jerusalem, fearing, so Jerome affirms, to condemn what he really approved, or to incur the reproach
of heresy by an open resistance.[2] John of Jerusalem
was equally indignant at the accusation, but displeased
with Jerome for publicly exculpating himself independently of his bishop. In fact, the episcopal pride of the
Bishop of Jerusalem was severely wounded at this time,
both by the pre-eminence of the metropolitan See of
Cæsarea,[3] and by the reputation of Jerome's monastic
establishment at Bethlehem, which attracted visitors from
all parts of Christendom.

When the minds of all were thus ruffled, a second and
far more mischievous visitor arrived in the person of
Epiphanius, the octogenarian Bishop of Salamis and
Cyprus. He was one of those men who, joining some
erudition and a high reputation for rigid orthodoxy to
a narrow mind and impulsive temper, figure prominently
in theological warfare as the very personifications of
discord. Shocked at the intelligence of the heretical
tendency in Palestine, and vexed that it should have
been detected by a stranger rather than by himself, who
was a native of Palestine, and the visitor of a monastery
between Jerusalem and Hebron, he lost not a moment in

---

[1] Jerome in Ruf. iii.; and Ep. lxi.

[2] In Ruf. iii. 33.

[3] The contest for precedence was
eventually decided in favour of Jerusalem. The See was made a Patriarchate in the reign of Theodosius II.,
and its jurisdiction fixed to the three
Palestines by the Council of Chalcedon, A.D. 451.

setting out for the Holy City. He accepted the hospitality of the Bishop John, and spent the evening in all
amity with him, nor was the obnoxious subject of dispute
mentioned between them.[1]

A strange scene took place on the following day.

In the Church of the Holy Sepulchre, in the presence
of a large congregation, Epiphanius fulminated a discourse against Origen, his doctrines, and all who favoured
them. Bishop John and his clergy expressed their contempt by grimaces, sneers, and impatient scratchings of
their heads. At last an archdeacon stepped forward, and
required Epiphanius, in the name of the bishop, to desist
from his discourse. The assembly was dissolved, but
met again in the afternoon, largely augmented, in the
Church of the Holy Cross. This time Bishop John dis-
coursed, and denounced the Anthropomorphites, or Hu-
manisers, under which opprobrious name the partisans
of Origen endeavoured to include all their opponents.
Pale and trembling, and in a voice quivering with passion,
the bishop directed his discourse, and turned his body
towards Epiphanius, who sat motionless in his chair. The
invective being concluded, the aged Bishop of Salamis
rose and pronounced these words with solemn delibe-
ration: 'All that John, my brother in the priesthood, my
son in age, has just said against the heresy of the Anthropomorphites I thoroughly approve; and as we both
condemn that absurd belief, it is only just that we should
both denounce the errors of Origen.'[2] A general laugh
and acclamation on the part of the assembly proclaimed
their sense of this speech as a successful hit. John made
one more effort to right himself. He preached again in
the Church of the Holy Cross, this time on the chief
verities of the faith, the Trinity, the Incarnation, the
Atonement, the condition of souls before and after this

[1] Jerome, Ep. xxxviii.   [2] Ibid.

life. It was intended to be a grand and convincing display of his orthodoxy, and at the moment Epiphanius
expressed even approbation. On subsequent reflection,
however, the aged critic thought he discovered that it
teemed with error. He abruptly quitted Jerusalem, repaired to Bethlehem, resisted the solicitation of Jerome
and his friends to be reconciled, and addressed a circular letter to all the monasteries of Palestine, requiring
them to break off communion with the Bishop of Jerusalem.

Rufinus ranged himself immediately on the side of
Bishop John; but Jerome, though with somewhat balanced
feelings, sided on the whole with Epiphanius. Then the
pent-up jealousy of John towards the monasteries of
Bethlehem burst forth; they were placed under interdict,
and the Church of the Holy Manger closed against them.
They were in despair for want of a priest to celebrate
the Eucharist; but Epiphanius provided one through a
forcible ordination. The young Paulinian had always
stedfastly declined holy orders, though considered eminently qualified by his learning and virtue. He was now
on a visit to the monastery of Epiphanius, near Eleu-
theropolis. When Epiphanius was celebrating the Eucharist, the young man was seized by the deacons, dragged
to the steps of the altar, and there made to kneel. Epiphanius approached, cut off some of his hair, ordained
him deacon, and obliged him to assist in the celebration
on the spot. At a fresh sign from the bishop he was a
second time seized, gagged to prevent his adjuring the
bishop in the name of Jesus Christ, and when he rose
from his knees he was pronounced to be priest.[1] The
joy which filled the monasteries of Bethlehem was only to
be equalled by the indignation of their opponents at Jerusalem. John actually applied (not without money, it is said)

[1] Jerome, Ep. cx.

to Rufinus at Constantinople, then Prætorian Prefect, and
even procured a decree of banishment against Jerome;[1]
but, the murder of Rufinus taking place soon afterwards,
the Governor of Cæsarea evaded the execution of the
decree. Jerome retaliated by one of those fierce, nervous
philippics which exhibit more command of language than
of temper. The Governor of Palestine made a praiseworthy but ineffectual effort to bring about a reconciliation. John had determined to invite an arbitrator,
from whom he expected a strong partiality for his own
cause. He appealed to Theophilus, from whom Rufinus,
the monk, had derived his first acquaintance with Origen.
Jerome indignantly complained of this invocation of a
foreign jurisdiction. Was not Cæsarea the metropolitan
see of Palestine? why this contempt of ecclesiastical
law?[2] Theophilus, however, had no scruples in accepting the appeal. It was just one of those recognitions of
pre-eminence which the Patriarch of Alexandria, like the
bishops of Rome, joyfully welcomed. The gratification
of ambition was pleasantly disguised from others, and
perhaps from themselves, under the semblance of peace-
making. Theophilus despatched Isidore as his legate to
Palestine. His arrival was preceded by two letters, one
intended for the Bishop of Jerusalem, the other for Vincentius, the presbyter and friend of Jerome at Bethlehem.

Unfortunately the letter intended for the bishop was
delivered to Vincentius, and he and Jerome read with
indignation assurances of sympathy and friendship towards John, and expressions of contempt for Jerome and
his party, the language, in short, of an accomplice rather
than of an arbitrator. It set forth in flowery oriental
terms the confidence of the legate in the success of his
mission; 'as smoke disperses in the air, as wax melts
before the fire, so will these enemies, who always resist

---

[1] Jerome, Epp. xxxviii. and xxxix.   [2] Ibid. xxxviii.

.the faith, and seek to disturb it now, by means of simple ignorant men, be dispersed on my arrival.'[1] The legate took up his abode at Jerusalem, and spent his time in familiar intercourse with the bishop and Rufinus. To Bethlehem he paid occasional visits, where he conducted himself with dictatorial haughtiness. Jerome and the monks plainly perceived that the so-called arbitrator was committed to one side—which was not theirs.

But on a sudden, in A.D. 398, the Patriarch wheeled round; he discovered that he had been in error. ' The writings of Origen were fraught with danger to the unlearned, however profitable to philosophic minds.' Such was the reason alleged for this sudden revulsion of opinion. The real reasons appear to have been of a less calm and philosophic character. One of the most distinguished presbyters in Alexandria at this time was Isidore, an octogenarian. His youth had been spent in pious seclusion, among the monks of Scetis and Nitria, and his piety had attracted the notice of Athanasius, whom he accompanied to Rome in A.D. 341, and by whom he was afterwards ordained priest. He became the Hospitaller of the Church in Alexandria, whose duty it was to attend to the reception of Christian visitors. In spite of great personal austerity, he was, as became his position, gentle and amiable to all men, even pagans, when brought into contact with them. In A.D. 398, at the age of eighty, he had been employed to carry to Rome the recognition by Theophilus of Flavian as Bishop of Antioch; and now, in the extremity of age, he was destined to become the first victim of a persecution from Theophilus, which, beginning with him, culminated in the deposition and exile of Chrysostom.[2]

An opulent widow committed to Isidore a large sum of money to be expended on clothing for the poor of Alexandria, and adjured him by a solemn oath to conceal the

---

[1] Jer. Ep. xxxviii.   [2] Pallad. Laus. p. 901.   Tillemont, vol. xi.

trust from Theophilus, lest the Patriarch's well-known cupidity should be tempted to appropriate the money to aid his grand operations in building. The precaution, however, was vain: nothing said or done in his diocese could escape the vigilance of informers in the employ of Theophilus. Isidore was questioned by the Patriarch concerning the charitable gift, and required to place the money at his disposal; but the hospitaller refused, and boldly maintained that it would be better bestowed on the bodies of the sick and poor, which were the temples of God, than on the erection of buildings. The Patriarch was astounded at the temerity of his disobedience, but dissembled for the moment the depth of his resentment. Two months later, in a convocation of the clergy, he produced a paper containing the charge of a horrible and unmentionable crime against Isidore, which the Patriarch said he had received eighteen years ago, but had been unable to prove from the absence of the principal witness. The whole charge turned out to be a baseless fabrication ; but Isidore was ejected from the priesthood by the contrivance of Theophilus.[1]

The aged hospitaller fled to the peaceful retreat of his earlier days, the desert of Nitria. The most distinguished of the monks in this seclusion were four brothers —Ammon, Dioscorus, Eusebius, and Euthymius—eminent alike for their piety and the height of their stature, whence they were known by the name of the 'tall brethren.' They were venerated as the fathers of the Nitrian monks. Theophilus had in former times professed the highest admiration and respect for their virtues. He had made the eldest, Dioscorus, Bishop of Hermopolis, and had persuaded, if not compelled, Eusebius and Euthy-

---

[1] Pallad. Dial. c. 6. Other causes of the enmity of Theophilus are mentioned by Socrat. vi. 9. and Sozomen. viii. 12. but not incompatible with the account of Palladius.

mius, much against their will, to be presbyters in Alexandria.[1] Their simple piety was so much shocked by the
avarice and other failings of the Patriarch, that they
implored to be released from clerical duties and restored
to the freedom of the desert. When Theophilus discovered their real reason for requesting this permission
he was furious, and tried to intimidate them into submission by fierce menaces, but in vain. They withdrew,
and for a time the Patriarch was at a loss how to execute
vengeance on men who had few possessions of any kind
to be deprived of. But now the opportunity arrived.
Isidore, the excommunicated hospitaller, had been sheltered in their friendly retreat. Theophilus devised a
malignant plan for disturbing their peace. The ' tall
brethren ' belonged to that more mystical order of monks
which embraced Origen's doctrine of a purely spiritual
Deity, and were determined adversaries of the more
sensuous and anthropomorphite school. Theophilus now
scrupled not to declare himself in favour of the Anthropomorphites, whom he had formerly denounced. He encouraged the more coarse and ignorant to make violent
and tumultuous assaults on the monastic retreat of
Nitria, and directed the bishops of the neighbourhood to
eject several of the most distinguished monks, including
Ammon. They repaired to Alexandria, sought an interview with Theophilus, requested to hear the cause of their
ejection, and remonstrated on the treatment of Isidore.
Theophilus burst into a violent rage, changed colour at
every moment, glared on them with bloodshot eyes, dealt
blows to Ammon on his face, and, while the blood trickled
down, shouted ' Heretic, anathematise Origen.' One of
the number was put in prison to intimidate the rest ; but
they all entered it voluntarily together, and refused to
come out unless their companion also was released. This

---

[1] Socrat. vi. 7.

was at length permitted, but the design of persecution
was followed up. The Patriarch's paschal letter of A.D.
401 is chiefly occupied with a condemnation of Origen
and his disciples. He confesses, indeed, that he had
himself at one time been cast into that fiery furnace of
error, but, like the three children, he had come out unscathed; 'not even his hair or garments had been singed,'
figurative language to imply that his orthodoxy had not
been in the minutest degree impaired. He describes
himself as having now returned from the land of captivity to the true Jerusalem; Origen and his doctrines are
condemned with much heat; and a prominent place is
assigned to him and all his disciples in the infernal
regions.[1]

But Theophilus was far from being contented to stop
at this point. He convoked a synod of neighbouring
bishops. The monks were not informed of it, nor invited
to appear and make their defence. Three of the most
eminent were excommunicated as heretics and magicians.
It was in vain that the monks protested against the
injustice of condemning Origen or his readers on the
strength of a few passages only, and those, as they maintained, in many instances garbled or interpolated. A
synodical letter was published, addressed to the Catholic
world, reprobating the writings of Origen. It produced
a profound sensation in Rome, where the Pope Anastasius anathematised Origen.[2] But the humiliation of
the Nitrian brethren was not yet complete. Five most
insignificant monks, scarce worthy, according to Palladius,
to discharge menial offices as lay brethren, were ordained
by Theophilus, one to a bishopric, one to be priest, and
the three others to be deacons. A small town was created
a see, there being none vacant to receive the new bishop.

---

[1] Pasch. Epist. of Theoph. quoted
in Tillemont, xi. p. 470. Pallad. Dial.

3. Sozom. viii. 12.
[2] Sulpic. Sever. lib. i. c. 3.

With these tools the Patriarch could rapidly execute his designs. His creatures prepared, under his direction, a list of complaints and charges against the Nitrian monks, which they publicly presented to him in church. Armed with this, he had an interview with the governor of Egypt, and obtained from him an order for the forcible expulsion of insubordinate monks from the settlement at Nitria. With a troop of soldiers and a rabble of rascals, such as in all large towns are ready for the perpetration of any mischief, whom he had previously primed with drink, the Patriarch fell by night upon the monastic dwellings. Dioscorus was the first victim of his rage. He was one of the 'tall brethren,' who had been compelled by Theophilus to become Bishop of Hermopolis. He was now dragged before the Patriarch by some rude Ethiopian slaves, and told that he was deprived of his see. Diligent search was made for the three other brethren, but they were undiscoverably hidden in a well. The fury of the Patriarch expended itself principally upon inanimate objects; the dwellings of the monks were pillaged and, burned, together with their valuable libraries, and, to the horror of the pious, some of the Eucharistic elements [1] also.

The work of destruction being accomplished, Theophilus returned to Alexandria. The terrified monks came out of their hiding-places, and, wrapping themselves in their sheepskins, their only remaining property, set out from their beloved solitudes to seek shelter and a new home elsewhere. Three hundred, following the 'tall brethren,' took their journey towards Palestine; the rest dispersed in different directions. Not more than eighty arrived with the four brethren at Jerusalem, whence they shortly afterwards withdrew northwards to Scythopolis, a place eminently adapted to their wants by its situation in a

[1] Pallad. Dial. c. 7.

well-watered valley rich in palm trees, of which the leaves
furnished materials for mats, baskets, and the other
articles usually wrought by monkish labour.[1] But distance
did not diminish the malice of their persecutor. They
were pursued by letters from Theophilus addressed to all
the bishops of Palestine, who were admonished not to
grant ecclesiastical communion or shelter to the heretical
fugitives. Jerome mentions two commissioners who
scoured Palestine, and left no hole or cave unexplored in
the diligence of their search for the offenders.[2] Thus
hunted and harassed, the poor monks at length resolved
to embark for Constantinople, throw themselves on the
generosity of the Emperor and Archbishop, and submit
their cause to their decision. They reached the capital,
fifty in number; their foreign aspect, bare arms and
knees, and primitive garb of white sheepskins, excited
much curiosity and interest among the people of Constantinople. They repaired first of all to Chrysostom, in
the hope that his authority would be sufficient to procure
them justice, without an application to the civil powers.
The Archbishop received them with great kindness and
respect, and shed tears of compassion when he heard the
tale of their sufferings and wanderings. But he acted
with caution; he consulted some Alexandrian clergy who
were at this time in Constantinople engaged in distributing
presents to conciliate, or, more properly speaking, to bribe,
the favour of persons just appointed to civil offices in
Egypt. They admitted the virtues and hard usage of
the monks, but recommended him not to incur the displeasure of Theophilus by admitting them to communion.
The monks were lodged in the precincts of the church of
Anastasia; Olympias and other pious women attended to
their wants, which were to some extent supplied by the
produce of their own manual labour. They were ad-

[1] Sozom. viii. 13.   [2] Jer. Ep. lxx.

mitted to prayer in the church, but excluded from the Eucharist until the merits of their cause should have been carefully sifted, and their excommunication revoked. Chrysostom, unsuspicious of others, in his own innocence, was sanguine of his power to obtain their restitution. He despatched a letter to Theophilus, in which he besought him in courteous and friendly terms to be reconciled with the fugitives, and thereby to confer a favour on himself, his spiritual son and brother. But no notice was taken of the request; and meanwhile the agents of Theophilus were busily employed at Constantinople in disseminating injurious tales about the monks—they were heretics, magicians, rebels.

Throughout the rest of Christendom Theophilus pursued a different method. He toiled with diligence worthy of a better cause to obtain a wide condemnation of Origen and his works. Could he once secure such a general condemnation, and then prove Chrysostom and the monks to be at variance with it, he would possess a powerful engine in working the ruin of both. It is difficult to believe that even Theophilus would have pursued the monks with such insatiable animosity had they not fled to the patriarch of that see which was regarded with peculiar jealousy by the bishops of Alexandria, and had not the present occupant of that see been elected in preference to the candidate put forward by himself. Thus he clutched at the opportunity of depressing his rival, and punishing his victims, the monks, at the same time.

He found a faction hostile to the Archbishop already existing in Constantinople, and quite ready to submit the management of their interests to his skilful direction. The persecution of the monks was quickly dropped. Their supposed offence was only the handle by which to compass the destruction of a more formidable foe. Jerome contributed powerful aid to the designs of Theophilus by favourable notices of him in his letters, depreciating the conduct of the monks.[1]   But a more active auxiliary appeared in the Bishop of Salamis, whose advanced age seems never to have diminished the alacrity with which he entered the lists of controversy. Theophilus, in his Origenistic days, had attacked Epiphanius with some vehemence as an anthropomorphite; but he now wrote a letter to the bishop expressing regret for his former language, and his increasing conviction of the mischievous tendency of Origen's doctrines.[2] He implored his holy brother to convene a council of the bishops of Cyprus without delay, for the purpose of condemning the heretic, and of drawing up letters, announcing their decision, to be sent round to the principal sees, especially Constantinople, where the heretical and contumacious monks were harboured. Epiphanius flattered himself that he had converted the Patriarch, and was delighted to receive such a powerful accession to his side. The council was summoned, the condemnation carried, and the letters despatched.[3] Theophilus himself, at the commencement of A.D. 402, issued a paschal letter, which contained a subtle exposition and refutation of the Origenistic errors. The letter was translated, and highly commended, both for matter and expression, by Jerome.[4]

To Chrysostom himself Theophilus wrote a sharp complaint of his protecting heretics, and violating the canon of Nice, which prohibited any bishop from exercising jurisdiction in matters relating to another see.   The cause of the Nitrian monks, he asserted, could not be decided legally anywhere but in a council of Egyptian bishops. It will be borne in mind, however, that Chrysostom had carefully abstained from pronouncing any

---

[1] Jer. Ep. lxxviii. in Ruf. Epp. lxvii. lxxiii.

[2] Socr. vi. 9. Soz. viii. 14.

[3] Socr. (vi. c. 13) says that the writings only of Origen, not the man himself, were condemned.   [4] Ep. lxxviii.

decision, through a council or otherwise, on the affair of the monks. They, indeed, became provoked with him that he did not espouse their cause more heartily. The agents of Theophilus were busily engaged in damaging their character; a little money easily persuaded the sailors and others employed in the Alexandrian corn trade to point at the monks in the streets as magicians and heretics. The monks declared to Chrysostom their resolution to appeal to the civil powers to obtain a formal prosecution of their accusers as base calumniators. Chrysostom remonstrated, and declined, if that step was taken, to mediate any more in their affair. Some of his enemies in Constantinople did not fail to make capital out of this also, as a cruel desertion of those whom he had at first befriended.[1]

Thus hostile forces were on all sides closing round the Archbishop, but he continued apparently unconscious of the snares which were being woven for him. The Origenistic controversy, into the vortex of which his enemies sought to drag him, possessed little interest for him. The more mystical, abstract speculations of Origen's theology were alien from his practical sphere of work and practical habit of mind; and, in common with the other chief representatives of the Antiochene school, Diodorus and Theodore, he neither wholly embraced nor wholly rejected his system of doctrine. At any rate, he paid no attention to the letter from Salamis, which requested him to join in the condemnation of Origen and his writings. This was precisely what his enemies wanted.

The Nitrian monks, cast off by the Archbishop when they had announced their intention of appealing to secular authority, drew up documents filled with charges of the most flagrant crimes against their accusers and against Theophilus. They demanded that their calumniators in

[1] Pall. Dial. c. 8.

Constantinople should be immediately tried by the prefect,
and that Theophilus should be summoned to defend his
conduct before a council under the presidency of Chrysostom.   One day, as the Empress was riding in her litter to
worship in the church of St. John the Baptist at Hebdomon, she was accosted by some of those strange skin-
clad beings of whom, and of whose wanderings and
wrongs, she had heard much.   She caused her litter to
stop, bowed graciously to the monks, and implored the
favour of their prayers for the Empire, the Emperor,
herself, and her children.   The monks presented their
petition; Eudoxia courteously accepted it, and promised
them that the council which they desired should be convened; that Theophilus should be summoned to attend it,
and that the accusers now in Constantinople should either
substantiate their charges, or suffer the penalties of
calumnious defamation.   This enquiry was immediately
instituted; the poor culprits confessed that they had been
paid agents of Theophilus, and that their accusations had
been dictated by him.   They therefore entreated that
their trial might be deferred till his arrival.   Meanwhile,
however, they were put in prison, where one of them died;
and as the arrival of Theophilus continued to be delayed,
they were banished to Proconnesus for libel.   An officer
was despatched to Alexandria to serve Theophilus with a
peremptory summons to appear at Constantinople, and
empowered to enforce his obedience if he was reluctant.[1]

Thus the preparations for a judicial investigation of the
affair of the monks emanated not from Chrysostom, but
from the throne, although he was represented by his
enemies as the originator, and by Jerome he is styled a
parricide for labouring to condemn Theophilus.[2]   Chrysostom seems, in fact, to have dismissed alike the business
of the monks and the theological question of Origenism

---

[1] Soz. viii. 13.   Pall. Dial. c. 8.   [2] Ep. xvi.

from his mind. Intent on edifying the Church, instead of agitating it by personal or polemical strife, he quietly pursued his daily routine of duties as chief pastor, feeding his flock with the wholesome food of the Word and of the bread of life.

Theophilus was unable to evade obedience to the summons which commanded him to repair to Constantinople. His only hope now was to change his position from that of the accused into that of the accuser. The council which was called together for the purpose of investigating his conduct should, by his contrivance, be transferred into a council for arraigning Chrysostom of heresy and misdemeanour. The letters of Epiphanius and Theophilus having failed to obtain from Chrysostom that condemnation which they demanded of the writings of Origen, the Bishop of Salamis, at the urgent request of Theophilus, set forth at the beginning of A.D. 403 for Constantinople, bringing the decree of the Council of Cyprus for the signature of the Archbishop. Theophilus slowly proceeded overland from Egypt through Syria, Cicilia, and Asia Minor, in order to bring up as many bishops as possible to the council, who would be prepared to act under his direction. Epiphanius, having landed, halted at the church of St. John, outside Constantinople, held an assembly of clergy, and even, it is said, committed the irregularity of ordaining a deacon.[1] Chrysostom, however, acted with all due courtesy and discretion. He sent out a large body of clergy to welcome the visitor by inviting and conducting him to the hospitable lodging prepared for him in the archiepiscopal palace. Epiphanius, acting on preconceived judgment of the two chief subjects in dispute, declined the offer unless the Archbishop would consent to expel the monks, and to sign the decree against Origen. Chrysostom justly replied that

---

[1] Socr. vi. c. 12.

he could not anticipate the decision of a council which
was being summoned for the very purpose of considering
both these questions.   Epiphanius, therefore, found a
lodging elsewhere, and diligently strove to induce such
bishops as he could collect to sign the decree.[1] His
reputation for learning, orthodoxy, and piety secured the
consent of many, but on the part of many more there was
determined opposition.   Eminent among these was Theotimus, a Goth by birth, but educated in Greece, who had
been made Bishop of Tomis and Metropolitan of Scythia.
He was a man of genuine sanctity, ascetic habits, and
courageous spirit.   Tomis was a great central market of
Gothic and Hunnish tribes, and the bishop used boldly to
enter the motley concourse and try to win converts.   He
would invite savage Huns to partake of some hospitable
entertainment in his house, and by gifts and little attentions, and courteous treatment, he sought to soften their
ferocity, and effect an opening in their hearts for the
reception of Christian teaching.   He came to be regarded
by them with a kind of superstitious reverence, and was
commonly called by them 'the god of the Christians.'
Over his half-episcopal, half-barbarian costume flowed the
long hair which betokened his Gothic origin.   He lifted
up his voice with boldness to denounce the present ill-
considered condemnation of the works of Origen.   It was
unseemly and unjust, he maintained, to pass a coarse and
sweeping sentence on the entire works of one whose genius
had been acknowledged by the whole Church.   He produced a volume of Origen, and from it read some beautiful,
powerful passages of irreproachable orthodoxy.   Then,
turning to Epiphanius, he asked him how he could attack
a man to whom the Church owed a thousand similar, and
even more beautiful passages.   'How call him a son of

[1] Soc. vi. 12.   Soz. viii. 14.

Satan? Place what is good in him on one side, and what is bad on the other, and then choose.'[1]

This courageous protest, however, did not divert Epiphanius and his partisans from their course of action. In fact, they proceeded a step further. It was arranged that when a large congregation was collected in the Church of the Apostles, Epiphanius should enter and harangue the assembly, denouncing both the writings of Origen and his admirers, especially the 'tall brethren,' and even Chrysostom himself as their protector. Chrysostom, however, received intimation of their design, and by his direction Serapion confronted Epiphanius at the entrance of the church, and told him that ' he had already violated ecclesiastical law by ordaining a deacon in the diocese and church of another bishop, but to minister and preach without permission was a still grosser outrage; a popular tumult would probably ensue, and Epiphanius would be held responsible for any violence which might be committed.' Epiphanius, though not without angry remonstrances, desisted.[2]

Eudoxia seems to have placed special faith in the intercessions of ecclesiastical visitors of distinction. As she had formerly asked the prayers of the 'tall brethren,' so now, the young prince her son (afterwards Theodosius II.) being attacked by an alarming illness, she implored the prayers of Epiphanius on his behalf. The bishop replied that her child's recovery depended on her repudiation of the heretical refugees. The Empress, however, declared that she should prefer simply to resign her son's life to the will of God who gave it, without complying with the requisition of Epiphanius.[3]

It may be that these incidents were beginning to tell upon the reason of the aged zealot, and open his eyes to the irregularity of his proceedings; at any rate, shortly

---

[1] Sozom. viii. 14 and 26.   [2] Socr. vi. 14.   [3] Soz. viii. 14.

after this, he granted an interview to Ammon and his
brothers. The record of the conversation is instructive.
'Allow me to ask, holy father,' said Ammon, 'whether
you have ever read any of our works or those of our disciples?' Epiphanius was obliged to confess that he had
not even seen them, and that he had formed his judgment
simply from general report. 'How then,' replied Ammon,
'can you venture to condemn us when you have no proof
of our opinions? We have pursued a widely different
course. We conversed with your disciples, we read your
works, among others one entitled the "Anchor of Faith";
and when we met with persons who ridiculed your opinions,
and asserted that your writings were replete with heresy,
we have defended you as our father. Is it just on such
slender ground as common report to condemn those who
have so zealously befriended you?' These bold and
pungent remarks are represented to have wrought compunction in the heart of the aged bishop. He began to
perceive that he had been made the agent of a plot, and
he lost no time in extricating himself from it by departing
from Constantinople. His farewell words to some of the
bishops who accompanied him to the ship were, 'I leave
to you the city, the palace, and this piece of acting.'[1] If
the historians speak truly, however, he and Chrysostom
entertained to the last no very kindly feelings towards
each other. Each predicted the misfortune about to befall
the other. When they took leave, Chrysostom said, 'I
hope you will not return to your diocese;' to which
Epiphanius rejoined, 'I hope that you will not die a
bishop.' The wishes of both were fulfilled. Epiphanius
died on the voyage to Cyprus; the deposition of Chrysostom will presently be related.[2]

[1] Soz. c. 15.   [2] Ibid. and Socr. vi. 14.

CHAPTER XVIII.

REGARDLESS of the forces which had been set in motion
against him, Chrysostom pursued his usual course of work
without any variation. The reins of discipline were held
tightly as ever; the Word was preached, in season and
out of season, with unabated diligence; the people were
exhorted, admonished, rebuked with the same irrepressible
earnestness. His enemies took advantage of a sermon,
specially directed against the follies and vices of fashionable ladies, to represent it as an attack upon the Empress
herself.[1] Eudoxia, credulous and impulsive by nature,
and probably irritated because the Archbishop did not
pay her subservient homage, complained to the Emperor
of the insult which had been cast upon her, and was
induced by the hostile party to expect the arrival of
Theophilus as an opportunity for redressing her wrongs.
That prelate was now rapidly approaching, with a large
number of bishops collected from Egypt, Syria, and Asia
Minor. Twenty-eight, on whose partisanship he could
reckon, travelled by sea to Chalcedon. Many bishops had
become disaffected to Chrysostom in Asia Minor, owing to
the rigorous investigation recently made by him into the
state of the Church in that region, and they readily joined
the camp of Theophilus. Prominent among them was

[1] Socr. vi. 15. Soz. viii. 15.

Gerontius of Nicomedia, whom, as will be remembered, he had deposed. The whole force was at length, June 403, assembled at Chalcedon, and a council of war was held to determine the plan of operations. None was more virulent in his denunciation of Chrysostom, as tyrannical, proud, and heretical, than Cyrinus, Bishop of Chalcedon. He was an Egyptian by birth, and Theophilus reckoned on him as a valuable ally, but was deprived of his services by a curious incident. Maruthas, Bishop of Mesopotamia, accidently trod on the foot of Cyrinus; a wound ensued, the wound gangrened, the foot had to be amputated, but the mortification spread, and, after two years of lingering pain, put an end to his life.[1]

Theophilus made his entrance into Constantinople about the middle of June. He had been summoned as a defendant, but, according to his design already indicated, he appeared surrounded by all the pomp and dignity of a judge. None of the bishops, indeed, or clergy of Constantinople came to greet him on landing, but the crews of the Alexandrian corn-fleet gave him a hearty welcome, and he was accompanied by a large retinue, not only of bishops and clergy, but of Alexandrian sailors, laden with some of the costliest produce of Egypt and the East, a very potent auxiliary in obtaining partisans. As on the arrival of Epiphanius, so now, Chrysostom did not fail to offer the customary hospitality due to a brother bishop; but Theophilus disdainfully declined it, passed by the palace and the metropolitan church, which episcopal visitors usually entered on their arrival, and proceeded to the suburb of Pera, where a lodging had been prepared for him in a house of the Emperor's, called the Palace of Placidia.

During the three weeks that he resided here, he refused to hold any communication with Chrysostom, or to

[1] Socr. vi. 15. Soz. viii. 16.

enter his church; nor did he vouchsafe any reply to the frequent entreaties of the Archbishop that he would assign his reasons for such conduct. His house became the resort of all the disaffected clergy or affronted ladies and gentlemen in the city, who were drawn thither, not only by a common hatred to Chrysostom, but also by the handsome gifts, the elegant and dainty repasts, and the winning flattery with which they were treated by Theophilus.[1] These arts were the more necessary because Theophilus had a double task to perform; to arrest the course of the accusation instituted against himself, as well as to organise a powerful cabal against Chrysostom. In the former he was helped by the scruples or peacefulness of Chrysostom himself. The Archbishop was directed by the Court to repair to Pera, and preside over an enquiry into the crimes of which Theophilus was accused. But he declined, on the plea that the ecclesiastical affairs of one province could not, according to the Canons of Nice, be judged in another; partly also, as he affirmed, out of respect for his brother patriarch. The truth probably was, that he foresaw the vindictive and turbulent spirit of Theophilus would never submit to the decisions of a council under the presidency of his rival in that see of which Alexandria was especially jealous. Otherwise there is no doubt that a General Council at Constantinople would have been competent to judge the Patriarch of Alexandria; whereas a provincial council in Egypt could not have judged him, he being supreme there by virtue of his position as Patriarch.[2] Chrysostom himself also might legally have been arraigned before a General Council; but, as will be seen, the synod composed by Theophilus was far from being entitled to that appellation.

---

[1] Pall. Dial. c. 2 (Epist. of Chrys. to Innocent), and c. 8.

[2] See Tillem. xi. ch. 71.

Y

The obstacle of his own trial being thus disposed of, it only remained for Theophilus to prosecute his design against his rival with mingled subtlety and boldness. The first step was to secure a sufficient number of witnesses, and a list of accusations, which, being presented to the Emperor, would furnish a plausible reason for summoning a council. The next step would be to pack that council with bishops hostile to Chrysostom. Two despicable deacons, who had been expelled from their office by the Archbishop for homicide and adultery, were well content to draw up such a list of charges on a promise from Theophilus that they should be restored to their former position. The accusations seem to have been of a puerile character; and if the source of them was known, it would seem inconceivable that the Court should have entertained them, did we not remember that the influence of the Empress, as well as many of the most powerful courtiers, was now turned or rapidly turning against the Archbishop, and that the bribes of Theophilus were permeating the whole city.

The attachment of the people, however, to Chrysostom was known to be so strong, that it was deemed prudent by the enemy to hold the synod at a safe distance from the city. A suburb of Chalcedon, called 'the Oak,' where Rufinus, the late prefect, had built a palace, church, and monastery, was selected as a convenient place for the assembly.[1] The bishops, after all the exertions of Theophilus, did not amount to more than thirty-six, of whom twenty-nine were Egyptians.[2] Among the latter was Cyril, the successor of Theophilus. Chrysostom was summoned to appear before the synod. The scene in the archiepiscopal palace immediately preceding the

[1] Vide ante, Ch. XIII.
[2] So Pallad. c. 8; on the whole the most trustworthy authority. Photius

Biblioth. (c. 59) says there were forty-five.

summons has been described by Palladius, with the vivid and minute exactness of an eye-witness.

'We were sitting, to the number of forty bishops, in the dining-hall of the palace, marvelling at the audacity with which one, who had been commanded to appear as a culprit at Constantinople, had arrived with a train of bishops, had altered the sentiments of nobles and magistrates, and perverted the majority even of the clergy. Whilst we were wondering, John, inspired by the Spirit of God, addressed to us all the following words: "Pray for me, my brethren, and, if ye love Christ, let no one for my sake desert his see, for I am now ready to be offered, and the time of my departure is at hand. Like Him who spoke these words, I perceive that I am about to relinquish life, for I know the intrigues of Satan, that he will not endure any longer the burden of my words which are delivered against him. May ye obtain mercy, and in your prayers remember me." Seized with inexpressible sorrow, some of us began to weep, and others to leave the assembly, after kissing, amid tears and sobs, the sacred head and eyes, and eloquent mouth, of the Archbishop. He, however, exhorted them to return, and, as they hovered near, like bees humming round their hive, "Sit down my brethren," he said, "and do not weep, unnerving me by your tears, for to me to live is Christ, to die is gain. Recall the words which I have so frequently spoken to you. Present life is a journey; both its good and painful things pass away. Present time is like a fair: we buy, we sell, and the assembly is dissolved. Are we better than the Patriarchs, the Prophets, the Apostles, that this life should remain to us for ever?" Here one of the company uttering a cry exclaimed: "Nay, but what we lament is our own bereavement and the widowhood of the Church, the derangement of sacred laws, the ambition of those who fear not the Lord, and

violently seize the highest positions; the destitution of
the poor, the deprivation of sound teaching." But John
replied, striking, as was his custom when cogitating, the
palm of his left hand with the forefinger of his right:
" Enough, my brother—no more; only, as I was saying,
do not abandon your churches, for neither did the office
of teaching begin with me, nor in me has it ended.   Did
not Moses die, and was not Joshua found to succeed
him ?   Did not Samuel die, but was not David anointed ?
Jeremy departed this life, but Baruch was left; Elijah
was taken up, but Elisha prophesied in his place; Paul
was beheaded, but did he not leave Timothy, Titus, Apollos,
and a host of others to work after him ?"   To these words
Eulysius, Bishop of Apamea, in Bithynia, observed: " If
we retain our sees, it will become necessary for us to hold
communion with the authors of your deposition, and to
subscribe to your condemnation."[1]   To which the holy John
replied: " Communicate by all means, so as to avoid rending the unity of the Church; but abstain from subscribing,
for I am not conscious of having done anything to deserve
deposition."[1]

At this point in the conference it was announced that
certain emissaries from the 'Synod of the Oak' had
arrived.   Chrysostom gave orders that they should be
admitted, enquired, when they entered, to what rank in
the hierarchy they belonged, and, on being informed that
they were bishops, requested them to be seated, and to
declare the purpose of their coming.   The two bishops,
young men recently raised to the episcopate in Libya,
replied, ' We are merely the bearers of a document which
we request that you will command to be read.'   Chrysostom gave the order, and a servant of Theophilus read the
missive.   'The holy Synod assembled at the Oak to John'

---

[1] The language is not very clear in this passage, but such is, I conceive, the
drift of it. C. S.

(thus did his enemies deprive him of all his titles). 'We have received a list containing an infinite number of charges against you. Present yourself, therefore, before us, bringing with you the priests Serapion and Tigrius, for their presence is necessary.' The bishops who were with Chrysostom were very indignant at the insolent tenor of the message. A reply to the following effect was drawn up, addressed to Theophilus, and despatched by the hand of three bishops and two priests : 'Subvert not nor rend the Church for which God became incarnate ; but if, in contempt of the canons framed by 318 bishops at Nice, you choose to judge a cause beyond the boundaries of your jurisdiction, cross the straits into our city, which is at least strictly governed by law, and do not, after the example of Cain, call Abel out into the open field. For we have charges of palpable crimes against you, drawn up under more than sixty heads ; our synod, also, is more numerous than yours, and is assembled, by the grace of God, after a peaceful manner, not for the disruption of the Church. For you are but thirty-six in number, collected out of a single province ;[1] but we are forty, from several provinces, and seven are metropolitans. It is only reasonable that the less should be judged, according to the canons, by the greater.'

Chrysostom approved of this answer of the bishops, but sent a separate letter on his own behalf. 'Hitherto I am wholly ignorant whether anyone has anything to say against me ; but if anyone has assailed me, and you wish me to appear before you, eject from your assembly my declared enemies. I raise no question respecting the place where I ought to be tried, although the most proper place is the city.' He proceeds to say that he objected to his declared and implacable enemies, Theophilus,

---

[1] This must have been a slight exaggeration, but the members do seem to have been mainly Egyptian.

Acacius, Severian, and Antiochus, being allowed to sit on the council at all. 'He could convict Theophilus of having said in Alexandria and Lycia, " I am setting out for the capital to depose John ;" which, indeed, is true, for, since he set foot in Constantinople, he has refused to meet or communicate with me. What, then, will one do, after the trial, who has acted as my enemy before it ? ' 'When these men should have been eliminated from the synod, or legally constituted as his accusers, he would appear before a council even if composed of members from all Christendom; but till this condition was complied with, he would refuse to present himself though summoned ten thousand times over.'[1]

He demanded, in short, to be tried by an œcumenical synod, as the only tribunal which could legally exact obedience from him. The Synod of the Oak, composed as it was mainly of Egyptians and of declared enemies, could not possibly pretend to that character. If the Imperial Court had been upright and courageous, not open to be cajoled by flattery and bribes, not induced by personal animosity against the Archbishop to connive at, if not favour, the proceedings of his enemies, such a synod could not have been held. That it was held, and succeeded in the purpose for which it met, will ever be a stain upon the Church and the Empire of the East.

But although viciously constituted, and, indeed, all the more on that very account, the synod made much display of complying in formalities with the established order of an ecclesiastical court of judicature. The prosecution was to be carried on in the name of a plaintiff who was to be present, and to submit his charge in writing. The defendant was to be cited to appear and defend himself; and if he failed to appear after three or four citations, he would be pronounced contumacious, and as such be

[1] Pall. Dial. c. 8.

punishable by the synod with excommunication and deposition. The further penalties of imprisonment, exile, or death could not be inflicted by any but the secular power.

Theophilus was president of the synod, and the prosecution was conducted in the name of John, Archdeacon of Constantinople, who cherished malice against Chrysostom because he had once been suspended by him for ill-treating a slave, though afterwards restored. The charges were drawn up under twenty-nine heads. The evidence of most worthless witnesses was accepted, or, more properly speaking, invited. A strange medley of monstrous and incredible offences was included in the list of charges prepared by the Archdeacon John—acts of personal violence, as well as violations of ecclesiastical discipline. ' He had struck people on the face, had calumniated many of his clergy, had called one Epiphanius fool and demoniac, had imprisoned others, had accused his archdeacons of robbing his pallium for an unlawful purpose ; he had despotically and illegally deposed bishops in Asia, and had ordained others without sufficient enquiry into their qualifications, mental or moral ; he had alienated the property and sold the ornaments of the Church, he held private interviews with women, he dined on Cyclopian fare, he ate a small cake after holy communion, he had administered both sacraments, after he himself or the recipients had eaten.' [1] The crowning charge was that of treasonable language against the Empress—' he had called her Jezebel.' This was the trump card of the cabal. If

---

[1] Phot. c. 59. Chrys. Ep. 125 ad Cyr., where he indignantly repels the charge. ' Had he done so, might his name be blotted out from the roll of bishops ;' but at the same time he deprecates the treatment of such an offence (had it been committed) with extreme severity : for had not our Lord Himself instituted that holy feast, and had not St. Paul baptised without previously fasting? Chrysostom shrinks in horror from the supposition of such a gross violation of ecclesiastical rule as the act in his case would have been, but refuses to place it on the same footing with the commission of a flagrant moral crime, or direct disobedience to any command of Christ.

the Emperor's Court could be persuaded to believe him guilty on this point, exile at least, and probably death, would be the inevitable consequence.

Such were the principal charges in the list presented by the Archdeacon John. A second list, presented by Isaac the monk, accused him of extending sympathy and hospitality to Origenists, of instigating the people to sedition, of using unseemly expressions in his sermons, such as 'exsulto, insanio,' or language which gave a dangerous encouragement to sinners; for example, ' as often as you sin, come to me and I will heal you.' By artfully making slight alterations in expressions actually used, and tearing them from their context, it was easy to represent them as mischievous or blasphemous.

It is not surprising that Chrysostom should stedfastly have refused to answer in person such a list of partly monstrous, partly puerile accusations before such a synod. He pursued the only dignified course possible under the circumstances. When a notary from the Emperor came to him with a rescript, and showed him the petition inserted in it from the synod that the Emperor would compel the attendance of the Archbishop; and when, presently, a second deputation from the synod, consisting of a renegade priest of his own clergy, and Isaac the monk, brought a peremptory summons from the synod, he inflexibly maintained the same attitude. 'I will not attend a synod which is composed of my enemies, and to which I am summoned by my own clergy. I appeal to a lawfully constituted General Council.' The citations were rapidly repeated three or four times, and always met by the same response. The cabal expended their fury on the messengers of the Archbishop; they beat one bishop, tore the clothes of another, and placed on the neck of a third the chains which they had designed for the person of Chrysostom himself, their intention having been to put him secretly on board ship, and send him off to some remote part of the Empire. Some of the clergy were so much intimidated by these violent proceedings that they dared not return to Constantinople. Demetrius, however, Bishop of Pessina, denounced the conduct of the synod, quitted it, and returned to the Archbishop. After several more ineffectual citations, the synod, at its twelfth session, declared that it would proceed to judgment against Chrysostom as contumacious. Either by a happy coincidence, or by the contrivance of Theophilus, a message arrived from the Court on the same day, urging the bishops to decide the cause as speedily as possible. With much alacrity the request was obeyed. They drew up a despatch to the Emperor—a formal statement: 'Whereas John, being accused of crimes, has declined to appear before us, and that in such cases ecclesiastical law pronounces deposition, we have hereby deposed him; but as the indictment against him contains charges of treason as well as ecclesiastical offences, we leave these to be dealt with by you, since it belongs not to us to take cognisance of them.' The synod waited for the Imperial ratification of their verdict, and meanwhile issued a circular to the clergy of Constantinople, informing them of the deposition of their spiritual father.[1]

Having attained, as he believed, the object of his intrigue, Theophilus went through the form of reconciliation with the 'tall brethren' in the presence of the synod. The facility with which they were restored to favour on a simple request for pardon is in strange contrast to the relentless animosity with which they had been hitherto pursued, and indicates that their persecution had been maintained simply as the means to securing a more important prey.

Dioscorus and Ammon had both recently died, the

[1] Pall. Dial. 8. Socr. vi. 15. Soz. viii. 17.

latter predicting with his dying lips that the Church was
about to be distressed by a furious persecution, and torn
by a deplorable schism. He was buried in that Church
of the Apostles, in the suburb of the Oak, where, nine
years before, he had baptised the founder, the Prefect
Rufinus. The monks of the foundation celebrated his
obsequies with great pomp; and Theophilus, his bitter
persecutor, condescended to weep over his death, and
publicly declare that he had never known a monk of more
exalted saintliness.[1]

The triumph of the synod seemed to be completed by
the receipt of an Imperial rescript, ratifying the sentence
of deposition, and announcing that the Archbishop would
be banished. Many members of the synod were probably
disappointed at the mildness of the penalty; but the
people of Constantinople were enraged, and impeded the
execution of the sentence. It was evening when the impending degradation of their Archbishop became known.
During the whole of the night, crowds of people watched
outside the Archbishop's palace and the cathedral to
guard against his forcible abduction. Early in the morning they thronged the church, loudly protested against
the injustice of the sentence, and demanded with shouts
the submission of his cause to a General Council. For
three days and nights the flock incessantly guarded their
beloved pastor. Under their protection, he passed to and
from the palace and the church. On the second day he
delivered a discourse to them in the cathedral. The first
portion of it is in all respects worthy of Chrysostom; the
conclusion, involved and rugged, seems to have been
added by another hand, and extracts will not be made
from it here.[2]

---

[1] Tillemont, v. xi.

[2] It contains the celebrated passage,
' Herodias again dances and demands
the head of John:' which recurs as the
exordium of another and spurious
homily (vol. viii. p. 485), and also an
indignant repudiation of the offence
of administering baptism after eating.
— Vol. iii. 127. Socr. vi. 16. Soz. viii.
17, 18.

'Many are the billows, and terrible the storms, which threaten us; but we fear not to be overwhelmed, for we stand upon the rock. Let the sea rage, it cannot dissolve the rock; let the billows rise, they cannot sink the vessel of Jesus Christ. Tell me, what is it we fear? death? "To me to live is Christ, and to die is gain." Or exile? "The earth is the Lord's and the fullness thereof." Or confiscation of goods? "We brought nothing into this world, and it is certain we can carry nothing out."' . . . 'I fear not poverty, I desire not wealth; I dread not death, I do not pray for life, save for the sake of your advancement. I beseech you be of good courage; no man will be able to separate us, for "that which God hath joined together no man can put asunder." If man cannot dissolve marriage, how much less the Church of God. Thou, oh my enemy! only renderest me more illustrious, and wastest thine own strength, "for it is hard to kick against the pricks." Waves do not break the rock, but are themselves dispersed into foam against it. Nothing, oh man! is stronger than the Church. . . . it is stronger even than Heaven, "for Heaven and earth shall pass away, but my words shall not pass away." What words? "Thou art Peter, and on this rock I will build my Church, and the gates of hell shall not prevail against it." If thou disbelievest the words, yet believe the facts. How many tyrants have attempted to overcome the Church; how often have wild beasts, and the sword and the furnace, and the boiling caldron, been employed against it, yet have they not prevailed. Where are those who made war upon it? They have been silenced and consigned to oblivion. Where is the Church? It shines above the brightness of the sun. Let none of the things that have been done disturb you. Grant me one favour only, unwavering faith. Was not St. Peter on the point of sinking, not because of the uncontrollable onset of the waves, but because of the weak-

ness of his faith? Did man's votes bring me here, that
man should put me down? I say not this in a spirit of
boastfulness—God forbid—but in the desire to settle your
agitated minds.' . . . 'Let no one trouble you; give heed
to your prayers. This disturbance is the devil's work,
that he might destroy your zeal in the sacred Litanies;
but he does not succeed. We find you even more earnest
than before. To-morrow I shall go out with you in the
Litany, for where you are, there I am. Though locally
separated, we are in spirit united; we are one body, the
body is not separated from its head; even death cannot separate us.' . . 'For your sakes I am ready to be slaughtered
ten thousand times over, since death is to me the warrant
of immortality. These intrigues are to me but the occasion of security. I say these things to listening ears; so
many days have you watched, and nothing has moved you
from your purpose. Neither length of time nor threats
have enervated you; you have done what I have always
been desiring, despised the things of this world, bidden
farewell to earth, released yourselves from the fetters of
the body: this is my crown, my consolation, my anoint-
ing; this the suggestion to me of immortality.'

Another discourse[1] contains much to the same effect,
and a declaration of his belief that the real cause of
his deposition was his sturdy opposition to the corrupt
manners and morals of the age. 'You know,' he says,
'why they are going to depose me—because I spread no
fine carpets, and wear no silken robes; because I have
not pampered their gluttony, or made presents in gold
and silver.' He would comfort and encourage himself
with the prospect of being reckoned among those who
had suffered for righteousness' sake. The cruel and capri-

[1] The authenticity of which has
been questioned. The style is perhaps
not quite worthy of Chrysostom; but
in one of his sermons after his return
from exile he apparently alludes to
some quotations from Job made in
this discourse.

cious woman, who one day called him 'a thirteenth apostle,' and the next 'a Judas,' would receive a just retribution for her conduct.

The attachment of the people to the Archbishop, and their sense of the injustice with which he was treated, were so strong that, with his powers of swaying their feelings, he might easily have raised a formidable sedition, and defied for an indefinite time the sentence of the synod and the edict of the Emperor. But his sentiments were too loyal, too Christian, too peaceful, for any such desperate and violent measures. He might have continued to demand the reference of his cause to a General Council; but, had this been granted, there was the extreme probability that his enemies would refuse, and persuade many more to refuse, a recognition of its decision. Then would follow one of those melancholy schisms, of which the Church already knew too well the misery. He determined to bow to the storm. On the third day after his deposition by the council, and about noon, when the people were not guarding the approaches to the church quite so vigilantly, he passed out, unperceived, by one of the side entrances, and surrendered himself to some of the court officials, who conducted him at nightfall to the harbour. In spite of the darkness, he was recognised by some of the people, who followed him with loud cries of distress. He besought them to abstain from the commission of violence, commended them to the care of Jesus Christ, cited the example of Job blessing and thanking God in the midst of trouble, and declared that he patiently waited for the decision of an Œcumenical Council. The vessel in which he embarked conveyed him the same night to Hieron,[1] on the Bithynian coast, at the mouth of the

---

[1] More strictly speaking, 'the Hieron,' 'the sacred spot' where the Argonauts were supposed to have offered sacrifice to Zeus on their return from Colchis.

Euxine. Perhaps, owing to the dangerous proximity of this place to Chalcedon, the head-quarters of his enemies, he removed (being apparently uncontrolled in his movements) to a country house belonging to a friend, near Prænetum, on the Astacene gulf, just opposite Nicomedia.

When the departure of the Archbishop became generally known on the succeeding day, the indignation of the people burst into a blaze. The places of public resort were thronged with clamorous crowds denouncing the synod, and demanding a General Council. They flocked into the churches to pour forth their lamentations, and to invoke the Divine intervention on behalf of their injured Patriarch. A revulsion of feeling in his favour took place among many of the clergy who had hitherto been opposed to him. The arrival of Theophilus with a large retinue was not calculated to allay the agitation. Force was employed to dislodge the people from the churches; the struggle occasioned bloodshed, and even some loss of life, chiefly among monks. The worthless clergy who had been deposed by Chrysostom, some of them for flagrant crimes, were restored by Theophilus. Severian of Gabala mounted a pulpit in one of the churches, and extolled the act of deposition. 'Even were the Patriarch,' he said, 'guiltless of other offences, the penalty was due to his arrogance, for "God resisteth the proud," even if He forgave other sins.' The people were furious at this barefaced attempt to justify injustice. They thronged the approaches to the Imperial palace itself, and with loud shouts demanded the restoration of the Patriarch.[1]

A natural phenomenon, not rare in Constantinople, but regarded under the circumstances as a Divine visitation, opportunely concurred with this demand. The city, the palace, but more especially the bed-chamber of the Empress, were agitated by a severe shock of earthquake.

---

[1] Soz. viii. 18, 19. Socr. vi. 16, 17. Zosim. v. 23.

The friends of Chrysostom rejoiced at this manifestation of the wrath of Heaven ; his enemies were alarmed. The terrified Empress eagerly promoted the demand of the people for the restoration of the exile. Messengers were sent across the Bosphorus to seek him, for the exact place of his retreat appears to have been unknown. Briso, the Empress's chamberlain, a man of Christian piety and a personal friend of Chrysostom, discovered him at Præ-netum. He was the bearer of a humble, we might say abject, letter of self-exculpation from the Empress. ' Let not your holiness (ἡ ἀγιωσύνη) imagine that I was cog-nisant of what has been done. I am guiltless of thy blood. Wicked and corrupt men have contrived this plot. I remember the baptism of my children by thy hands. God whom I serve is witness of my tears.' She informs him how she had fallen at the feet of the Emperor, and had represented to him that there was no hope for the Empire except through the restoration of the Archbishop.[1]

Chrysostom yielded to the solicitation so far as to embark and cross the Bosphorus, but he declined at first to advance nearer Constantinople than the suburb of Mariamna, two leagues from the capital by sea. He de-clared that he would not enter the city until he had been acquitted by a General Council. But the impetuosity of the people would brook no delay. Tidings of his approach had preceded him. The waters of the Bosphorus were studded with boats crowded with his friends, bearing torches and chanting psalms of welcome. The halt at Mariamna was suspected to be a contrivance of the enemy, who wished to deprive the Patriarch of the honours awaiting him. Their denunciations of the Emperor and Empress grew loud and menacing. An Imperial secretary arrived at Mariamna, urging Chrysostom to enter the city without loss of time. The Archbishop consented, and,

[1] Theod. v. 34. Chrys. vol. iii. p. 446.

attended by about thirty bishops, amidst the acclamations
of the populace, was conducted to the Church of the
Apostles. Again he remonstrated, and expressed scruples
at entering till the sentence of deposition should have
been revoked by a legitimate council. But the eagerness
of the people was irrepressible. He was borne into the
church, and compelled to take his seat on the episcopal
throne and pronounce a benediction upon the assembly.
When he had complied with their request, they would not
be satisfied till he had addressed them in an extempore
discourse. The address exists only in a Latin translation.
Its brevity, and the abrupt style of the opening sentences,
indicate the extemporaneous character of it.[1]

'What shall I say, or how shall I speak? "Blessed
be God." So spoke I when I departed, and I utter the
same again; yea, even in my exile I did not cease to say
these words. Ye remember how I quoted Job, and said,
"Blessed be the name of the Lord for ever." Such was
the pledge I left with you when I set forth; such is the
thanksgiving I repeat on my return. "Blessed be the
name of the Lord for ever." Our lot varies, but our
manner of giving glory is one. I gave thanks when I
was expelled, I give thanks when I return. The conditions of summer and winter are different, but the end
is one—the prosperity of the field. Blessed be God who
permitted the storm, blessed be God who has dispersed it
and wrought a calm. These things I say, that I may prepare you to bless God at all times. Have good things
happened to you? Bless God, and the good remains;
have evil things occurred? bless God still, and the evil is
removed.' . . . . . 'Behold what great results have been
wrought by the stratagems of my enemies. They have
augmented your zeal, inflamed your affectionate longing
for me, and procured me lovers in hundreds. Formerly

---

[1] Socr. vi. 16. Soz. viii. 18. Chrys. Ep. ad Innoc. in Dial. Pall. p. 10.

I was beloved by my own people only; now even the Jews pay me respect. My enemies hoped to sever me from my own friends; and, instead, they have brought even aliens into our ranks.' . . . . . 'To-day the Circensian games take place, but no one is present there; all have poured like a torrent into the church, and your voices are as streams which flow to Heaven and declare your affection towards your father.' He congratulates them on putting the enemy to flight. 'Many are the sheep, yet nowhere is the wolf seen; the devouring beasts are overwhelmed, the wolves have fled. Who has pursued them? Not I the shepherd, but ye the sheep. O noble flock! in the absence of the shepherd ye have routed the wolves. O beauty and chastity of the wife! how hast thou repulsed the adulterer, because thou lovedst thy husband!' . . . 'Where are our enemies? in ignominy;—where are we? in triumph.' [1]

On the following day the Archbishop delivered another address, pitched in the same strain, but amplified and more ornate. It opens with a singular comparison between the meditated seduction of Abraham's wife by Pharaoh, and the plot of Theophilus to corrupt the chastity of the Church of Constantinople. The courage and faith of the flock in resisting the wolf during the absence of their shepherd, their enthusiastic welcome of his return, when the sea, as he expresses it, became a city (alluding to the crowds who had gone out to meet him on the Bosphorus), and the market-place was converted into one vast church—these are again the topics on which he dilates with thankful joy. He applies to himself the verse, 'They that sow in tears shall reap in joy; he that now goeth on his way weeping and beareth

---

[1] It appears from subsequent events that Theophilus had not yet actually quitted Constantinople, but he and his partisans had retired for the time discomfited from the field of active opposition; and this would justify the language of Chrysostom, who is speaking under excitement.

forth good seed shall doubtless come again with joy and
bring his sheaves with him.' The Empress is extolled in
language which to any but Oriental ears must sound
painfully fulsome and adulatory. She had sent a message
to him on the previous evening, saying, ' my prayer is
fulfilled, my object accomplished. I have obtained a
crown better than the diadem itself. I have received
back the priest, I have restored the head to the body, the
pilot to the ship, the shepherd to the flock, the husband
to the home.' In return for this complimentary greeting
(complimentary, it must be confessed, to herself as much
as to the Archbishop) she is styled by him, ' most devout
Queen, mother of the churches, nurse of monks, protectress of saints, staff of the poor.' The people were so
much delighted with these laudations of the Empress,
that the address was constantly interrupted by their
acclamations.[1]

When the object of the Synod at the Oak had eventually failed through the recall of Chrysostom, many of
the members lost no time in returning to their several
sees. Theophilus and a few of his most resolute partisans
appear to have lurked in the city, waiting a possible
opportunity for resuming their intrigues. This they attempted, according to two historians,[2] by instigating accusations against Heracleides, who had been consecrated
Bishop of Ephesus by Chrysostom. The friends of Heracleides and of the Archbishop protested against the illegality of such proceedings in the absence of the defendant.
The question was taken up by the populace. Fierce and
sanguinary frays were fought in the streets between the
citizens and the Alexandrian followers of Theophilus.
At length he and his followers consulted their safety by
a precipitate flight. This account is not incompatible

with the assertion of Chrysostom himself in his letter to Innocent, that after his recall he incessantly demanded the convocation of a General Council to absolve him from the verdict of the false synod, and to reinstate him in possession of his see; that the Emperor consented, and that, as soon as the Imperial summonses were issued in all directions, Theophilus, dreading the scrutiny of his conduct, embarked in the dead of night, and sailed in haste for Alexandria.[1] The citation of the council, and the hostility of the people, may well have concurred to hasten his departure. The General Council seems never to have regularly assembled. Theophilus was cited to attend it after he had returned to Alexandria, but excused himself on the plea that the Alexandrians were so deeply attached to him, he feared a sedition would take place if he were again to absent himself. No less than sixty bishops, however, who had congregated in Constantinople, though not apparently convened in synodal form, solemnly declared their sense of the illegality and injustice of the late proceedings at the Synod of the Oak, and confirmed Chrysostom in the resumption of his see.

[1] Ep. ad Innoc. in Pall. Dial. p. 10.

CHAPTER XIX.

THE storm had passed over for the moment, and the
atmosphere seemed serene; but in reality it was charged
with all the old elements of disturbance. The Archbishop owed his restoration to a mere superstitious
impulse on the part of the Empress, seconded by the
enthusiastic devotion of the common people to his person
and his cause. But as the revulsion of feeling which had
led to his recall died away, and he himself resumed with
unabated zeal his former work of moral and ecclesiastical
reformation, the irritation and animosity of the more
corrupt portion of the clergy and laity revived. In two
months after his return, an occasion arose which brought
him into serious collision with the Court. This was the
signal for the reappearance of his enemies; they flocked
from far and near—Egypt, Syria, Asia, as well as his own
more immediate diocese—and swooped down upon their
prey with the avidity of vultures.

The pride and ambition of Eudoxia were not satisfied
by the enjoyment of a power really greater than her
husband's, and of respect outwardly equal; she was determined to receive that half-idolatrous kind of homage
which custom, handed down from pagan times, still paid
to the Emperor, but to him alone. The smaller forum of

Constantinople was a great square,[1] on one side of which
stood the grand curia or senate house, which Constantine
had enriched with the sumptuous spoils of many pagan
temples, and especially with the statues of the Muses
brought from the grove of Helicon; opposite to it was
the entrance of St. Sophia, and the remaining sides of the
forum were bounded by handsome public and a few
private buildings all faced with colonnades. In the centre
was a stone platform paved with various marbles, from
which speeches were delivered on great public occasions.
On this platform the Empress determined to gratify her
vanity by the erection of a lofty column of porphyry surmounted by a silvern image of herself. This design was
accomplished in September A.D. 403, and the erection of
the statue was celebrated by all the pagan ceremonies
and festivities, including music and dancing, with which
the adoration of the Emperor's image was usually attended. These rites had been retained by the Christian
Emperors because they were supposed to be useful in
maintaining a loyal spirit among the people, but the pagan
elements were afterwards suppressed by Theodosius II.[2]

The position of Eudoxia's column in front of the vestibule of St. Sophia, and the disturbance caused to the
sacred services within by the noisy, tumultuous proceedings
outside, was regarded by the Patriarch as a disgrace to an
Empress calling herself Christian, an outrage and insult
flung in the very face of the Church. He denounced the
heathenish ceremony with his usual vehemence before
the people, and complained of it to the prefect of the city.
The prefect was a Manichæan, and no friend to Chrysostom. Instead of endeavouring to conciliate both parties,
he reported to the Empress, probably with some exaggeration, the condemnation pronounced by the Patriarch

---

[1] As distinguished from the Forum of Constantine, which was elliptical in
shape.   [2] Cod. Theod. vi. 102.

on the indulgence of her pride. The resentment of
Eudoxia was fierce. She rallied the enemies of Chrysostom around her to devise means for crushing the
audacious prelate. Acacius, Severian, and others of the
old troop were soon upon the scene, and conferring with
their old confederates, the Marsas and Castriccias, the
rich worldly dames, and the dandy young clergy of Constantinople. There was no diminution meanwhile in the
tide of invective poured forth from the golden mouth,
and the pungency of his sarcasms did not lose force in
the reports of them which were carried to the royal ears.[1]

Once more the faction applied to the Patriarch of Alexandria, inviting him to come and conduct their operations.
But he was too wary to involve himself personally in
another campaign, to terminate perhaps in a second ignominious flight. His influence, however, even at a distance
was potent. The stratagem adopted this time was to
counterfeit that General Council which had been constantly demanded by Chrysostom; packing it with hostile
bishops who were ostensibly convened to revise, but in
reality to confirm, the decision issued by the Synod of the
Oak. Theophilus, then, having excused attendance at
Constantinople in person, sent three 'pitiful bishops'
(ἐλεείνους ἐπισκόπους), creatures of his own on whom he
could rely, to execute his designs.[2] They were armed
with the 12th Canon of the Council of Antioch held in
A.D. 341, which declared that any bishop who, after

---

[1] The celebrated exordium of a
homily supposed to be directed a-
gainst Eudoxia, 'Again Herodias
rages, again she demands the head
of John,' if actually spoken with
reference to John the Baptist, may
easily have been represented by the
malevolent as aimed at the Empress.
But the whole homily has been pronounced spurious by Savile and
Montfaucon, and on perusal of it

their verdict seems reasonable. The
discourse is the production of a
thorough misogynist, describing with
much coarseness and acrimony the
misery and trouble caused by the
wickedness of women. Most will
agree with Savile, that it is 'scarcely
worth reading, and quite unworthy
emendation.'—Vol. viii. p. 485.

[2] Pall. Dial. c. 9.

deposition, appealed to the secular power for restoration should, for that very act, be regarded by the Church as permanently and irrevocably deposed. The Council of Antioch had been swayed by Arian influence, and this same canon had been aimed against Athanasius, who had returned from exile to Alexandria under the Imperial sanction. It had been repudiated by the Western bishops, and some of the Eastern, at the Council of Sardica, and, indeed, by all who maintained communion with Athanasius. Theophilus, however, proposed to base the present proceedings against Chrysostom on this foundation; to turn, in fact, against the greatest luminary of Constantinople the engine which had been originally constructed against the greatest ornament of the Alexandrian see. The instrument would work well if proper hands could be procured to work it. Syria, Cappadocia, Pontus, Phrygia, were once more ransacked to supply the council with disaffected prelates. To the old names of Acacius of Berœa, Severian of Gabala, Antiochus and Cyrinus may be added as leaders of the malignants Leontius, Bishop of Ancyra in Galatia, Brison of Phillipopolis in Thrace, Ammon of Laodicea in Pisidia; among those honourably distinguished as friendly to the Patriarch one Theodore of Tyana, Elpidius of Laodicea, Tranquillus (see unknown), and Alexander of Basilinopolis in Bithynia. Theodore, however, perceiving the malevolent intention with which the council was convoked, quitted Constantinople soon after his arrival.

The council met about the close of the year A.D. 403. It was customary for the Emperor to attend Divine service in state on Christmas Day, but he was induced by the enemies of Chrysostom to refuse on this occasion, alleging that it was impossible to be present where the Patriarch officiated till he had been cleared of the serious charges brought against him. It was proposed at first to affect to

meet the demand of Chrysostom for an equitable trial,
and to hear all the charges which had been preferred at
the Synod of the Oak. But the witnesses were so back-
ward to appear, and the attitude of the defendant betokened such confidence in his cause, that it was deemed
more prudent by his enemies to stake the whole issue on
the canon of the Council of Antioch. If that was once admitted, there would be an end of the whole matter. The
Archbishop, having been deposed already once for all, was
not competent to appear and plead his cause before a council.
Chrysostom and his friends opposed the adoption of such
a course with two powerful arguments. They represented
that the Council of Antioch had been managed by an
Arian bishop and influenced by an Arian emperor, and
the object of it had been to harass the great Athanasius.
In the next place, the Synod of the Oak had been illegally constituted; sixty-five bishops had repudiated its
decision; Chrysostom, therefore, was not legally deposed,
and the canon of Antioch was in consequence not applicable to his case. This last objection was not permitted
by his enemies. Leontius boldly declared, what appears
to have been a palpable lie, that a larger number of
bishops than sixty-five had voted against Chrysostom in
the synod.[1]

Thus the question as to the validity of the Council of
Antioch became the knot of the whole affair. It was
debated with such vehemence on both sides, that at length
the adversaries of the Patriarch proposed that a deputation from the two contending parties should plead the
case before the Emperor, and submit the decision to him.
It may be presumed from their making the proposal that
they felt secure of a verdict favourable to their side, and,
at the same time, by this step a semblance of impartiality
would be imparted to the proceedings. The deputies met in

[1] Soz. viii. 20. Socr. vi. 18. Pall. Dial. c. 9.

the royal presence. When the heat which marked the beginning of the discussion had cooled down a little, Elpidius
of Laodicea with much gentleness of manner made an
astute proposal. He was an old man, eminent for stain-
lessness of character, as well as for learning in ecclesiastical lore. 'Let us not,' he said, 'weary the clemency
of your Majesty any longer; only let our brethren, Acacius
and Antiochus, subscribe a declaration that they are of
the same faith with those who promulgated these canons,
which they maintain to be the production of orthodox
men, and the controversy will be at an end.' The Emperor perceived the adroitness of the proposal, and observed with a smile to Antiochus, that the plan struck
him as the most expedient which could be devised.
Antiochus and his colleagues turned livid with perplexity
and rage, but, being fairly caught in the dilemma, were
forced to dissemble their feelings, and simulated a willing
consent to sign the proposed declaration. The promise
was made but never executed. The deputies retired, and
the adversaries of the Patriarch laboured with redoubled
energy to procure his final condemnation; but we have no
record of any formal session or formally declared sentence.
Chrysostom continued to preach and discharge his other
functions with, if possible, increased diligence, and still
acted as president over the floating synod of more than
forty bishops who constantly adhered to his cause. His
enemies, on the other hand, acted as if the sentence of
condemnation had been passed, and continually requested
the Emperor to put it into execution.[1]

A.D. 404. As Easter approached, they became more im-
portunate in their demand. They dreaded the demonstrations which might be made in favour of their victim
by the large congregations which on Holy Saturday and
Easter Day were wont to assemble in the churches. They

[1] Pall. Dial. c. 9.

succeeded in prevailing on the Emperor to prohibit the
Patriarch, as having been deposed and excommunicated
by two councils, from entering or officiating in the church
at Easter-tide. Chrysostom had always expressed an
earnest desire to be tried before a lawful council, and to
abide by its decision. This request had been systema-
tically evaded even when ostensibly complied with. His
whole soul rebelled with honest indignation against these
insidious and persistent attempts to misrepresent his
conduct, and he determined now to resist them by taking
his stand on the lofty ground of his Divine mission. ' I
received this church from God my Saviour, and am
charged with the care of the salvation of this flock, nor
am I at liberty to abandon it. Expel me by force if you
will, since the city belongs to you, that I may have your
authority as an excuse for deserting my post.' [1]

The Emperor, though with some shame, sent officials
who removed the Archbishop from the church to his
palace, with a strict injunction that he should not attempt
to leave it. This was a cautious preliminary to final
expulsion, suggested by superstitious dread of any earthquake or other manifestation of Divine displeasure. Should
any such occur again, the Archbishop could be released in
a moment; if not, they might proceed to further measures.

Easter Eve arrived, the greatest day in the year for
the baptism of converts. Three thousand were to be
' initiated ' this year. Chrysostom was again commanded
to abstain from entering the church, but answered according to the tenor of his former reply, that he would
not resist from officiating unless compelled by actual
force. The feeble Arcadius was alarmed, and hesitated
how to act. He scrupled to use force on so sacred a day,
and dreaded an insurrection of the populace. As usual,
he tried to shift responsibility from his own shoulders.

[1] Pall. Dial. c. 9.

He sent for Acacius and Antiochus, and requested their advice in the present emergency. They were too far committed now to draw back, and promptly replied that they would take on their heads the deposition of the Archbishop.

One more effort was made to avert the impending calamity. The forty bishops who maintained a close friendship with Chrysostom accosted the Emperor and Empress as they were visiting, according to their custom at this season, some of the martyr chapels outside the city. They entreated their majesties with tears to spare the Church her chief pastor, especially on account of the seasons, and for the sake of those who were about to be baptized. But Arcadius and Eudoxia turned a deaf ear to their piteous appeal. The bishops retired, grief-stricken, to mourn over the wrongs of their Church and Patriarch; but not before one of them, Paul, Bishop of Crateia, had lifted up his voice in bold and solemn warning. 'Take heed, Eudoxia; fear God; have pity on your children. Do not outrage by bloodshed the sacred and solemn festival of Jesus Christ.' [1]

The Church of St. Sophia became the scene, on the night of that Easter Eve, of shocking tumult. A vast congregation from the city and surrounding towns, including many of the catechumens, was keeping vigil to greet the dawn of the Resurrection morning. Suddenly a body of soldiers burst in with noise and violence, and took possession of the choir. The confusion may be imagined. Women and children fled shrieking in wild disorder. Many of the female catechumens, only half-dressed, in preparation for the reception of baptism, were hurriedly driven out of the baptistry with the deaconesses who attended them. Some were even wounded, and the

---

[1] Pall. Dial. c. 9. Chrysostom (Ep. ad Innoc. vol. iii.) speaks of more than forty friendly bishops.

sacred fonts stained with blood.   Some of the soldiers, unbaptized men, penetrated even to the chamber where the Eucharistic elements were kept, and profaned them with their gaze and touch.   The clergy were forcibly ejected in their vestments, and several were wounded. The pitiable spectacle of the mingled troop of men, women, children, and clergy, violently chased along the streets by the brutal soldiery, moved even Jews and Gentiles to compassion.   The clergy, however, rallied the scattered flock in the Baths of Constantine, the largest public baths in the city.   Here they proceeded with the Easter services in due order; some reading the Scriptures, others baptizing.   The churches of Constantinople were deserted, which the adversary wished to force the people to attend in the absence of the Archbishop, in the hope that the Court might thus suppose him to be unpopular.

Such is the description of these violent scenes as drawn by the pen of Chrysostom himself, in a letter[1] written soon after the occurrences and addressed to Innocent I., Bishop of Rome, Venerius, Bishop of Milan, and Chromatius, Bishop of Aquileia.   'You may imagine the rest,' he concludes; 'great as these calamities are, there is no prospect of their immediate termination; on the contrary, the evil extends every day.   The spirit of insubordination is rapidly spreading from the capital to the provinces, from the head to the members.   Clergy rebel against their bishop, and one bishop assails another.   People are, or soon will be, split into factions.   All places are racked by the throes of coming trouble, and the confusion is universal.   Having been informed of all these things, then, my most reverend and prudent lords, display, I pray you, the courage and zeal which becomes you in restraining this lawlessness which has crept into the churches.   For if it were to become a prevailing and

[1] Vol. iii. p. 533.

allowable custom, for any at their pleasure to pass into
foreign and distant dioceses, and to expel whomsoever
anyone may choose, and act as they like on their own
private authority, be sure that all discipline will go to
pieces, and a kind of implacable warfare will pervade the
world, all expelling or being themselves expelled. Wherefore, to prevent the subjection of the world to such confusion, I beseech you to enjoin that these acts so illegally
performed in my absence, when I had not declined fair
judgment, may be reckoned invalid, as indeed in the
nature of things they are, and that those who have been
detected taking part in these iniquitous proceedings may
be subjected to the penalty of ecclesiastical law; while
we who have not been proved guilty may continue to
enjoy your correspondence and friendship as aforetime.'
He closes his letter by affirming that he was still prepared to prove his innocence and the guilt of his accusers
before a legally constituted council.

This letter is interesting not only in itself, but because it illustrates remarkably the growing tendency of
Christendom to appeal to the arbitration of the Western
Church, and especially of the Bishop of Rome, in matters
of ecclesiastical discipline. The law-making, law-protect-
ing spirit of the West is invoked to restrain the tur-
bulence and licentiousness of the East. The Patriarch
of the Eastern Rome appeals to the great bishops of the
West, as the champions of an ecclesiastical discipline
which he confesses himself unable to enforce, or to see any
prospect of establishing. No jealousy is entertained of
the Patriarch of the old Rome by the Patriarch of the
new. The interference of Innocent is courted, a certain
primacy is accorded him, but at the same time he is not
addressed as a supreme arbitrator; assistance and sympathy are solicited from him as from an elder brother,
and two other prelates of Italy are joint recipients with

him of the appeal. The effect of this letter will shortly
be related; for the present, the course of events at Constantinople must be followed.

It did not suit the purpose of Acacius and his party to
allow the congregation which had been hunted out of St.
Sophia to proceed with their service in the baths unmolested. If the Emperor entered the church in the
morning and found it deserted, the vacancy on so great a
day would reveal too plainly the intense devotion of the
people to their bishop. The aim of the conspirators was
to force the people to attend the services, which were to
be marked by the absence of Chrysostom alone. They
accordingly applied to Anthemius, Master of the Offices,
to disperse the congregation if necessary by force. Anthemius, however, was a moderate, prudent man, and
kindly disposed towards the Patriarch. He refused to
interfere, pleading the advanced hour of the night, the
vastness of the assembly, and the risk of serious tumult.
He yielded, however, to their persevering and urgent
demands so far as to direct Lucius, a subordinate officer,
commander of a Thracian corps called the Scutarii, to
present himself with his troops at the entrance of the
baths, and exhort the people to return to the church, as
the more proper place for conducting the services. He
was strictly charged to abstain from violence. He acted
on his instructions, and harangued the congregation, but
without effect. The chanting of the Psalms and the administration of baptism to crowds of catechumens were
proceeded with. Lucius returned and reported his errand
ineffectual. Acacius and his colleagues urged him with
all their eloquence, and with promises of rich reward,
probably more effective than their golden words, to make
another effort, and to use force if persuasion were not
regarded. They gave him some ecclesiastics to accompany him, and as it were sanction their proceedings.

Whether they began by exhortation is not recorded; at any rate, if it was given, no attention was paid to it, and it was quickly seconded by barbarian violence. Lucius himself pushed his way to the place of baptism, and laid about him with a truncheon upon candidates, deacons, and priests, some of them aged men, and dispersed them in all directions. The soldiers seized and plundered the women of their ornaments, the clergy of their vestments, and the sacred vessels belonging to the Church; they beat the fugitives and dragged them off to the prisons. The natural solitude and silence of the streets, in the hour immediately preceding dawn, were disturbed by the cries of the captives and the shouts of their brutal captors.

In the morning the street walls were covered with proclamations, menacing with severe punishment any who persisted in maintaining intercourse with the Patriarch.[1]

The baths were effectually emptied of the congregation; but to fill the churches could not so easily be accomplished—in fact, they were entirely deserted. Large numbers of the dispersed congregation who had escaped the hands of the soldiers fled outside the walls of Constantinople, and, with indefatigable zeal, sought to complete the celebration of the Paschal rites as best they could in the secure recesses of woods or valleys. A large number assembled in a field called Pempton, because five miles from the Forum of Constantine, an open space surrounded by wood and intended to be used as a Hippodrome. In the course of the day—Easter Day—the Emperor and his retinue happened to ride, or perhaps were maliciously conducted, near the spot. The eye of Arcadius was attracted by the sight of a large body of people, many of them clothed in white, crowded together outside the Hippodrome. Unhappily, the Emperor was attended by courtiers inimical to the Archbishop. They replied to

[1] Pall. Dial. c. 9.

his enquiries respecting the nature of the concourse, that it was a body of heretics who had met to worship there in order to escape interference. Arcadius was weak enough to allow, without further enquiry, a number of soldiers who formed part of his escort to ride in upon the assembly and seize the most conspicuous leaders. A number of priests were captured and several rich and noble ladies, whom the soldiers despoiled of their head-dresses and earrings with great barbarity, in one instance even tearing away with the appendage a portion of the ear itself.

One more attempt was made to assemble in a wooden hippodrome, built by Constantine, called the Xulo Circus; but once more they were driven out, and hunted from place to place with relentless diligence. These repeated assaults broke up the flock of Chrysostom, the prisons were filled with the Johnites, as they were called after the name of their bishop, and the churches were empty. The prison walls echoed to the sound of the chants and hymns of the martyrs, but the churches to the noise of scourge and fierce threats administered to those who ventured to enter. This was done in the hope that they might be coerced by torture to anathematise the Archbishop.[1]

He himself, however, meanwhile continued to reside two months in his palace, though not without risk. Twice, as it was believed, attempts were made to assassinate him, but frustrated. Suspicion fell first on a man who affected demoniacal possession, and hovered much about the pre-cincts of the palace. A dagger was found upon his person; the people seized him and dragged him before the prefect; but Chrysostom procured his release through the inter-cession of some bishops, just as he was about to be ex-amined by torture. A second attempt was supposed to be intended by a slave, who ran at full speed towards the

[1] Pall. Dial. c. 9.   Sozom. viii. 21.

entrance of the palace, and plunged a dagger, in some
instances with fatal effect, into several passers by who
endeavoured to stop him. He was at last surrounded and
captured by the people, when he confessed that he had
been bribed by his master, a priest named Elpidius, to try
and assassinate the Archbishop. The fury of the people
was appeased by the imprisonment of the man; but they
now resolved to take the protection of their Archbishop
into their own hands. They divided themselves into com-
panies, which kept watch by turns, night and day, over the
episcopal palace. The hostile party, dreading any further
impediments to the execution of their iniquitous sentence,
now hurried matters to their conclusion. Five days after
Pentecost, four bishops—Acacius, Antiochus, Severian,
and Cyrinus—obtained an interview with the Emperor.
They represented that the city never would be tranquil
till the removal of the Archbishop had been effected, and
that his remaining in the palace after his condemnation
was a gross violation of ecclesiastical law. They avowed
themselves willing to take the responsibility of his deposition on their own heads, and besought the Emperor not
to be more lenient and concessive than were bishops and
priests.[1]

June, A.D. 404. The long hoped-for mandate was at
length issued. It was conveyed to the Archbishop by the
notary Patricius, and informed him that Acacius and
three other bishops having charged themselves with the
responsibility of his deposition, he must commend himself
to God, and quit the church and the palace without delay.
The martyr received the cruel order with meek submission,
and prepared to act upon it with prompt obedience. He
passed from his palace to his church, saying to the bishops
who accompanied him, ' Come, let us pray and say farewell
to the Angel of the Church. At my own fate I can rejoice,

---

[1] Pall. Dial. 10.   Soz. viii. 21. 22.   Socr. vi. 18.

I only grieve for the sorrow of the people.' One of his friends, a nobleman, conveyed a warning to him to avoid by a secret departure the risk of exciting popular tumult. He informed him that Lucius was waiting with troops in one of the public baths to compel his removal in the event of any delay or resistance, and that the consequences of any attempt at a rescue by the populace might be serious.

Chrysostom acted on his advice. He entered the choir with his friendly bishops, bestowed on them a farewell kiss and farewell words; then bidding them wait for him there while he went to repose, he entered the baptistry, and sent for the deaconesses, Olympias, Pentadia, Procla, and Sylvina. 'Come hither, my daughters,' he said, 'and hearken to me; my career, I perceive, is coming to an end; I have finished my course, and perchance ye will see my face no more. Now I exhort you to this, let not any of you break off her accustomed benevolence towards the Church. If any man is appointed my successor without having canvassed the office, and against his own will, but by the common consent of all, submit to his authority as if he were Chrysostom himself; so may ye obtain mercy. Remember me in your prayers.' The women threw themselves at his feet, dissolved in tears. The Archbishop made a sign to one of the priests to remove the women, lest, as he said, their wailing should attract the attention of the people outside. He directed that the mule on which he was accustomed to ride should be saddled and taken to the western gate of the cathedral; and while the people's attention was diverted by this feint, he passed out, unobserved, by a small door near the east end, and surrendered himself to some soldiers who were at hand to convey him to the port. So he departed from the church, the scene of his indefatigable labours, whose walls were never again to resound to his eloquence. He went out, and, in the emphatic words of the historian to whose narrative we are indebted for the minute picture of these occurrences, 'the Angel of the Church went out with him.' Two bishops, Cyriacus of Synnada in Phrygia, and Eulysius of Apamea in Bythinia, accompanied him on board the vessel which conveyed him across the straits to the Bythinian coast.[1]

[1] Pall. Dial. c. 10.

CHAPTER XX.

THE people meanwhile, both within the church and outside, were not long in discovering that the Archbishop had
disappeared from the building and its precincts. They
became furiously agitated: some rushed to the harbour,
but too late to obstruct the embarcation. The doors of
the cathedral, which had been locked by some of the cabal,
who anticipated a rush of the people as soon as the
departure of Chrysostom should have been discovered,
were fiercely battered by the crowd on both sides. Jews
and pagans looked on, and jeered derisively at the tumult.
The horror of this scene of wild confusion was suddenly
increased by the apparition of fire bursting forth from the
building. How kindled, by accident or design, it is impossible to determine. Each party fiercely charged the
other with the guilt of the catastrophe, and some attributed it to miraculous interference of heavenly powers.
The conflagration broke out in or near the throne of the
Archbishop, which it consumed, and thence spread to the
roof. In three hours the edifice, whose erection and
embellishment had been the work of many years, was
reduced to a heap of cinders. The only portion not
destroyed was the treasury, which contained the sacred
vessels of silver and gold, as if expressly to confute one

of the charges made against the Archbishop, that he had sold all the most valuable ornaments belonging to the church. Germanus and Cassian, the custodians of the treasury, when they fled to Rome, carried with them a copy of the inventory of all these articles, which, when they surrendered their office, had been handed over to the prefect and some of the other chief functionaries of the city.

The conflagration, however, did not confine itself to the cathedral. A violent north wind carried the flames across the Forum, and ignited the great curia or senate house; not, however, that side of it which faced the cathedral, but the further side, which looked into the little forum where the royal palace was situated. The whole senate house was destroyed. The statues of the Muses which Constantine had brought from Helicon were consumed, and all the other principal adornments. The images of Zeus and Athene alone were found intact, beneath a heap of ruins and of masses of molten lead which had dropped upon them from the burning roof.[1]

The real or affected suspicion that the Archbishop and his flock were the incendiaries was quite a sufficient pretext for treating them with rigour. He himself, with Cyriacus and Eulysius, was detained in chains under a strict guard in Bythinia. These two companions were taken from him and conveyed bound to Chalcedon, but after examination were dismissed as innocent. But at Constantinople the persecution was enforced with merciless severity under the auspices of Optatus, a pagan, now prefect in the place of Studius. All the followers of the Archbishop, clerical and lay, high and low, were subjected, if caught, to rigorous inquisition, and most of them to severe punishment. Chrysostom wrote a letter from Bythinia to the Emperor, imploring that he might at least be allowed to appear and defend himself and his

[1] Pall. Dial. c. 10. Zosim. v. 24. Sozom. viii. 22.

clergy from the atrocious charge of incendiarism, but the
letter received no attention; and as the poor exile continued his journey to Nice, his sufferings were enhanced
by pitiable intelligence of the persecution inflicted on
bishops, priests, and deacons who refused to anathematise
him or recognise the validity of his deposition.   But the
spirit of the exile was not only brave to support his own
troubles, but could spare some of its energy to encourage
those who were suffering in his cause to patience, fortitude, resignation, and even joy.[1]

In times of religious persecution, the language of the
New Testament, about the blessedness of tribulation as
a pledge of future happiness and a means of preparation
for it, comes home to men's hearts with a reality and
force which seem to exceed our present application of it
to the ordinary troubles of sickness and the like.   Those
who were firmly persuaded that their cause was the cause
of truth and of Jesus Christ read the words, ' Blessed are
ye when ye are persecuted for righteousness' sake,' or
' Happy are ye when men revile you and persecute you,'
as if spoken directly to themselves; and they really did
' rejoice in that day and leap for joy.'   Such are the texts
which Chrysostom cites for the consolation of his suffering friends.   He speaks of their exposure to intimidation
by threats, imprisonment, frequent appearance in judges'
courts, torture at the hands of the executioner, shameless
false evidence, coarse ribaldry, and scurrilous jests; but
' blessed were they, yea, thrice blessed, and more than that,
to endure imprisonment and chains, for not only was
their fortitude the subject of admiration everywhere, but
their present sufferings were the measure of their future
happiness, and their names had been inscribed in the
Book of Life.'[2]

The destruction of the church and senate house was

[1] Pall. Dial. c. 11.   [2] Ep. ad Episcop. vol. iii. pp. 541 and 673.

the first pretext for instituting persecution against the
adherents of Chrysostom; the second was, their refusal
to recognise his successor. One week after his deposition,
Arsacius, brother of Nectarius the predecessor of Chrysostom, was, apparently by the simple exercise of Imperial
authority, elevated to the see. He was eighty years old,
and is quaintly described by Palladius as 'muter than a
fish, and more incapable than a frog.'[1] The probable aim
of the Empress was to secure a man whose servility might
be depended on. His brother, Nectarius, had once desired
to make him Bishop of Tarsus; and, on his declining to
accept the promotion, had taunted him with ambitiously
reserving himself for the See of Constantinople; where-
upon Arsacius had taken an oath that he never would
accept any bishopric. But ambition and Imperial authority overcame his scruples. He is described by the
historians as a man of pious disposition and mild conduct;
with one exception, that he persecuted with relentless
vigour the contumacious adherents of his predecessor.
By Chrysostom he is denounced as a wolf, and in a figurative sense as an adulterer, on account of his usurpation
of the see during the lifetime of its legitimate occupant.[2]
Arsacius applied to the civil powers for assistance, to
compel the Johnites to attend the churches where he and
his clergy officiated. A tribune was directed to attack a
body of them who had assembled for worship in some remote part of the city. The soldiers dispersed the assembly, took several of the most eminent persons prisoners,
and, as usual, stripped the women of their golden girdles,
and jewels, and earrings. The only consequence of this
was, that the Johnites became more attached to the cause
and memory of their late Archbishop. Some of them
fled the city, and many more refrained as much as possible from appearing in public places, such as the Forum

<hr>

[1] C. 11.   [2] Epist. cxxv.

and the baths. Meetings of some kind for worship were not discontinued, or were soon resumed, for we find Chrysostom, in one of his letters written during his exile, reproving two priests, Theophilus and Salustius, for slackness in attending such assemblies.[1] But worshippers ran great risks. The Prefect Optatus, who succeeded Studius, probably because the latter was considered too lenient, appears to have entertained all the animosity of a thorough pagan against Christians, and to have rejoiced in the present opportunity of inflicting sufferings upon them. He combined the two charges of incendiarism and contumacy in his prosecution of the Johnites, and endeavoured to extort confessions of guilt from his victims with merciless barbarity.

A few instances are recorded, and they are quite enough to sicken us of the tale of such horrors. Eutropius, a reader, was commanded to name the persons who had set fire to the church. He refused. He was young and delicate, and it was thought a confession might be wrung from him under the agony of torture. He was lashed with a scourge, his cheeks were scraped, and his sides lacerated with iron teeth, after which lighted torches were applied to the wounded parts. No information could be extorted from him : he was, therefore, conveyed to prison, and thrown into a dungeon, where he expired. Some priests, adherents of Arsacius, buried him by night, that his mangled body might not be seen by any eyes but those of his enemies. Celestial music was said to have been heard at the time of his interment.

Tigrius, the priest, whose presence with Serapion had been demanded at the Synod of the Oak, was another victim. He was stripped, scourged on his back, and then stretched on the rack till his bones were dislocated. He survived the torture, and was banished to Mesopotamia. Serapion

---

[1] Epist. ccxii.

himself, now Bishop of Heraclea in Thrace, was seized, tried on several calumnious charges, barbarously scourged, and sent into exile.

Those ladies also who were most distinguished for their friendship with the deposed Archbishop, and for the dedication of their time and money to the Church, were marked objects of persecution. They were brought before the prefect, and admonished by him to acknowledge Arsacius, and so save themselves from future annoyance. A few from timidity complied; but Olympias, who was subjected to a severer examination, confronted it with a dauntless spirit. She was bluntly asked why she had set fire to the 'Great Church.' 'My manner of life,' replied the accused, 'is a sufficient refutation of such a charge; a person who has expended large sums of money to restore and embellish the churches of God is not inclined to burn and demolish them.' 'I know your past course of life well,' cried the prefect. 'If you know aught against it, then descend from your place there as judge, and come forward as my accuser,' replied the undaunted Olympias. Perceiving that she was not to be brow-beaten, Optatus proposed the same course to her which had been adopted by some other women as a means of exemption from further persecution, namely, communion with Arsacius; but she scornfully rejected the base compromise. 'I have been publicly calumniated by a charge which cannot be proven, and I will not accede to any terms till I have been cleared from this accusation. Even if you resort to force, I will not hold communion with those from whom I ought to secede, nor do anything contrary to the principles of my holy religion.' She made a request, which was granted, that she might be allowed a few days to consult with lawyers on the proper means of legally refuting the libellous accusation. The prefect, however (on what pretence is not stated), sent for her again, and exacted a heavy fine, in the hope that she would be induced to yield. The fine was paid without any reluctance, but her refusal to acknowledge the usurper was inflexible; and to avoid, if possible, further pressure and persecution, she retired to Cyzicus, on the other side of the straits.[1]

The tidings of her fortitude and loyalty were conveyed to the exiled Chrysostom, and so cheered his spirit in the midst of depression and sickness that his sufferings seemed to him as nothing. 'When many men and women, old and young, highly reputed for their virtue, had turned their backs on the enemy almost before the conflict had begun, she, on the other hand, after many encounters, so far from being enervated, was even invigorated; she spread forth the sails of patience, and floated securely as on a calm sea; so far from being overwhelmed by the storm, she was scarcely sprinkled by the spray. In the seclusion of her little house she was able to inspire courage into the hearts of others, and had been to them a haven of comfort and a tower of strength.'[2]

The deaconess Pentadia, widow of the consul Timasius, was another victim. She led the life of a recluse, never going beyond the walls of her house except to church. She was now dragged from her retreat through the Forum to the prefect's tribunal, and thence to prison, charged with being an accomplice in the late fire. Several persons were put to the torture before her eyes, in order to intimidate her into a confession; but in vain. Her firm demeanour, courageous answers, and powerful demonstrations of her innocence confounded and silenced her adversaries, and elicited the admiration of the public. Beyond imprisonment no indignities seem to have been inflicted on her; and when desirous to quit the capital, she was persuaded by Chrysostom to remain, who represented the great value of her presence and example in

animating others to support their present afflictions. She
had apparently intended to try and join him in his place
of exile, when he had been removed to Cucusus, on the
confines of lesser Armenia, for he dwells on the great
risk to her delicate health from a journey in winter, and
the danger of being plundered by the Isaurian robbers,
who were just then, he says, in a powerful condition.
He, therefore, on all grounds, begs her to remain where
she is, but to relieve his mind from anxiety about her
affairs and health by constantly writing to him.[1]

Meanwhile, the injured Church of Constantinople did
not cease through letters and emissaries to solicit the
interference of the Western Church. The first intimation
of the calamities we have been describing which reached
the ears of Rome, was through a messenger despatched
by Theophilus. The letter which he brought was inscribed 'From Pope Theophilus to Pope Innocent,' and
stated in the barest manner, without assigning his reasons
or mentioning any assessors in his judgment, that he had
deposed Chrysostom, and that it behoved Innocent to
break off communion with him. The Pope was displeased
by the cool and curt character of the letter, and somewhat
perplexed how to notice or reply to so inexplicit a despatch. Eusebius, a deacon from Constantinople, who
was in Rome at the time on some ecclesiastical business,
obtained an interview with Innocent, and entreated him
not to act till information should be received from Constantinople, which, he added (on what grounds does not
appear), he had good reason to expect would arrive in a
short time. Three days afterwards four bishops did arrive,
bearing the letter from Chrysostom to Innocent which
contained that pathetic and perspicuous narrative of the
recent occurrences, from which extracts have been made
in the preceding chapter. They brought two other letters,

[1] Epp. xciv. and civ.

one from the forty friendly bishops, another from the
clergy of Constantinople.

Innocent no longer hesitated to pronounce an opinion.
His letter to Theophilus is brief, decisive, almost peremptory in tone. 'The See of Rome,' he said, 'would maintain
communion with Alexandria and Constantinople to avoid
rending the unity of the Church ; but he annulled
(ἀθέτησας) the deposition of John, apparently made by
Theophilus. It was impossible to recognise the validity
of a sentence pronounced by such an irregular synod as
that lately convened at Chalcedon. If Theophilus had
confidence in the justice of that sentence, he must appear
in person to prove it before a General Council called
together and regulated according to the Canons of Nice.'
A few days after the despatch of this letter, Peter, an
Alexandrian priest, arrived with a deacon from Constantinople, bearing another letter from Theophilus, and
certain minutes, so called, of the acts of the Synod at the
Oak. Innocent, having perused the minutes, was indignant
at the mingled monstrosity and levity of the charges
brought against Chrysostom, and at the condemnation
having been pronounced in the absence of the defendant.
He ordered special prayers and fasts to be observed by the
Church for the restoration of concord, and addressed to
Theophilus a sharp letter of reproof.[1]

It is not easy to make out precisely how many communications passed each way between the Churches of
Rome and Constantinople, or the exact date of each, but
several letters are distinctly mentioned. Theotecnus, a
priest from Constantinople, brought a letter from twenty-
five of the forty bishops who had constantly adhered to
Chrysostom, in which they described the expulsion of the
Patriarch and the conflagration of the church. Innocent
replied by a letter of condolence, and exhortation to bear

[1] Pall. Dial. cc. 1, 2, 3.

their trial with Christian fortitude and patience, for at
present he confessed, with deep regret, that he saw small
prospect of rendering much effectual aid, 'owing to the
opposition of certain persons powerful for evil,' alluding
probably to the jealousies between the Courts of the two
brothers, Honorius and Arcadius. The cabal also sent a
letter to Innocent, containing their version of the late
transactions. Their emissary was Paternus, who called
himself a priest of Constantinople; 'an ugly little fellow,'
says Palladius, 'and very unintelligible.' The letter was
written in the names of Arsacius, Paulus, Antiochus,
Cyrinus, Severian, and some others; and, among other
opprobrious charges, distinctly accused Chrysostom of
setting fire to the church. Innocent treated the letter
with much disdain, and would not condescend to answer
it. Some days afterwards, Cyriacus, Bishop of Synnada,
arrived in Rome as a fugitive, in consequence of an Imperial edict, which directed the deposition of any bishop
who refused to communicate with Arsacius and Theophilus, and the confiscation of his property, if he had any.
After Cyriacus arrived Eulysius, Bishop of Apamea in
Bithynia, bringing a letter from fifteen of the forty
friendly bishops, which described all the past and present
distress of the Church caused by Chrysostom's enemies,
and in all respects confirmed the oral account of Cyriacus.
In the course of another month, Palladius, Bishop of
Hellenopolis, fled to Rome from the intolerable harshness
of magisterial decrees, which now subjected to confiscation the house of anyone who should be found to have
harboured bishop, priest, or even layman, who communi-
cated with Chrysostom. From a letter of Chrysostom[1]
it appears, that Palladius and many others lived for some
time in concealment at Constantinople, in the hope of
escaping persecution. They were courteously lodged in

[1] Ep. cxiii.

Rome by one Pinianus and his wife, by Juliana, Proba, and other Roman ladies, whom Chrysostom warmly thanks for their kindness in letters written by him from Cucusus.[1] Germanus the priest, and Cassian the deacon, custodians of the Church treasury at Constantinople, also came to Rome, bringing a letter from the whole body of the clergy who adhered to Chrysostom, describing the violent deposition and expulsion of the Archbishop, and the tyranny of their adversaries under which they were now suffering.[2]

The reply of Innocent to this letter from the clergy of Constantinople is dignified as well as sympathetic. He exhorts, as usual, to patience, and to the derivation of comfort from the remembrance of the sufferings of all God's saints in past times. But he deeply deplores their wrongs, and again expresses his reprobation in the strongest terms of the illegality of the late proceedings. 'The canon which prohibited the ordination of a successor during the lifetime of the reigning bishop had been grossly violated. The Canons of Antioch, on which the synod had relied, were invalid, having been composed by heretics, and they had been rejected by the Council of Sardica. The Canons of Nice alone were entitled to the obedience of the Church; but adversaries and heretics were always attempting to subvert them.' . . . . 'What steps, then, should be taken in the existing crisis? Plainly a General Council must be convoked; that was the only means of appeasing the fury of the tempest. He was watching an opportunity to accomplish this; meanwhile, they must wait in patience, and trust the goodness of God for the restoration of tranquillity and good order.'

To Chrysostom Innocent wrote, as friend to friend, as a bishop to a brother bishop, a letter of Christian consolation and encouragement, not entering into the legal questions of the case, and not pledging himself to decisive

---

[1] Epp. clxviii. clxix. et aliæ.   [2] Pall. Dial. c. 3.

action of any kind. 'It was not necessary to remind one, who was himself the teacher and pastor of a great people, that God often tried the best of men, and put their patience to the severest tests, and that they are firmly supported under the greatest calamities by the approving voice of conscience.' . . . 'A good man may be severely tried, but cannot be overcome, since he is preserved and guarded by the truth of Holy Scripture. Holy Scripture supplied abundant examples of suffering saints who did not receive their crowns until they had undergone the heaviest trials with patience. Take courage then, honoured brother, from the testimony of conscience. When you have been purified by affliction, you will enter into the haven of peace in the presence of Christ our Lord.'[1]

At the same time, Innocent took all possible measures to obtain the council which he had recommended to the Church of Constantinople as the only means of redressing her wrongs. He wrote a letter to Honorius, then at Ravenna, representing the lamentable condition of the Church of Constantinople, which elicited from the Emperor an order for the convention of an Italian synod. This synod, after a due consideration of all the circumstances, was to submit its decision and suggestions to himself. The result of the deliberations of the Italian bishops, swayed no doubt by Innocent, was to request the Emperor to write to his brother Arcadius, urging the convocation of a General Council to be held in Thessalonica, which would be a convenient meeting-point for the prelates of East and West. Honorius complied, and the letter was despatched under the care of a deputation from the Italian Church, consisting of five bishops, two priests, and a deacon. The Emperor calls it the third letter[2]

[1] Soz. viii. 26.

[2] One previous letter we possess in Chrys. vol. iii. p. 539, in which he expresses his horror at the late outrages in the Church of St. Sophia, and at the gross violation of justice and law in the recent so-called trial of Chrysostom.

which he had written relative to the affairs of Constantinople. He professes great solicitude for the peace of the
Church, ' on which,' he observes, ' the peace of our Empire
depends ; ' and with a view to this object, he urges the
convocation of a council at Thessalonica, and specially
entreats that the attendance of Theophilus, who was, he
is informed, author of all these disturbances, should be insisted upon. He commends the deputation to the honourable care of Arcadius ; and that he may know the sentiments of the Italian Church on the present state of affairs,
he sends him two letters as samples of many, one from the
Bishop of Rome, the other from the Bishop of Aquileia.

The only bishop on the deputation whose see is mentioned was Æmilius, Bishop of Beneventum. The Oriental refugees, Cyriacus, Demetrius, Palladius, and Eulysius, accompanied the Italians. They were the bearers
not only of letters from Honorius, Innocent, and the
bishops Chromatius of Aquileia and Venerius of Milan,
but also of a memorial from the Italian synod, which
recommended that Chrysostom should be reinstated in
his see before he was required to take his trial before a
council. He would then, it was observed, have no reasonable excuse for declining to attend it. The deputation
was absent four months. On their return the members
had a pitiful tale to tell of failure in their errand, and of
personal suffering from maltreatment. They touched at
Athens on their voyage out, whence they had intended to
proceed to Thessalonica, and lay the letters first of all
before Anysius, bishop of that place ; but at Athens they
were arrested by a military officer, who placed them on
board two vessels under charge of a centurion, to be conveyed to Constantinople. A furious southerly gale sprang
up soon after their departure, and, after a voyage of some
danger, they arrived, late on the third day, at the suburb
of Constantinople called Victor. But, instead of being

permitted to proceed to the city, they were shut up in a fortress named Athyra, on the coast—the Romans in a single chamber, the Orientals in separate apartments. No servant even was permitted to attend them. They were commanded to deliver up the letters which they had brought, but refused, as being ambassadors, to surrender them to any but to the Emperor himself. Secretaries and messengers were sent in succession, but the ambassadors stedfastly adhered to their refusal. The letters were at length wrested from their possession by sheer violence: one bishop's thumb was broken in the struggle. On the following day a large bribe was offered them if they would recognise Atticus (the aged Arsacius was now dead) as Patriarch, and say no more about the trial of Chrysostom. This base proposal was firmly resisted; and, seeing the utter hopelessness of their mission, they requested to be released as soon as possible, and suffered to return to their dioceses in safety. The Italians saw no more of their companions from the East. They themselves were thrust into a miserable vessel, with twenty soldiers of various grades, and conveyed to Lampsacus, on the Asiatic coast, where they embarked in another vessel, and, after a tedious voyage of twenty days, arrived at Hydruntum, in Calabria.[1]

Neither the Papacy nor the Empire of the West were sufficiently powerful at this time to insist further upon justice being done to the Patriarch, in the face of the determined animosity of the ruling powers at Constantinople; but the friends of the martyr deemed that they read unequivocal signs of the Divine displeasure in the misfortunes which befell some of Chrysostom's greatest personal enemies. Thrace and Illyria were ravaged by an incursion of Huns, and the Isaurians, a predatory barbarian race, which inhabited the fastnesses

[1] Pall. Dial. c. 4.

of Mount Taurus, committed fearful havoc in Syria and
Asia Minor. Cyrinus, Bishop of Chalcedon, one of the
four who had taken on them the responsibility of Chrysostom's condemnation, died in great agony from the
wound in his foot, originally caused when his foot had been
trodden upon by Bishop Maruthas, more than a year ago,
just before the Synod of the Oak. At the end of September, Constantinople was visited by a destructive fall of
hailstones of extraordinary size; and on October 6, A.D.
404, died the Empress Eudoxia. Nilus, one of the most eminent anchorites of the day, once Prefect of Constantinople,
who had abandoned wealth, family, and position for the
solitudes of Mount Sinai, addressed two letters of reproof
and warning to Arcadius on the iniquitous banishment
of Chrysostom and inhuman persecution of his followers.
' How can you expect to see Constantinople delivered from
visitations of earthquake and fire from Heaven, after the
enormities which have there been perpetrated; after crime
has been established there by the authority of laws; after
the thrice-blessed John, the pillar of the Church, the
lamp of truth, the trumpet of Jesus Christ, has been
driven from the city? How can I grant my prayers
(Arcadius had apparently begged the intercession of the
saint to remove the national troubles) to a city stricken
by the wrath of God, whose thunder is every moment
ready to fall upon her?'[1]

But human and divine warnings were alike wasted; the
enemies of the Patriarch had complete sway over the
Court, and suffered it not to swerve from the path of
persecution. The Western bishops and presbyters, after
the disastrous termination of their embassy to Constantinople, returned home, without honour indeed, but unmolested. Their Eastern colleagues did not escape so
easily. They were conveyed to places of exile in the most

[1] Nilus, 2 Epp. cclxv. and cclxxix.   Soz. viii. 25.

distant and opposite quarters of the Empire. Cyriacus
was confined in a Persian fortress beyond Emessa;
Eulysius in Arabia; Palladius on the confines of Ethiopia;
Demetrius was to have been confined in one of the Egyptian oases, but died of the harsh treatment to which he
was subjected on the journey. The exiles suffered such
brutal insults and indignities from the soldiers who conducted them to these places, that the desire of life was
extinguished. The little money which they had collected
for the expenses of their journey was taken from them by
their guards, who divided it among themselves. They
were forced to perform in one day the distance of two
days' journey. They were not permitted to enter any
churches on their route, but forced into Jewish or Samaritan synagogues, and lodged at night in low inns, where
their ears were shocked by the filthy conversation of
abandoned characters of both sexes. Yet even some of
these degraded people were won to a more respectful
behaviour, if not actually converted, by the Christian exhortations and instruction of the captives. The 'Word
of God was not bound.' Some of the bishops friendly
to Theophilus bribed the soldiers to hurry the exiles out
of their dioceses as quickly as possible. Distinguished
among these malignants were the Bishops of Tarsus, Antioch, Ancyra, and of Cæsarea in Palestine. Most of the
bishops of Cappadocia, on the other hand, especially
Theodorus of Tyana, and Bosporius of Colonia, accorded
them a compassionate and courteous reception.[1]

Arsacius died in November, A.D. 404. Out of many
ambitious candidates for the vacant throne, Atticus, a
presbyter, who had taken an active part in the persecution of Chrysostom, a native of Sebaste in Armenia, was
appointed. He was a man of moderate abilities and
generally mild disposition, but relentless in his deter-

---

[1] Pall. Dial. 20.

mination to crush out the party of the exiled Patriarch.
By his influence an Imperial rescript was obtained, which
decreed that 'any bishop who did not communicate with
Theophilus, Porphyry of Antioch, and Atticus, should be
ejected from the Church, and his property confiscated.'
The wealthy, for the most part, bowed to the storm; the
poor sought peace of body and of conscience in flight
either to Rome or monasteries. This rescript, aimed at
the bishops, was followed up by another directed against
the laity. Any layman who refused to recognise the above-
mentioned prelates was, if a civilian, to be deprived of
any office which he might hold, if a soldier, of his military girdle, if an artisan, to be heavily fined or banished.
Bishops and presbyters were dispersed as fugitives into
all parts of the Empire. Some sought retirement in
some secluded little country property of their own, and
obtained a precarious livelihood by manual labour, farm-
ing, or even fishing.[1]

But, in spite of all the various means of coercion at
Constantinople, in spite of trials, torture, imprisonment,
banishment, the bulk of the people could not be brought
to attend the ministration of Atticus and his clergy.
Their churches were comparatively empty, while the
persecuted adherents of the exile persistently held their
services in some sequestered valley, or on some lonely hill-
side. In fact, persecution, as has always been the case,
brought out and intensified the attachment of many to
the person and the cause which it was intended to crush,
and so far defeated its own object. Chrysostom himself
observes,[2] that many of those who had enjoyed a high
reputation for piety were the first to fall away when
brought to the test of persecution; whereas others who
had formerly been abandoned to frivolity and vice, now
renounced the theatre and circus, hastened into the

---

[1] Sozom. viii. 27. Pall. Dial. 20.   [2] Ep. ad eos qui scandalizati sunt, c. 19.

desert to attend the assembly of the Catholics at worship,
and displayed the greatest fortitude before the judge
when brought to trial, in the face of torture, and with the
prospect of imprisonment or exile.

The party now in power could not convert the hearts
of clergy or people to their side, but they could, and did,
change the outward aspect of the Church. The men of
probity and piety with whom Chrysostom had replaced
the six simoniacal bishops deposed in Asia were expelled,
and the delinquents restored. The Church in that region
was reduced to a disgraceful state. Ordinations were
conducted, not amidst prayer and fasting, but feasting,
drunkenness, and gross bribery. The See of Heracleides,
the good Bishop of Ephesus, appointed by Chrysostom,
was occupied by a eunuch, a monster of iniquity. The
people in disgust deserted the churches.

The death of Flavian, Bishop of Antioch, nearly coincided with the banishment of Chrysostom. The people
of Antioch were much attached to a priest named Constantius, a man described by Palladius as a faithful and
incorruptible servant of the Church from his earliest
youth, first as a messenger who carried ecclesiastical
despatches, then as reader, deacon, priest. He had won
the love and admiration of the people by his gentle,
amiable disposition, his intelligence, strict integrity, and
exemplary piety. There was a general desire to make
him bishop, but an ambitious priest named Porphyry
frustrated the design. By bribery, and calumnious stories
conveyed to the Court at Constantinople, he procured an
Imperial rescript, condemning Constantius to be banished
to one of the oases as a disturber of the people. With
the assistance of his friends Constantius escaped to
Cyprus. Porphyry meanwhile imprisoned several of the
clergy of Antioch, and seized the opportunity of the
Olympian festival (when most of the inhabitants had

poured out to the celebrated suburb of Daphne) to enter the church with a few bishops and clergy; and then, with doors fast closed, he was hurriedly ordained, so hurriedly that some portions of the service were omitted. Acacius, Severian, and Antiochus, who had officiated, immediately fled. The people were enraged when they discovered the trick, surrounded Porphyry's house, and threatened to burn it to the ground. He applied for protection to the prefect, who lent him a body of troops, with which he forcibly took possession of the church. He contrived to get an unscrupulous and cruel man sent from Constantinople to be captain of the city guards, terror of whom drove the people to attend the churches, though they did so with disgust, and earnestly prayed for retribution from Heaven on the authors of this wickedness.[1]

Innocent remained inflexibly attached to the cause of Chrysostom. The Church of Rome and the Italian bishops broke off all communion with Theophilus and Atticus, and ceased not to demand the convocation of a General Council, as the only tribunal by which the Patriarch could be lawfully acquitted or condemned.[2] But the Court of Ravenna was not in a position to support these demands by intimidation or actual force. All the skill of Stilicho and all the resources at his command were barely sufficient to repel the persevering efforts of Alaric and Rhadagaisus to take the great prize which they so eagerly coveted, the capital of the Roman Empire. The inevitable fall of Rome was averted only for a little while.

Thus the spirit of lawlessness and selfishness took advantage of the impotence of the secular power both in Rome and Constantinople to work its will upon the Church. It dealt a blow to Christian morality and ecclesiastical discipline from which the Church at Constantinople never recovered, and which caused a throb of pain

[1] Pall. Dial. cc. 15 and 16.   [2] Theod. v. 31.

from one end of Christendom to the other; for, in spite of all differences and divisions, Christendom was one then, so that, if one member suffered, all the members suffered with it; and what was done and said, and thought and felt, in the Church of Alexandria, or Antioch, or Constantinople, was not unknown or unregarded by the Churches of Rome or Milan, and through them made its impress on the Churches even of Gaul and Spain.

CHAPTER XXI.

CHRYSOSTOM ORDERED TO BE REMOVED TO CUCUSUS — PERILS EN-
COUNTERED AT CÆSAREA — HARDSHIPS OF THE JOURNEY — REACHES
CUCUSUS — LETTERS WRITTEN THERE TO OLYMPIAS AND OTHER
FRIENDS. A.D. 404.

It now only remains to follow the illustrious exile along
his painful journey to its melancholy, or, regarding him
as the Christian martyr, its glorious termination.

He was removed, as has been already seen, from Constantinople on June 20, and conveyed, in the course of
a few days, to Nice. Here he remained till July 4,
and several of his letters to Olympias were written from
this place. The air of that locality, soft yet freshened by
the sea, revived his health, which had suffered from the
feverish and harassing scenes which he had gone through
at Constantinople, and from the journey begun in the
very middle of the summer heat. Nothing could exceed
the kindness of the soldiers under whose custody he
travelled, who discharged towards him all the duties of
servants as well as of guards.[1] His ultimate destination
was not known for some time by himself or his friends.
Common report sent him to Scythia,[2] but the intention
of his enemies appears to have changed from time to time.
Sebaste in Armenia had been first proposed, but finally
Cucusus, a village in the Tauric range on the edge of
Cilicia and the lesser Armenia, was fixed upon. It was a
remote and desolate spot, subject to frequent attacks from
the marauding Isaurians; and at first Chrysostom earnestly entreated his friends in Constantinople to try and

[1] Epp. x. xi.   [2] Ep. xiii.

procure a more agreeable place of exile, a favour frequently granted to criminals. Olympias, Bishop Cyriacus,
Briso the chamberlain, and a lady named Theodora,
repeatedly interceded on his behalf; but their efforts were
ineffectual.[1] The Empress herself, it would appear, selected
Cucusus, and was inexorable in her decision.[2]

From beginning to end of his exile Chrysostom's mind
was occupied with organising such work as yet remained
possible to him. It has been seen with what zeal he had
planted a missionary settlement in Phœnicia. This project continued to the close of his life to be an object of
his most solicitous interest. On July 3, the eve of his
departure from Nice, he addressed a letter to a priest
named Constantius,[3] apparently the surperintendent of
the missionary work in Phœnicia and the surrounding
countries. He implores him to prosecute his labours for
the extirpation of paganism with zeal undiminished, and
undismayed by the present afflicted state of the bishop
and the see, to whom the mission owed its origin. ' The
pilot and the physician, far from relaxing their efforts
when the ship and the patient are in peril, redouble their
efforts to save them.' He begs Constantius to inform
him year by year how many temples are destroyed, how
many churches built, how many good Christians immi-
grate into Phœnicia. He had himself persuaded a recluse, whom he found at Nice, to go and place himself
under the direction of Constantius in the missionary
work. He had, he says, happily concluded, just about the
time of his deposition, arrangements for the suppression
of Marcionism, which was very prevalent at Salamis, in
Cyprus. He begs Constantius to write to his friend
Bishop Cyriacus, if still in Constantinople, and request
him to carry these plans into effect. Finally, he implores
the prayers of Constantius and all faithful people for the

---

[1] Epp. cxx. cxxi.   [2] Ep. cxxv. in fine.   [3] Ep. ccxxi.

cessation of the present calamities of the Church, especially of the intolerable evils which had befallen it in Asia; alluding no doubt to the restoration of the simoniacal bishops.

On July 4 or 5 the exile started from Nice on his toilsome and perilous journey in the midsummer heat, across the scorching plains of Galatia and Cappadocia. He describes himself[1] as an object of great compassion to travellers whom he met coming from Armenia and the East, who stopped to weep and wail over his distress. His route lay in a diagonal line across the centre of Asia Minor, ascending first of all near the stream of the river Sangarius, which in its upper course winds through vast plains of black bituminous soil, scantly cultivated, but supplying pasture to great herds of cattle. Chrysostom had always been an ascetic liver, but he had not a robust frame, and he had been accustomed to wholesome food and the frequent use of the bath. Continuous travelling by night as well as day, the scorching sun, hot dust, hard bread, brackish water, and deprivation of the bath, threw him into a fever; but, either from fear of the Isaurians, or of Leontius, Bishop of Ancyra, in Galatia, one of his most virulent enemies, the journey was prosecuted without intermission, till he arrived, more dead than alive, at Cæsarea, in Cappadocia.

He has left us a detailed account of the perils which befell him here, and a melancholy picture indeed it is of the ferocity and cunning of which bishops and monks were capable under the influence of fanatical partisanship.[2] Having escaped, he says, from the Galatian (probably meaning Leontius), he was met, as he approached Cæsarea, by several persons, who informed him that Pharetrius the bishop was eagerly expecting him, and preparing to welcome him with affectionate hospitality. He

[1] Ep. viii.   [2] Ep. xiv.

confesses that he himself mistrusted these specious offers, but he kept his suspicions to himself. On his arrival at Cæsarea, in a state of extreme exhaustion, Pharetrius did not appear, but he was enthusiastically received by the people as well as some monks and nuns. The extreme kindness and skill of physicians (one of whom declared his intention of accompanying him to the end of his journey), wholesome food, and the use of the bath so much renovated his strength and diminished his fever, that he became anxious in a day or two to resume his journey. But just at this juncture the city was thrown into consternation by tidings that a large body of Isaurians was ravaging the neighbourhood, and had already burned a town with much slaughter. All the available troops in Cæsarea were marched out, and the whole male population, including old men, turned out to man the walls. During this time of suspense, the house in which Chrysostom lodged was besieged by a large body of monks, who with furious cries and gestures demanded the surrender of Chrysostom. The prætorians who guarded him were terrified by the fierce behaviour of these fanatics, and declared that they would rather face the Isaurians than fall into the hands of these 'wild beasts.' The governor of the city succeeded in protecting the person of Chrysostom, but not in quelling the fury of the monks, who renewed their assault still more hotly on the following day. The Bishop Pharetrius was very generally suspected to be the instigator of these attacks, and an appeal was made to him to interpose his authority, that the Archbishop might at least enjoy a few days' repose, which the state of his health greatly needed. But the envy of Pharetrius was embittered by the popularity of Chrysostom, and the great kindness and compassion which his hardships had elicited from clergy and people. He refused to interfere; but Chrysostom's friends took advantage of

a brief lull in the hostile visits of the monks to convey
him in a litter outside the town, amidst the lamentations
of the attendant people, and imprecations on the author
of the malevolent assaults. When he was once outside
the town several of the clergy joined him, and besought
him not to think of trusting himself to Pharetrius; it
would be worse they declared than falling into the hands
of the Isaurians: 'only escape from our hands, and
wherever you fall you will fall safely.'

At this crisis a lady named Seleucia, the wife of Rufinus, a man of rank and a friend of Chrysostom, entreated
him to accept a lodging at her country-house, about five
miles out of the city. He accepted the offer; but, unknown to him, Pharetrius, whose rage was inflamed by
the rescue of his prey, visited the house, and threatened
to take vengeance on the mistress if her guest was not
surrendered. This demand was refused, and the lady
gave orders to her steward, in the event of any attack by
monks, to collect all the labourers on the estate and repel
the assault by force. But her courage at last gave way
under the pressure of incessant menaces from Pharetrius,
and it was resolved to remove the Archbishop, not less
for his own safety than for that of the person whose roof
had afforded him shelter. In the dead of night, when
Chrysostom was sleeping, unconscious of impending danger, he was roused by a companion, the priest Evethius,
who told him that he must instantly prepare for flight.
It was midnight, and the sky murky and moonless; but
they dared not light torches for fear of attracting the
observation of their enemies. The road was rugged and
rocky; the mule which carried the Archbishop's litter fell,
and he was thrown out. Evethius took him by the hand
and led, or rather dragged, him along. In such a pitiable
plight, faint with fatigue and fever-stricken, did the bishop
of the second see in Christendom stumble and totter

in the darkness along the Cappadocian mountain path.
'Were not these calamities,' he writes to Olmpias, 'sufficient to blot out many sins, and suggest to me a hope
of future glory?'

Of the remainder of his journey to Cucusus we possess
no detailed narrative. He only speaks in general terms
of his sufferings for thirty days from fever, aggravated by
deprivation of the body, and by deficient accommodation of
every kind in a journey made along a rough road, through
a desolate mountainous country, liable to an attack at
any moment from Isaurian bandits.[1] Desolate though
the region was, however, he speaks of monks and nuns
occasionally meeting him in large numbers, and loudly
bewailing his calamities, exclaiming that it 'had been
better the sun should have hidden his rays, than that the
mouth of Chrysostom should have been closed.[2] About
seventy days[3] after his departure from Constantinople,
that is, about the end of August or beginning of September, Cucusus was reached. After the fatigues and
dangers of his journey, it was a haven of rest to the
exhausted exile, though he describes it as in itself the
most desolate place in the world; a mere village high up
in the eastern range of Taurus, on the confines of lesser
Armenia, Cilicia, and Cappadocia.[4] But it was protected
from the Isaurians by a strong garrison, and it contained
many warm-hearted friends of the Archbishop, who emulated one another in showing him attention. Several had
sent invitations to him, before he left Cæsarea, to accept
a lodging at their houses, but more especially one whom
he calls 'my Lord Diodorus,' who had known him in Con-

[1] Epp. xiii. lxxxiv.
[2] Ep. cxxv.
[3] Ep. ccxxxiv.
[4] Epp. ccxxxiv. ccxxxvi. It is not
mentioned in Pliny or Ptolemy, but
appears in the Itinerary of Antonine

as Cocusus (pp. 10, 13). It stood at
the confluence of several roads, but
apparently not high roads, one of
which connected Antioch with Asia
Minor.

stantinople. This generous personage not only placed
his whole house at the disposal of Chrysostom, betaking
himself to a country villa to make room for his guest, but
furnished it with every possible defence against the cold
of the approaching winter, in that altitude very severe.
The Bishop of Cucusus not only received him with great
civility, but was even desirous that his own throne should
be occupied by the illustrious exile, that his flock might
profit by the eloquence of the greatest teacher and
preacher of the day; but Chrysostom thought it prudent
to decline the honour.[1]

Many of his friends in Constantinople and other places,
who owned property near Cucusus, directed their stewards
to provide in various ways for the comfort of the exile,
and some of his friends actually came to share his fortunes
in person. The aged deaconess, Sabiniana, arrived from
Constantinople with the fixed determination of accompanying him to his final place of exile, whatever that
might be. Constantius, the presbyter of Antioch, whom
the people had wished to make bishop, also took up his
abode at Cucusus, as well to escape from the persecution
of Porphyry as from his zealous attachment to Chrysostom.[2] Thus the natural disadvantages of the place, the
want of good physicians and of a plentiful market, the
severity of the heat in summer and cold in winter, were
largely compensated by the enjoyment of freedom, rest,
and the kind attention of friends. He warns his supporters in Constantinople, who were endeavouring to
procure a change of destination for him, to be careful
that he was not removed to a place worse than Cucusus,
where he possessed all substantial necessaries and comforts
of life. If, however, they thought there was a chance of
obtaining Cyzicus or Nicomedia, they were not to desist
from their efforts; but he was convinced that another

---

[1] Ep. cxxv. in fine.   [2] Ep. xiii.

long and fatiguing journey to a spot as remote and
desolate as Cucusus would kill him.[1]

The leisure of the exile was profitably employed in
writing letters to every variety of friends—men of rank,
ladies, deaconesses in Constantinople, bishops, clergy,
missionary monks, and his kind acquaintances in Cæsarea,
especially the physician Hymnetius, who had attended
him there with affectionate care. As might be expected,
none of his letters describe his condition so minutely or
pour forth so unrestrainedly his fears, hopes, his causes of
distress or joy, as those written to Olympias. The style
in which she is usually addressed is at once respectful,
affectionate, and paternal: 'To my lady, the most reverend and religious deaconess Olympias, Bishop John
sends you greeting in the Lord.' They are seventeen in
number, written at different stages of his exile; nor is it
possible to determine precisely the date of each. The
first three seem to have been written from Cucusus, and
are mainly devoted to the aim of consoling her under the
present calamities of the Church, to dissipating, as he
expresses it, that cloud of sorrow which surrounded her.[2]
' Come now, let me soften the wound of your sadness, and
disperse the sad cogitations which compose this gloomy
cloud of care. What is it which upsets your mind, and
occasions your grief and despondency? Is it the fierce
and lowering storm which has overtaken the Churches
and enveloped all with the darkness of a moonless night,
which is growing to a head every day, and has already
wrought many lamentable shipwrecks? All this I know,
it shall not be gainsaid; and, if you like, I can form an
image of the things now being done so as to represent the
tragedy more distinctly to thee. We behold a sea heaved
up from its lowest depths, some sailors floating dead,
others struggling in the waves, the planks of the vessel

---

[1] Epp. xiii. xiv. ccxxxiv.   [2] Vol. iii. p. 549 et seq.

breaking up, the masts sprung, the canvas torn, the oars
dashed out of the sailors' hands, the pilots, seated on the
deck, clasping their knees with their hands, and crying
aloud at the hopelessness of their situation; neither sky
nor sea clearly visible, but all one impenetrable gloom,
and monsters of the deep attacking the shipwrecked crew
on every side. But why attempt further to describe the
indescribable? Yet, when I see all this, I do not despair,
when I consider who is the Disposer of this whole universe—One who masters the storm not by the contrivance
of art, but can calm it by his nod alone. He does not
always destroy what is terrible in its beginning, but waits
till it has come to its consummation; and then, when most
men are in despair, He works marvels and does things
beyond all expectation, displaying a power which belongs
to Him alone. Wherefore, faint not, for there is only
one thing, Olympias, which is really terrible, there is only
one real trial—and that is sin. All things else, whether
they be insidious assaults of foes, or hatred, or calumny,
or abuse, or confiscation of goods, or exile, or the sharp-
ened sword, and war raging throughout the world, are but
as a tale; they endure but for a season, they are perish-
able, and have their sphere in a mortal body, and do no
injury to the vigilant soul.' . . . 'Why, then, do you fear
temporal things, which flow away like the stream of a
river?' . . . 'Let none of these things which happen vex
you; cease to entreat the help of this person or that, but
continually beseech Jesus Christ, whom you serve, merely
to bow the head, and all these troubles will be dissolved;
if not in an instant of time, that is because He is waiting
till wickedness has grown to a height, and then He will
suddenly change the storm into a calm. . . .'

He enters into an eloquent review of the sufferings and
persecution to which our blessed Lord was subjected from
his birth to his death, in order to prove that apparent

failure is a fallacious test of the truth and real value of man's character and work.

‘ Why are you troubled because one man has been expelled and another introduced into his place? Christ was crucified, and the life of Barabbas, the robber, was asked. How many must have been shocked and repelled by this ignominious termination to a life of miracles! But in every stage of his life there was much to surprise and offend, and try the faith. His birth was the cause of death to many innocent children in Bethlehem; poverty, danger, exile, marked his infancy. He was misunderstood and suspected throughout his ministry. "Thou art a Samaritan and hast a devil;" "He deceiveth the people;" "He casteth out devils through the chief of the devils;" "He was a gluttonous man and winebibber, a friend of publicans and sinners." His discernment of purity and goodness was questioned, because He permitted the sinful woman to approach Him; " neither did his brethren believe on Him." You speak of many having been frightened out of the straight path by the present calamities. How many of Christ's disciples stumbled at the time of his crucifixion! One betrayed Him, another denied Him, the others fled, and He was led to trial bound and alone. How many, think you, were offended when they beheld Him, who a little while ago was raising the dead, cleansing the lepers, expelling devils, multiplying loaves, now bound, forlorn, surrounded by coarse soldiers, followed by a crowd of tumultuous priests? How many when He was being scourged, and they saw Him torn by the lash, and standing with bleeding body before the governor's tribunal? How many, again, when He was mocked, now with a crown of thorns, now with a purple robe, now with a reed in his hand? How many when He was smitten on the cheek, and they cried, " Prophesy, who is he that smote thee?" and dragged Him hither and

thither, consuming a whole day in jesting and revilement
in the midst of the throng of Jewish spectators? How
many when He was led to the cross with the marks of
the scourge upon his back? How many when the soldiers
divided his raiment among themselves? How many
when fastened to the cross and crucified? And, after our
Lord's Ascension, what had been the lot of the early
Church? Calamity, persecution, discomfiture, weakness,
the offence of many and the defection of many. Yet the
truth of Jesus Christ's Gospel had not been obscured; it
had shone more and more brightly: God had wrought out
the triumph of his Church.'

The above is a much-condensed rendering of passages
which can hardly be too much admired for the spirit as
well as style in which they are written. The union of a
Christian philosophy and a Christian faith, a philosophy
which traces a principle in God's modes of operation, and
a faith which contentedly accepts whatever happens, in
the firm belief that, be it pleasant or painful, it is part of
some purpose of God; a philosophy which traces in every
suffering of Christ's servants for the cause of truth a
reflection of the Master's sufferings, and a faith which
enables the sufferer not only to be cheerful himself, but
to cheer others, form, indeed, a noble object of contemplation. In a letter written to Olympias, just after his
hardships and perils at Cæsarea, he begs her to rejoice,
as he declares he can himself rejoice, in suffering as a
pledge of future glory. 'He never had desisted, and never
would desist, from declaring that the only real distress to
a man's self was sin; all other evils were as dust and
smoke. Spoliation of goods was freedom; banishment was
but a change of abode; death was but the discharge of
nature's debt, which all must eventually pay.' So much
has been at all times, and is still, said by Christian books
and preachers about patience and joy in affliction, that

we may be disposed to pass over language of this kind
sometimes as a hackneyed commonplace; but it must
be remembered that. in Chrysostom's case, the speaker
was an actual sufferer. His words were not the senti-
mental utterances of a rhetorical preacher addressing an
admiring audience, but convictions deliberately expressed
by a persecuted sufferer, who was really living by the
principles which he was accustomed to preach.

The bold and lavish praise which in some of his letters
he bestows upon the virtues of Olympias would be by a
lady of piety in modern times distrusted as flattery,
and distasteful as a dangerous encouragement to self-
righteousness and pride; but a highly wrought complimentary language which would be offensive to Western
taste, seems the natural expression of sincere feeling, and
is tolerated and taken for granted by Orientals; and it
may therefore be supposed that its effect in elating the
mind of the recipient is faint in proportion. He begins
his second letter by recommending her to divert her mind
from those calamities and sins, for which she was no way
responsible, by directing it to the final judgment. The
awe with which she must contemplate that scene, in which
she, together with all others, is individually concerned and
interested, will expel the useless grief which mourns over
iniquity wrought by others. But he breaks off suddenly
from such a line of argument, as inapplicable to the case
of so angelic a being as Olympias. 'To me, indeed, and
those who, like me, have been plunged beneath a sea
of sins, such discourse is necessary, for it excites and
alarms; but you, who abound in goodness and who have
already touched the very vault of Heaven, cannot even be
pricked by such language; wherefore, in addressing you,
I will chant another strain and strike another string.'
He does indeed; he invites her to count over her own
perfections, and to dwell with complacent satisfaction on

the heavenly rewards which are surely in store for her.
. . . 'It would fill a volume to relate the history of her
patience, tried in such a variety of ways from her youth.
She had laid such vigorous siege to her body, though
naturally delicate and nurtured in the lap of luxury, that
it might truly be called dead; and these austerities
had raised for her such a swarm of maladies as defied
the skill of physicians, and involved her in continual
suffering.   To speak, indeed, of patience and self-
control, in reference to her fasts and vigils, would be in-
accurate, because those expressions implied a conquest
over oppugnant passions. But she had no desires to
conquer; they were not merely subdued but extinguished.
It was as easy and natural to her to fast as it was to
others to eat, as natural to her to pass the night in vigil
as to others to sleep.' With an admiring comment on her
squalid and neglected attire he closes this singular enumeration of her perfections, lest, as he expresses it, he
should lose himself in an illimitable sea if he attempted
to wade further; his object being, not to make an exhaustive catalogue of her virtues, but only such as might
be sufficient to lift her out of her present state of depression.

It is worth making such extracts as these, because they
enable us to see how widely remote Chrysostom was from
the mind and taste of our own times in some points,
although in others he seems so nearly congenial.   There
is another vein of thought in this letter which is still
more alien. 'If,' he says, 'in addition to the rewards of
her chastity, her fasts, her vigils, her prayers, her boundless hospitality, she wishes to enjoy the sight of her
adversaries, those iniquitous and blood-stained men, undergoing punishment for their crimes, that pleasure also shall
be hers. Lazarus saw Dives tormented in flames. This
you will experience. For if he, who neglected but one

man, suffered such punishment, if it was expedient for the man who should offend one little one to be hanged or cast into the sea, what penalty will be exacted of men who have offended so large a part of the world, upset so many churches, and surpassed the ferocity of barbarians and robbers? You will see them fast bound, tormented in flames, gnashing their teeth, overwhelmed with useless sorrow and vain remorse; and they, in their turn, will behold you wearing a crown in the blessed mansions, exulting with angels, reigning with Christ; and they will cry aloud and groan, repenting of the contumely which they fastened upon thee, supplicating, but in vain, thy pity and compassion.'[1]

To our ears of course such language is extraordinarily shocking; but, in estimating the character of Chrysostom, it is valuable as a warning not to judge him or any individual by words or deeds, which belong not so much to him personally as to the age and circumstances in which he lived. Chrysostom had exercised as well as taught meekness, forbearance, and charity towards all men, enemies as well as friends; but he lived when the minds of Christians had for generations been inured to scenes of persecution, and to such a rigorous system and barbarous execution of criminal law as is hardly conceivable by us. Fierce opposition of party against party, violence and bloodshed put down, if at all, by the stern hand of force, harden public feeling, and the individual, however amiable and gentle by nature, inevitably becomes infected by the prevailing mode of thought; he must look at things and judge of things more or less from the same point of view as the generality of men amongst whom he lives. What would seem revoltingly cruel to a humane man now, appeared to a man who lived some hundreds of years ago, though perhaps equally humane by nature, and in

[1] Ep. ii. c. 10.

private life amiable, a merely natural and just retribution.

The letters of Chrysostom to those bishops [1] who remained loyal to his cause, are full of asseverations that his affection for them cannot be diminished by separation or distance. He exhorts them to continue their labours with unabated zeal, and carefully to abstain from all communion with the adverse party. Small though their numbers were, yet their fortitude under persecution would so much encourage others that their conduct might be the salvation of the Church. Several of his letters to laymen in Constantinople are models of wise Christian counsel. He is never less than the pastor, while he is always the friend. He writes to one Gemellus,[2] on his promotion to some high magisterial office, that, 'while others congratulated him merely on his new honours, *he* would rather dwell with thankfulness on the abundant opportunities Gemellus would now possess of exercising wisdom and gentleness on a large scale. He doubted not Gemellus would prove to those who were attached to the vain glories of this earth, that the true dignity of the magistrate consisted not in the robe or the girdle of office, or in the voice of the herald, but in reforming what was evil, and repairing what was falling to pieces, in punishing injustice, and preventing the right from being oppressed by might. He knew the boldness of Gemellus, his freedom of speech, his magnanimity, his contempt for the things of this world, his mildness, his benevolence ; and he was persuaded that he would be as a haven to the shipwrecked, as a staff to the fallen, a tower of defence to those who were oppressed by tyranny.' Gemellus appears to have been on the point of receiving baptism, and perhaps on that account to have been exposed to a rather trying degree of persecution. Chrysostom begs

[1] e. g. Epp. lxxxviii. lxxxix. et aliæ.   [2] Ep. cxxiv.

him not to delay baptism in the hope of receiving it from his hands, because the grace of the sacrament would be equally effectual by whatever hands administered, and his own joy would be none the less.[1]

So again, in his letter to Anthemius, who had recently been made prefect and consul. 'Nothing has been really added to you; it is not the prefect or the consul whom I love, but my most dear and gentle Lord Anthemius, full of philosophy and understanding. I do not felicitate thee because thou hast climbed to this throne, but because thou hast gained a grander sphere wherein to exercise thy benevolence and wisdom.'[2]

He was less distant from Antioch than Constantinople, and was cheered by visits from not a few of his old friends in his native city, and maintained a correspondence by letter with many more; but intercourse of either kind was much impeded by the dangers and difficulties of the roads, and at times by the severity of the climate.[3] The illegal seizure of the see of Antioch by Porphyry, and the harsh treatment to which the orthodox were subjected under his administration, caused them to turn to Chrysostom, not only with sympathy as a fellow-sufferer, but also for guidance, comfort, and some kind of episcopal superintendence. Their presents to him were so numerous that he felt compelled sometimes to decline them, or to request permission that they might be transferred to the aid of the missionary work in Phœnicia.[4]

Much of his thought and correspondence was concerned in providing for the welfare of the Church in Persia, Phœnicia, and among the Goths. In his fourteenth letter to Olympias he begs her to use her best endeavours to detach Maruthas, Bishop of Martyropolis in Persia, from the influence of the hostile party; 'to lift him out of the

---

[1] Ep. cxxxii.   [2] Ep. cxlvii.   [3] Epp. cxxx. ccxxii.
[4] Epp. l. li. lxi. et aliæ.

slough ' is his expression, 'for he greatly needed his
assistance on account of affairs in Persia; and he was
very anxious to know what Maruthas had accomplished
there, and whether he had received two letters recently
sent by himself.' From this it would seem as if Maruthas,
who had been present at the Synod of the Oak (when he
caused the fatal injury to the foot of Cyrinus), had
returned to Persia and again visited Constantinople, and
that Chrysostom had hopes of working in connection with
him for the good of the Church in Persia.[1] In the same
epistle he expresses his sorrow at having heard, through
some Gothic monks with whom Serapion had sought
shelter, that the Gothic bishop Unilas, whom he had
recently consecrated, was dead, after a short but active
career, and that the Gothic king had written to request
that a new bishop should be sent out. Chrysostom was
fearful lest Atticus and his party should appoint one; and
he urges that everything should be done to delay the
appointment if possible till winter came, when the season
would prevent anyone being sent till the following spring.
Meanwhile, Moduarius, the deacon who had brought the
letter from the Gothic prince, was to repair secretly and
quietly to Cucusus, and there confer with Chrysostom on
this important matter, to avert if possible the appointment of an improper person to so difficult a charge.

But of course the exile's interest was pre-eminently
centred on that city of which he could not but consider
himself still the chief pastor, although deprived of his
external authority over it. Banishment, imprisonment,
and intimidation had thinned the community of the
orthodox; and among the remaining pastors there were
some whose neglect of duty, the result of indolence or

---

[1] There seems no doubt that Maruthas was an able and active missionary
bishop. Socrates (vii. 8) tells strange
stories of his skill in exposing some
tricks of the magi, by which they attempted to prejudice the Persian king
Isdigerdes against Christianity.

faintheartedness, called forth severe rebukes from their former chief. 'He had heard with concern, and was vexed that the information had not come direct from the clergy themselves, that a priest, Salustius, had preached only five times between the end of June and October, and that he and Theophilus, another priest, rarely attended Divine service at all.'[1] To Theophilus he writes a letter of mingled sorrow and reproof, expressing a hope that the report may be incorrect, and begging him to refute it, or to amend his conduct. He reminds him of the dreadful punishment which was inflicted on the servant who buried the talent which he ought to have used, and of the fearful responsibility of neglecting that most beautiful flock, which, by the grace of God, was being strengthened in goodness, though now agitated by so terrible a tempest.[2] Several of his clergy and friends are upbraided with more or less of affectionate expostulation for slackness in writing to him; others are praised for their unshakable fortitude, patience, and zeal under affliction. He had learned with much concern from Domitianus, to whom the care of the widows and virgins of the Church was confided, that they were reduced to extreme indigence, and he entreats his friend Valentinus to sustain his well-known character for benevolence by relieving their necessities.[3]

Peanius, a man of rank and position in Constantinople, is thanked and praised for the unremitting zeal, yet tempered with moderation, with which he had resisted the usurping party, had stood inflexible in loyalty when others had fled, and had exerted himself for the welfare of the Church, not only in Constantinople, but also in Phœnicia, Palestine, and Cilicia. Chrysostom observes in the same letter that the members of the Church in

---

[1] Ep. ccx.   [2] Ep. ccxii.   [3] Ep. ccxvii.

these regions had, with very few exceptions, refused to recognise Arsacius.[1]

Those clergy and other persons who had been imprisoned on the charge of incendiarism were released in the beginning of September;[2] and Chrysostom, having heard of their liberation, was eagerly expecting a visit from them when he wrote (about the end of October probably) to Elpidius, Bishop of Laodicea,[3] in Syria, a prelate venerable in years and eminent in piety, who had as a priest accompanied Meletius to the Council of Constantinople in A.D. 381, and was his counterpart in the moderation and gentleness of his disposition. Chrysostom wrote to thank him for his zeal in endeavouring to retain the bishops, not only in his own region, but in all parts of the world, in loyal fidelity to the exiled Patriarch. Elpidius proved the sincerity of his own attachment to his friend by suffering deposition from his see, and imprisonment for three years in his own house. Alexander, the successor of the usurper Porphyry in the see of Antioch, restored Elpidius to his see about A.D. 414—a recognition of his merits which received the high approbation of Pope Innocent.[4]

Thus by letters did the exile maintain his influence over all varieties of people in distant and opposite quarters of the Empire. Exhortation and reproof, consolation and encouragement, or the mere expression of affectionate goodwill, are the main chords struck, as circumstances require. But there is one tone which pervades all alike— the unshakable Christian faith of the writer; his deep belief that all suffering was sent for a remedial chastening purpose, and that, if resignedly borne, it enhanced the glory of the reward reserved for those who should suffer

---

[1] Ep. cciv.
[2] As appears from an edict dated August 29, addressed to Studius, Prefect of Constantinople.—Cod. Theod. vol. ii. p. 16.
[3] Ep. cxiv.
[4] Tillemont, xi. 274.

for righteousness' sake ; that sin is the only real evil, that expatriation and persecution, and even death, since they touch only the external and temporal, are to be regarded as mere shadows, cobwebs, and dreams; that distance and material obstacles cannot impede the wings of affection and prayer, and that the cause of right and truth, although long depressed, will eventually triumph—these are principles, convictions firmly rooted, which he never tires of repeating, and on the strength of which he lived cheerful and contented.

The wide range of his influence, and the nobility of his Christian resignation and fortitude, maintained during his exile, have elicited the admiration of an historian not lavish of his compliments to Christian saints. ' Every tongue,' says Gibbon, ' repeated the praises of his genius and virtue ; and the respectful attention of the Christian world was fixed on a desert spot among the mountains of Taurus.'[1]

[1] Vol. v. ch. 32.

CHAPTER XXII.

THUS the autumn of A.D. 404 wore away.   The time of the
exile was occupied, not unpleasantly, by sending and receiving letters, and his spirits were cheered by occasional
visits from friends.   The destitute in the neighbourhood of
Cucusus were relieved by his alms; the mourners com-
forted by his affectionate sympathy; some persons taken
captive by the Isaurians obtained a release through his
intercession or ransom.   But the winter, always severe in
that elevated region, set in this year with unusual rigour:
all communication with the outer world was cut off by the
impassable condition of the roads, and the cold told
cruelly on the delicate constitution of the poor exile.   In
a letter to Olympias, written just on the return of spring
A.D. 405, he draws a pitiable picture of his winter sufferings.   For days together he lay in bed; but, in spite of
being wrapped under a very pile of blankets, with a fire
constantly burning in his room, he could not exclude the
cold.   He suffered from constant sleeplessness, headache,
sickness, and aversion from all food; but, with the return
of milder weather in spring, 'he was brought up again
from the gates of death;' and he compares the softness
of the climate at that season to the amenity of the
air of Antioch.   His spirits also were raised by the

arrival of messengers from Constantinople, bringing letters from Olympias and other friends.[1]

But the blessings of restoration to health and warm weather were counterbalanced by the misery of constant disturbance from the Isaurian bandits, who commenced their marauding campaigns as soon as the break-up of winter made the country practicable for their operations. They swarmed over the whole neighbourhood, and the roads which had been impassable from snow were now impassable from robbers, who mingled much merciless bloodshed with their plunder. When the full blaze also of summer heat came, Chrysostom found it almost as injurious to his health as the excessive cold; but he kept up his correspondence with his friends with unabated assiduity.[2]

The mission in Phœnicia occupied a great deal of his attention during this year. He had written, as already related, from Nice to Constantius, the superintendent of the mission, exhorting him not to allow the work to flag, owing to his own deposition and banishment, but rather to carry it on with additional energy. The efforts of the missionaries had begun to provoke a rather fierce opposition on the part of the Pagans, and attempts were made to deprive them of the bare necessaries of life. But Chrysostom's confidence and zeal never failed for a moment. 'The missionaries were to keep him informed of their wants, for, through the liberality of his friends, he could supply them with all that they required.' He was ably seconded by Nicolaus, a priest, who, though living at a distance, supplied the mission not only with money but with men. Gerontius, a presbyter whom Chrysostom had persuaded to abandon a solitary ascetic way of life for missionary work, was anxious to visit Cucusus on his way to Phœnicia; but Chrysostom begs him not to delay, as the work was urgent

[1] Ep. vi.   [2] Epp. cxl. cxlvi.

and winter was approaching. He represents the greater advantages of the active life Gerontius was now embracing. 'There would be nothing to prevent him observing his fasts, vigils, and other ascetic practices, as before, for the good of his own soul, and at the same time, by his missionary labours, he would reap the reward of those who save the souls of others.'[1]

The pagan resistance assumed more alarming proportions as time went on. A letter written to the missionaries seems to imply, by its tone of mingled warning and exhortation, that their courage was beginning to fail. Chrysostom has recourse to his favourite comparisons of the pilot and the physician, who exert twofold energy as the violence of the storm and the disease increase. Rufinus, a presbyter, seems to have been sent into Phœnicia as a kind of special agent to restore peace, and is stimulated to his work by an animated letter. 'I hear that the rage of the Greeks in Phœnicia has burst forth again, that several monks have been wounded, and some even killed. Wherefore I urge you the more earnestly to set out upon your journey with great speed, and take up your position.' . . . 'If you saw a house in a blaze you would not retreat, but advance upon it as quickly as possible, so as to anticipate the flames. When all is tranquillity it is within the compass of almost any one to make converts, but when Satan is raging and the devils are in arms, then, to make a gallant stand and rescue those who are falling into the hands of the enemy, is the work of a noble, vigilant spirit, a work which befits an alert and lofty mind like yours, an apostolic achievement worthy of crowns innumerable and rewards which defy description.' He entreats Rufinus to write to him from every halting-place on his journey, and to keep him constantly informed of all which might take place after his arrival. He would send, if necessary, ten

---

[1] Epp. liii. liv.

thousand times to Constantinople, in order to provide
Rufinus with all things necessary to facilitate his journey
and procure his ultimate success. The letter closes with
a passage which remarkably illustrates the importance
attached to reliques. 'With regard to the reliques of the
holy martyrs, feel no anxiety, for I immediately despatched
the most religious presbyter, my Lord Terentius, to my
Lord Oneius, the most religious Bishop of Arabissus, who
possesses many reliques indisputably genuine, which in a
few days we will forward to you into Phœnicia.' . . . 'Use
diligence to get the churches which are yet unroofed completed before the winter.'[1]

There is no further record of the future progress or
ultimate issue of this mission, in which the heart of the
exile was so deeply wrapped up. Theodoret (v. 29) merely
says that, through the energy of Chrysostom, the extirpation of idolatry in Phœnicia, and the destruction of pagan
temples, were successfully carried on. But there are
instances of the existence of Paganism mentioned in the
middle of the fifth century;[2] and it is only too certain that,
under the feeble and degenerate successors of Chrysostom,
the work would not receive any powerful impulse. Partly
from the absence of a great central organising force like
the Papacy, partly from the irregular and unpractical temperament of the Eastern nature, missionary enterprises
have not proceeded in great number from the Eastern
Church. The preaching of Ulphilas to the Goths, the
missions organised by Chrysostom among the Goths and
in Phœnicia, and the missionary labours of the Nestorians
in Asia, are but the rare exceptions which prove the rule.

The misery and desolation caused in the neighbourhood
of Cucusus by the Isaurians seem to have culminated in
the winter of A.D. 405–406 and the ensuing spring. The
inhabitants of the villages fled from their homes at the

---

[1] Epp. cxxiii. cxxvi.   [2] Photius, p. 1048.

approach of these formidable robbers, and sought a precarious refuge in woods and caves. Many perished from cold in these wild retreats, and many more at the hands of the ruffian robbers, who showed no mercy even to the aged, the women, and children. Chrysostom himself was, like others, frequently moving from place to place, now in this village, now in that, sometimes in the woods or secluded places. The only spot in which the poor harassed people seem to have found tolerable security was in the strong fortress of Arabissus, a neighbouring town. Yet even here they ran considerable risks. A body of 300 Isaurians attacked and very nearly captured it in the middle of the night; and the discomfort was extreme at all times, for the castle was crowded like a prison; the difficulty of obtaining food was often very great, and the difficulty of corresponding with friends still greater. Privation, anxiety, and frequent hurried movements in cold weather brought severe illness on Chrysostom again. Physicians attended him with great kindness, but the impossibility of procuring comforts and wholesome food rendered their services almost nugatory. His greatest grief, however, seems to have been the difficulty of maintaining regular correspondence with friends. The bearer of a letter from Olympias actually fell into the hands of the robbers, but was released; in consequence of which Chrysostom entreats her not to send any more special messengers, but only to avail herself of such persons as were obliged by business to pass through his place of exile. He would not add to his present sufferings the distress of knowing that any life had been lost on his account.[1]

To the year A.D. 406 belong those letters of affectionate gratitude, written to the bishops of the West for their zeal in supporting his cause, especially those who had

[1] Epp. lxi. lxix. cxxvii. cxxxi.

undertaken a long and perilous voyage to Constantinople to intercede in his behalf. These letters were sent by the hands of Evethius, the presbyter, who had for some time been his companion in exile. One letter may be quoted as an example: 'I had already been amazed at your zeal, on behalf of the reformation of the Church, displayed for a long time; but most of all am I now astonished at your great earnestness, in having undertaken so long a journey by sea, full of labour and toil, on behalf of the interests of the Church. I have longed continually to write to you, and offer you the salutation due to your piety; but since that is not possible, living as I now am in a region almost inaccessible, I take advantage of a most honourable and reverend presbyter to send you greeting, and to beseech you to persevere to the end in harmony with such a noble beginning. For ye know how great will be the reward of your patience, how vast the return from a benevolent God to those who labour for the common peace, and undergo so great a conflict.' [1]

To Chromatius, Bishop of Aquileia, he writes thus: ' The loud-voiced trumpet of your warm and genuine affection has sounded forth even as far as to me, a clear and far-reaching blast indeed, extending to the very extremities of the world. Distant as we are, we know, not less than those present with thee, thy exceeding and burning love; wherefore we long extremely to enjoy a meeting with thee face to face. But, since the wilderness in which we are imprisoned precludes this, we fulfil our desire, as well as we can, by writing to you through our most honourable and reverend presbyter, expressing our great gratitude for the zeal which you have for so long a time displayed in our behalf; and we beg you, when he returns, or by the hands of chance messengers who may visit this desolate spot, to send tidings of your health, for you

---

[1] Ep. clvii.

know how much pleasure it will afford us to hear frequently of the welfare of those who are so warmly disposed towards us.'[1]

The letter written by Chrysostom in A.D. 406 to Innocent is full of grateful acknowledgments for all the efforts which he had made, and was still making, on his behalf. 'Though separated by so vast a length of journey, yet are we near your Holiness, beholding with the eye of the soul your courage, your genuine, inflexible firmness, and the constant and abiding consolation we derive from you. For the higher the waves are lifted up, the more numerous the rocks and reefs, the more does your untiring vigilance increase.' . . . 'This is now the third year of my exile, spent in the midst of famine, pestilence, continual sieges, an indescribable wilderness, and the pillage of the Isaurians. In the midst of these distresses and dangers, your constant and firm affection is no ordinary solace to me.'[2]

There is a letter also addressed to Aurelius,[3] Bishop of Carthage, thanking him for bold and persevering intercession in his behalf. The Church of Africa appears to have adhered to what was at first the resolution of the Roman Church, to maintain communion with both Chrysostom and Theophilus. St. Augustine has bestowed a high eulogium on Chrysostom.[4] An African council, in A.D. 407, passed a resolution to address a letter to Innocent, praying that the intercourse between the Churches of Rome and Alexandria might be resumed.

The health of the exile appears to have suffered less than usual, in the winter of A.D. 406–7, from the effects of the cold. By carefully remaining in the house, and for the most part in bed, wrapped up in blankets in an apartment where a fire was kept constantly burning, and by

---

[1] Ep. clv.
[2] Vol. iii. p. 535.
[3] Ep. cxlix.
[4] Aug. cont. Jul. p. 370.

use of a medicine sent him by a lady, his attacks of head-ache and of sickness were averted or alleviated. He had become inured to the want of exercise, and the depriva-tion of the bath, and the smokiness of the room; and even the natives were astonished at the firmness with which so feeble and 'spidery' a frame supported the severity of the climate. He began to feel a persuasion that God would not have preserved him so miraculously through such various perils, if it were not his purpose to restore him to his former position, that he might accomplish some work for the Church.[1]

But the chief work which he was destined to ac-complish was to exhibit to the close of his life, now rapidly approaching, a noble spectacle of Christian forti-tude and patience, of one continuing to the last to hope in God, to put his trust in God, and still to give Him thanks. The malicious envy of his enemies was aug-mented by the admiration and affection which pursued their victim from all parts of Christendom, and the cor-respondence which was maintained with him even in the mountain fortress which they had selected for his prison. The only remedy was to remove him yet further, to a more remote and still more inaccessible region. They worked upon the Emperor and the Court, whose jealousy had been already excited by the interference of the West; and, in the middle of June, A.D. 407, an order was obtained by them for the removal of the exile to Pityus, on the eastern coast of the Euxine, near the very frontier of the Empire, in the most desolate country inhabited by savage, barba-rous people. The two prætorian soldiers charged with conveying him thither were instructed to push on the journey with the most inexorable haste, and encouraged to hope for promotion should their prisoner die on the road. One of the two had some sparks of humanity, and

[1] Ep. v.

furtively showed some little kindness to the sufferer; but
the other followed out the cruel directions given him
with merciless fidelity. Chrysostom had, some time ago,
expressed his conviction that he could not survive the
fatigue of another long and laborious journey, yet for
three months his fragile frame endured the strain till he
reached Comana in Pontus. A former bishop of that
place, Basiliscus, had suffered martyrdom in the persecution of Maximinus, together with Lucian of Antioch.
Chrysostom was lodged in the precincts of the church
erected in honour of Basiliscus, about five miles outside
the town. Here, so runs the story, the martyred bishop
appeared to him in the night, stood beside him, and said,
' Be of good cheer, for by to-morrow we shall be together.'
A similar vision was vouchsafed to one of the presbyters
of the church. He was bidden ' to prepare a place for
our brother John.' In the morning, Chrysostom entreated his guards to allow him to stay where he was till
eleven o'clock; but they were inflexible, and the weary
march was resumed. When, however, they had proceeded
about thirty stadia, he became so ill that they were compelled to return to the martyry. Here he asked for white
garments, and having been clothed in them, he distributed his own raiment among the clergy who were present. The Eucharist was administered to him, he spoke
a few farewell words to the ecclesiastics who stood around
him, and with the words ' Glory be to God for all things,
Amen,' on his lips, he expired. The promise of Basiliscus
was literally fulfilled—he was buried in the same grave
with the martyr, in the presence of a large concourse of
monks and nuns.[1]

The enemies of Chrysostom thus succeeded in wreaking

---

[1] Pall. Dial. pp. 38, 39, who says
that they came out of Syria, Cilicia,
and Armenia: but how could this be
if it took three months to convey
Chrysostom from Cucusus to Comana?

their vengeance to the full upon the person of their victim—'Non missura cutem nisi plena cruoris hirudo;' but they were powerless to obliterate his memory. A sense of the cruelty and injustice with which he had been treated grew throughout Christendom, and he was more honoured and admired after his death than he had been during his life. His followers in Constantinople, under the appellation of Johnites, persisted in refusing to hold any communion with Atticus; and in the course of ten years, Atticus himself was constrained, by the solicitations of the Court and people, by the example of other prelates, especially Alexander of Antioch, and by a natural desire to maintain communion with the Western Church, to admit the name of Chrysostom into the diptychs of the Church of Constantinople. Cyril, the nephew and successor of Theophilus, who inherited in too many points his uncle's spirit as well as his see, yielded a more tardy and reluctant consent to the recognition of his uncle's foe.[1]

But a still higher honour was yet to be paid to his memory by the Church from which he had been so violently expelled. In A.D. 434, Proclus, formerly a disciple of Chrysostom, was elevated to the See of Constantinople. He conceived that the only effectual means of doing justice to the injured saint, and reconciling the Johnites to the Church, would be to transport his remains to the city. The consent of the Emperor Theodosius II. was obtained. On January 27,[2] A.D. 438, the reliques of the banished Archbishop were brought to the shores of the Bosphorus. As once before in his lifetime, to greet him on his return from exile, so now, and in still greater numbers, the people, bearing torches, crowded the waters of the strait with their boats to welcome the

[1] Till. xi. 349.
[2] This is his day in the Calendar of the Eastern and Western Church.

return of all which remained of their beloved and much-
wronged spiritual father. The young Emperor, stooping
down, laid his face on the reliquary, and implored forgiveness of the injuries which his parents had inflicted
on the saint whose ashes it contained. That reliquary
was then deposited near the altar of the Church of the
Apostles.[1] It is the sad story, so often repeated in history, of goodness and greatness, unrecognised, slighted,
injured, cut short in a career of usefulness by one generation, abundantly, but too late, acknowledged in the next;
when posterity, paying to the memory and the tomb the
honours which should have been bestowed on the living
man, can only utter the remorseful prayer—

> ' His saltem accumulem donis, et fungar inani
>   Munere . . . .'

[1] The Roman martyrology states that the remains of the saint were afterwards translated to St. Peter's, Rome, but the statement is not supported by any trustworthy historical evidence.—Till. xi. 352.

CHAPTER XXIII.

SURVEY OF CHRYSOSTOM'S THEOLOGICAL TEACHING — PRACTICAL TONE
OF HIS WORKS—REASON OF THIS—DOCTRINE OF MAN'S NATURE—
ORIGINAL SIN—GRACE — FREE-WILL—HOW FAR CHRYSOSTOM PELA-
GIAN— LANGUAGE ON THE TRINITY—ATONEMENT—JUSTIFICATION—
THE TWO SACRAMENTS—NO TRACE OF CONFESSION, PURGATORY, OR
MARIOLATRY—RELATIONS TOWARDS THE POPE—LITURGY OF CHRY-
SOSTOM—HIS CHARACTER AS A COMMENTATOR—VIEWS ON INSPI-
RATION—HIS PREACHING—PERSONAL APPEARANCE—REFERENCES TO
GREEK CLASSICAL AUTHORS—COMPARISON WITH ST. AUGUSTINE.

THE main characteristics of Chrysostom as a theologian
and interpreter of Scripture, as well as a pastor and
preacher, have, it is hoped, been already indicated in the
course of the preceding narrative; but it may be desirable to supplement, by a fuller and more methodical
survey, notices which were necessarily sometimes brief and
incidental in the biographical chapters.[1]

Some evidence, therefore, of his theological teaching
and method of interpretation will first of all be collected
from his writings, and arranged under different heads.
Two difficulties in the way of executing this task faithfully should be borne in mind : first, the voluminous
bulk of Chrysostom's works (as Suidas observed, that it
belonged to God rather than man to know them all),
which renders a successful search, for the selection of
what are really the most telling passages in illustration
of each point, far from easy; secondly, that Chrysostom,
being a preacher rather than a writer, was of course liable

[1] I must acknowledge my obligations in the composition of this chapter to the very useful and instructive
work of Dr. Th. Foerster, Berlin,
entitled, 'Chrysostomus in seinem
Verhältniss zur Antiochenischen
Schule.'—Gotha, 1869.

to slip into inexact or exaggerated language, under the
influence of excitement, or a desire to make an impression
on the feelings of his hearers. An attentive perusal,
however, of his writings leads the reader to the conclusion
that he was very seldom carried away by the impulse of
the moment into merely vague or rhetorical expressions,
and that he was especially preserved from this failing by
his habit of combining the expository with the practical
and hortatory line of preaching. His discourses are careful commentaries as well as practical addresses. Week
after week it was his custom to go through some book of
Holy Scripture, verse by verse, clause by clause, almost
word by word; endeavouring with all diligence and
patience to ascertain the exact meaning of the passage
before him, to place it clearly before his audience, and
to base his practical exhortation upon it.

The remark has been so often repeated, as to have
become almost a truism, that the theology of the East
is distinguished from the theology of the West by its
more speculative, metaphysical character. It deals more
especially with the most profound and abstract mysteries—
the being and nature of the Godhead, of angels, of the
whole spiritual realm. It might, therefore, occasion some
surprise to find the homilies of Chrysostom marked by
such an eminently practical tone. But the apparent con-
tradiction is easily explained. It is precisely because
Greek philosophy and theology were chiefly concerned
with the most abstract questions, that the Greek preacher,
speaking on matters not abstract, but practical, relating
to moral conduct, is especially free in his language from
philosophical or technical terms. On the other hand, in
the Western Church exactly the reverse occurs. The
best intellectual powers of the Roman having been mainly
exercised on jurisprudence, the mind of Roman theologians
naturally turned most powerfully towards practical ques-

tions which had most affinity to that science with which they were chiefly conversant—such as the relation of man to God, the nature of sin, the means of discharging the debt owed by man, the problem of the free-will of man, and providence of God. Western theology is coloured by the language of Roman law, as Eastern theology is coloured by the language of Greek philosophy. 'Merit,' 'satisfaction,' 'decrees,' 'forensic justification,' 'imputed righteousness,' are terms which do not occur in the writings of the Greek theologian, because they are the expressions of ideas in which he felt no interest. They are the offspring of the Roman mind, in which legal ideas were dominant. Hence the Western theologian is most technical and scientific in the region of practical questions; the Greek, on the other hand, is more entirely free from the influence of philosophy in that region than in any other.

In accordance with this distinction, we find that Chrysostom, in treating of those practical questions with which, as a preacher and pastor, he was mainly concerned—the nature and the work of Jesus Christ, providence, grace, the nature of man, sin, faith, repentance, good works, and the like—casts his thoughts into the most free, natural, untechnical, and therefore forcible language possible.

To consider first of all his exposition of man's nature. The majority of the Oriental fathers made a triple division, into body, soul, and spirit—the soul ($\psi\upsilon\chi\acute{\eta}$) being equivalent to the animal life, the spirit ($\pi\nu\epsilon\hat{\upsilon}\mu\alpha$ or $\psi\upsilon\chi\grave{\eta}$ $\lambda o\gamma\iota\kappa\acute{\eta}$) to the reason. Chrysostom makes a twofold division only, into body and soul, and reserves the word spirit to designate the Holy Spirit.[1] Man, when first created, came like a pure golden statue fresh out of the artist's hands, destined, if he had not fallen, to enjoy a yet higher and nobler dignity than he then possessed.[2] His being made

---

[1] In Rom. Hom. xiii. 2. 1 Cor. Hom. xiii. 3. In Phil. vii. 5.
[2] Hom. de Stat. xi. 2.

'in the image of God' Chrysostom interprets to signify
that dominance over the lower animals which God Himself
exercises over the whole creation, and the peculiar superiority of man's nature to theirs consists in his reasoning
power, as well as in his endowment with the gift of
immortality.[1] Man fell through his own weakness and
indolent negligence (ῥαθυμία), and then became deprived
of that immortality and divine wisdom with which he had
been previously gifted; but his nature was not essentially
changed, it was only weakened.[2] Evil is not an integral
part of man; it is not an inherent substantial force (δύναμις
ἐνυπόστατος):[3] it is the moral purpose (προαίρεσις) which
is perverted when men sin. If evil was a part of our
nature, it would be no more reprehensible than natural
appetites and affections. If man's will was not unfettered,
there would be no merit in goodness and no blame in evil.
There is no constraint either to holiness or to sin; neither
does God compel to the one, nor do the fleshly appetites
compel to the other.[4] The body was not, as the Manichæans erroneously maintained, the seat of sin; it was the
creation of God equally with the soul: the whole burden,
therefore, of responsibility in sin must be thrown on the
'moral purpose.' Here was the root of all evil; the conception of necessity and immutability is bound up with
the idea of nature. We do not try to alter that which is
by nature (φύσει): sin therefore is not by nature, because
by means of education, laws, and punishments we do seek
to alter that.[5] Sin is through the moral purpose which
is susceptible of change, and till the moral purpose has
come into activity sin cannot properly be said to exist:

[1] In Genes. Hom. xxi. 2.
[2] Ibid. xvi. and xvii.
[3] In Rom. Hom. xii. 6.
[4] In Genes. Hom. xx. 3. In 1 Cor. Hom. ii. 2. In Matt. Hom. lix. 1. 2.
[5] Comp. Jeremy Taylor, 'On Ori-

ginal Sin,' ch. vi.: 'A man is not
naturally sinful as he is naturally
heavy, or upright, naturally apt to
weep and laugh; for these he is
always and unavoidably.' Comp.
also Aristot. Eth. ii. c. 1.

infants, therefore, and very young children, are free from
sin.[1] Our first parents fell through moral negligence
($ῥᾳθυμία$); and this is the principal cause of sin now. They
marked out a path which has been trodden ever since;
they yielded to appetite, and the force of the will has
been weakened thereby in all their posterity, who have
become subject to the punishment of death; so that,
though sin is not a part of man's nature, yet his nature
is readily inclined to evil ($ὀξύρροπὴς πρὸς κακίαν$) : but this
tendency will be controlled by the moral purpose if that
is in a healthy condition.[2]

Chrysostom would thus readily allow the expressions
hereditary tendency to sin, hereditary liability to the
punishment of death, but he shrinks from the expression
'hereditary sin.' His anxiety to insist on the complete
freedom of the human will was very natural in the earnest
Christian preacher of holiness, who lived in an age when
men were frequently encountered who, in the midst of
wickedness, complained that they were abandoned to the
dominion of devils or to the irresistible course of fate.
They transferred all guilt from themselves to the powers
of evil, all responsibility to the Creator Himself, who had
withdrawn from them, as they maintained, the protection of
his good providence.   To counteract the disastrous effects
of such philosophy which surrendered the will to the
current of the passions, like an unballasted ship cast
adrift before the storm, it was indeed necessary to maintain very resolutely and boldly the essential freedom of
the will, to insist on man's moral responsibility, and the
duty of vigilant, strenuous exertion.   Chrysostom frequently exposes the absurdity as well as the moral evil of
a doctrine of necessity.   If human actions are necessary
and preordained results of circumstances, then teaching

---

[1] In Matt. Hom. xxviii. 3, and lviii. 3.
[2] In Heb. Hom. xii. 2 and 3.

and government become mere pieces of acting, destitute of any practical influence; they are also unjust, since you have no right to punish a person who has acted under compulsion. Such a theory ought, also, logically to paralyse human industry. If a plentiful harvest is predetermined by the decrees of fate, you may spare yourself the trouble of ploughing, sowing, and other laborious operations; or, if Clotho has turned her distaff in the other direction, all your exertions will fail to produce an abundant crop. Such a doctrine is repugnant to our natural sense, and contradicts our own consciousness and inward experience. We feel that we are free, and all human action proceeds on the principle of supposing man to be free. We teach and we punish. The plea of necessity would be rejected in a court of law as an impudent and futile excuse for crime. Such a theory is utterly at variance also with God's mode of addressing man, which always implies freedom of volition; as, for instance, ' If *ye will* hearken unto me, ye shall eat the fat of the land; but if *ye will not* hearken, the sword shall devour you.'[1]

Profoundly convinced, therefore, of a universal tendency to sin on the one hand, but of an essential freedom of the will on the other, Chrysostom sounds alternately the note of warning and of encouragement—warning against that weakness, indolence, languor of the moral purpose which occasions a fall; encouragement to the full use of those powers with which all men are gifted, and to avoid that despondency which will prevent a man from rising again when he has fallen. St. Paul repented, and, not despairing, became equal to angels; Judas repenting, but despairing, was hurried into self-inflicted death. Despair was the devil's most powerful instrument for working the destruction of man.[2] Chrysostom therefore earnestly com-

---

[1] De Fato, Hom. iii.–vi. Comp. Jer. Taylor, unum necessar. ch. 6. sec. 5.

[2] De Penit. Hom. i. 2; et ad Theod. lapsum.

bated any view of Christian life which daunted and discouraged man's efforts, by winding them too high, or placing before them an unattainable standard. Men sometimes said we cannot be like St. Peter and St. Paul, because we are not gifted with their miraculous power. But he replies, you may emulate their Christian graces : these are within the reach of all, and these are, by our Lord's own declaration, the most important. ' *By this* shall all men know that ye are my disciples, if ye have love one to another;' the moral works of the Apostles, works of love, mercy, and faith, were far more instrumental in the conversion of the world than their merely miraculous powers.[1]

Urgently, however, as Chrysostom, in his desire to stimulate exertion and strengthen the moral life, insists on the absolute freedom of the will, he maintains no less clearly the insufficiency of man's nature to accomplish good without the Divine assistance. No one has described in more forcible language the powerful hold of sin upon human nature. Sin is like a terrible pit, containing fierce monsters, and full of darkness.[2] It is more terrible than a demon,[3] it is a great demon ;[4] it is like fire ; when once it has got a hold on the thoughts of the heart, if it is not quenched it spreads farther and farther, and becomes increasingly difficult to subdue ;[5] it is a heavy burden, more oppressive than lead.[6] Christ saw us lying cast away upon the ground, perishing under the tyranny of sin, and He took compassion on us.[7] In the infant weakness and liability to sin are inherent, though not sin itself. The moral nature of the infant is like a plant, which will grow healthily by a process of natural development, unless exposed to injurious influences ; but it requires the protection of grace, ' therefore we baptise

[1] In Inscrip. Act. ii. 6.
[2] In Psalm cxlii. 5.
[3] In Act. Hom. xli. 4.
[4] In Matt. xxxii.
[5] De Sanct. Babyla, vol. ii.
[6] In Johan. vol. viii. p. 482.
[7] In Hebr. Hom. v. i.

infants, to impart holiness and goodness as well as to
establish a relationship with God.' This passage is
quoted by St. Augustine in his earnest vindication of
Chrysostom from Pelagianism.[1] But the passages on which
Augustine mainly depends, to prove Chrysostom's adherence to the tenet of original sin, are in his exposition
of Romans v. 12–14 :—' Death reigned from Adam to
Moses. How reigned? In likeness of the transgression
of Adam, who is a figure of One to come. How a figure?
Because, as he became a cause of death to those who were
born from him, although they had not eaten of the tree,
even so Christ has become to his posterity the procurer
of righteousness, though they have not done righteousness,
which He has bestowed upon us all through his cross.'
Augustine quotes also his observation on Christ's tears
over the grave of Lazarus :—' He wept to think that men,
who were capable of immortality, had been made mortal
by the devil;' and his remarks on Genesis i. 28, about
the subjection of the lower animals to man, ' that man's
present dread of wild beasts was entirely owing to the
fall, and had not existed previous to that: it was inherited
by all Adam's posterity, because they inherited his degradation through the fall.' All these passages, however, do
not amount to more than the doctrine of a universally
inherited tendency to sin, and therefore liability to its
punishment, death. In his interpretation of the passage,
' the free gift is of many offences unto justification,' this
last word is plainly taken by him in the sense of making
man righteous, not accounting him as such.[2]

His conception of the relation between the will and
power of God on the one hand, and man's freedom on the
other, appears to be this :—All men, without exception,
are through Christ called to salvation; predestination

<hr />

[1] Contra Julianum, bk. i. ed. Bened.
p. 630; but I have failed to find the
passage in Chrysostom's works.
[2] In Rom. Hom. x. 2.

means no more than God's original design, conceived prior to the Fall, of bringing all men to salvation. So, after the Fall, his redemptive plan or purpose embraces all men; but, on the other hand, it constrains no one. According to his absolute will all men are to be saved; but the accomplishment of his purpose is limited by the freedom of choice which He has Himself bestowed on man, whereby man may either accept the proffered favour and be eternally blessed, or reject it and be eternally condemned. God's election of those who are called is not compulsory, but persuasive;[1] hence, many of those who have been called perish through their rejection of grace: they, and not God, are the authors of their own condemnation. God knows beforehand what each man will be, good or bad; but He does not constrain him to be one or the other.[2] The illustration of the potter in Romans ix. 20, must not be pressed too closely; St. Paul's object simply is to enforce the duty of unconditional obedience. A vessel of wrath is one who obdurately resists God's grace; he was never *intended* by God to be a vessel of wrath. 'The vessels of mercy are said to have been prepared afore by God unto glory,' but the vessels of wrath to be fitted (not by God—He is not mentioned—but by sin) unto destruction.[3] So again, he acutely observes that, in the account of the final judgment (St. Matt. xxv.), the destiny of the *good* only is referred to God. 'Come, ye blessed *of my Father*, inherit the kingdom prepared *for you*;' but, 'Depart, ye cursed' (not 'of my Father'), 'into everlasting fire prepared' (not for you, but) 'for the devil and his angels.'

On St. John vi. 44, he remarks, it is perfectly true that only they who are drawn and taught by the Father can

---

[1] προτρεπτικὴ οὐ βιαστικὴ, in John, Hom. xlvii. 4; et in Matt. H. lxxx. 3.
[2] In 1 Cor. Hom. vii. 2. In Ephes.
Hom. i. 2. In 1 Cor. Hom. ii. 2.
[3] In Rom. Hom. xvi. c. 8, 9.

come to Christ; but away with the paltry pretence that those who are not thus drawn and taught are emancipated from blame; for this very thing, the being led and instructed, depends on their own moral choice. Two factors, therefore, Divine grace which presents, and human will which appropriates, are co-efficients in the work of man's salvation; God's love and man's faith must work hand in hand. On the whole, Chrysostom seems to assign the initiatory movement to man's will. God provides opportunities, encourages by promises, arouses by calls; and the moment these are responded to, the moment man begins to will and to do what is right, he is abundantly assisted by grace. But Chrysostom recognises nothing approaching the doctrine of final perseverance. St. Paul might have relapsed, Judas might have been saved (De Laud. Ap. Pauli, Hom. ii. 4). In his commentary on Phil. ii. 12–13, 'It is God which worketh in us both to will and to do of his good pleasure,' the spontaneity of man's will is carefully maintained. It may be said, if God works the will in us, why does the Apostle exhort us to work? for if God wrought the wish, it is vain to speak of obedience; the whole work is God's from the beginning. No! Chrysostom says, what St. Paul means is, that if your will works, God will augment your will, and quicken it into activity and zeal. Hast thou given alms? you are the more prompted to give; hast thou abstained from giving? negligence will increase upon you. The histories of Abraham, Job, Elijah, St. Paul, and other saints, are frequently cited to prove his central principle, that God in the moral and spiritual sense helps those only who help themselves. 'When He, who knows the secrets of our hearts, sees us eagerly prepare for the contest of virtue, He instantly supplies us with his assistance, lightening our labours, and strengthening the weakness of our nature. In the Olympian contests the trainer stands by as a spectator merely, awaiting the issue, and unable to contribute anything to the efforts of the contender; whereas our Master accompanies us, extends his hand to us, all but subdues our antagonist, arranges everything to enable us to prevail, that He may place the amaranthine wreath upon our brows.'[1] God does not anticipate ($\phi\theta\acute{a}\nu\epsilon\iota$) man's own volitions ($\beta o\upsilon\lambda\acute{\eta}\sigma\epsilon\iota\varsigma$), but, when these are once bent in the right direction, God's grace powerfully promotes them; and without this divine co-operation holiness is unattainable.[2]   But as, according to Chrysostom's conceptions, the first movement towards good moral practice comes from the man himself, he often speaks of a man's salvation depending on his own moral choice.   He is not, therefore, in harmony with the mind of our Church as expressed in the Article, that 'we have no power to do good works, pleasant and acceptable to God, without the grace of God *preventing* us, that we may have a good will;' but his language thoroughly concurs with the subsequent clause, 'and working with us when we have that good will.'   In the technical language of theology, he recognises assisting, but not prevenient, grace.

It has been well remarked by Mr. Alexander Knox ('Remains,' vol. iii. 79), that 'the advocates for efficient grace have been too generally antiperfectionists, and the perfectionists, on the other hand, too little aware that we are not sufficient so much as to think anything as of ourselves, but that it is God which worketh in us both to will and to do of his good pleasure.'   The perfect conception of the true Christian standard of character could only be found, he thought, in a union of the systems of St. Chrysostom and St. Augustine.   It must not be imagined, however, that Chrysostom regarded Divine grace as accessory or subsidiary merely to man's own will and

---

[1] In Genes. Hom. xlii c. 1.   [2] In Johan. Hom. xviii. 3.

purpose. He fails not to represent it as indispensable to
every human soul, however powerfully inclined of itself to
good. The human will, weakened and depraved by evil,
is not for a moment to rank as co-ordinate in its action
with the work of the Holy Spirit : the real efficient force
in the work of sanctification is the Holy Spirit. The
beginnings, indeed (ἀρχαί), are our own, and we must
contribute what we can, small and cheap though it be,
because, unless we do our part, we shall not obtain the
Divine assistance ; but though the initiatory step is ours,
the accomplishment of the work is altogether God's, and,
since the major part is his, we commonly say that the
whole is his.[1]

He invariably speaks of the Old Dispensation as a period
when Divine grace was given in less measure than under
the Gospel, because then sin had not been blotted out,
nor death vanquished. The achievements of holy men like
Abraham and Job in this period were therefore deserving
of peculiar praise, and their faults, on the other hand,
were entitled to more indulgent judgment, because they
laboured under disadvantages. When the Lamb which
taketh away the sins of the world had been slain, and the
reconciliation between man and God had been effected,
then spiritual gifts of a higher order were imparted, as
a sign and a pledge that the old hostility had ceased.[2]

Turning now to theology, strictly so called, to the being
and nature of the Godhead, we find comparatively little
said by Chrysostom, except incidentally, on a subject more
congenial to the theologian and student than to the
earnest, practical preacher. In opposition to the mate-
rialising doctrine of the Arians, who affected to compre-
hend the Divine Nature, he strenuously maintained, as we
have seen,[3] its inscrutability, and denounced any curious
investigation of it as at once foolish and profane. God

---

[1] In Heb. Hom. xii. c. 3.   [2] De Mac. i. 3.   [3] Ch. VIII.

has condescended to appear to us in a form which is intelligible, and it is presumption to attempt to penetrate beyond the limits which He has placed to a knowledge of Himself. Chrysostom takes the dogma of the one substance (ὁμοουσία), established at Nice, as the basis of his position against the Arians, and seeks to prove it, not by speculative argument, after the manner of the Alexandrian school, but by reference to Holy Scripture. He uses the word 'substance' (οὐσία) to designate the essential nature, and 'person' (ὑπόστασις), the personality of the Godhead, and points out that words which relate to the οὐσία, as Lord and God, are applied to all the Persons; whereas the other terms—Father, Son, Holy Spirit—indicating distinction of personality, are each applied to one Person only in the Godhead. Yet the Persons are not related to the substance as parts to the whole: God the Son is to God the Father as a beam of the sun, inseparable from Him, identical with Him in substance, yet retaining his own personality.[1] He is equally careful to guard the divinity of Christ against the rationalising spirit of the school of Paul of Samosata, and the distinctness of his personality as against the Sabellians. St. Paul, he observes, does not dwell too much upon the abasement of Christ, lest Paul of Samosata should take advantage; neither does he dwell exclusively upon the exaltation, lest Sabellius should spring upon him.[2]

The equal divinity and distinct personality of the Holy Ghost are no less clearly and forcibly demonstrated by a collection and comparison of passages. St. Paul, for instance, in 1 Cor. xii. 6, speaks of God as 'working all in all;' in verse 11 of the same chapter, he uses the same language of the Holy Spirit. Into any metaphysical, abstract discussion of the nature of the Godhead Chrysostom does not enter. He simply endeavours to guard

[1] In John, Hom. iii. 2.   [2] In Heb. Hom. ii. c. 2.

the faith of the Church by a careful exposition of Holy
Scripture, on which that faith was based, and by an
exposure of the one-sided, or perverted, interpretations on
which the current forms of heresy depended.

The union of the two natures in the person of our
blessed Lord was, as is well known, a subject of constant
speculation in the first five centuries, and of prolific error.
Here, again, the good sense of Chrysostom, united to his
careful study of Holy Scripture, enabled him to hold the
balance between two divergent methods—one which attended too exclusively to the humanitarian point of view,
the other which brought out the divinity, but at the
expense of the manhood. He earnestly maintains the
veritable assumption of humanity by the Word. Our
nature could not have been elevated to the divine if the
Saviour had not *really* partaken of it; neither could He
have brought help to our race if He had appeared in the
unveiled glory of his Godhead, for sun and moon, earth
and sea, and even man himself, would have perished at
the brightness of his presence. Therefore He veiled his
Godhead in flesh, and came not as the Lord in outward
semblance, but in lowliness and abasement.[1] And this
very condescension enhanced his dignity and extended
his dominion : before the Incarnation He was adored by
angels only, but afterwards by the whole race of redeemed
man.[2] He assumed our nature, even in its liability to
death, but not as contaminated by sin.[3] There were in
Him three elements—body and soul making up the human
nature, and the Logos or Word making up the divine.
These two natures were *united* but not *fused*. ' We,
indeed, are body and soul, but He is God and soul and
body; remaining what He was, He took that which He
was not, and having become flesh, He remained God, being
the Word. The one He became, He assumed; the other

---

[1] In Psal. li. expos.　[2] In Heb. Hom. iv. 2, 3.　[3] In Rom. Hom. xiii. 5.

He was. Let us not then confound, neither let us divide;
one God, one Christ the Son of God; and when I say one,
I speak of union, not fusion' (ἕ. ωσιν λέγω οὐ σύγχυσιν).[1]
Jesus Christ was subject to death, susceptible of pain and
all those emotions and sensations which belong to the
human body, otherwise his would not have been a real
body, but the weakness pertaining to human nature was
entirely overruled by the constant operation of the Logos.
If He is said to have been lowered or exalted, this was
only as man, since the Godhead was incapable of either,
being absolutely perfect. When the Holy Ghost is said
to have descended upon Him at his baptism, this must be
considered to refer to his human nature only; the manhood, not the Godhead, is anointed. Or when we read that
He walked not in Judæa, because the Jews sought to kill
Him, and then, just afterwards, that He passed through the
midst of his enemies unscathed, we have a direct manifestation, in close juxtaposition, of the Godhead and the
manhood.[2]

In speaking of the redemptive work of our blessed
Lord, Chrysostom's language is too rapturously eloquent
to be very precise. There are in him several traces of the
idea which began with Irenæus, and was developed by
Origen, that the devil through the Fall acquired an
actual right over man, and that a kind of pious fraud was
practised upon him to deprive him of this right through
the Incarnation and death of Jesus. By the noiseless,
unostentatious manner in which our Saviour assumed
humanity, veiling his Godhead under it, He, as it were,
stole unawares upon the devil, who was not fully conscious
of the majesty and might of his adversary. The devil
assaulted Christ as if Christ had been merely man, and he
was disappointed in his expectation. He was vanquished

---

[1] In Phil. Hom. vii. c. 3.
[2] In Heb. Hom. iii., Hom. iv. c. iii. In Philog. Beat. In John, Hom.
xlviii. c. i.

by his own weapons, his tyranny was destroyed by means
of those very things which were his strength; the curse
of sin and of death were his most trusted pieces: Christ
submitted Himself to be bruised by them, and yet crushed
them by his submission.[1]

On the other hand, we find also in Chrysostom the
customary conception of a debt discharged, a ransom
paid, a sacrifice offered once for all. 'Adam sinned and
died; Christ sinned not and yet died. Wherefore? that
he who sinned and died might be able, through Him who
died but sinned not, to throw off the grasp of death. This
is what takes place also in money transactions. Often
some one who is a debtor, not being able to pay, is detained in bonds; another, who owes nothing but is able
to lay down the sum, pays it and releases the responsible
person. Thus has it been in the case of man. Man was
the debtor, was detained by the devil, and could not pay;
Christ owed nothing, nor was He holden by the devil, but
He was able to pay the debt. He came and He paid down
death on behalf of him who was detained in bondage.'[2]

From this point of view the person to whom the debt
is due and is discharged is the devil; from another, the
satisfaction is regarded as due to God, owing to the violation of man's obedience, and is paid to Him through the
sacrifice of a sinless life. 'It was right that all men
should fulfil the righteousness of God; but, since no one
did this, Christ came and completely fulfilled it.'[3] He
was Himself both the sacrificer and the victim; the cross
being the altar. He suffered outside the city that the
prophecy, 'He was numbered with the transgressors,'
might be fulfilled, and also that the *universality* of the
sacrifice might be proclaimed.[4] Chrysostom is not careful

[1] In Matt. Hom. iii.; Expos. in Ps. li.;   [3] De Bapt. Christi, c. 3.
in 1 Cor. Hom. xxiv. 4.   [4] De Cœmet. et Cruce, i.

[2] De Resur. J. Chr. c. 3.

to distinguish between the alienation of man from God, and of God from man through the Fall. He represents the hostility as in some sort existing on both sides. Christ did the work of a mediator by interposing Himself between the two parties, and reconciling each to the other. The references to such a fundamental verity are of course numerous, often full of beauty of expression and tenderness of feeling, and glowing earnestness. What he specially delights to dwell upon, as might be expected from his warm, affectionate disposition, is the exceeding love of Christ to man, and the hearty return which gratitude for such a benefit ought to draw forth from us. Like St. Paul, he often will break forth, in the midst of some argument or practical address, into a burst of rapturous and adoring praise. 'What reward shall I give unto the Lord for all the benefits which He hath done unto me? Who shall express the noble acts of the Lord, or show forth all his praise? He abased Himself that He might exalt thee; He died to make thee immortal; He became a curse that thou mightest obtain a blessing.' . . . . 'When the world lay in darkness, the light of the Cross was held up like a torch shining in a dark place, and the light at the top of it was the Sun of Righteousness Himself.'[1]

Chrysostom's doctrine of justification is naturally coloured by his ethics. Maintaining, as he did, that the corruption of man's nature consisted in a weakness of the moral purpose, a crooked tendency of the will, rather than in any inherent indelible stain in that nature itself, his exhortations are directed rather to inculcate energetic action, a gradual process of improvement of the will with the Divine help, than that entire dependence through faith on the mercy of God which springs out of a deep conviction of the sinner's own insufficiency. The logical

---

[1] De Cœmet. et Cruce, 3. See also in Ephes. Hom. xx.; and esp. In Ascens. J. Chr. c. 2.

tendency of the Augustinian view of the intense and radical depravity of man's nature is to induce a total distrustfulness of the efficacy of personal effort, a total disavowment of all personal merit. Hence justification comes to be regarded as purely an act of acquittal on God's part, a boon which the despairing sinner by an act of faith thankfully accepts. Such is not the position of Chrysostom, or of those who, like the Cambridge divines of the seventeenth century, have trodden in his footsteps. With him the condition of a pardoned sinner consists rather in that renovation of the spiritual and moral life, which is the result of long and laborious effort, aided of course by Divine grace, a succession of moral acts eventually producing 'a new creature.' Faith is not so much regarded merely as the instrument or hand held out by which God's gift is appropriated, as the first in a row of good works, a fruitful source of all good action. 'Abraham,' he says, 'believed God, and it was counted to him for righteousness. Why? to prove that belief itself, in the first instance, and obedience to the call of God, come from our own good judgment (εὐγνωμοσύνη); but as soon as the foundation of faith is laid, we require the alliance of the Holy Spirit, that it may remain constantly unshakable and inflexible.'[1] . . . . 'Faith is the mother of all good, the sure staff of man's tottering footsteps, the anchor of his tempest-tossed soul, without which he would be like a ship cast adrift on the sea to the mercy of winds and waves.'[2] . . . . 'It is more stable and secure than reason, for it carries its own proof with it; the conclusions of reason may be diverted by counter-arguments, but faith stands above argument, and is not distracted by it.'[3]

He does not, indeed, shrink from a bold declaration of

[1] De Verb. Apost. vol. iii. p. 276.   [2] In Joh. Hom. xxxiii. c. 1.
[3] In Rom. Hom. viii. c. 5.

the value of good works, but he is far from teaching men
to depend on them as efficient causes of salvation. They
are to be stored up as a kind of viaticum for our journey
to the other world. 'As those who are in a foreign
country, when they wish to return to their own land, take
pains, a long time beforehand, to collect means sufficient
for their journey, so surely ought we, who are but strangers
and settlers on this earth, to lay up a store of provisions
through spiritual virtue, that when our Master shall command our return into our native country, we may be
prepared and may carry part of our store with us, having
sent the other in advance.'[1] On the other hand, he constantly insists that it is the favour and mercy of God
alone which, in the end, bestows salvation on us. Faith
and good works are necessary conditions, but not efficient
causes of salvation. God has graciously willed that they
who have faith and good works shall be saved: let no
man, therefore, boast. We could not do good works
without God's assisting grace, nor could they in the end
and at the best save us if it were not his merciful and
gracious will.[2] Therefore, let no one pride himself on his
good works; above all things, guard a spirit of humility
and modesty: St. Paul, after all his labours, confessed
that he was not meet to be called an Apostle, but was
what he was by the grace of God.[3] 'What is impossible
with men is possible with God.' 'Tell me not I have
sinned much, and how can I be saved? *Thou* art not
able, but thy Master is able so to blot out thy sins that
no trace even of them shall remain. In the natural body,
indeed, though the wound may be healed, yet the scar
remains; but God does not suffer the scar even to remain, but, together with release from punishment, grants
righteousness also, and makes the sinner to be equal to him

---

[1] In Gen. Hom. v. c. 1.   [2] In Ephes. Hom. iv. c. 2.
[3] In Gen. Hom. xxxi. 2.

who has not sinned. He makes the sin neither to be nor to have been.' . . . 'Sin is drowned in the ocean of God's mercy, just as a spark is extinguished in a flood of water.'[1]

It was, no doubt, the trustful dependence of Chrysostom on Divine grace, coupled with his firm conviction of the free capacity of man to turn to what is good, which enabled him to pitch all his exhortations to Christian holiness in such a singularly cheerful, hopeful tone. To his sanguine temperament it seemed as if man's natural capacities for good, aided by grace obtained through prayer, could accomplish anything. 'The effect of prayer on the heart is like that of the rising sun upon the natural world; as the wild beasts come forth by night to prowl and prey, but the sun ariseth, and they get them away together and lay them down in their dens, so, when the soul is illuminated by prayer, the irrational and brutal passions are put to flight, anger is calmed, lust is extinguished, envy is expelled; prayer is the treasure of the poor, the security of the rich, the poorest of all men is rich if he can pray, and the rich man who cannot pray is miserably poor. Ahab without prayer was impotent amidst his splendour; Elijah with prayer was mighty in his coarse garment of sheepskin.'[2] . . . 'It is impossible, impossible that a man who calls constantly on God with proper zeal should ever sin; his spirit is proof against temptation so long as the effect of his praying lasts, and when it begins to fail, then he must pray again. And this may be done anywhere, in the market or in the shop, since prayer demands the outstretched soul, rather than the extended hands.'[3] Long prayers were to be avoided, they gave great opportunities to Satan to distract the attention, which could not easily bear a lengthened strain. Prayers should be frequent and short; thus we should best comply with the direction of St. Paul to pray without ceasing.[4]

[1] De Penit. Hom. viii. 2.   [2] De Anna. iv. 5.
[3] Cont. Anom. vii. 7.   [4] Ibid. ii. 2.

It remains to collect some notices of Chrysostom's teaching with reference to the two Sacraments.

The number of those who, as Christian children of decidedly Christian parents, were baptised in infancy appears to have been small at this period, compared with those who, like Chrysostom himself, joined the ranks of the Church at a later epoch of life. There were many whose parents, one or both, or who themselves, hovered not so much between Christianity and any definite form of paganism, as between Christianity and worldliness. The sermons addressed by Chrysostom and his contemporaries to catechumens, and the frequent allusions to them, the minute directions respecting their instruction, their division into classes, the custom of calling the first part of the service to which they were admitted the Missa Catechumenorum, prove that numerous they must have been. I have failed to find any passages in which Chrysostom urgently inculcates infant baptism, and, considering his views respecting original sin, this is not surprising; but he earnestly denounces a custom of deferring baptism, prevalent among those who were already believers, or professing to be such. Often it was delayed till men believed themselves to be at the point of death—a practice which he especially deprecates, because at such a time ‘the recipient was often in a restless, suffering state of mind and body, most unfit to receive that holy sacrament; the entrance of the priest was regarded by the sorrowful attendants as a certain evidence of the approaching end ; and when the rich man could not recognise those who were present, or hear a voice, or answer in those words by which he was to enter into a blessed covenant with our Lord, but lay like a log or a stone, what possible advantage could there be in the reception of the sacrament?’ [1] Again, it was often delayed till a man conceived that he

[1] Ad illum. Catech i. c. 3.

had received a distinct call and intimation that it was
the will of God. This Chrysostom regarded as being too
often a mere cloak for moral indolence, a reluctance of
men to bind themselves under the high responsibilities of
the Christian vocation.[1]

He certainly considered baptism as being not merely a
solemn initiation into the Christian covenant, and instrument of remission of sin, but also of moral renovation.
This, however, is represented as a blessing naturally
derivable from the entrance into the new and holy federal
relation with God. In his comment on the passage,
'and such were some of you; but ye are washed, but ye
are sanctified, but ye are justified in the name of our
Lord Jesus Christ,' he observes that such words signify
that they were not only purified from past uncleanness,
but had become holy and righteous. 'For such is the
benevolence of the Divine gift; if an imperial letter consisting of a few lines discharges men from liability to
punishment for any number of offences, and advances
others to great honour, much more will the Holy Spirit
of God, which can do all things, release us from all
wickedness, bestow on us abundant righteousness, and fill
us with much confidence.' The nature of the baptised was,
therefore, like a vessel which had not only been cleansed
from past defilements, but recast in the furnace so as to
come out in a new shape.[2] He is far, however, from
regarding such a change as final. The virtue of baptism is
effectual at the time, but the grace then given is as a trust
to be carefully guarded; a talent to be traded with, a
seed of righteousness to be diligently cultivated, the
dawning of a light to shine more and more unto the
perfect day. As Christ becomes at that time the clothing,
the food, the habitation of the Christian, the recipient of
these favours has to take care that he does not wrong this

---

[1] De Mut. Nom. iv. in fine.   [2] Ad illum. Catech. i. 3.

intimate relationship. Therefore he is ordered to say at baptism, ' I renounce thee, Satan ; ' that is the declaration of a covenant with his Master. A firm determination to abandon past sin, and eradicate evil habits—in a word, repentance—should take place previous to baptism. ' Just as the painter freely alters the lineaments of his picture, when it is sketched in outline, by rubbing out or putting in, but when once he has added the colour, he is no longer at liberty to make alterations ; in like manner erase evil habits before baptism, before the true colouring of the Holy Spirit has been thrown over the soul : take care when this has been received, and the royal image shines forth clearly, that you do not blot it out any more, and inflict wounds and scars on the beauty given thee by God.'[1]

In another place he contrasts the baptism of the Jews, of John the Baptist, and of Jesus Christ. ' The first was only a cleansing of the body from ceremonial defilements, the second was a means of enforcing an exhortation to repentance, the third was accompanied by remission of sins : it releases and purges the soul from sin, and gives a supply of the Holy Spirit.'[2] . . . . ' When the merciful God saw the extremity of our weakness, and the incurable nature of our sickness, requiring a great work of healing, He conferred upon us that renovation which comes through the laver of regeneration, in order that, being divested of the old man, that is, of evil works, and having put on the new, we might go forward in the path of virtue.'[3]

In considering those passages which relate to the Holy Eucharist, it must be constantly borne in mind that Chrysostom lived in an age when that Sacrament had not become a battle-field of controversy. He was under no

[1] Ad illum. Catech. ii. 3.   [2] De Bapt. Chr. c. 3.
[3] In Gen. Hom. xl. c. 4.

constraint in his language, because he did not feel that
every word he used was liable to be criticised, or misunderstood, or torn to pieces in the strife of contending parties.
He enjoyed because he disputed not. Filled with thankfulness and joy to overflowing for the unspeakable benefits
derived from that Sacrament, he is not cautious or scrupu-
lously precise in his expressions, but gives the freest rein
to the enthusiasm of his feelings; his object being not
to support any rigidly defined theory or system, but to
infuse a certain spirit, to encourage a proper moral tone
and temper in reference to the whole subject.

Three ideas, however, are apparent as dominant in his
mind—a sacrifice, a presence of Christ, a reception of
Christ. In several of the passages about to be presented,
all the three points will appear in similar and simulta-
neous force. In one homily,[1] where he severely censures
the custom among many of attending the Eucharist on
great festivals only, and then behaving in a disorderly
manner, hustling and trampling on one another in their
tumultuous haste to approach the holy table, and then
hurrying out of church immediately after the reception, without waiting for the conclusion of the service—
'What,' he exclaims, 'O man, art thou doing? When
Christ is present, and the angels are standing by, and the
awe-inspiring table is spread before thee, dost thou withdraw?' . . . 'If you are invited to a feast and are filled
before the other guests, you do not dare to withdraw
while the rest of your friends are still reclining at the
table; and here, when the mysteries of Christ are being
celebrated, and the holy feast is still going on, dost thou
retreat in the middle?' Again: 'Since, then, we are
about to see this evening, as a lamb slain and sacrificed,
Him who was crucified, let us approach, I pray you, with
trembling awe. The angels, who surpass our nature, stood

[1] De Bapt. J. Chr. c. 7.

beside his empty tomb with great reverence; and shall
we, who are about to stand beside, not an empty sepulchre,
but the very table which bears the Lamb, shall we approach with noise and confusion?'[1]   Again : 'It is now
time to draw near the awe-inspiring table ' . . . 'Christ is
present, and He who arranged that first table, even He
arranges this present one.   For it is not man who makes
the things which are set before us become the body and
blood of Christ, but it is Christ Himself, who was crucified
for us.   The priest stands fulfilling his part ($\sigma\chi\eta\mu\alpha$)
by uttering the appointed words, but the power and the
grace are of God.   " This is my body," he says.   This
expression changes the character ($\mu\epsilon\tau\alpha\rho\rho\nu\theta\mu\iota\zeta\epsilon\iota$) of the
elements, and as that sentence, " increase and multiply,"
once spoken, extends through all time, enabling the pro-
creative power of our nature, even so that expression,
" this is my body," once uttered, does at every table in
the churches from that time to the present day, and even
till Christ's coming, make the sacrifice perfect.'[2]   Speaking
of the sacrifice of Isaac, he observes that it was perfect so
far as Abraham was concerned, because his *intention*
did not fail, though the knife was not actually drawn
across his son's throat; ' for a sacrifice is possible even
without blood—the initiated (i.e. the baptised) know what
I mean : on this account, also, that sacrifice was made
without blood, since it was destined to be a figure of this
sacrifice of ours.'[3]

Perhaps the most significant passage with reference to
the sacrificial idea is one where, after contrasting the
many and ineffective sacrifices of the Jews with the one
perfect, efficacious sacrifice of Christ, he proceeds : ' What
then? do we not offer every day ?   We do offer certainly,
but making a memorial of his death ; and this memorial

---

[1] De Cœmet. et Cruce, in fine, vol. ii.   [2] De Prod. Jud. vol. ii. Hom. i. c. 6.
[3] In Eustath. Ant. vol. ii. p. 601.

is one, not many. How one, not many ? Because the
sacrifice was offered once for all, as that great sacrifice
was in the Holy of Holies. This is a figure of that great
sacrifice as that was of this; for we do not offer one
victim to-day and another to-morrow, but always the
same : wherefore the sacrifice is one. Well, on this ground,
because He is offered in many places, are there many
Christs ? Nay, by no means, but one Christ everywhere,
complete both in this world and in the other; one body.
As then, though offered in many places, He is but one
body, so is there but one sacrifice. Our High Priest is
He who offers the sacrifice which cleanses us. We offer
that now which was offered then; which is indeed incon-
sumable. This takes place now for a memorial of what
took place then : " Do this," said He, " for my memorial."
We do not then offer a different sacrifice as the high
priest formerly did, but always the same; *or, rather, we
celebrate a memorial of a Sacrifice.*' [1]

There are other passages in which the idea, no less
prominently set forth, is that of a holy feast. Elijah
bequeathed his mantle and a double portion of his spirit
to Elisha, ' but the Son of God, when He ascended, left us
his own flesh.' . . . ' He who did not decline to shed his
blood for all, and imparts to us again his flesh and blood,
what will he refuse to do for our salvation?' [2] Again:
' Consider, O man, what kind of sacrifice thou art about
to touch, what kind of table to approach; reflect that
thou who art but dust and ashes receivest the body and
blood of Christ.' [3] The sedulous care with which he
urges the duty of moral cleansing before venturing to
approach the holy table, proceeds chiefly from regarding
it as a holy feast. 'How shall we behold the sacred
passover ? How shall we receive the sacred feast? How

---

[1] In Ep. ad Hebr. Hom. xvii. c. 3.   [2] Hom. ii. De Stat. c. 9.
[3] De Nat. Christi, c. 7.

partake of the adorable mysteries with that tongue whereby we trampled on the Law of God and defiled our soul? for if one would not touch a royal robe with defiled hands, how shall we receive the Lord's body with an unclean tongue?' [1]

These passages, which are but a few specimens extracted from a large number on the same subject, are yet sufficient to show how easy it would be for the partisans of contending schools to press the language of Chrysostom into support of their own system. The truth is, that in the case of this, as of other subjects, we find in Chrysostom and his contemporaries the raw material, which has been wrought out by the toil and strife of later times into definite sharply chiselled dogmas. Nothing, therefore, can really be more unfair than to regard, as a direct friend or opponent, one who lived and wrote long before controversy had arisen on the subjects of which he treated. He might innocently employ expressions which we should deem it incautious to use, because we know the interpretation of which they are susceptible, or because we see in them incipient symptoms of an idea which in process of time grew into a mischievous error. It is instructive also to notice how harmless, doctrines, afterwards mischievous, were when not pushed to an extremity; not made integral parts of a system of belief. It does not occur to us, for instance, for a moment to suppose that such invocation of saints as was manifestly approved by Chrysostom was the least detrimental to that free intercourse which ought to exist between the soul of man and God Himself. As Dr. Pusey has observed, 'through volumes of St. Augustine and St. Chrysostom there is no mention of any reliance except on Christ alone.' [2]   There

---

[1] De Stat. xi. c. 5. The authenticity of the letter to Cæsarius is so doubtful that I have not ventured to introduce here the celebrated passage which it contains on this subject. It will be found in the Appendix, where the curious history of this letter is related.

[2] Eirenikon, part i. p. 112.

is not the least approach to that system of stepping-stones or halting-places between God and man, which the Roman Church established by means of confession, saint-worship, and, above all, Mariolatry.

There is no trace in Chrysostom of priestly confession as an ordinance of the Church. When he speaks of the misery which ensues on the commission of sin, he urges the sinner to relieve his conscience by a free confession with repentance and tears. 'And why are you ashamed to do so?' he proceeds, 'for to whom do you confess? Is it to a man or a fellow-servant who might reproach or expose you? Nay, it is to the Lord, tender and merciful: it is to the physician that you show your wound.'[1] Again, in speaking of prayer, he contrasts the freedom of access to God with the difficulties and impediments which encounter the delivery of a petition to some great man. 'This last could be reached only through porters, flatterers, parasites; whereas God is invoked without the intervention of anyone, without money, without expense of any kind.'[2] This reads like a prophetical sarcasm on a Church which ultimately made a traffic of dispensing what cannot really be dispensed by man, because it is the free gift of God.

Nor is there any symptom in Chrysostom of a tendency to the theory of Purgatory. The condition of man after death is always represented by him as final and irrevocable. His tone, when exhorting to repentance, is always in harmony with the following passage: 'For the day will come when the theatre of this world will be dissolved, and then it is not possible to contend any longer: this is the season of repentance, that of judgment; this of contest, that of crowning; this of labour, that of repose.'[3]

But of all mediæval additions to the purer faith of primitive times, Mariolatry has grown to the most extra-

[1] De Laz. Hom. iv. 4.   [2] De Pœnit. Hom. iv. 4.   [3] Ibid. ix.

ordinary dimensions.[1] Of any tendency to this error
there is in Chrysostom a remarkable absence. In fact, his
notices of the Blessed Virgin, not very frequent, are on
the whole, we might almost say, unnecessarily disparaging. In his commentary on the Marriage Feast at
Cana, he suggests that the Virgin, in mentioning the
failure of wine to our Lord, may have been anxious to
draw out his miraculous powers, partly to place the guests
under an obligation to Him, partly to enhance her own
dignity through the display of her Son's divine powers.
He considers that the appeal sprang from the same feeling
which prompted his brethren to say, ' Show Thyself to the
world ; ' and he proceeds to observe that our Lord, while
never failing to manifest dutiful reverence and affectionate
care towards his mother, has taught us, by his conduct
and language to her, that the tie of mere earthly kindred
entitled her not to higher privileges, and placed her in no
more intimate spiritual relationship with Himself, than
anyone might through love and obedience enjoy. ' Who is
my mother, and who are my brethren ? ' and looking round
about on his disciples, He said, ' Behold my mother and
my brethren, for whosoever shall do the will of my Father,
the same is my brother, and my sister, and mother.'
' Heavens ! ' Chrysostom exclaims, ' what honour ! what
reward ! to what a pinnacle does He exalt those who
follow Him ! How many women have blessed the Holy
Virgin and her womb, and have longed to be such mothers !
What then prevents it ? Behold, He opens a broad way
for us : not women only, but men also are permitted to
be placed in the same rank.' ' The demand to see Him
was made by his mother in an ambitious spirit : she
wished to show to the people how much authority she
possessed over Him ; at any rate, the request was un-

---

[1] See Dr. Pusey's history of the cultus and its mischievous effects, in Parts
i. and ii. of the ' Eironikon.'

reasonable and unseasonable. If she and his brethren desired to speak with Him on matters of doctrine, they
might have done so in the presence of the others; but if
on private matters, it was an ill-timed interruption to his
discourse on weightier subjects.'[1] Again : 'When a woman
in the company cried out, "Blessed is the womb that bare
Thee!" He instantly corrected her, "Yea, *rather* blessed
are they that hear the word of God and keep it."' It is
possible that the general sentiment of the age may have
regarded the Virgin with more veneration, but Chrysostom could not have ventured to use such language
had the cultus been in any but its very earliest stage, if
then. She is called holy by him; she intercedes [2] for
Eve, who is a type of herself, but of worship paid to her
there is not the slightest evidence.[3]

It is almost superfluous to observe that Chrysostom
knew and acknowledged nothing of papal supremacy, in
the sense which those words conveyed to the minds of
later generations. In common with the rest of Christendom, he paid great deference and respect to the metropolitan at Rome, and he was quite free from those feelings
of jealousy which were entertained by the patriarchs of
Constantinople, as time went on, owing to the increasing
pretensions and exactions of the Roman See. If he
respects Innocent, partly because occupying the chair of
St. Peter, he equally respects Flavian, Bishop of Antioch
(who was not in communion with Rome), for the same
reason; he calls him 'our common father and teacher, who
has inherited St. Peter's virtue and his chair.' The letter
written to Innocent during exile was addressed also to

[1] In John, Hom. xxi. 2; and in Matt. Hom. xliv. 1.

[2] De Mundi Creat. vi. 10.

[3] Vide Dr. Pusey, Eiren. i. p. 113: 'We could preach whole volumes of the sermons of St. Augustine or St. Chrysostom to our people, to their edification and without offence: were a Roman Catholic preacher to confine himself to their preaching, he would (as it has been said among themselves) be regarded as "indevout towards Mary."'

the Bishops of Milan and Aquileia. In his commentary on Galatians ii., he proves the equality of St. Paul with St. Peter. No doubt he assigns an eminent rank to St. Peter, speaking of him as 'leader of the band' (κορυφαῖος) of Apostles, and as entrusted with the 'chieftainship' (προστασίαν) of the brethren: but these words do not imply absolute authority, and the same appellations are applied to St. Paul also.

Scattered up and down the discourses of Chrysostom there are abundant references to the liturgical forms, and manner of using them, which were in vogue in his time. If we had no other authority, we could learn from him alone that the service consisted of two parts—the first, called Missa Catechumenorum, because the catechumens were permitted to be present at it, which included an opening salutation of 'Peace be with you,' with the response, 'And with thy Spirit,' psalms sung antiphonally, appointed lessons according to the season or the day (as Genesis was read during Lent, the Acts of the Apostles in Pentecost, that is, during the fifty days between Easter and Whitsun Day), the sermon, frequently in Chrysostom's case, on the lesson for the day, the preacher usually sitting, and the people standing ; then prayers, announced by the deacon, for the catechumens, the 'possessed,' and the penitents; the benediction by the bishop, and dismissal by the deacon, who bade them 'depart in peace.' The second part of the service then began, called Missa Fidelium, because the baptised only were permitted to be present. Chrysostom strongly denounces an increasing tendency on the part of many to remain during this second and more sacred portion without participating. He plainly declares that all those who were baptised should communicate, and tells them, if they were not worthy to receive the Eucharist, neither could they be worthy to join in the prayers which preceded the reception, and

therefore they ought to quit the church, with the catechumens and penitents, when the deacon commanded all
unbaptised, ungodly, and unbelieving persons to depart.[1]
The usual order of the Missa Fidelium was 'the silent
prayer' (εὐχὴ διὰ σιωπῆς), on part of the priest and people
(which the latter too often abused, Chrysostom feared, to
imprecate vengeance on their enemies[2]); then a prayer
somewhat equivalent to our bidding prayer in form, and
to our prayer for the Church Militant in substance, the
deacon bidding or proclaiming the forms, and the people
responding; then a prayer of invocation made by the
bishop, which was also called 'collecta,' because in it the
prayers of the people were considered to be gathered or
summed up; the oblations of the people presented by the
deacons; the kiss of peace, the reading of the diptychs,
the ablution of the priest's hands, the bringing of the
elements to the bishop at the altar, while the priests
stood on each side, and deacons held large fans to drive
away the flies; a secret prayer offered by the bishop; the
benediction, 'The Grace of our Lord Jesus Christ,' etc., to
which the people responded, 'And with thy Spirit;' followed by 'Lift up your hearts'—'We lift them up unto
the Lord;' 'Let us give thanks to our Lord God'—'It is
meet and right so to do;' a long thanksgiving, terminating
with the Ter Sanctus, in which the people joined; the
consecration prayer, including the words of our Lord at
the time of institution, and an invocation of the Holy
Spirit to make the elements become the body and blood
of Christ; a prayer for all members of the Church, living
and dead; the doxology, the Creed; a prayer of the bishop
for sanctification; the words pronounced by him, 'Holy
things for holy people' (τὰ ἅγια τοῖς ἁγίοις); the reception
by the clergy and laity in both kinds, taking the elements
into their hands; concluding prayers, and dismissal by

---

[1] In Ephes. Hom. iii. in fine.   [2] Vol. iii. p. 362.

the deacon proclaiming, 'Go in peace.' Nearly all of the forms indicated in this sketch are more or less clearly referred to or quoted in Chrysostom's works, and from these, with the aid of other contemporary writers and documents, we might construct a liturgy, which would more nearly resemble that actually used by him than the liturgy called by his name resembles it.[1] For in this, as in the so-called liturgy of Basil, it is impossible now to determine how much was actually composed by the Father who gave his name to it. It cannot be proved that Chrysostom actually corrected or improved at all the liturgy which he found in use at Constantinople. It may only have come to be called after him as being the greatest luminary who ever occupied the see. The statement, however, made in a tract ascribed to Proclus, Patriarch of Constantinople in the fifth century, is not in itself improbable, that Chrysostom found the existing liturgy so long that many of the congregation, being men of business, and pressed for time, left before the service was concluded, or came in after it had begun, and therefore he abridged and otherwise altered it. In any case, many alterations were made by different churches and bishops in the course of time, as in other liturgies, so also in those which bear the name of Basil and Chrysostom; and hence, as Montfaucon, Savile, Cave, and others have remarked, you cannot find any two copies which are exactly alike.

A critical estimate of Chrysostom's value as a commentator hardly falls within the scope of an essay on his life, but a few general observations on this head may not be deemed out of place here. The same fact was the cause in him of much excellence and some defect in this depart-

---

[1] I have not thought it expedient to crowd the margin with references to Chrysostom's works, for every one of the liturgical forms above-mentioned. They may nearly all be consulted in Bingham, book xv., who has collected them with great care. The fullest passages occur in vol. ii. p. 345 iii. p. 104 ; x. pp. 200 and 527 ; xi. p. 323.

ment. He was a preacher whose primary object was to convert souls. This earnest, practical aim, of which he never lost sight, helped to protect him from lapsing into idle, fanciful, mystical interpretations of Scripture; but, on the other hand, it hindered his entering so fully into all the historical, grammatical, or even doctrinal questions which might be raised about a passage as he would have done had he been exclusively a commentator. His dominant aim being to affect the heart and the moral practice of his hearers, he is content when he has elicited from the passage all that will be most useful for that purpose, and the continuity of the commentary is frequently marred by sudden digressions. His ignorance of Hebrew was of course fatal to his being an accurate interpreter of the Old Testament, since he was entirely dependent on the Septuagint translation. And even in Greek, though few would deny him the merit of fine scholarship on the whole, though his command of the language as an orator is masterly, his style luminous, his diction copious and rich without being offensively ornate or redundant, yet his hold upon the language for critical purposes is neither that of a man who spoke it when it was in its purest stage, nor that of a scholar who, living in a later age and speaking a different tongue, has made of Greek a careful, laborious study.

But two invaluable qualifications for an interpreter Chrysostom did possess—a thorough love for the Sacred Book, and a thorough familiarity with every part of it. There is no topic on which he dwells more frequently and earnestly than on the duty of every Christian man and woman to study the Bible; and what he bade others do, that he did pre-eminently himself. He rebukes the silly vanity of rich people who prided themselves on possessing finely written and handsomely bound copies of the Bible, but who knew little about the contents. Study of the

Bible was more necessary for the layman than the monk, because he was exposed to more constant and formidable temptations. The Christian without a knowledge of his Bible was like a workman without his tools. Like the tree planted by the water-side, the soul of the diligent reader would be continually nourished and refreshed. There were no difficulties which would not yield to a patient study of it. Neither earthly grandeur, nor friends, nor indeed any human thing, could afford in suffering such comfort as Holy Scripture, for this was the companionship of God.[1]

The honest, straightforward common-sense which marks his practical exhortations was a useful quality to him also as an interpreter. One of his principles is, that sound doctrine could not be extracted from Holy Scripture but by a careful comparison of many passages not isolated from their context.[2] Allegorical interpretations were by no means to be rejected, but to be used with caution; men too often made the mistake of dictating what Scripture should mean instead of submitting to be taught by it: they *introduced* a meaning instead of *eliciting* it.[3] Thus, though he often accepts popular types—as Boaz and Ruth are figures of Christ and his bride the Church; and Noah, Joseph, Joshua, are all in different ways representative of our Lord; though sometimes particular expressions in Messianic prophecies are forced, for instance, in Isaiah's description of Immanuel, the 'butter and honey' there spoken of he supposes to be intended to indicate the reality of our Lord's humanity --yet his customary aim is to discover the literal sense and direct historical bearing of the passage. At the same time he fully recognises a general foreshadowing of Jesus Christ, and the complete fulfilment in Him ultimately of prophe-

---

[1] Vol. ii. pp. 17, 92, 522 et passim.
[2] Vol. vi. 157.
[3] In Isai. v. 3, and vi.
[4] Ibid. vii. 6.

cies which immediately refer to persons and events nearly,
if not quite, contemporaneous with the utterance. He
fails not also to point out the moral aspect of prophecy
as a system of teaching rather than prediction, as preparatory to the advent of Jesus Christ in the flesh, not
only by informing men's minds, but disciplining their
hearts to receive Him.[1] Hence the holy men who lived,
under the Old Dispensation, in faith on God's promises
knew Christ as it were by anticipation, and were to
be reckoned as members of the one body.[2]

He had a clear conception of the essential coherence
between the Old and New Testament. He observes that
the very words 'old' and 'new' are relative terms: new
implies an antecedent; old, preparatory to it. The condition of the recipients, the circumstances and age in
which they lived, being different, necessitated a difference
in the treatment. A physician treated the same patient
at different times by directly contrary methods; sometimes
administering sweet, sometimes bitter medicines, sometimes using the lancet, sometimes cautery, but always
with the same ultimate end in view—the health of his
patient. So the Old and New Testaments were different,
but not, as the Manichœans maintained, antagonistic. The
commandment, 'Thou shalt not kill,' attacked the fruit
and consequence of vice; the precept, 'Whosoever is
angry with his brother without a cause,' &c., struck at
the root. This was an illustration in a small instance of
the general truth that the New Dispensation was only a
completion and expansion of the Old. Those, therefore,
who rejected the Old Testament, dishonoured the New,
which was based upon it, and presupposes it.[3]

He is equally rational in his manner of accounting for
the variations in the Gospel narratives. That they differ

---

[1] In Is. vii. c. i.   [2] In Ephes. Hom. x. 1.
[3] De Verb. Apost. vol. iii. p. 282.

in details, but agree in essential matters, he regards as
a powerful evidence of veracity. Exact and verbal coincidence in every particular would have excited in the
minds of opponents a suspicion of concerted agreement.[1]
Authors might write variously without being at variance;
if there had been ten thousand evangelists, yet the Gospel
itself would have been but one.[2] Each evangelist tells
substantially the same tale, but varied according to the
readers for whom he wrote, and the special object which
he had in view. So St. Matthew wrote in Hebrew for the
Jews, St. Mark for the disciples in Egypt, St. John to set
forth the divine aspect of our Lord's life. Thus we have
variety in unity, and unity in variety.[3]

In his commentaries on the Epistles he is careful to
consider each as a connected whole; and, in order to impress this on his hearers, he frequently recapitulates at the
beginning of a homily all the steps by which the part under
consideration has been reached. In his introductions to
each letter he generally makes useful observations on the
author, the time, place, and style of composition, the
readers for whom it was intended, the general character
and arrangement of its contents. He regarded the Bible
as in such a sense written under the inspiration of God,
that no passage, no word even, was to be despised;[4] that
men wrote as they were moved by the Holy Spirit, but
not to the total deprivation of their own human understanding and personal character. The prophet was not
like the seer who spoke under constraint, not knowing
what he said; he retained his own faculties and style;
only all his powers were quickened, energised by the
Spirit to the utterance of words which unassisted he
could not have uttered.[5]

[1] In Matt. Hom. i. 2.
[2] In Galat. i. 6.
[3] In Matt. i. et in Johan. i.
[4] In Rom. Hom. xxxi. 1.
[5] In Psalm xliv.; in 1 Cor. Hom.
xxix. 1.

Chrysostom's influence as a preacher was not aided by any external advantages of person. Like so many men who have possessed great powers of command over the minds of others—like St. Paul, Athanasius, John Wesley— he was little of stature; his frame was attenuated by the austerities of his youth and his habitually ascetic mode of life; his cheeks were pale and hollow; his eyes deeply sunken; his forehead ample, but wrinkled; his head bald. He frequently delivered his discourses sitting in the ambo, or high reading-desk, just inside the nave, in order to be near his hearers and well raised above them. But these physical disadvantages were more than compensated by other more important qualities. A power of exposition which unfolded in lucid order, passage by passage, the meaning of the book in hand; a rapid transition from clear exposition, or keen logical argument, to fervid ex- hortation, or pathetic appeal, or indignant denunciation; the versatile ease with which he could lay hold of any little incident of the moment, such as the lighting of the lamps in the church, and use it to illustrate his discourse; the mixture of plain common-sense and simple boldness, and yet tender affection, with which he would strike home to the hearts and consciences of his hearers—all these veins are not only general characteristics of the man, but are usually to be found manifested more or less in the compass of each discourse. It is this rare union of powers which constitutes his superiority to almost all the other Christian preachers with whom he might be, or has been, compared. Savonarola had all, and more than all, his fire and vehemence, but untempered by his sober, calm good sense, and wanting his rational method of interpretation. Chrysostom was eager and impetuous at times in speech as well as in action, but never fanatical. Jeremy Taylor combines, like Chrysostom, real earnest- ness of purpose with rhetorical forms of expression and florid imagery; but, on the whole, his style is far more artificial, and is overladen with a multifarious learning from which Chrysostom's was entirely free. Wesley is almost his match in simple, straightforward, practical exhortation, but does not rise into flights of eloquence like his. The great French preachers, again, resemble him in his more ornate and declamatory vein, but they lack that simpler, common-sense style of address which equally distinguished him. Whether the sobriquet of Chrysostomos, 'the golden mouth,' was given to him in his lifetime is extremely doubtful; at any rate, it seems not to have been commonly used till afterwards. John is the only name by which he is mentioned in the writings of historians who were most nearly contemporaneous, but the other was a well-known appellation before the end of the fifth century.[1]

The preservation of Chrysostom's discourses we owe mainly to the custom, prevalent in the Eastern Church at that time, of having the sermons of famous preachers taken down by shorthand writers as they were spoken; but some of them Chrysostom published himself.[2] To what extent they may have been written before preaching it is impossible to say. The expository parts were evidently the result of previous study and preparation; the actual diction of the practical portions he may have left to the suggestion of the moment, though the main subjects of his address had been always decided upon beforehand. Extempore remarks were frequently called forth by the behaviour of the congregation, or some passing incident. The discourse delivered after his return from exile we also know to have been purely impromptu; and Suidas observes that he 'had a tongue which exceeded the cataracts of the Nile in fluency, so that he delivered many of

---

[1] Vide Tillemont, xi. p. 37.   [2] Socr. vi. 4.

his panegyrics on the martyrs extempore without the least hesitation.'[1] His hearers were sometimes wrapt in such profound attention that pickpockets took advantage of it:[2] sometimes they were melted to tears, or beat their breasts and faces, and uttered groans and cries to Heaven for mercy; at other times they clapped their hands or shouted—marks of approbation frequently paid at that time to eloquent preachers, but always sternly reproved by Chrysostom.

Although his style is generally exuberantly rich, yet it is seldom offensively redundant, for every word is usually telling; and at times he is epigrammatically terse. A few instances will suffice :—' The fire of sin is large, but it is quenched by a few tears;' 'Pain was given on account of sin, yet through pain sin is dissolved;' 'Riches are called possessions (κτήματα) that we may possess them, not be possessed by them;' 'You are master of much wealth, do not be a slave to that whereof God has made you master;' 'Scripture relates the sins of saints that we may fear, the conversion of sinners that we may hope.' He refers to a visitation of Antioch by an earthquake, as God 'shaking the city, but establishing your minds; making the city crumble, but consolidating your judgment.'

His familiarity with classical Greek authors is apparent sometimes in direct references. He speaks of 'the smoothness of Isocrates, the weight of Demosthenes, the dignity of Thucydides, the sublimity of Plato.'[3] He quotes the beginning of the 'Apology,' to show that if Socrates did not put a high value on mere fine talking, how much less should the Christian.[4] He illustrates the readiness of men to supply the wants of the monk by a passage from Plato, where Crito says that his money, and that of Cebes and

---

[1] Suid.; vide verb. Johannes.
[2] Cont. Anom. Hom. iv.
[3] De Sacerd. iv. 6.
[4] Adv. Oppugn. Vit. Mon. iii. 2.

many others, is at the disposal of Socrates ; and, go where
he will, he may rely on finding friends.[1]   Sometimes we
detect a thought derived, it may have been unconsciously,
from classical sources. When he compares the crowd
of the congregation before him to the sea, and the play
upon the surface of that sea of heads to the effect of a
strong west wind stirring and bending the ears of corn,[2]
it is impossible not to think that the idea was suggested
by the well-known simile in Homer (Il. ii. 147).   Again,
when, in speaking of David's sin, he compares the body to
a chariot, the soul to the charioteer, and says that, when
the soul is intoxicated by passion, the chariot is dragged
along at random, it can hardly be fanciful to see a reflection of Plato's celebrated image of the charioteer and
horses in the ' Phædrus.'[3]

But, whatever admiration Chrysostom may have retained of those authors whom he had studied in his
youth, it was confined to their language, for with their
ideas and modes of thought he had, so far as we can
judge, abandoned all sympathy. Nor was this unnatural.
Christianity existed in such close contact with pagan corruption, it had suffered so much from pagan persecution,
that the revulsion of earnest Christians from all things
pagan was total and indiscriminating. 'The old order
changeth, yielding place to new;' and the new, having
fought a hard struggle with the old, is for a long time
incapable of recognising merit in anything belonging to
it.   There are several allusions in Chrysostom to the
' Republic ' of Plato, but they are always depreciative. He
fastens on a few points, such as the regulations about
marriage and female work, and condemns it on these as
absurd and childish, quite failing to consider the idea in its
grandeur as a whole.[4] Yet it is instructive to notice that

---

[1] Adv. Oppugn. Vit. Mon. ii. 4.   [3] Ibid. ii. 1.
[2] De Pœnit. vi. 1.   [4] In Johan. Hom. ii. 2, and vol. vii. 30.

he never hesitates to assign to Plato the first place among the heathen philosophers, dignifying him with the title of Coryphœus.[1] He often compares the failure of Plato's teaching to regenerate men in every rank with the successful labours of St. Paul and the other apostles; but, while he rejoices that the writings and doctrine of the philosopher were eclipsed by the tentmaker and fisherman, and well-nigh forgotten, he evidently regarded it as the most signal triumph which Christianity had achieved.[2]

Unquestionable as the intellectual genius of Chrysostom was, yet it is rather in the purity of his moral character, his single-minded boldness of purpose, and the glowing piety which burns through all his writings, that we find the secret of his influence. If it was rather the mission of Augustine to mould the minds of men so as to take a firm grasp of certain great doctrines, it was the mission of Chrysostom to inflame the whole heart with a fervent love of God. Rightly has he been called the great teacher of consummate holiness, as Augustine was the great teacher of efficient grace;[3] rightly has it been remarked that, like Fénelon, he is to be ranked among those who may be termed disciples of St. John, men who seem to have been pious without intermission from their childhood upwards, and of whose piety the leading characteristics are ease, cheerfulness, and elevation: while Augustine belongs to the disciples of St. Paul, those who have been led astray by the allurements of the world, but in later life are brought back to the love and service of God, and whose characteristics are gravity, earnestness, depth.[4] If Augustine has done more valuable

---

[1] Vol. xi. p. 694.

[2] Vol. ix. p. 407. Comp. Jerome: 'Quotusquisque nunc Aristotelem legit? quanti Platonis vel libros novere, vel nomen? Vix in angulis otiosi eos senes recolunt; rusticanos vero et piscatores nostros totus orbis loquitur, universus mundus sonat.' — In Galat. iii.

[3] Al. Knox, 'Remains,' vol. iii. pp. 75–77.

[4] Jebb, 'Pastoral Discourses,' ii.

service in building up the Church at large, Chrysostom
is the more loveable to the individual, and speaks un-
constrained by the fetters of a rigid, exclusive system.
out of a heart overflowing with love to God and man.
Yet it is precisely on this account that he has not
been so generally appreciated as he deserves. His tone is
too catholic for the Romanist, or for the sectarian par-
tisan of any denomination. ' It would be easy to produce
abundant instances of his oratorical abilities; I wish it
were in my power to record as many of his evangelical
excellencies.' Such is the verdict of a narrow-minded
historian,[1] and the comparative estimation in which he
held St. Augustine and St. Chrysostom may be inferred
from the number of pages in his history given to each:
St. Augustine is favoured with 187, Chrysostom with 20.
But he whose judgment is not cramped by confinement
in the shackles of some harsh and stiff theory of Gospel
truth will surely allow that Chrysostom not only preached
the Gospel, but lived it. To the last moment of his life
he exhibited that calm, cheerful faith, patient resignation
under affliction, and untiring perseverance for the good of
others, which are pre-eminently the marks of a Christian
saint. The cause for which he fought and died in a
corrupt age was the cause of Christian holiness; and,
therefore, by the great mediæval poet of Christendom he
is rightly placed in Paradise between two men who, widely
different indeed in themselves, time, and place from him
and from one another, yet resembled him in this, that
they freely and courageously spoke of God's ' testimonies
even before kings, and were not ashamed'—Nathan the
Seer, and Anselm the Primate of all England:—

> ' Natan profeta, e 'l metropolitano
> Crisostomo, ed Anselmo. . .'[2]

---

[1] Milner, Hist. ii. p. 302.   [2] Dante, Parad. xii. 136.

APPENDIX.

[Vide ante, p. 433, note.]

ON THE LETTER TO CÆSARIUS, CHRYS. OP. vol. iii. p. 755.

THE history of this letter, and the controversy connected with it, are curious and interesting. Peter Martyr transcribed a Latin translation of it, which he found in a manuscript at Florence, carried it with him to England, and deposited it in the library of Archbishop Cranmer. After Cranmer's death, and the dispersion of his library, the letter disappeared. Peter Martyr had not stated the source from which he had derived it, and, therefore, when the assailants of the doctrine of Transubstantiation wished to make use of it, their opponents always maintained that it did not exist. In 1680, however, Emericus Bigotius discovered a copy in the library of St. Mark's Convent, at Florence, probably the same which Peter Martyr, himself a Florentine, had transcribed. Emericus appended it to his edition of 'Palladius's Life of Chrysostom,' and in his preface endeavoured to vindicate its authenticity; but the doctors of the Sorbonne suppressed the letter, and such portions of the preface as related to it. Emericus, however, had retained in his own possession some of the entire copies after they were printed, before they came into the licenser's hands. The translation was published by Stephanus Le Moyne in 1685, by Jacob Basnage in 1687, and in 1689 by Harduin, a Jesuit, who strenuously maintained the Roman Catholic interpretation of the passage on the Eucharist. Montfaucon adopted Harduin's version of it, annexing a few fragments in the Greek, picked out of Anastasius and John Damascene.

John Damascene, Anastasius, and Nicephorus refer to the letter as authentic, nor does Harduin venture to dispute it; but there are several points of evidence which seem to mark it as belonging to a later age than that of Chrysostom. It is not

quoted before Leontius, in the latter part of the sixth century,
although it might usefully have been employed against the
Eutychians. There are expressions in it which were not in
common use till after Cyril of Alexandria had employed them
against Nestorius. The language generally is that of one who had
lived in the midst of the Nestorian and Eutychian controversies,
and the style of the Greek fragments, as well as the tone of the
Latin translation, are extremely unlike Chrysostom's manner:
the sentences are abrupt and rugged, and a kind of scholastic,
dogmatic tone pervades the whole composition. The general
scope of the letter is clear: it is to maintain the doctrine of the
two natures under one person in Jesus Christ, against the heresy
of the Apollinarians; or, if we accept the theory of Montfaucon,
the intention of the author, living in the time of the Eutychian
heresy, was to strike a blow at that by forging a letter supposed
to be addressed by Chrysostom to a friend, warning him against
Apollinarian errors, which had much in common with the Eutychian. The passage in which the writer illustrates his position
by a reference to the Holy Eucharist has been construed by Roman Catholics and Protestants in a sense agreeable to their own
views on the subject. The writer has been labouring to prove
that there were two distinct natures in the one person of God
the Son Incarnate, and he proceeds as follows:—' Just as the
bread before consecration is called bread, but when the Divine
grace sanctifies it through the agency of the priest it is liberated
from the appellation of bread, and is regarded as worthy of the
appellation of the Lord's body, although the nature of bread
remains in it, and we speak not of two bodies, but one body of
the Son; so here, the Divine nature being seated in the human
body, the two together make up but one Son, one Person.'

INDEX.

urges the Emperor to remove Chrysostom from Constantinople, 353; his death, 320, 371

Cucusus, a village in the Tauric range, subject to attacks from Isaurians, 376; selected by Eudoxia as the place of Chrysostom's exile, 377; arrival of the archbishop at, 381; ravaged by the Isaurians, 397

DAMASUS contests the see of Rome, 50

Damophilus exiled by Theodosius, 149

Dante, the position assigned in Paradise to Chrysostom by, 449

Daphne, grove of, 96; description of, 105; destruction of its temple, 107

Deacons, duties of, 91; called 'Levites of the Christian Church,' 91; their peculiar office in the early Church, 92–93

Death, Chrysostom on, 98, 168

Decius, persecution of, 64

Demetrius, bishop of Pessina, Chrysostom's epistle to, 74–75; denounces the 'Synod of the Oak,' and returns to Chrysostom, 329; accompanies the Italian deputation, 368; dies of harsh treatment when being conveyed to the Egyptian oases, 371

'De Sacerdotio,' Chrysostom, 43–49

Diocese, meaning of, 285 *note*

Diodorus, influence of, upon Chrysostom and Theodore, 29; founder of a method of Biblical interpretation, 30; made bishop of Tarsus by Meletius, 30; attacked by Julian, 30; commentary on the Old and New Testaments, 30–31; his theology, 31–33; its rationalistic tendency, 32; writings condemned by the Fifth Œcumenical Council, 33; rational system of conducting monasteries, 70

Diogenes, 99

Dionysius, the tyrant of Sicily, 81

Dioscorus, a Nitrian monk, one of the 'tall brethren,' 306; made bishop of Hermopolis by Theophilus, 306; a victim of the rage of Theophilus, 309; his death, 329

Dispensations, teaching of the Old and New, 104

Divination, arts of, 150

Domitianus, widows and virgins in the care of, 393

Domninus blinded to the preparations of Maximus, 199

Doxology, Arian form of the, 18

EASTER-DAY, vast crowds attend the church on, 244, 345

Easter-Eve, a great day for the baptism of converts, 346; the vigil on, interrupted at St. Sophia, 347

Easter kept according to Jewish calculation, 136; this practice condemned by the Council of Nice, 137; and denounced by Chrysostom, 137

Eastern Church, the, acknowledges Meletius, 21; the parent of asceticism, 63; the festival of Christmas in, 141; favourable to clerical celibacy, 228; finds the teaching of Origen congenial, 299; the 'Synod of the Oak' a stain upon, 326; appeals to the Western Church, 349, 363; not famed for missionary enterprise, 399; desirous of communion with the West, 405

Education in monasteries, Chrysostom urges the advantage of, 84

Elpidius, a priest, bribes a slave to assassinate Chrysostom, 353

Elpidius, bishop of Laodicea, friendly to Chrysostom, 345; his adroit proposal, 345; deposed and imprisoned for his attachment to Chrysostom, 394; the archbishop writes thanking him for his zeal, 394; restored to his see by Alexander, bishop of Antioch, 394

Elvira, synod of, enjoins celibacy of the clergy, 228

Emperors, fate of, 98–99; half idolatrous homage paid to, 340-341; custom of attending church in state on Christmas-day, 343

Epaminondas not allured by ambition, 99

Ephesus, Chrysostom arrives at, 282; election of a bishop to the see of, 282; synod at, 283; worship of Midas suppressed at, 285; its see occupied by a monster of iniquity, 373

Epiphanius, bishop of Salamis and Cyprus, 301; visits Jerusalem, and accepts the hospitality of Bishop John, 302; preaches against the doctrines of Origen, 302; leaves Jerusalem, and breaks off communion with its bishop, 303; forcibly ordains Paulinian deacon and priest, 303; receives an apologetic letter from Theophilus, 312; goes to Constantinople, irregularly ordains a deacon, and refuses the hospitality of Chrysostom, 315; his attempt to enter the church and denounce the writings of Origen prevented by Serapion, 317;

LONDON: PRINTED BY
SPOTTISWOODE AND CO., NEW-STREET SQUARE
AND PARLIAMENT STREET